Dancing for Degas

A NOVEL

Kathryn Wagner

BANTAM BOOKS TRADE PAPERBACKS

NEW YORK

A Bantam Books Trade Paperback Original

Copyright © 2010 by Kathryn Wagner

Reading group guide copyright © 2010 by Random House, Inc.

All rights reserved.

Published in the United States by Bantam Books,
an imprint of The Random House Publishing Group,
a division of Random House, Inc., New York.

BANTAM BOOKS is a registered trademark of Random House, Inc., and
the colophon is a trademark of Random House, Inc.

RANDOM HOUSE READER'S CIRCLE & Design is a trademark of Random House, Inc.

Library of Congress Cataloging-in-Publication Data
Wagner, Kathryn
Dancing for Degas : a novel / Kathryn Wagner.
p. cm.
ISBN 978-0-385-34386-2
eBook ISBN 978-0-440-33871-0
1. Ballerinas—Fiction. 2. Degas, Edgar, 1834–1917—Fiction.
3. Painters—France—Fiction. 4. Paris (France)—Fiction. I. Title.
PS3623.A35633D36 2010
813'.6—dc22   2009042938

Printed in the United States of America

www.bantamdell.com

2 4 6 8 9 7 5 3 1

Book design by Diane Hobbing

"Must we admit that the center of this powerful city...is today an opera house? Must our glory in the future consist above all in perfecting our public entertainments? Are we no longer anything more than the capital of elegance and pleasure?"

Le Temps editorial, 1867

Contents

Intermission

Act III

Act IV

Introduction

1872

*A*imagine the lines he is drawing are causing me to dance. I extend my leg in the air, holding my pose, and imagine he is in the audience drawing me once again. I expect to see his hand extended to the top of his paper, and as my leg begins to feel the strain, I picture how the flick of his wrist makes me relax. I'm ready to bring my leg down, but wait, he seems to smile to himself, not just yet. His pencil remains pressed to the top corner of his paper, watching me, knowing he can control my every move. Then another girl whirls past me, my cue and his distraction. His pencil whips away from the page and my toe plummets to the floor of the stage, launching me in graceful *pirouettes,* my arms fluttering around me, his pencil moving in spirals across the page until I leap into the air, breaking free from the page entirely.

Raising my head and using his empty seat in the balcony loges as a focal point, I push off into a series of *fouetté en tournants.*

Even though I remain in one place, I've broken free and he cannot keep up with my movements as I spin around and around. The orchestra consumes my mind as each note plays for me and me alone. I reach a point where the visual performance meets the melodic and for a moment I wish I was in the audience so I could see how it all unfolds. I wish he was here to see it. The lanterns cast yellows and whites into the tulle of our rose-colored skirts, the colors bouncing until I can't distinguish where one ends and the next begins. The orchestra becomes all arms, moving back and forth, dancing to their own music. The gilded walls of the Opera House contrast against the black tuxedos in the seats. The twinkle of the women's jewels makes the entire audience glitter. I imagine that when I leapt off the pages of his sketchbook I caused everything around me to dance.

As the production of *Coppélia* moves along, I become lost in the character I'm portraying—Swanilda, a peasant girl. Rapid *pirouettes* transform me, and in my mind I cast the Ballet Master as the story's scheming inventor, Doctor Coppélius, who creates the dancing doll Coppélia and tricks Swanilda's fiancé into falling in love with the doll.

The music slows and I feel every muscle of my body stretch as I bend and lean my head back, arms flowing over my head, knowing what it is like to try to become something you are not. As I raise myself up to *relevé* on one toe while slowly extending my leg to the ceiling, I pretend I'm reliving my own journey through Swanilda as I try to capture the love of one man by becoming someone else. Deception is the theme of the next scene and I leap through the air, trying to run away from all the hidden truths that have shaped who I am today. With each *ballon,* I imagine I am crushing them and flying higher and higher as they diminish. As the production ends with a grand reconciliation,

Swanilda and her true love are reunited. The entire cast convenes at a spirited wedding, showing the audience that a woman with faults is better than a flawless doll.

As the curtain closes and I exit the stage with heavy limbs and heart, I can only hope that this will be true in my life as well. My entire being depends on it.

Act I

No. 1 Scène:
The Fiery Side of France

1859

I wasn't always filled with such anxiety. The inescapable need for perfection was cultivated during many years of training—just as my body was strengthened to complete a flawless *pirouette,* my mind underwent vigorous instruction until I believed that I was better than all others and entitled to nothing short of the riches of an empress. Yet it was no secret that I could be dethroned without a second thought. My success was nothing but an illusion, which I find especially ironic because I was not born into such complications. I sought them out.

At the age of twelve, when all the girls around me seemed to be blossoming, I was painfully average. Others received praise for their looks and talents, while I faded into the background. Once in a while someone would compliment my startling green eyes, but this only happened when there was no one else in the vicinity and nothing else to focus on. And, believe me, one had to put quite a bit of focus into the task of taking notice. They had to overlook my gangly, awkward body, my clothes that always seemed to attract dirt, my drab, brown hair that always managed to become unruly. It was a wonder to me how other girls seemed to not have to give their hair a second thought. I couldn't stop staring at the locks that cascaded over their shoulders in one fluid motion like corn silk. My wavy hair seemed to feed off of hairbrushes, growing larger and larger with each stroke. Like a horse running wild, I could not control it so I chose instead to suppress it under limp bonnets.

My hair was only the start of my ordinary existence. I grew taller than most girls my age, but not so tall that I drew attention, only tall enough to look clumsy by comparison. I loathed running into the Neville family at the market. Madame Neville had given birth to a staggering number of children, ten the last time I counted and all girls, all names beginning with *N*—Nathalie, Nicole, Naomi, and so on. I was sure they would run out of N names if she didn't stop having children. The Neville girls were tiny, so tiny that they drew crowds as they followed behind their mother like a row of ducklings with shiny white heads of hair. I hated when my mother would stop to pay her respects to Madame Neville and I would find myself stuck in the middle of the group, my head rising above the girls like a large, scruffy dog amongst a litter of kittens. The only company I kept was my mother's, with just one brother who mimicked my father's apathy toward me as if neither could be bothered with the trivial thoughts of a girl, and thus I really had no idea how to talk to children my own age. When passersby would stop and coo that the Neville girls looked just like a group of porcelain dolls, my face would grow red and I would stare down at my shoes. I remember peering over at Madame Neville, who basked in the glow of the compliments, a baby thrust onto her hip, and noticing how her body resembled a pyramid, becoming wider and wider until her bottom sagged down so low that it seemed it would surely touch the ground. I thought with some satisfaction that these tiny girls would grow to be only as tall as their mother. They wouldn't be able to grow higher, so they would grow wider until each of the little dolls resembled walking pyramids as well.

While I was much too shy and proper to have said such a terrible thing aloud, I did constantly think terrible thoughts of others. Perhaps it was from being overlooked so often; I had nothing else to do but observe those around me and find faults to rival the compliments they were given. If a girl received praise for her exquisite needlework while I tried to hide the knots that formed in mine, I would shrug my shoulders and console myself with the thought that of course her needlework was perfect, she had such large bug eyes that the tiny stitches must surely be magnified to her!

Such thoughts entertained me as I began morning chores each day at our tiny farmhouse which meandered off the path from the small winding streets of our little town of Espelette. Espelette was as painfully ordinary as myself, with only its spicy pepper crop bringing it any recognition. Locals called it the fiery side of France, although there was nothing sizzling about it in my opinion. My father grew hot peppers, just like every other farmer in the town.

"Alexandrie, don't let the eggs sit over the fire, keep stirring them so they scramble properly," my mother's shrill voice interrupted my thoughts as she cut thick slices of bread, spreading butter over them. "Your father and brother have a long day of work ahead and they need a hearty breakfast."

As I whipped the fork through the eggs, I paused to watch

them puff up, letting a huge bubble form and then poking my fork in the center so it burst.

"Alexandrie, I told you if you let the eggs sit they become rubbery," my mother said, exasperated.

"You should know these things by now," she added while guiding my hands. "I can only pray that one day you'll make a good wife." I saw how effortless it was for her and wished she would just finish it since her arms were so much larger and stronger than mine.

"What difference does it really make?" I complained. "We spend all of this time making breakfast and then Denis and Papa rush in and eat it in minutes. Why can't we eat before them so we can have eggs too? Most of the time there isn't anything left for us but a slice of bread."

"If we eat first, then there might not be enough for them," she told me in a singsong voice that made me wonder how she could sound so happy about something that was so unfair.

I felt as if we lived in the kitchen. As soon as one meal ended we had to begin preparing for the next. We never stopped throughout the day. In between our kitchen duties we would hang freshly harvested peppers on our front and back porches to dry. We worked quickly, throwing the dried ones in a bag to be ground into a fine powder. I spent each afternoon hunched over the funny red vegetables, smashing them into dust to be sold at the market, all the while careful not to touch my face. I once made the mistake of rubbing my eye in the midst of my work only to be met with a fire that seemed to ignite underneath my eyeball and burn for hours. I was sure I would be blinded for life.

Whenever I thought we might have time to ourselves between preparing meals, my mother would drag me around the house and we would make the beds, sweep, and dust. My father and brother dirtied everything and we dutifully followed behind cleaning it up. On the weekends we rose at dawn to weed the garden so our vegetables wouldn't be ruined, washed the laundry, and swept the porches and floors again. On Sundays we traveled to the market to sell our peppers to the merchants who would distribute them all across France and to buy food for the week. I looked forward to each Sunday, if only for a break in a routine that I grew to resent almost as much as I resented my mother. I despised working in the garden the most. As the sun rose, we hunched over pulling out weeds, my mother going into near hysterics when I inevitably pulled out a carrot or beet. "Pay attention! That could have been your dinner," she screamed.

"They all look the same!" I complained back to her, my legs cramping as I stood to brush off the dirt caked on my knees. I looked down at my hands, which had dirt underneath the fingernails, and I knew that as soon as the dirt finally disappeared it would be time to come back into the garden and my fingernails would be dirtied again. I wiped my hands together hopelessly, and untied my bonnet in order to lift my sweaty hair away from my neck. "Put your bonnet back on," my mother said without looking up. "But it's so hot," I whined. How had she seen me? "If you don't wear your bonnet, you will get sunburned and ruin your skin," she declared, her arms moving down the row of weeds. "And the sun will lighten your hair, then once you stay inside during the winter your hair will grow in darker, leaving it half light and half dark and you'll look despicable. Once you're married you can burn your skin and lighten your hair to your heart's content, but until then you need to take care of yourself."

My mother was obsessed with looking proper for the sole purpose of attracting a stable husband. I peered at her, scrutinizing her weathered look from sunburned skin, her dry hair, her yellowed teeth that she long ago stopped taking care of. Looking proper didn't apply to her because both my brother and I were supposed to correct the mistakes that she had made. It was no secret that she had expected a certain kind of life. She was an educated woman, able to read and write, which was something that had been very important to my grandparents, may they rest in peace. Their philosophy had been to give their only daughter the freedom to make her own decisions, with the belief that it would lead her to happiness. It didn't and she vowed not to raise us the same way.

My mother had been overly praised as a child and thought that the world would bend to her will. She never would have pictured herself weeding in the hot sun behind a tiny home with a roof that leaked when the heavy rains came through. My father swept her off her feet with his grand ideas. She looked into the future and saw the two of them acquiring much land and supervising farmhands, not tilling the earth with their own hands. Only years into the marriage, and after the birth of my brother and me, did she see that while my father's ideas were bountiful, they were never put into action. They spent more than they had, with the thought that in a few years when one of these ideas became a reality, they could easily pay off the many debts they had been acquiring. I could see for myself that merchants would no longer offer them credit because they also knew by now that my father would never attempt to see any of his moneymaking ideas through.

I knew I was supposed to do as Maman said, that I should look forward to growing up and marrying a successful farmer, but it was the last thing I wanted for myself. I didn't want to spend the rest of my life waiting on my father and brother, and then having to do the same thing for my husband and sons. I wanted to be able to do something more important than clean, and to afford to have someone else make all of my meals. I felt sorry for my mother, pulling weeds constantly. As the sun beat down on me, I realized my mother and I had one thing in common—I would do whatever it took not to have her life.

No. 2 Scène:
The Market

As the sun rose each morning, it first illuminated the narrow, winding road through the center of Espelette, the light moving out toward the church, the feed store, the fish market, then trickling down the road to the meadows, where black night turned into bright green and finally woke the peppers and livestock of our house. My family would be ready to greet the morning and embark on a day that was exactly the same as the day before. But my routine existence was forever disrupted when I awoke one morning to the raised voice of my father and the hysterical sobbing of my mother. Curious, I tiptoed closer to the noise coming from our kitchen and stopped behind the door to hear my brother speaking in a hushed tone.

"Maman, please stop crying," he said. "We love each other completely and will be bringing a child into the world. Nothing is more important than that. You'll see. I'll stay here and work the fields and Luce will be able to help you and Alexandrie. Wouldn't you like another hand?"

I slapped my palm against my mouth to muffle a gasp. Denis and Luce? In love and having a baby? Luce's family lived in one of the smallest, shabbiest homes in Espelette. Whenever I passed it I was happy with our modest farmhouse. When I saw chickens pecking away at dirt and messy toddlers wearing only diapers chasing them it made me thankful that we didn't live in such conditions. Thinking back, I had noticed that Denis always took a moment to give his regards to Luce. One year his senior, she would reply with a shy smile and a blush when he spoke to her. I assumed he was being polite, but listening at the door I realized they must have been tiptoeing out to see each other and were very much in the midst of a relationship when they spoke in public.

"Denis, you are eighteen and should know things are not that simple," my father bellowed. "Your engagement to Claire was set up to benefit our family. Our farms are situated in the ideal location to merge together and we have been planning exactly that from the time you were both born. Everything depends on it! You must take care of this mess with Luce and never speak of it again. And you had better make damn sure Claire's family doesn't hear about it."

"I'm not going to marry Claire," Denis replied calmly. "I love Luce and will marry her. You cannot force me into a marriage I do not desire only because you have been careless with your finances."

At this point, I turned to creep back to my room. Surely such an insult would enrage my father and I didn't want to witness how the conversation ended. In my haste to retreat, my hand hit a basket filled with jars of crushed peppers. I watched as the basket teetered and I tried to catch it but I was too slow. The jars clanged down to the floor, rolling and making a huge noise. I stood, frozen, not sure whether I should dash to my room, but it was too late for action. I turned to see my parents standing in the doorway staring at me.

"I'm sorry," I said meekly, as much for knocking over the basket as I was for eavesdropping. "I'll go check to see if the peppers have dried."

"No, stay." My father put a hand on my shoulder and guided me to the kitchen. He stood in front of my brother with both hands on my shoulders. "Now it's up to Alexandrie to support our family."

I stared uncomfortably between my father and brother, not used to Denis being out of favor with my parents. My mother sat down at the table, her eyes red and misty, watching her husband dismiss one child and turn his attention to the other. The following days were the most unordinary of my life thus far. After exhausting all pleas for Denis to rethink his marriage, my parents relented and Luce moved into our home. I would have liked to have a sister, but Luce was an outcast in our house and my parents barely tolerated her. Denis overcompensated for their behavior by encouraging her to get involved in the household work, but my mother only ordered her to do tasks far away from us. When we were in the garden, Luce would crush peppers quietly on the porch. No one spoke to her during meals and I wondered if she missed her small home with the dirty chickens.

The rift between my parents and Denis widened as news of his new bride spread quickly throughout Espelette. My father called on every adequate-size farm in town that had grown sons, desperately trying to reach a compromise. But no one would touch my family. My father's debts coupled with Denis' indiscretion made me a less than desirable bride.

So after only a few weeks as the favored child, my father began to turn his attention to the farm's cows. By selling a few animals, he would be able to buy more time from his debtors. When he announced that he would be showing cattle to Monsieur Belmont at next week's market, I quietly hid my excitement, for this would be the first time I could observe a truly wealthy man. My secret scrutinizing of others wasn't reserved just for the Neville girls. I observed the differences between the farmers and the fishermen, how large each home was, what dress each woman wore to church, and how many sacks of food each family purchased at the market.

Monsieur Belmont was a well-respected banker living in the next town over. He began his career by financing farmland around the South of France and then moved toward larger investments in Paris. He traveled to Paris during the week and returned to the South of France each weekend because he loved the fresh air. The people of Espelette adored him and made themselves feel better about their run-down farms by telling one another that even though Monsieur Belmont made more money than the entire town combined, there was not a better place in the country to be than their own little fiery side of France. I was very curious to see what the famous Monsieur Belmont was like in person.

However, my mother managed to take the joy out of the anticipation. All week long she prattled on about how important the Belmonts were and how we needed to make a good impression. I wondered why she thought it was so important to impress them. We were selling our cows out of desperation, so why would what we looked like or said make a difference? I was thankful when Sunday finally arrived because it meant an end to her fretting. I followed my father and brother as they herded the cattle out of our fields and led them into Espelette's center to the market. My hair with its halo of fuzz was pulled back in a ribbon and my mother had made me scrub my face so thoroughly that my skin felt tight. I walked slowly with my family so we would not become dirty from the journey.

When we arrived at the market, the cows were herded into a small fenced-in area and my father and brother sat down on bales of hay waiting for Monsieur Belmont to arrive. "Come along," my mother pulled my hand, "let's go do our shopping so they can take care of business."

Reluctantly, I followed her. After all her chattering, I had thought I would be there when Monsieur Belmont made his entrance. I glanced over my shoulder and saw a tall, lean man dressed in a full suit and carrying a cane approach my father and shake his hand while a woman wearing layer upon layer of lace stood at his side. I stared in awe at how every movement he made was so graceful and refined. He ran his hand through a head of thick, gray hair and beamed at my father, revealing the whitest teeth I have ever seen. I suddenly felt self-conscious about my family's appearance, and even more so when I looked at the pretty woman with him and her gloved hands and her parasol to shield her from the country sun. I was craning my neck to see more, but they disappeared from my view as my mother rounded the corner to haggle with the bread merchant. "I'm going to look around on my own," I told her and eagerly separated myself from her.

I walked through the market, ignoring looks from others, who I knew were talking about my family. They smiled at me as I passed, then dropped their heads together in whispers. I tried to think of something that would make the situation worse. This was a trick of mine; I knew things could always be worse so I tried to imagine how a bad predicament could be even worse. Many times, my daydreams would run wild with unrealistic scenes that ended up making me giggle. If the pepper plants grew taller than the house and I had to grind a giant pepper, then that would surely be worse than grinding the week's crops. If I woke up dreading pulling weeds, I imagined that an overnight storm caused our garden to expand throughout the entire town. And I would have to weed the whole thing. Today, I thought of a more realistic situation: If Luce were here waddling around, then everyone would focus even more on my family's embarrassment.

Turning past a vegetable stand, I stopped worrying about others' thoughts and my face broke out in a smile as I spotted my favorite stand at the market. The Tibbit family sold ground peppers just like my family, except they had much more fun, making musical instruments out of everyday items. The Tibbits turned crates into drums and sang while ringing bells, and by the end of the day they would have everyone at the market either dancing or singing with them. I joined a group already moving to their music and forgot about my neighbors' gossip, and Luce waiting for us at home, and my family's desperate situation. I twirled around, dancing with people my parents' age and with other children, imagining that I was at a grand ball. Only when I turned to see my mother standing by the vegetable stand did I stop dancing and rejoin her.

"You're quite a talented dancer," a voice said and I looked up to see the woman with the parasol beside me. She was much older than I had thought, with crinkles around her eyes and

mouth and streaks of gray in her chignon. Even so, she had a refined elegance that I had never encountered before. She was very
serene in comparison to Espelette's women, even Madame
Neville, who constantly wore a look of worry on her face. My
mother stood next to her, beaming. "Yes, Alexandrie always runs
off to the Tibbits' stand," she said as if I were a toddler, and I
immediately became embarrassed.

We all walked back to where my father was talking to Monsieur Belmont. He was patting the cows on the flanks as Monsieur Belmont nodded approvingly. I watched my father and
brother taking in Monsieur Belmont's every move, jumping up
as he pointed his finger at each cow, all the while their heads
bobbing up and down like chickens. I thought of my mother,
and wondered if Madame Belmont had seen her gesturing wildly
with the bread merchant like she did every week so she could
save a few francs. I didn't want to admit it, but I was ashamed
that this was my family. I would have preferred to be Madame
Belmont's daughter. I pictured their life as calm and quiet, without any worries.

Madame Belmont bid us farewell and joined her husband,
who was watching my father herd the cattle away for him. I immediately felt guilty for not wanting to be part of my family. My
father was selling his cattle to take care of us and my mother was
haggling with the merchants so we had food to eat. I should be
proud to call them my family, but instead I wanted to distance
myself from them.

The following morning I was knee-deep in manure when my
mother altered the course of my future. Shoveling out the stalls

was oddly my favorite morning chore. The cows rose up and mooed at my arrival; it was the only time I received such an enthusiastic greeting. As I cleaned out their little living quarters, the few cows we had left inclined their heads toward me and watched my actions with such curiosity that it made me laugh, which sent them into louder vocals. They always became silent when my mother entered to milk them, as if we had been sharing a secret.

"Good morning," my mother interrupted, gesturing for me to come over to her. "Madame Belmont was quite taken with you yesterday," she said, and I felt a nervous fluttering in my stomach. "We were watching you dance at the market and she was very impressed. She told me you have a natural talent and could become a professional ballerina."

I imagined myself as a ballerina like I had heard about in fairy tales. In my imagination I was poised and graceful, like a princess with wings who danced on clouds. I tried to see myself dressed in a delicate outfit, my hair pulled back, green eyes shining like emeralds as I danced.

"Perhaps we were looking in the wrong direction for your future," my mother continued. "Most girls begin training when they are very young, so you'll be getting a late start. I need you to be serious about this. You're going to have to work twice as hard as the other girls to get a spot in the Paris Opera Ballet. Can I depend on you to do this?"

I looked at her face, hard with tension, and nodded. She smiled at me, but her eyes remained serious. "Alexandrie, this will offer us more opportunity than we could ever have here." She moved closer to me, sitting on a stool and motioning to me to do the same. I brushed hay from the seat and perched beside her. "In Paris, no one will know of your brother's indiscretion or your father's finances," she whispered as if she was afraid some-one would hear her. "Marriage will be much easier for you there and the men you meet will have more wealth to offer than any-one in Espelette. In Paris, you can be anyone you want. You will have no past."

This appealed to me like nothing else I dared to dream of. I imagined being married to a man like Monsieur Belmont and the wealth and freedom to be so much more than just a farmer's wife. My mind immediately filled with images of a city I had never seen. My imagination built museums full of art and his-tory, shops with gorgeous dresses, and so many restaurants I could dine at a different one each night.

"Alexandrie," my mother's voice interrupted my daydream. "This is very serious."

I turned toward her, taking in her dry, cracked fingers as she swept a piece of long hair away from her tired face. "I can do this," I said to her with a determined glint in my eye. "When can I begin training?"

No. 3 Scène:
Madame Channing's Studio

*N*early every afternoon for the next year, I tucked my pale pink ballet slippers with the tiny bow on the top safely into a bag and rode in our rickety carriage two towns over to join the other young girls studying ballet at Madame Channing's Studio, one of the only dance classes in the South of France. My first day was the most humiliating experience of my life. Without any prior experience, I was placed in a class of eight-year-olds. I looked like a fully grown woman next to them and I wanted to cry and return home. But my mother's words, "In Paris, you will have no past," rang in my head. I still awoke before the sun came up, but after lunch, Luce took over my chores while my mother and I left for ballet practice. By the end of the year, my father had sold two more cows, Luce gave birth to a healthy boy, and I turned thirteen and moved up to a class with girls my own age. My mother, motivated by her plan of being rewarded by my success, made arrangements to clean the studio and maintain the yards at Madame Channing's every weekend in order to pay for my classes. I saw her sacrifice for me and took my lessons seriously, striving to excel beyond the other girls in the class.

Madame Channing was an overweight woman with incredible grace for her size. She was admired because one of every twenty girls in her classes had been accepted into the Paris Opera Ballet. I listened eagerly as she told us stories of those girls who had moved on to better lives. "I still receive letters thanking me for instructing them when they were young girls just like you," she said as she walked back and forth observing us lined up at the *barre,* correcting our *pliés* and *relevés.* She stopped by my side, opened up my hand, which was balled tightly into a fist as I con-centrated on my legs, and guided my middle finger to rest on my thumb. "Much more graceful," she whispered. "These young women dine in the company of the rich, refined gentlemen of Paris," she continued her story while moving down the line of girls. "One young woman wrote to me that she wears a different dress every day and she lives in a huge apartment overlooking the city, which a handsome gentleman bought for her. You see, girls, the dance can enthrall a gentleman like nothing else."

My eyes widened as I absorbed this. From the sound of it, in Paris, ballerinas were like royalty. I had heard that dancers re-ceived flowers after an outstanding show, but an apartment? This was astonishing.

For the first time in my life, dance gave me something to sep-arate myself from the other girls in Espelette. When we went to the market our neighbors would inquire how my ballet classes were and the other girls would always ask me of my plans to move to Paris to become a famous ballerina. My brown hair was now referred to as chestnut and my long limbs were called dancer's legs and I felt as if I had a purpose. But just as I was beginning to fully embrace my dream and believe that I could achieve it, my family intervened as if they intentionally plotted ways to make my life difficult.

"Alexandrie," Madame Channing's voice seemed to blend in with the music box as our class practiced an ensemble routine. "More fluid, more grace." I nodded slightly so that she would recognize that I heard her and concentrated with all of my will to transform my stiff arms into featherlike limbs. Each time I raised myself from the toe of my shoe, my calf muscles screamed. I had been practicing so much that my muscles began to get sore, but I pushed through, thinking they would catch up to my will. Yet today they seemed to be saying to me that they were quite finished and would not take any more. Every inch of my body ached, my torso felt like it was ripping apart with even the slightest turn. Our routine was nearing the end and I forced myself to leap into the air, but I could see the other girls far above me, and I felt like an elephant struggling to get off the ground. We all gazed straight ahead for the closing pose, leg extended, but mine was visibly shaking. It was without a doubt my poorest performance and I knew that I would need to find a balance in practicing just enough to excel beyond the other girls without abusing my body. Without it, I would never get to Paris. Relieved to have both feet on the floor once Madame Channing dismissed us, I was astonished to see my mother leaning against the studio's door, arms crossed, with a concerned look on her face.

Of course this is the one practice she has shown up to watch, I thought with a sigh. I walked over to her and before I could say anything she told me in a curt voice to get my things. When I glanced back I saw her approaching Madame Channing on the other side of the studio. While I changed out of my shoes, I wondered why today she had decided to watch my practice. All of the girls' mothers, at one time or another, had stayed to watch and I had always felt jealous when they would finish the day with a proud hug from their mothers while I sat outside waiting for mine to pick me up, usually quite later than when practice actually ended. I felt a strange sort of justification that now the other girls knew I actually had a mother, and I was no different than they were. I scurried toward the studio to tell my mother how happy I was that she had come. I could see her in animated conversation with Madame Channing, and I imagined they were complimenting how hard I worked both at the studio and practicing at home. Neither could see my dedication at both places, so now they were filling each other in. I smiled, then slowed down as I could see from their faces that they weren't having a friendly conversation.

"Why am I breaking my back cleaning your studio if this is all that I get?" my mother asked angrily. "Is this some kind of scam you're running? Putting up the guise of a dance studio so every mother in the area will come and willingly take care of your property?" Madame Channing looked shocked at these words but quickly composed herself. "Madame," she said crisply but politely, "a girl will not become a prima ballerina overnight. It takes much practice, which Alexandrie is doing wholeheartedly. Her performance today shows it, her legs are tired from pushing herself so hard. If you had come to other practices you would see how much she has progressed."

My mother snorted at this. "As if I have nothing but idle time to come sit here and watch the progression of a snail!" My face burned with humiliation and hot tears enveloped me as I turned away and started back toward the dressing room. But my mother called out to me, "Good, you're ready," in a tone that made it sound as if I had been holding her up and forcing her to speak to Madame Channing. I didn't turn around but stood where I was and waited for her. "I'll see you tomorrow morning, Alexandrie," Madame Channing called out cheerfully. "Keep up the good work and give your legs a rest tonight!" I nodded, embarrassed that she should feel the need to overcompensate in kindness where my mother lacked.

"That woman has no idea what an effort it is for you to be in her class," my mother ranted loudly as we made our way to the carriage. I wished I could put a hand over her mouth when some of the other girls looked over in curiosity as they departed for home with their mothers. I decided to not answer her until we were well down the road without anyone around to hear. "Is that really what you think of me?" I looked at her with hurt, *like a snail* repeating over and over in my head as the tears threatened to return.

"Now, now, don't be upset," she said dismissively while rubbing my back. "Not everyone is a natural dancer. We gave it a good try, now, didn't we?" She gave me a smile and I jerked away from her touch. She continued to smile as if I should agree with her and perhaps even feel relieved. "I've been working very hard at this," I said defensively. "And I'm improving every day and getting further and further ahead."

"When you were with the eight-year-olds, sure," she replied absently, watching the road. "But it's not as easy to keep up with girls your own age, is it?"

"I'm keeping up just fine," my voice began to rise. "You've never even asked me to show you what I'm learning. I admit I was not my best today, but it's one practice, Maman. One. And from this you think that I'm a talentless snail and you criticize Madame Channing and completely embarrass me!"

"You can stop scowling at me, because it won't happen again," she said shortly, flipping the reins for the horse to move forward at a faster pace. I sat back smugly and waited for her apology while the insects of the approaching night chirped around us. "You won't be taking ballet lessons anymore."

"No!" I screamed into the still dusk so loudly that I was sure people seated in their homes for dinner must have heard me. "These classes were your idea. You can't give me something that I love so much, something I'm actually good at, and then just take it away from me!"

She turned to me so I could see her hateful glare. "You're not the only one in this family who needs me. There's simply too much work to be done and I can't keep up with it if I have to go traipsing to the studio every weekend. We're behind in grinding peppers for the market. I hadn't expected your classes to take so much of my time."

"But when I go to Paris, you won't have to grind peppers all day." I looked at her in confusion.

"We just started this all too late," she sighed. "I saw the other girls in your class. They're so far ahead of you and they'll be going to Paris in a year or two. It will be less of a risk if you come back to work at home. As you get older you'll be able to take on more work at the farm and that will give us a little more to sell at the market."

"Let me finish this," I pleaded with her. "If I'm not one of the best dancers by the end of this year, then I will work on the farm for the rest of my life and you will never hear me complain about it."

She was silent for a few moments and then nodded. I felt differently about my dancing than my mother did and was going to prove it to her. So I took it upon myself to replace her and soon found myself cleaning Madame Channing's studio each Saturday so I could remain in class. As I scrubbed the floors, my anger at my mother grew. But I had fallen too deeply into my dream of becoming a Parisian ballerina to give up so easily.

My new job did nothing for my social standing amongst the other girls in my class. As we changed into our slippers, a fellow classmate, Laure, picked up her mud-caked boot, wiping it on the long lace curtains that hung from the studio's dressing room door. "Oh, no! What a mess I've made," she said in mock horror. The rest of the girls watched her curiously. "I suppose Alexandrie-the-Maid will have to clean it. Haven't you heard? She's cleaning the studio to pay for her lessons. It's bad enough when mothers have to do that, but could you imagine how poor you must be if you have to do it yourself?"

The rest of the girls stared at me as if I was a dirty orphan. Some looked uncomfortable at the position Laure had put me in but most just laughed. I refused to comment on my predicament and walked with my head down into the studio, taking my place at the *barre*. I felt breathing behind my ear and jerked my head away, assuming Laure had thought of another not-so-witty thing to say to me. "Do not let them break you," Madame Channing whispered to me and I smiled sheepishly at her for having jerked away. "Cleaning the studio shows great dedication on your part. Focus on the dance." I nodded and tried to pretend it didn't bother me to be ostracized. But of course it did. The worst part about Laure's comment was that it was true, and I found myself scrubbing the mud out of the intricate lace pattern that Saturday.

No. 4 Scène:
Destined for Greatness

I followed Madame Channing's advice and concentrated only on practicing. I became stronger, more graceful, so much so that by my fourteenth birthday even my mother began to notice I had some promise. In order to properly train for the Paris Opera Ballet, a young girl must first condition her body and then strengthen her mind. Once properly trained, a dancer's body can take on the most challenging moves. The mind, I have learned when looking back on those days, requires more time to adapt.

In an effort to prepare us for encounters with the wealthy patrons of the ballet, Madame Channing announced that a class of boys from the local academy would be attending practice to watch our dance routine. "Think of it as a mock recital," she said as we listened intently. "Pretend you are at the Opera Ballet and these boys are the gentlemen of Paris."

While we perfected our routine, she taught us how to make eye contact with the audience. "Men love it when you look them in the eye," she said teasingly, which was met by nervous giggles from the group. "But don't stare at them; that will only make them uneasy. Try to glance over and hold it for a second, then smile slightly and look away. You need to learn how to enthrall the audience."

I practiced this in the mirror when I returned home, but I thought I looked eerie with my eyes boring into my reflection and my mouth breaking into a forced grin before I whipped my face away. I remembered Madame Channing's advice of "subtle flirtation" and I worked on making my eyes and smile more demure until I felt that perhaps I did look as if I knew a secret that would draw the audience to me. At the time, I thought nothing odd of our mock recital. Later I would revisit that day as one of the many pieces of the puzzle that combined to form the *true* tradition of the grand Paris Opera Ballet.

I joined the rest of the class, all nervously waiting in the dressing room on the afternoon of our performance. The boys were already in the studio, all seated in a row. We moved toward the studio and stood by the door waiting to go on the mock stage. Madame Channing had brought her violin. She told us to pretend it was a full orchestra and to imagine a velvet curtain of the deepest red separating the boys from the stage. As she began to play and we sashayed toward the middle of the room, I watched the boys' reactions. Some watched curiously, others looked bored, and some laughed with one another as if this was the dullest way to spend the afternoon. When we finished the routine they all clapped obligingly and Madame Channing walked with a graceful dancer's stride to the center of the room, her huge backside bobbing up and down behind her.

"Aren't they talented?" she beamed. "We have a few minutes left, so please mingle."

The boys rose to their feet as we approached and then we all stood there awkwardly. "Are your skirts itchy?" a freckle-faced boy asked me, pointing at my tutu. "Not really," I replied. "My tights are more uncomfortable than the skirt."

He nodded. "I'm glad I'm not a girl so I don't have to wear all of that," he said. I wanted to tell him that his plain clothes were ugly and boring but I just smiled and nodded, remembering Madame Channing's words that gentlemen do not like women who talk back. If we were to use this recital as a learning experience for our days to come in Paris, then I would treat these boys like the gentlemen we would join when we were grown.

I looked around the room and saw most of the girls huddled up together pointing and giggling at the groups of boys. Sophie, the youngest girl in our class, was showing off for one of the boys, leaping about and bragging about how high she could kick her leg. He kicked his leg up and she laughed at his stiff attempt. I saw Madame Channing raise an eyebrow at him and he smiled back at her, then he glanced at Sophie in the middle of a *pirouette,* and walked away to talk to the giggling group of girls. Sophie stopped mid-*pirouette* and stomped after him. "I was in the middle of showing you something!"

"I'll talk to whoever I want," he yelled rudely at her, which caused her to burst into tears. Soon the boys were shuffled out of the room and Madame Channing gathered us to her to review how we performed during the recital. "I'm very proud that you all kept up with the routine and no one's timing was off. You are all well on your way to becoming professional ballerinas. Now, as far as interacting with the audience, you do have some more learning to do. Boys are shy; they won't approach a group of girls. Always separate yourselves so you look approachable.

Alexandrie, you did well, but you were a little too quiet. You must ask the boys questions about themselves to keep the conversation going. Sophie, you would be thrown out of the ballet for behavior like that. Your outburst is an example to always remember the number one rule—jealousy has no place in the ballet. You cannot expect a gentleman to only pay attention to you. You must be graceful and demure while he interacts with every dancer in the room. He will return to you, but you must not show that it bothers you when he goes to others. You must hide all ill feelings and appear as he wishes you to be."

I told my mother about this conversation on the way home. "That's good advice," she said while maneuvering the horse forward. "It certainly would be something if everyone's wife said what she was really thinking." She chuckled to herself but I failed to see the humor in it.

"But what if he's mean to you?" I asked. "Why do we have to make sure not to say or do anything to upset a man? Why isn't it their job to make us happy?"

"If you keep him happy he won't be mean to you," she replied. "And if he's happy, then you will be too. That's what you call a partnership."

"It sounds more like what you would call a maid," I mumbled.

"You'll be living on the street with that attitude," she said sternly. "Just because you don't want to raise a family on a farm does not mean that you can do whatever you want. You will need to learn to be accommodating toward men, even in Paris. It's the same in all walks of life."

"Isn't part of becoming an adult being able to finally voice your opinions?" I asked her, thinking of all of the times I had kept quiet because I was just a child and not old enough to join adults in conversation. "Yes," she nodded. "But with maturity comes knowing when to keep quiet." She stared off into the distance, reliving her memories out loud. "You know I thought your father was going to do great things. I thought we would be like the Belmonts—a well-to-do couple with everything to live for. But it has been harder to live as each year goes by," she added bitterly.

"But, Maman," I said. "You remind Papa of this all of the time. How can you say Madame Channing's words are good advice when you don't follow them?" She snorted and shook her head. "My dear girl, I very much censor my words. What I say out loud is only the half of what I'm actually thinking."

I cocked my head to the side and looked at her, really looked at her deeply. She had always appeared worn-out to me, and I had assumed that it was from the many tasks at the farm that she constantly reminded us that she had to do. But now I saw her weariness in a different light, that of a woman who had not only given up on her looks but had completely given up on life. "Are you that unhappy, Maman?" I asked her with concern. She patted my hand. "At times, but you mustn't blame yourself. In fact, it is you who will bring me happiness again."

"I think it will bring both of us happiness," I smiled at her. "Every single day I think about what I will be doing in Paris at this very moment. Right now, I could be waiting for the curtain to rise, ready to dance for hundreds of people. Or maybe I'm at a fancy restaurant having dinner with a man like Monsieur Belmont. Maybe if I go to Paris I'll fall in love with a man like that, just like you had wanted when you were my age."

But her reply was not what I expected. "Don't start with your daydreaming now," she said harshly. "A rich, handsome man like Monsieur Belmont would never look twice at a girl like you.

Even if you can clean yourself up, your incessant blushing will give away your self-consciousness and he'll know that you're beneath him. Don't go to Paris expecting a great love affair. If you can actually become a ballerina and can manage to find some man, any man—old, bald, or fat—who can pay off all our debts, then that will be all I need to be happy."

My face flushed with anger and shame and I turned away so she wouldn't be able to see it. "So it is only money that will make you happy," I said quietly, the connection I'd felt with her only moments ago gone. "That is a very rude thing to say, Alexandrie. Children bring you more joy than you can ever imagine, you'll see one day, but they can also cause you more pain than you ever thought possible. Just look at your brother. A fine way to repay me for bringing him into the world."

"Maman!" I said in shock.

"Don't act like you don't think the same thing," she said to me as if we were cohorts. "If he hadn't made such a mess you wouldn't need to be in ballet classes and you wouldn't be cleaning the studio each week. If he had thought of anyone besides himself, we would be partners with Claire's family, our farms thriving together, and you could have the pick of any boy who wanted your hand. Your life would have been easy. His selfishness has affected you as well."

"He's happy, Maman," I defended him. "And I love dancing and would choose being a ballerina over a farm wife any day of the week. I'll make it to the auditions, and I'll be accepted. I'll marry the wealthiest man in all of Paris!"

My mother chuckled sharply. "You think you are so charming, so witty, that no man will be able to resist you? And what will you dazzle the men of Paris with? Talk of peppers and cows and life on a farm?" Suddenly she sighed, exhausted, and looked at me in consternation. "I only want what's best for you, you know. And I want you to succeed. You've got years of training for the ballet ahead of you before you even try out in Paris. And we'll have to use that time to get your manners in shape."

She drove in silence for a while, reflecting, then finally said, "Monsieur Aston, a retired teacher, lives at the edge of town. He's a friend of our family and taught my brothers and me how to read and write when we were young. It was part of my father's idea to raise me as an independent child. He thought a basic education would help me to make smart choices in my life. Except that my education was very limited because I met your father not too long after I began, and abandoned my studies. But Monsieur Aston is a wonderful teacher and it will benefit you to get an education in order to make it in Paris."

"I would be able to take classes like Denis?" I asked, my eyes brightening at the thought. I didn't know any girls in town who went to school and this was truly something special. But my mother's fist slammed down, hard, on the seat, jolting me out of my thoughts.

"This is nothing like going to school," she said, her voice rising with each word. "This is one more hassle that I have to fix because you are not polished enough to go to Paris. Madame Channing told me that it would do you well to work on becoming more refined. Did you know that? She said you weren't reaching your full potential."

"That sounds like she thinks I have a lot of potential," I countered, but my mother cut me off. "She thinks you can make it into the ballet, but after that you'll never be able to attract a wealthy suitor. I don't care if you become a ballerina or a seamstress. But the ballet is where the type of man you need to find is." She fell silent for a few moments, clutching the reins of the horse tightly. "The more I think about this, the more I am certain that you need to be educated. You need to make yourself shine so only the highest class of men will pay you attention. There will be dozens of ballerinas in Paris, all of whom can dance and wear a pretty dress. But you'll be able to converse, which will make you acceptable to bring to high society events without making a fool of yourself or saying something ignorant."

I straightened in my seat. "I'm training to be a ballerina, not a society woman," I protested. "Why can't I concentrate on dancing and learn to read and write just a little? I doubt anyone expects me to be a scholar when I arrive. And if a gentleman was interested in marrying me, he would know I don't come from a wealthy family and would be drawn to me because he had seen me dance. That's where my passion is, and that's what is going to attract my husband!"

"Once you arrive in Paris, you'll find that you'll need more than dancing if you are to get ahead," my mother said firmly. She spoke again about how everything depended on me finding security for my family. "I need you to be a more logical thinker and to make wiser choices than I did, Alexandrie. At the very least it will scare off men who think they can get by on charm alone. Most men are intimidated by an educated woman, you'll soon learn this, so with some book smarts in your back pocket, you'll be able to reach a wealthy man in Paris, not some common imposter. I don't want you to run off with the first handsome man who pays you attention. Your life will be on an entirely different level, and Monsieur Aston will be the one to get you there."

I opened my mouth to respond but realized that she was really thinking out loud and not talking directly to me. I gazed out at the fields as we drove down the road. I felt completely overwhelmed. Yet the idea of being trained to become a fine lady was tantalizing.

"I will see if I can get him to tutor you one day a week so you can learn a basic education," my mother continued. "You need to think of this as part of your training for the ballet. It will benefit you greatly to know literature and how to manage your finances. We'll make you more than a dumb farm girl."

"I'm not a dumb farm girl," I said defiantly, even though I knew she was correct. Perhaps a bit of education was exactly what I needed to become extraordinary.

"Well, you're certainly not an educated well-to-do mademoiselle," she shot back, and guided the carriage down the long dirt road home.

The next morning, an hour's drive brought us to a small house in the middle of a meadow. My mother knocked on the door. It creaked open and a tall, thin old man with a great white mustache and thick glasses stood at the door. His skin was like tough leather and his face was wrinkled into a permanent smile. He squinted at us with kind eyes as he and my mother caught up on their lives, my mother finally explaining that I was bound for the ballet and would need academic training to help me along the way.

He smiled down at me and invited us inside. I took a seat on a chair and looked around the room. It was cluttered with books piled along the windowsills and tall bookshelves overrun with more threadbare books, crammed into the shelves and stacked on top of one another. He brought us both cups of tea and took a seat opposite us.

"So you have big dreams of moving to Paris?" he said to me and I nodded. Before I could answer, my mother interjected, "She has been studying at Madame Channing's Studio for the last two years. She's shown great talent. She does cleaning and yard work there to pay for lessons. I'm having a hard time driving her back and forth and keeping up my own home."

My face reddened. I knew we were poor, but would there ever be a time when everyone in Espelette didn't know it and look down on us?

"Well, I would be happy to teach Alexandrie," Monsieur Aston said, his hands shaking as he brought his cup to his lips. I watched it, waiting for it to spill. He took a long sip, droplets glistening on his mustache, and I shifted forward in my seat as his trembling hands set it back down on the saucer. "An old man like me could use the company of a bright, young child. Since my wife passed away, the garden has been all but ignored. Perhaps if Alexandrie arrived here early in the morning she could work in the garden until the sun becomes too hot, and then she can come inside and we can study."

I slumped in my chair, horrified. Separating myself from the other ballerinas was what I desired more than anything, but gardening? That was a price I wasn't willing to pay.

My mother, on the other hand, was beaming. "That sounds wonderful," she said, nodding at me like I should be grateful to pull weeds each week. "Luce and I can handle the market ourselves. Sundays would be perfect."

That Sunday, I sat in the carriage sulking. As we pulled into Monsieur Aston's drive, my mother pinched my arm and said,

"Don't ruin this or you'll be pulling weeds for the rest of your life."

"I'll be the perfect lady," I rolled my eyes and hopped out of the carriage. Walking behind the house to the garden, I sighed as I looked at the rows and rows of plants overgrown with weeds. Weeds were just like preparing meals. Once you finish one meal, there's another one waiting around the corner. By the time you reach the end of the garden, new weeds have sprouted up at the front. The sun was already beating down but I kept pulling weeds until I heard Monsieur Aston's voice. "Young Alexandrie, you're going to cook like an egg out there." I shielded my eyes from the glare and saw his stooped frame standing by the door waving me inside. I stood up, brushing off dirt, and trotted to the house.

"Sit down," he said while he shuffled around the kitchen. He had set out biscuits and he gestured to me to help myself. I was starving from working in the garden all morning and gladly smeared butter onto a warm biscuit. He brought a pot of tea over and then sorted through a muddle of books on the windowsill. "First I will teach you how letters form words," he said, sitting down beside me. "Once you understand this, your mind will open up to a whole new world and anything you wish to learn will be within your reach." He sharpened a pencil, squinting at it, his shaky hands pressing down hard on the knife and moving in short, strong swipes. I watched him over my teacup, afraid that he would cut himself. He passed a pencil to me and kept one for himself. "Once you learn how to write you can preserve all of the thoughts that run through that little head of yours." He smiled at me, tapping my forehead with his pencil, and I couldn't help but smile back.

I left his house that day in a completely different form than I had arrived. I couldn't stop talking about our study session and how his house was full of books and soon I would be able to read every single one of them. Each Sunday, I awoke eagerly in anticipation of poring over books and learning how to write over biscuits and tea.

As his garden transformed from a jumble of weeds to neat rows of plants, I grasped basic reading and writing skills, and Monsieur Aston eventually showed me a book of poems by Margaret Cavendish. I was in awe of a woman writer and devoured the pages. "Her stories are short and I'm afraid I don't follow them," I said, quite frustrated. Monsieur Aston nodded. "These are poems," he explained. "They follow a different structure with rules of their own."

He showed me how my words could be arranged in a type of meter that brings a distinct rhythm to the piece, creating a poem. I was intrigued and, after countless frustrating attempts, I soon began to find it cathartic to write down what I was feeling at that very moment and then work the lines into a poem. "You have finally caught on!" Monsieur Aston said months later, proudly reading a poem I composed about his garden. "I shall hang this up and tell everyone who visits that my best student composed it!"

Soon my room was filled with poems. It had been nearly five years since I stepped foot in Madame Channing's Studio, and I felt I had complete control over my life of training. After ballet class, I helped prepare dinner, and after cleaning, I retired to my room where I would quietly practice the steps I had learned. When my legs began to ache, I studied by candlelight until I could no longer keep my eyes open. I slept with a pride in knowing that my muscles were getting stronger and the book on my bedside table was larger than the last. But the problem with a routine is that it can only go smoothly for so long. Eventually it will unravel.

"Do one thing at a time," Monsieur Aston said gently as I grew more and more frustrated with an arithmetic problem. "Don't get overwhelmed by the entire picture. Just concentrate on one aspect of it. Once you've completed that, then move to the next task, and keep going until the entire picture is finished. Then you'll find yourself looking at a masterpiece."

I smiled and wiped a tear from my cheek. "If only it were that easy," I sniffled. "I need to become an accomplished dancer, scholar, and lady all at the same time. I think if I only concentrated on one of those, then I wouldn't have time to complete the rest before going to Paris. I cannot arrive with a half-finished picture—as a work in progress."

He smiled sympathetically and put down his pencil. "I know your mother is pushing you hard," he said. "And you push yourself too!" I managed a small laugh at this. "It seems she has aspirations for you to become a *lorette* of the highest class."

I tilted my head and laughed. "But no, Monsieur. Maman would certainly be shocked to hear you suggest such a thing—to become a man's mistress! I love the ballet but Maman sees it as only a route to marriage, since no man in Espelette will have me." An odd expression washed over Monsieur Aston's face. "She has not told you?" "Told me what?" I asked, frowning. He didn't answer and I suddenly felt chilled, as if the happiness ballet had given me was about to slip from my grasp. My voice came out quavering and childlike, "Please, Monsieur, you have to tell me."

"Ah, Alexandrie, it's not my place," he said, dropping his eyes. But looking back into my watery gaze he seemed to change his mind. "Your mother should have told you." He let out a great sigh. "Alexandrie, while the ballet is one of the most beautiful things anyone can experience, it has a history of attracting powerful men who think they can buy any beautiful thing they see. Most of the girls who become ballerinas are from very poor families and are trying to make a better life for themselves."

"Girls like me?" I asked, thinking I understood. "No, Alexandrie." He placed his hand on mine. "They are nothing like you."

I squeezed his hand, rough and arthritic, and breathed in, somehow knowing that what I heard next would change everything. "Many of these girls think their looks are the only thing they can offer to a man, especially of a higher station. As a result, it has become common for patrons to take a ballerina as a mistress, a *lorette*."

"The gifts of apartments," I murmured, realizing how stupid I had been in Madame Channing's class. "But you said many of the girls, not all of them. Surely some of them fall in love and marry."

"Some," he acknowledged. "It really becomes somewhat of a trap. The ballet provides the opportunity to earn your own wages and become a glamorous fixture of Parisian society, yet you will always be just a dancer—never a real society woman whom a ballet patron would court for marriage."

"So that is the life my mother wishes for me," I said, deflated. I had gotten quite used to the idea of separating myself from my family, creating my own life in Paris, and marrying the type of man I would never find in Espelette—not just rich and handsome, but able to appreciate cultural things like the ballet. I had a fantasy that a handsome man in the audience would see my passion for dancing and fall in love with me. I hadn't considered the reality of the situation. I never thought the patrons would already have preconceived notions of ballerinas and view them as not good enough to marry. My first instinct was to abandon my training and accept my life on the farm as all that I would ever have. Only I didn't want to be in the family selling cattle to the Belmonts—I wanted to *be* the Belmonts. I didn't want to stay here where everyone already knew me and had formed their opinions of me based on my family.

"Did you know I was once in love with a ballerina?" Monsieur Aston said, his eyes gazing off toward the window.

I raised my eyebrows in shock and he chuckled at this. "Yes, there was a time when I wasn't an old man living in this little cottage. When I lived in Paris, I met her at a lecture and she was so beautiful that I couldn't take my eyes off her. And smart too. I knew immediately that I would marry her."

"What happened?" I asked, trying to imagine Monsieur Aston as a young man.

"We were engaged, but soon it became clear that I wasn't going to be able to provide her with anything more than a modest home. This was fine at first, but as time went by, she was drawn more and more to the life that other ballerinas were living as *lorettes*. She wanted to wear fine clothes and jewels and ride in large carriages with their own drivers. She became the mistress of a man older than her father," he sighed at the memory. "I was heartbroken and moved here to live away from the materialism of the city."

"But I'm nothing like that," I said. "I want to dance in Paris and find love, even if my mother would want me to find someone like your fiancée's monsieur."

"Then use everything you're learning and everything that you're working so hard at achieving to benefit *you*," Monsieur Aston told me earnestly. "Become the best ballerina Paris has

ever seen and earn the highest wages. Use your knowledge to engage in all that Paris has to offer. Converse with those people
who are interested in you, not in a faceless dancer. Make your life
your own, Alexandrie."

I wanted to confront my mother immediately, but each time I
saw her, the words wouldn't come. Even in arranging Denis' engagement to Claire in order to secure our farm, I knew my parents had wanted him to find happiness and a respectable, full life.
I didn't want to know that my mother had never cared if *I* married or found happiness, as long as I brought her wealth. With so
much weighing on my mind, I didn't even realize that it was my
seventeenth birthday, and I arrived at dance class as if it was any
other day. No one in my family wished me happy birthday, as it
would seem they were also too preoccupied to remember. At the
studio, I could forget about the thoughts that kept me up at
night. I could become lost in the dance, transported to a different world, where nothing could hurt me. When the music ended,
I always felt let down to see the uneven floorboards and hazy
mirrors of the studio, knowing that I had to pick up my life
where I left it.

When Madame Channing asked me to stay after class, I wondered what I had done wrong to be detained. "Someone's in
trouble," Sophie hissed as she walked by and the other girls giggled, following closely behind her. I slowly walked toward
Madame Channing, going over the day's practice in my head. I
had definitely drifted off into my own world, which happens
quite a lot when I dance. I had imagined myself on a cloud,

lightly bounding into the sky and returning to the fluffy starting point. Perhaps I had been so wrapped up in my daydreaming that I had performed an entirely different routine!

But instead Madame Channing beamed at me. "You did an outstanding job today." I breathed a sigh of relief. "Give me one minute to put the music away and then I have some very exciting news to speak to you about."

When she returned I took the opportunity to ask her what I had wanted to for so long. Looking around, I saw no one else was in the studio to overhear. "Madame, remember when you told us about the ballerina who was given an apartment?"

"Of course! She is one of my most successful students." Her eyes lit up with pride. "She lives such an exciting life now."

"Is she a *lorette*?" I whispered the word as if it was obscene.

"Of course, my dear." Madame Channing looked at me in puzzlement. "Why ask with such secrecy?" she whispered, imitating my tone in amusement. Then she smiled broadly. "Did you think there was nothing else to ballet but dance? My dear, it is an honor to be a *lorette*! You are more dedicated to dancing than I had thought if you had believed that is all you would get out of becoming a ballerina! It was my life's ambition to perform as part of the Paris Opera and have everything taken care of for me. I was so close to it," she said wistfully. "I was accepted into the ballet, but only a few weeks into it, I landed wrong and injured my knee. I was never able to dance professionally again."

"I'm so sorry," I replied genuinely, knowing how difficult it must have been for her to work so hard for something only for it to fall apart as soon as she had arrived. She smiled and waved her hand as if it was not that traumatic. "If I hadn't fallen, then I wouldn't be here teaching you. And telling you that you have nothing to be worried about! One day you'll see how exciting it is to live right in the middle of such a vibrant city, and how frustrating it is to not have any money to enjoy it. Paris is truly a *lorette*'s paradise—shopping and shows and parties. You can't do all of that if you have a family to take care of. So let someone else take care of you and enjoy life!"

I nodded, and even though I felt some relief at Madame Channing's openness about *lorettes* and the ballet, I also felt more confused. I didn't want to believe that the vibrant, always cheerful Madame Channing could be like Monsieur Aston's fiancée, a woman to whom money was more important than love. But she interrupted my thoughts. "I want you to stop attending class." Madame Channing's eyes twinkled as my mouth dropped open. She began to laugh and gave me a great hug. "Oh, I shouldn't torture you so, but I cannot help but have a bit of fun. You have graduated! I want you to turn all of your attention to perfecting a routine of your own that you will perform in one month at the Paris Opera House."

"You mean it? Oh, Madame Channing!" I couldn't contain my excitement. I knew eventually I would be ready to audition, but I hadn't known how the news would be delivered, or that I would arrive to class one morning and leave ready to prepare for my Paris audition. I had always pictured the entire class going to Paris together.

"I am completely serious," she said. "I want you to practice every single day. On Saturday, instead of cleaning the studio, I want you to come here to show me your routine. We'll polish it up and make sure you're flawless for the Opera Ballet. You'll need to include your basic steps, along with *ronds de jambe, pirouettes, ballons, entrechats,* and *jetés,* at a minimum. How you put all of this together is at your own liking and, of course, I'll help you make sure it all comes together smoothly. They will play any music they choose at the audition, so keep in mind that your routine will need to complement whatever musical accompaniment is given to you. You're the only girl in the class who is ready for Paris, Alexandrie, this is a huge accomplishment. I know how hard you've worked for this, and I don't know anyone else who deserves it more than you."

Tears of gratitude welled up in my eyes as I thanked her over and over for everything she had done for me. If it had been up to my mother, I would have quit my classes long ago and given up on life, just as she had. Now I felt as if I had an entirely new world to explore, but there was just one thing I needed to sort out before I left.

I returned home that night determined. The fact that Maman thought I had been the worst girl in the class and now I was the only girl ready for Paris gave me the nerve to finally stand up for myself and confront her. I stood by the frame of the door, looking at her in the kitchen as she cut carrots, muttering under her breath. Every now and again a slice of carrot would drop to the floor and she would curse, pick it up, rinse it off, and throw it into the pot with the rest. Lifting the pot off the table as if it was a huge effort, she set it down on the fire with a thud. Turning around, she saw me and motioned to the table. "How about cleaning up the carrots before the table stains orange?" It wasn't a suggestion or a question.

I brushed the carrot peelings to the edge of the table and into my hand, and said matter-of-factly, "You must be tired from chopping all of these vegetables. I bet you would do anything to have farmhands and a maid or two around. Even sell your own daughter off as a mistress so that you can finally have the easy life you think you deserve." Color flooded my cheeks. The words were so satisfying, yet I couldn't look up to see her reaction. I had never thought something so harsh before, let alone said it aloud. I could hear my mother put down the knife she was using to chop an onion, and her footsteps told me she was approaching the table. I looked up to see her within arm's length of me and, in one quick flash, she slapped me across the face. I bit my lip and my hand immediately flew to my burning cheek, but I said nothing. I knew I deserved it, yet I also knew I couldn't apologize because she deserved those words as well. Perhaps she thought the same, because she lowered herself to a chair and, running a hand through her hair, all she said was, "Now you know what reality is. Daydreaming is a waste of time."

I grew up that day, sitting at the table with my mother. She talked to me not as a daughter, but as a woman about to venture into the world on her own with the burden of providing for her family. I thought about Madame Channing's words that I wouldn't be able to enjoy Paris to its fullest with a family to take care of. I smiled ironically, thinking that my mother wanted me to become a *lorette* so I could take care of her, not so I could enjoy myself without any worries like Madame Channing wanted for me. But my mother did share Madame Channing's opinion about the arrangement, describing the relationship of a dancer and patron as a romantic partnership that society was not ready for, and because of this, it was never spoken of outright. My mother explained that a man sacrificed his desires and kept his true love, the ballerina, near the Opera House while his legacy was ensured by a sensible woman from the same background as he.

But I wasn't as naive as I had been when I was twelve. I knew she wanted me to become a *lorette* because it was the fastest way to ensure a pile of francs would be delivered to her. I knew she doubted I would find a husband who could provide for both me and for her, and I knew she didn't think I was talented enough to become a great ballerina. Yet I had surpassed all the others in my class and would be auditioning soon. If I had listened to everything she said, I would have given up a long time ago. I knew she was wrong about my ability to find both happiness and success.

I told her Monsiuer Aston's opinions of the arrangement and watched her smile in amusement. "He is very much the overprotective grandfather, and a lover scorned," she said. "Do not let him worry you, a *lorette* is nothing to be ashamed of." I only nodded to acknowledge her opinion. Once I got to Paris I would decide for myself.

No. 5 Scène:
The Audition

I suggest you take her to Paris. She is ready," Madame Channing said to my mother as I finished the last of our Saturday sessions. I couldn't have been happier to hear this. I had been petrified when I arrived at the studio that morning that my routine would not be ready and I would need to wait. My mother was under the impression that I was working even harder now because I thought the life of a mistress sounded pretty good. While I still wanted to see this "prestigious tradition" with my own eyes, I also wanted to prove to her what I already knew—I could be more than that. I could be one of the few ballerinas who are exceptional dancers and marry because they want to, not because they need to. I knew my mother wouldn't understand this. I would send her money but, for once, I would make my own decisions about how I wanted to live my life. I had no idea what decisions I would come to, but they would be mine. The thought made me giddy with excitement and when my mother hugged me hard, I hugged her back with equal strength. With her voice full of excitement, she thanked Madame Channing for allowing me to join the class. "She has been a delight," Madame Channing replied. "Her routine is flawless. There will be hundreds of girls there, but she has something special."

My mother couldn't stop thanking her and Madame Channing modestly accepted her praise. I climbed into the carriage and she yelled out to me, "Good luck, Alexandrie. Be sure to write me of your adventures!"

"I will!" I shrieked back, overcome with excitement. "We'll be going to Paris tomorrow!" I turned to my mother, eyes shining with emotion.

"Yes, isn't it thrilling?" she said, her face breaking out in a smug smile. "You will become such a fine lady. Perhaps soon things will be looking up."

"I must tell Monsieur Aston good-bye," I interrupted in a panic. I thought of the windowsills full of books that would remain unread and the serene days in his home away from the chaos of farm life.

"There isn't time," my mother said. "We need to leave tomorrow before the sun rises to be in Paris by noon. I can send your brother over to let him know."

"No! I need to say good-bye." I looked at her, disbelieving. He had not only taught me how to read and write but how to calculate how much of a ballerina's stipend I would need to keep for myself, how much to send home, and how if I put away a small percentage each month it would grow so I could have something in the future. "You don't want to find yourself in a difficult situation," he had told me, and I agreed to always keep a percentage of my earnings for myself, rather than send the entire thing back to Espelette, as was my mother's plan. Each week, he gave me a new book to take with me when I finally went to Paris. "This will be helpful," he would say as I peered at the cover. My room had a stack of novels and books about architecture, the history of France, law, and ethics. They were all topics that we didn't have time to study together, but I promised him I would treat it as homework. I no longer stared at his shaking hands, now I only saw the great mind underneath it all. "Please, it is important to me," my voice cracked as I fought back tears.

"Very well," she sighed and I chose not to reply. When we arrived at Monsieur Aston's, I ran to his door, my mother reluctantly following me through the dim light of the evening. "Alexandrie! What a pleasant surprise," he shuffled to the door, a book in his hand and a pencil behind his ear. "Shall I make us some tea?"

"I'm afraid we're a bit short on time," my mother said apologetically.

"I'm going to be auditioning for the Paris Opera Ballet tomorrow!" I told him.

"You will?" His face broke out into a wide smile as he hugged me tightly. "Alexandrie, I am so proud of you and know you will be wonderful. But I see our time together must come to an end." I nodded, looking at his bushy eyebrows above his thick glasses. "I'm sad to see you go; you have become quite an accomplished student." He shuffled away from the door and began to sort through a pile of books. His hands shaking, he gave me a thick book with a tattered leather cover. "A parting gift."

"More homework," I laughed as I ran my fingers over the cover, a film of dust covering my fingertips, and saw it was a book of Margaret Cavendish poems. "But this is an original, and your favorite. I can't accept this," I said. "Of course you can," he assured me. "I hope that you continue to read and write poems; you have many gifts. I wish you all the luck in Paris. It's a big city and you'll meet people from all over the country, but do not lose sight of who you are. You have a strong will and you must promise me that you will always be true to yourself."

"That's the most important thing you taught me. Paris is where I am meant to make a name for myself," I grinned conspiratorially at him as my mother guided me away from the door while thanking him for my lessons.

He nodded in reply to her thanks and smiled at me in a mixture of sadness and concern, as if he knew what lay ahead for me. "I wish the world were different," he said.

The day of my audition I woke earlier than I ever had even when we had to weed the garden. My mother wet my hair with honey so the fuzz would not appear and harshly brushed it back, forming a tight chignon. As I felt the teeth of the comb struggle to smoothe my thick locks, I saw myself in this same position, my mother pinning back my hair, beaming at me proudly as she gently secured my wedding veil.

Looking toward the window at my final glimpse of the pepper fields, I began to tear up. "This day has come so quickly and I'm scared to leave," I admitted. "The entire family is depending on me and I only have one try to get it right." I couldn't imagine failing in Paris only to return home to grinding peppers and pulling weeds.

"Stop, your eyes will get red and puffy," my mother said, turning my head so she could continue combing my hair. "You must work harder than ever to develop yourself into a great dancer and society woman, and write to me of all your accomplishments. Paris is the theater of nations, with the Opera House at the very center of it. Your acceptance will offer you a world of opportunity that we cannot provide for you. You must use everything at your disposal to secure your place in that world. Remember that your family is depending on you."

I climbed into the carriage, careful to not get the dewy morning grass on my feet. As we traveled through the winding streets, I saw the tiny homes decorated with dried peppers for the last time. Excitement overtook my fear and I promised myself I would be a model ballerina and move up in society. I would not be another generation stuck in Espelette.

I couldn't wait to see the city I had heard so much about, yet it was so early that the sky was still dark, and the only thing I could distinguish were shadows of the rolling countryside meadows. I tried to stay awake, forcing my eyelids back open repeatedly to watch the landscape change from grassy fields to soaring buildings. I finally dozed off, telling myself the dawn would wake me and I would take in the towns along the way to Paris. But when I opened my eyes, the sun was shining brightly and I saw my mother's glance darting back and forth as she anxiously nudged me, telling me we had arrived. Indeed we had, I thought, as I gaped at the wide street that we had pulled our carriage to the side of, perfectly in line with a long row of other, much fancier, carriages. I stepped down from our small, rickety carriage ready to distance myself from it; embarrassed to admit it was our means of transportation as large, shiny buggies pulled by two horses passed by, making ours look even shabbier than I had suspected it to be. Our horse looked dirty and worn, dropping his head in what I understood to be shame as the freshly groomed horses trotted by with their heads held high.

While my mother tied our horse to a street post, I gazed at the city around me. The Paris Opera House, which I had only seen in pictures at Madame Channing's Studio, seemed to loom above the rest of the block, towering over the streetlamps and dwarfing the people walking up its steps. I looked curiously at the lamps, imagining how they glowed at night and wondering why we did not have these in Espelette so that we could stretch our day past the sun's setting. I shifted my gaze to the Opera House. It seemed that every inch was decorated with something ornate, from columns to sculptures. I had never seen a building so bejeweled. To me it looked like a castle and I couldn't believe this was where I hoped to dance for all of Parisian society. The sounds of the city buzzed around me as pedestrians strolled past us, men elongated in top hats and women floating by in full skirts. The women wore tightly fitted jackets over their dresses, stretching down to gloved hands, stiff bonnets protecting their eyes and hair from the sun. Many added extra flavor to their ensembles by arranging a silk scarf, matching the color of the jacket, around their necks. In Espelette we never dressed that well for the most important occasion let alone for just a regular day.

I brightened up when I saw a fruit vendor. Perhaps Paris was not that different from home. A woman approached the stand, and I expected to see a familiar exchange, but instead she pointed at various produce and the vendor would pick them up and show them to her. She moved her face in closely and would nod or shake her head no. It didn't make a lot of sense to me. If you were going to eat this food, then why wouldn't you pick it up yourself to inspect it?

For a moment I wanted more than anything to return to Espelette. I was intimidated by this elegant building and the people who didn't even seem to notice it. They walked about with looks of boredom, effortlessly wearing their rich clothes, used to this way of life and all of the fine things the city offered. I pulled self-consciously at the tutu I was wearing with its pieces of tulle pinned together. I had worn it for the entire trip, as I owned nothing but faded, drab peasant skirts and my mother decided that I would look best in the ballerina outfit. I had sat wrapped in a blanket until we reached Paris so the dust from the road wouldn't cover me. "We can't afford any mishaps," she had told me that morning while coiling my hair into its chignon. We had thought I looked quite elegant when I left the house, but now as I stood awkwardly amidst the hustle and bustle of Paris I felt like a beggar.

My feelings of inadequacy only heightened when we entered the Opera House. The grand arched doors were so tall that my mother had to pull with all of her strength to open them. I gasped as I gazed about at an interior equally as elaborate as the outside while my mother shot me a look that said "Be silent, we need to keep up the charade that we belong here." The foyer stretched up for stories and I felt incredibly small standing in the middle of it. Young dancers and their mothers hurried by, but I hardly noticed them. My feet planted on the marble floor, I stared at what I would later learn were moldings, columns, and archways framing balconies overlooking the entranceway. I felt as if I was standing atop a cake whose icing had been applied so carefully that not an inch was left undecorated. The entire place was lit up brightly with the sun flowing in through the large windows, and I envisioned myself completely at home here, leaning over the railing bathed in the glow of elegance. I was both awestruck and frightened as I followed my mother up the large, winding staircase.

Once we left the mesmerizing foyer, we followed a long hall-way leading to the backstage dressing room, and I was panic-stricken by the number of young girls gathered in the hall awaiting their auditions. We stood in a line to get to the dressing room where an older woman handed each of us a slip of paper with a number on it before allowing us to enter. Mine was two hundred and two. "When this number is called, it is your turn," the woman said brusquely and ushered us into the dressing room. I stayed close to my mother as we moved through the crowd of hopeful ballerinas. Many were so much younger than me and their mothers hovered over them, hands flying every-where, working their hair, fluffing their tutus, and applying color to their lips in the hopes that enhancing their physical beauty would augment the grace of their performance. I smoothed my hair, hardened with honey, and watched as the girls practiced their steps. A line of hopeful ballerinas stood nervously by the entrance to the stage waiting for their numbers to be called, and I felt the pressure that all of us were under to succeed. I stretched my legs and found an open corner of the room where my mother instructed me through my routine. As the numbers were called out, my heart beat faster and I numbly joined the queue waiting to go onstage. I heard music begin and just as sud-denly cut off when a thin, gawky girl scurried past me with tears streaming down her face. As her hysterical mother shook her shoulders and slapped her face, a booming voice yelled, "Num-ber *deux cent deux!*"

"That's you!" my mother said hurriedly, pushing me past the curtain. I shook away the image of the tearful girl receiving a beating for failing and walked onto the stage. The bright lights shocked me and I could barely make out the row of men who would judge whether I had enough talent to remain in Paris. Two hundred girls had already performed for the group and, in a panic, I wondered if perhaps they were growing bored and every dancer appeared the same to them by this point. Just as my mind began to wrap itself around the fact that only forty new ballerinas would be chosen, one man stepped to the front of the group, a silhouette of a short, refined gentleman in a top hat and holding a cane. He ceremoniously banged his cane down to the floor twice, which echoed throughout the large empty theater. Then the music of the orchestra began, swallowing the echo from the cane.

I immediately launched into my routine, not waiting for anyone to give me direction, knowing I had to give nothing short of a *tour de force*. I couldn't hear the music and I couldn't see anything but the glow of lanterns shining down on me. Instead of performing a well-known dance, I had chosen instead to create my own. I wanted to show the depth of my skill by combining difficult moves with classic ballet. While I was not the daintiest dancer, I knew I was strong, so I included a series of jumps to show off the height my muscular legs could achieve. I drew in my breath and leapt into a *ballon,* bounding up from the floor, pausing a moment in the air, and descending lightly and softly, then rebounding in the air like a feather. I was glad to hear no loud thud when my feet met the floor and I gained confidence as I prepared myself for a *grand jeté en avant,* springing from a *plié* so high into the air that I felt as if I had all of the time in the world to extend one leg forward and the other one up and back before descending into the most controlled and graceful *plié* I had ever accomplished. My head filled with every instruction I had accumulated in my young life—"head up to elongate your body, no stiff fingers, stomach pulled in so you don't look like a sausage, pointed toes, no flat feet, extend, extend, don't swing your leg, gracefully extend, don't strain your face, relax through your shoulders." I was lost in the routine, yet anxious to finish, and my stomach tightened in anticipation of my grand finale, a series of *pirouettes*. *Pirouettes* had always caused me problems because correct body placement was essential and I had a bad habit of rushing into the step. I loved the elegance that an accomplished dancer has of landing from the air and immediately breaking into a series of *pirouettes,* yet each time I tried to mimic this I lost my balance and spun onto the floor. Every night in my room since I had learned I was going to Paris, I practiced this move until I mastered it. Now I inhaled with determination and briefly made sure my body was lined up properly, fixing my eyes on a sconce and focusing on nothing but that sconce as my leg extended and swirled back in, leading my body into the turn. I gracefully built momentum and miraculously held my balance as I spun around and around to complete the series without toppling over. I fought breaking out into a huge smile as my head buzzed in a mix of pride at my flawless performance and relief that it was over. I stood in *arabesque* with my leg extended behind my body and my arms raised to form the longest possible line from my fingertips to toes. I tried to remain still and not shake from fatigue and nerves as I held my shoulders square to the line of my pose. I was grounded in profile, peering at the silhouettes from the corner of my eye for what seemed a lifetime. The silence was broken by the voice of the short man booming throughout the room at an alarming volume. "I like this girl. She can attain an extraordinary amount of height." His statement was quickly followed by the rustling of papers and I was handed a card.

I returned to my mother, who told me this was my ticket into the ballet. She held the card in both hands and tears ran down her face. "Oh, thank God, thank God," she pulled me to her and stroked my hair. "You've made me so proud. I knew we could depend on you; you're not weak like your brother." I was glad that another top-hatted gentleman whisked me away before I could reply. I knew that I would either turn out to be the child who completed what my mother had not, or I would disappoint her even more than my brother had. The man deposited me into a small room down the street from the Opera House and, in what seemed a haze to me, he pointed to the wall where a schedule was posted and departed with a thud of the door while I gingerly sat down on one of the room's small beds and waited. The short man's statement replayed over and over in my head. *Extraordinary.* I glowed from this word. Even at Madame Channing's class I believed the only thing that separated me from the other girls was that I cleaned the studio. I was no longer an ordinary girl from Espelette, but while I had achieved what I came here for, I didn't know what was next. My entire life had been guided by the strong hand of my mother and now that she wasn't here to tell me what the next step was, I had no idea what to do with myself. So I sat and waited for instruction.

Just as I began to nod off from the day's excitement, the door opened and a girl my own age entered, accompanied by the same gentleman. "Alexandrie, this is Noella," he said. "You will be sharing this room during your time as students."

I was glad to see she looked to be my age and I was not going to have to share my room with a fourteen-year-old. Noella gave me a huge smile as the man exited, and I welcomed the company. "Congratulations! We are officially the most talented dancers in the entire country," she bubbled over.

"I never thought of it that way," I said. "I was concentrating so hard on not messing up that I hadn't really considered where the rest of the girls had come from."

"You must be lying! My mother has been telling me since I can remember how I need to be better than not just the girls in my own dance class but better than all of the girls in all of the dance classes in the country," she said, her voice growing louder with excitement. She smoothed her bright locks back and sat gracefully onto her bed. Noella was unlike any girl I had met before. She spoke so rapidly I didn't have to worry about what to say to her, but only reply to her chatter. Her skin was so pale and her hair so fair that she would have looked like a ghost if it were not for her intensely blue eyes. They seemed to float out from her face, the only touch of color on her. She had an air of someone twice her age who had seen the world, and that added to her allure. I self-consciously touched my own chignon, which I thought looked drab in comparison.

"Can you read? I need to know what our schedule is." She passed off her embarrassment at her lack of education by replacing it with a sense of urgency.

I had not even looked at the schedule and felt dense for staring into space for so long, waiting for someone to tell me what to do. I got up and read out loud that every day was scheduled with ballet practice, character building classes, and end of the week exams. Sunday was titled "day of rest."

"Come on. Orientation is starting!" Noella cried impatiently as she scooped her ballet slippers into her arms. "My mother was right—this schedule is painful!"

I quickly did the same and followed her out of the room, practically running down the street to catch up to her as she trotted back to the Opera House and into a huge dance studio full of young ballerinas. Marbled pilasters stood tall throughout the room, and the floor-to-ceiling windows stretching for what seemed like miles made my jaw drop. An elaborately framed mirror stood opposite a grand piano, the source of the music I would soon be dancing to. We joined the rest of the dancers and soon learned why there were so many of us. Even though we had been accepted into the Opera Ballet school, it did not mean that we were going to be ballerinas. The short man from the audition entered the room carrying his cane and I could see him clearly now. He had unruly white hair and wore a long, black jacket hitting mid-thigh. He introduced himself as the Ballet Master, the one who would decide which of us were worthy to stay. "Many of you will not advance," he told us sternly and I was immediately afraid of him, for he held my future in his hands. "For the next year you will endure rigorous training that will make your previous training seem like a tea party. Here we will mold you into true Parisian dancers. Every day we will practice. Those who advance will attend the performances of the Opera and learn from the professional ballerinas. They have been in your shoes and have set themselves apart from the rest to perform in our prestigious ballet. Your natural ability has taken you this far. For the next year you will be judged not only on your talent but your improvement with the dance, how well you take direction, and your strength of character. Only when you achieve all of this will you be formally accepted into the Opera Ballet."

He reviewed the schedule and repeated that Sunday was our day of rest and we were to be in our rooms by sunset. I was thrilled to hear that we could venture out wherever we pleased as long as we returned by this time. He praised us for how we had sacrificed our family lives to find a better path for ourselves. We were the most talented, the chosen ones, and we were now property of the ballet.

When we returned to our room, Noella washed her face, slathering lotion over her hands and covering them with socks. "It keeps the moisture in," she explained, holding up her hands. "You don't wash your face or take care of your hands?" she asked as she looked at me tucked into my bed. I shook my head no. "You had better start! Our entire being depends on our looks. Hands are the most expressive part of a dancer. They not only complete every pose but will be the first contact you have with a gentleman when he meets you." I was too tired to contemplate such things so I reluctantly ran the bar of soap along my face and looked wearily at a pair of socks as Noella stared critically at herself in the mirror. "I'm so pale," she said hopelessly. "My mother tells me that's what sets me apart from other girls and she won't allow me out in the sun."

I giggled as I climbed back into my bed. "My mother won't let me outside without a bonnet and speaks about the dangers of sun streaks in my hair." I saw my mother chastising me in the garden for trying to remove my bonnet and a wave of sadness swept over me. I had never before been away from home for a night and I felt incredibly lonely without my family. I turned away from Noella, pretending to be asleep, so she would not see my tears and think that I was weak.

I awoke in the morning, my eyes itching from crying myself to sleep, overwhelmed with the haste at which I arrived at the ballet. I tiptoed to the window so as not to wake Noella, who was sprawled facedown on her pillow, her blond curls fanned out in all directions. I was used to waking early on the farm and as I looked out the window, I saw the city beginning to come to life.

Instead of dew glistening from pepper plants, I watched as shopkeepers swept the areas in front of their stores and set up small tables and chairs, cranking wheels in a circle to open their awnings. I watched the laborers lug their work through the city, the milliners holding hatboxes full of needlework in their arms, and the laundresses carrying large bundles of linens. I felt a flutter of excitement as I looked out onto the city. I was here; I had made it to Paris, and now I lived along the Grands Boulevards, the commercial center of Paris, a place I had only heard about. At Monsieur Aston's, I had once read that shops lined the streets, selling porcelains, perfumes, carpets, furs, mirrors, controversial caricatures in journals, the most sparkling champagne, and the best coffee anyone has ever had. Now I was looking at those words coming to life in front of me. I felt the motion of the city run through my veins and I wanted to stay here, far away from Espelette and its monotonous routine. I was still scared to be on my own, but my desire to become a famous dancer at the Opera Ballet was greater.

I threw myself into the classes and lived my life according to the schedule on the wall. The dance classes were unlike anything I had experienced before. We were worked past the point of exhaustion. My toenails felt as if they were being pried off as I pounded the floor with the stiffened tip of my toe shoes while the instructor made us practice our *pirouettes* over and over until we had perfected the step. I had envisioned dancing under the expertise of someone like Madame Channing, but it seemed there was a revolving door of instructors. I never knew which one would be teaching us on any given day. We never saw the

Ballet Master after our initial acceptance. He only worked with real dancers; his talents could not be wasted on those in training.

When we were not practicing to become the next class of ballerinas, Noella and I scraped together our francs and headed to the cafés. "What do you think of this hat?" she asked me while looking in our mirror. "You look like you're dressing up in your mother's clothes," I replied honestly. She sighed and removed it. "I can't wait until our stipends are larger and we can buy normal clothes," she complained as she bit into a piece of bread. "How can they expect us to be refined women if we can't afford to look like one?" I nodded, swallowing my own lunch. We couldn't afford to eat at the cafés, so we filled up on bread before leaving. "It looks like we'll be wearing the same dresses and hats we wear every week," I replied, looking down at the same peasant skirt I wore in Espelette. I didn't know how my mother thought I would attract a wealthy man when she refused to buy me at least one decent walking dress. I scowled for a moment but changed my tone when I saw Noella's fallen face. "Luckily there are so many different places to go that no one will know!" She brightened up at this and we left for our Sunday tea.

I took a few moments to look over the beverage menu while Noella tapped her fingers impatiently at me. She always ordered chamomile, but I wanted to try all of them. Settling on a pear-flavored brew, I turned my attention to the crowd. Noella and I sat up straight, nearly on the edges of our seats, imitating the other women. A stunning redhead sat opposite an equally stunning man. I watched her as she waited until he took a sip from his mug and then slowly removed her gloves. She loosened each finger and then delicately pulled the glove off, repeating the other side, then gently laid them down on the table beside her. It was such a ladylike gesture, and I wondered if she had eaten before coming out so she would not be tempted to rip off her gloves and dive into her entrée out of hunger. Perhaps when I began to dine out with gentlemen, I would keep some peanuts or something in my purse so I was not famished by the time I sat down to eat.

The waitress returned, placing tiny porcelain teapots and delicate cups with saucers in front of both of us. She poured the hot water into the cup and I watched it swirl into a deep green. I felt like I didn't belong here. Everyone was so at ease, not second-guessing any of their actions. You're just as good as them, I told myself, and began to slowly take off my gloves. I felt completely clumsy; the fabric was slick and I was having a hard time gripping it gently. I breathed in, remembered how effortlessly the woman removed her gloves, and tried not to concentrate on it so much. Once I relaxed, my gloves slipped off and I laid them beside me as if I could not be bothered. I smiled to myself; perhaps I can do this after all.

For every minor success I encountered, I was quickly met with a slap to the face. Each week dancers were cut from the school as they proved unable to keep up with the demands of a true Parisian ballerina. Becoming a Paris Opera Ballet dancer proved to be quite degrading. Our instructor lined us up each week as if we were cattle to measure our bodies with an orange tape measure that I came to fear. We were all growing into our womanly frames, some more gracefully than others. Most in our class came from tiny towns like me and marveled at the sweets displayed throughout the city. It was hard to practice restraint and not spend a Sunday afternoon gorging oneself on the abundance of desserts at every turn. Those that made a habit of this were ridiculed in front of the class for their weakness as the instructor read off how thick these girls' waistlines were and how heavy their legs were becoming. She chastised them for forgetting that a dancer's body is one of the many things that separate her from ordinary girls who grow plump as they become women. I avoided the public bathroom in our building after dinner because I couldn't stand to hear girls throwing up. I didn't want to see which girl's face matched the vile sound. Others who had the discipline to refrain from sweets had bodies that collapsed from lack of food during the rigorous practices. These girls dropped from fatigue and the instructors didn't even stop the music as they waved for us to remove the weaker girls from the room. After months of this we barely blinked when a girl collapsed from overexertion. When one lanky girl fell, crying out and reaching toward her ankles, Noella picked up her legs and I hoisted her up under her armpits and we carried her off the dance floor as the rest of the girls continued on as if nothing had happened.

"I was doing fine until I started to get taller," the girl wailed in desperation. "My parents aren't going to take me back home. They won't accept that I failed. I didn't mean to fail, but my feet don't work anymore."

She sobbed as she removed her worn toe shoes to reveal a foot so disfigured that I had to hold back from gagging. After witnessing that limb that I hesitate to call a foot, Noella and I began to steal the older girls' ballet slippers and hide them in our room underneath a panel in the floor. The image of the foot deformed into a horse's hoof motivated us to be prepared for any growth spurts waiting in the future. The probationary dancers were not provided new clothes or slippers, so we had to make do with what we had brought when we arrived for auditions.

We became obsessed with studying the size of each girl's feet and within a few weeks we had a collection of ballet slippers that would take us through the next four shoe sizes if we needed them. We would never have to endure a life of walking around on hooves like the most recently departed dancer. I had never felt more guilty in my life, but my drive to remain at the Opera and become a star was that strong. Life in the ballet was competitive and we were learning to look out for ourselves.

No. 6 Scène:

Petits Rats

*W*e're going to the ballet!" Noella's voice preceded her as she bounded down the hall after practice, the sconces bouncing against the walls as her eyes fixed on me as the target of her enthusiasm. "We're going to be the most stunning new girls there. Everyone will notice us and ask, 'Who are they? When will we see them onstage?' I don't know about you, but I'm going to spend the whole afternoon getting ready."

"Lower your voice," I cautioned, trying not to laugh as she grabbed my hands, jumping up and down. "Aren't you the least bit excited?" She dropped my hands, giving me a look of disbelief.

I was bursting with excitement but knew that, while we had advanced into the third quadrille, we were only halfway through the final probationary period and our making it into the ballet rested on our poise and elegance during these final weeks. Until we were formally accepted into the ballet, we were kept completely separated from the Opera ballerinas. Students were even housed in an entirely different building. Every day was a reminder that we had not made it all the way and any foolish behavior would derail our chances. I glanced nervously toward the studio's imposing doors in case our instructor would emerge and see us acting like giddy girls. My eyes left the heavy wood doors and turned toward my friend. "I'm looking out for both of us; you know every movement we make is judged."

Noella smiled widely at me, her bright blue eyes becoming enormous as her mouth stretched so far I thought it would surely split her face. "Those of us who still remain are being rewarded by attending a performance. Enjoy this and stop being so cautious. Soon we will be sitting with the elegant patrons and will be allowed backstage to see everything that goes into the production."

Now that we were trotting down the path of winding stairs, moments from breaking free into the outdoors, I allowed my enthusiasm to escape. "We have so much to do before tonight's performance. We must find the most beautiful dresses that will make us look like sophisticated Parisian women and try to get our hair into complicated updos like we've seen." I paused for a moment, letting the importance of our admittance to the night's performance sink in. "And we must take great care in choosing our gowns for the night." There were so many rules to keep track of for two seventeen-year-olds in a city like Paris. I had learned that respectable women shopped indoors, and negotiating with merchants on sidewalks and streets was morally risky. It would be extremely uncomfortable to see someone at the ballet who had witnessed us haggling for a dress. Or perhaps they would have seen the dress while passing by and know we had purchased it from a street vendor. I knew we must take every caution to appear flawless in all aspects.

Noella's blue eyes clouded as if reading my mind, her fervor turning into panic as she grabbed my arm and we walked away from the Opera House. "You're right! For heaven's sake, shopping alone is seen as excessive. If we enjoy it too much others will think we're shallow. We must act like true high society women and only spend modestly and not embellish ourselves too much. At least until our training is complete and we are no longer *petits rats*. And don't forget that our instructor has given us strict guidelines that we are there only as observers," Noella continued. "We can't talk to the patrons or dancers."

I was about to agree with her when we were interrupted. "Why, if it isn't a pair of little rats foraging for a gown to wear to their first performance," the loud, accented voice of an impeccably dressed woman cut into our conversation. "I remember when I was in your shoes and how I searched all of Paris for the perfect dress to wear to my debut."

I recognized her as the Opera's lead ballerina. She was famous throughout France, and Noella and I couldn't reply as we stared in awe at a true ballerina. She stood in front of us with such confidence, and I marveled at how she could have once been in our position. She appeared to me as if she was born at the ballet. It wasn't so much the way she moved, but more the attitude she gave off, as if we were two girls who had stumbled upon her front door. "I have dozens of dresses that I never wear anymore; perhaps you would like to borrow one of mine for the performance? I remember how little *petits rats* are given for a stipend," she smiled kindly at us.

Noella found her voice first. "That's very generous of you,

but I would prefer to buy my own dress." The ballerina's eyes narrowed, and Noella rushed to add, "It's such an important night that I would like to keep whatever gown I choose so that each time I wear it I will remember the first night I attended the Opera Ballet."

I also would have liked to have a sentimental gown, but I knew it would cost me all of my earnings. I had dutifully been following Monsieur Aston's formula and my mother's orders, so I sent the majority of my stipend to Espelette. I noticed the ballerina looking at me questioningly, waiting for my answer. I darted my eyes to Noella, who gave me an impatient look. "I cannot tell you how much it means to me that you would let me borrow a gown," I beamed at the ballerina while carefully choosing my words. "Wonderful!" she clapped her hands together. "Come along, I believe I have the perfect dress for you."

I followed her into the building where the ballerinas lived, as Noella set out to find her own dress for the night. "My name is Cornelie," she said to me as she opened the door to her room. "It's a pleasure to meet you," I replied, taking in a room that extended from the entrance in both directions. I could see a living area to my right but wasn't able to look further because Cornelie led me in the opposite direction to her bedroom. How nice it must be to have your own little home, I thought while looking at a shelf lined with the most fashionable shoes and parasols, in peach, lavender, blue, and pale green. "And do you have a name?" Cornelie grinned at me as she opened her armoire. "Alexandrie," I said, embarrassed that I was ogling her belongings. "How did you become the lead ballerina? It must be amazing to be recognized as the best and live in all of this space." I couldn't help but imagine myself here when I was older. I would definitely fill the balcony with flowers and get huge vases to put all around the rooms. She gave me an odd look and replied simply, "I couldn't picture myself anywhere else."

I became a little self-conscious when I realized she hadn't told me how she became the *étoile*, and it appeared she wasn't going to. I cleared my throat and ran my hand through my hair, still amazed that I was able to do this. Noella had watched me slick it back with honey each morning and was astounded that I didn't know how to manage my own hair. "You have to control it," she told me sternly, as if it were a rambunctious child. She showed me how to smooth lotion into the strands when it was wet and coil the hairs until it looked like spiral pasta was growing out of my head. Patiently, she wrapped each coil around a piece of cloth, securing each one to the top of my head. "When you wake in the morning, you'll have a head of shiny curls," she grinned, and to my great delight she was correct. I looked like an entirely different person.

Cornelie had her back to me while she spent quite a bit of time moving gown after gown around in her armoire. Finally she leaned over her shoulder to address me. "Well, Alexandrie, you must be a very brave little rat to not only speak to a ballerina but come into her room!" She turned back to the dresses and immediately my heart beat faster and I remembered that our instructor had told us we were to observe the night's performance and not speak to the dancers. Did she mean only at the performance? Could I be thrown out for borrowing Cornelie's dress?

"Here it is! This will look lovely with those eyes of yours." Cornelie swung a dark green dress into my arms and I had to steady myself from the weight of it. It was exactly my size and made of rich satin so that it was hard to hold on to and kept slipping from my hands, which were now sweating out of fear. "Will I get into trouble for borrowing this?" I asked quietly.

"No one has to know." Cornelie winked at me. "As I said, I never wear it anymore; in fact, it's too small for me. I couldn't possibly squeeze into it, so you're free to keep it. It is your dress now."

I couldn't thank her enough for her kindness and my stomach fluttered with anticipation as I hurried back to my room to prepare for the night. I couldn't believe my luck—a new dress and a new friendship, with none other than the lead ballerina. To be taken under the wing of the *étoile* would be far more than I could have hoped for. She could teach me and groom me to be the lead ballerina one day too. I floated down the street with a sense of pride in knowing that I was making my own life and everything was lining up for me to succeed. By the time I opened the door to my room I felt as if my heart was going to burst out of my chest with happiness.

No. 7 Scène:
The Debut

$\mathcal{I}$ had yet to attend a formal occasion, and the dress Cornelie had given me looked as elegant as those I had seen in books and paintings. But when Noella returned to our room from her shopping trip, after seeing all the dresses in the fine shops, she couldn't believe that I could be so stupid.

I proudly held up the dress and she bit her lip, wincing at its stiffened petticoat. She had spent her entire stipend to purchase a tasteful, elegant ruffled dress. She informed me that the crinoline petticoat dress Cornelie had given me was utterly out of style and would stick out like a bell while the other women's gowns would flow gracefully, gathering in the back in a bustle of cascading fabric.

"Couldn't you feel me staring at you when you agreed to take her dress? I was trying to tell you not to do it, to buy your own,"

Noella whispered to me, her face still in shock as she stared at the dress. "She gave you that hideous thing on purpose. It's completely out of fashion."

"Why would she do such a thing?" I wanted to believe that Cornelie wouldn't have pulled such a conniving trick. I had thought she saw Noella and me as younger sisters. But my enormous dress was evidence that she did not.

"We're her competition," Noella hissed. "Every ballerina is petrified that the wealthy patrons will turn their attention away from them once the younger ballerinas are debuted. She wanted to make sure that you won't get in her way. She's obviously threatened by us."

My lip trembled and when I tried to stop it, the trembling reached down to my chin and across my whole face and soon I was crying uncontrollably. Noella stood still for a moment, then wrapped her arms around me. "Stop," she said with a small laugh. "We can fix it up a little so it's not so wide." I smiled back at her reassurance. "I know a dress is a silly thing to cry about," I said, wiping my eyes. "But I feel like I should have known better. I should have realized this is not what the style is; I watch everyone in the city and try so hard to fit in. I was so distracted by being in the *étoile*'s apartment, and I was so nervous about spending so much on a dress. If I told my family I spent that much on a dress they'd be furious." I sighed as my tears stopped, and I walked over to the doorframe where the dress was hanging. "I thought I had the best of luck."

Noella followed me and we both stood looking at the dress. She attempted to move the petticoat to the back, but the entire dress clumsily moved with it. "There's not time for you to buy a new dress, so you have two choices," she said as she released it and the dress shifted back to its bell shape. "You can either wear it as it is and have a huge dress or we can remove the petticoat and you can have a flat dress."

We looked at each other's serious faces and began to laugh. "I have really messed this up, haven't I?" I shook my head at the dress, but the tears did not resurface. "What were the dresses like in the store? Which way do you think would be better?"

"None of the dresses were this big," Noella said. "They all bustle in the back and the front flows down. I would cut the petticoat out. You'll knock over the entire orchestra with that thing!"

This brought us into a fit of laughter as we triumphantly separated the petticoat and threw it aside. The dress flowed naturally to the floor, and to our great delight it was too long on its own, so we pinned it to the back, mimicking Noella's dress so it rippled in the same manner.

"It's not perfect, but it is pretty good." Noella emerged from behind the dress and motioned for me to have a look. I was impressed. I couldn't see any of the pins and, while the volume was not there, it did sweep and gather like her gown. But even with her creative handiwork, I knew it looked like an obvious attempt to mimic the rich. I helped Noella fasten her dress and we took one last glance in the mirror before leaving our room to see our first performance.

"I haven't been so nervous to enter the Opera House since my audition," Noella whispered to me as she held on to my arm.

"It seems like a completely different place," I replied as we maneuvered our way through the crowd. I allowed myself a moment to absorb the energy of the main foyer. I couldn't help but stare at the patrons dressed in such rich, luxurious clothing. They looked like royalty with their dresses embellished with so much detail, ruffles, and trains. I self-consciously glanced down at my own gown.

My jaw tensed in anger: at Cornelie's cruelness, at my naïveté, and at my parents for taking the stipend I should have used for a new dress. One woman caught me taking in her beautifully stitched leather heels and lace-covered dress and gave me a pitying look, her eyes full of sorrow and unease for me. Embarrassed at being so obvious with my envy, I blushed and turned away, quickly making my way backstage, where we were to meet the rest of our quadrille. As I rushed by, I caught a bit of her malicious whispered conversation. "Those girls live such a morally disgusting life that they have to be grouped together in one building."

At the time I believed that I must have happened upon a conversation about something else entirely, perhaps a bathhouse, but if I had kept up my childhood habit of observation instead of becoming obsessed with myself, certainly I would have put the entire story of the Paris Opera Ballet together long ago and saved myself the shock I felt when I finally opened my eyes to it. But for the moment, I was fixated only on the shiny green eyesore that I wore and the humiliation I felt when I joined my quadrille. The instructor laughed as if she was truly amused. "Oh, my, Alexandrie! It looks as if your dress is missing a few pieces! Wherever did you find a shop that sells dresses by the piece?" I gritted my teeth and looked at the floor. "It was a bit of bad judgment on my part," I said in a monotone voice that showed I wished to drop the subject.

I resolved to enjoy the experience of my first performance and not let Cornelie's spiteful trick ruin it for me. Backstage I noticed how the dancers of the Opera greatly contrasted with the women in the foyer who accompanied the patrons, holding on to their arms and wearing long, luxurious dresses. The dancers' satin, scoop-neck, sleeveless tops and their bare legs, arms, and back had an alluring, almost risqué quality.

"Observe how the dancers are transforming themselves from ordinary women into stars," our instructor said to us in a low voice as she motioned toward the ballerinas sitting before mirrors, applying heavy makeup and delicately placing flowers in their hair. A few smiled in our direction briefly before turning back toward the mirrors to tie a sash at the waist, satin ribbons catching the light as they ran down their calves to meet pink slippers.

"The only others who have the privilege of seeing this transformation are the season ticket holders, the *abonnés*." Our instructor hovered over us, whispering in an effort to remain an undetected observer. I looked around to see that the *abonnés* were all men. In their monochrome suits they all looked the same, as if they had been duplicated until the entire room was filled with refined gentlemen who watched the dancers with intensity and glanced toward our class with knowing looks, making me feel self-conscious. I tried to avoid eye contact with these men because their entitlement made me feel uncomfortable, yet I couldn't stop staring and wondering which of these men might choose me as his own. I saw how familiar they were with the dancers, touching them and whispering very closely to them, and I wondered which men kept which ballerinas in beautiful dwellings.

"There are so many men backstage with the dancers," I whispered to Noella as our instructor led us away.

"It is amazing how many fans the ballerinas have," Noella agreed as she followed our instructor past the mirrored stations. "Here they are simply getting ready for a performance and patrons are practically attacking them for attention."

I began to follow her but stopped to look back at the dancers. For the last five years I had been told what an honor it was to be accepted into the Opera Ballet. I smiled and thought that I was so close to my dream of stardom. Soon I would be one of the ballerinas being fawned upon.

"Taking in your future?" One dancer interrupted my observations. I knew I was not to speak to the dancers or patrons so I simply nodded. She looked down at me and I saw that while her body was youthful, with precise muscle tone, her eyes looked older than my own mother's, with lines and dark circles under them. "How does it feel to enter the dark side of society?" she asked in a tone that sounded friendly, but her bitter eyes led me to believe she was not being cordial. I looked at her quizzically, and broke the rules. "I'm here to become a great dancer," I whispered, not understanding why she had said such a thing.

She laughed a little too loudly and my heart pounded with the dread that my instructor would follow the noise and know I had disobeyed her. "Poor girl. There is no such thing as a career as a dancer. As soon as one enters the Opera she's nothing but a high-class whore in slippers."

She turned sharply and walked away just as I identified what it was about the men's looks that had made me uncomfortable. In the blink of an eye, I saw the patrons in a new light. They were inappropriately close to the dancers, who seemed to invite their suggestive looks. The Ballet Master was hunched over a book, writing hastily while keeping an eye on the clock as a crowd of gentlemen formed around him. I heard an obnoxiously loud laugh and turned to see Cornelie as the source. My eyes narrowed and I saw myself in her room, so grateful for her kind gesture. In an instant I recalled Noella's warning—"Every ballerina is petrified that the wealthy patrons will turn their attention away from them." Cornelie waved at me and I nodded back with a forced smile, annoyed that I had let the other ballerina rattle me with talk of being a whore. Of course, I thought, she was trying to eliminate the competition. I vowed to myself to not get caught up in their game of deceit as I caught up to my quadrille to take our seats for the performance.

As the lights dimmed, I diverted my full attention to the performance of *Giselle,* its heartbreaking plot coming to life before my eyes. As part of our training, we studied each ballet the Opera performed, and I couldn't wait to see how the story of the poor girl Giselle and her imposter fiancé, Albrecht, would be portrayed, and how an entire act set at her graveside would translate to the stage.

From my seat I could see the edge of the orchestra pit, the cello, bassoon, neck of double bass, a sea of middle-aged men dressed in tuxedos. I watched in amazement as the dancers floated to the side of the stage, turning toward the audience in a *grand assemblé en tournant* as if they were one. They moved into a perfectly executed *saut de basque,* swirling in the air together. While mid-air, each dancer drew one foot to the opposite knee at exactly the same time. I wanted to practice all night to reach the level of these girls. I tried very hard to look at Cornelie with scorn but my eyes widened to see her, the lead ballerina, playing Giselle, whip around in a series of turns, her leg extending out and bending back quickly as she performed a flawless *fouetté rond de jambe en tournant*. It made me respect her and hate her at the same time. The performance concluded with a classic *coda* and I watched the principal dancers take the stage one last time. The Opera House filled with thunderous applause and roses were thrown onto the stage just like I always imagined they would be.

I wanted more than ever to be part of the ballet. I imagined myself onstage, picking up roses, basking in the glow of adoration from the crowd. I was so taken with the performance that I forgot for a moment that I was wearing this hideous dress. As the lights came up, my shame resurfaced and I had a sudden urge to confront Cornelie to let her know that one gown would not be enough to make me back down from my dream. I separated myself from my quadrille and headed backstage, only to find it empty. I heard a great ruckus coming from the foyer adjacent to the dressing room and I followed the sound of laughter. I peered through the door into the foyer, to find the grandest party well under way. The dancers had changed out of their costumes into elegant dresses, and were shrieking in delight as men poured champagne, which bubbled over the rim onto their hands. Beautiful dresses and tuxedos danced throughout the entire room, unveiling trays of desserts and groups playing cards as they swished by. I nearly banged my head on the wall when I was startled by a hand coming down on my shoulder. "Only after you are formally accepted will you go into the Green Room," my instructor said sternly to me. I was relieved that she did not chastise me further and I returned to my room in shame at being discovered spying on the party. I gladly discarded the dress, throwing it across the room. I lay down on my bed but couldn't sleep, so I daydreamed for hours about the performance and the extravagant party I had glimpsed. From the corner of my eye I was aware of a large green lump staring at me. I glared back at the dress, lying in a heap, and its full petticoat standing next to it, as if a ghost was wearing it. The clock said it was one o'clock in the morning. I looked over at Noella, who was in a deep sleep. Quickly, I threw on a walking dress and scooped the green dress and petticoat up in my arms, thinking of Cornelie's face when she opened her door in the morning to find the dress standing upright to greet her.

I left the students' small building and scurried down the block toward the dancers' building across the street from the Opera House, as discreetly as I could while balancing the dress. As I approached the dancers' building I saw a couple walking toward it as well, so I stayed still, hoping they would not see me. The gas lamps illuminated the couple, laughing and swaying, the man holding an open bottle of champagne. The woman took a swig, opened the door, and they disappeared from my view. My heart beat rapidly as the dancer's harsh words reentered my mind. As I tried to make sense of what I had just witnessed, more and more couples made their way from the Opera House into the dancers' building. Some walked briskly as if they were nervous, while others groped each other as if they would fall if they let go. I was so consumed with monitoring the entranceway that I didn't notice someone was standing next to me and I screamed when I turned my head. "I didn't mean to scare you." A young man put his hands up, taking a few steps back to show me he meant no harm. But I didn't believe him and suddenly realized I was standing in the empty street with only a gas lamp giving off any light. I knew I should run away as fast as I could. In my mind, I had thought I would do something brave and heroic if I was ever in this type of situation. Perhaps throw the dress over his head and hit him in the stomach and run faster than any human being ever has. But, finding myself in danger, I couldn't move at all. It was as if

I was standing in a bucket of water that had frozen, locking my feet in one place.

"Are you watching the post-performances?" the man stammered nervously, cocking his head at the Paris Opera House and then at the dancers' quarters. I stared at him with wide eyes, gradually realizing that he was not dressed for the ballet at all but rather wore brown pants and a heavy sweater. "A what?" I asked in more annoyance than fear or curiosity.

"It's nothing to be ashamed of," he said, as if we were friends. "I purposely walk down this road on the nights of ballets so I can watch all of the ballerinas taking their men back to bed. Surely you're doing the same thing." I looked down at my walking dress and realized he didn't know I was a ballerina, and his words angered me.

"Sir, I am sure nothing of that sort is going on in that building," I said haughtily, picturing an extension of the Green Room. I imagined the dancers and the patrons were not quite ready to retire for the night, so they brought champagne across the street and were probably playing music and dancing and laughing and having a grand time. Or perhaps this was another secret party like the one I had spied, an even more glamorous and exclusive party. Maybe the party I'd seen was for the *corps de ballet* and this party was for the lead ballerinas and the most notable patrons. I imagined kings and queens being entertained away from the commoners. He shook his head and chuckled. "If that's the case, then don't look at that window." He pointed to a pane of glass illuminated by candlelight. I could see two shadows moving up and down, and while I wished my eyes could have interpreted it as dancing I knew better. I gasped as if I had just walked in on someone's private moment, and my face immediately flushed.

With shattering clarity, I understood that while Cornelie had been dishonest, the words the other dancer spoke were true. The dress slipped from my hands and I swallowed back tears as a well-dressed man exited the dancers' building, whistling as he walked down the street. The ice melted from my feet and I ran away from the building as fast as I could, wanting to get the image out of my head. But I couldn't, it was burned into my memory.

The chilly night air began to pierce my lungs and I slowed down to catch my breath. I walked slowly back to my room for the second time that night. I was no longer enthralled with the performance I saw tonight but felt numb instead. The delicate costumes no longer intrigued me. The bright white tights with their perfect seams running up the dancers' legs only seemed to guide leering men toward what lay underneath. The long satin ribbons of the ballet shoes no longer looked luxurious, but now seemed confining. I remembered how the dancers worked their tarlatan skirts until they puffed out like a light cloud, and I thought of how they would deflate and look dirty once the night was over. Just like the dancers.

Everything we had been taught by our fashionable instructor during character building classes now made sense.

"Once you present yourself onstage you are officially the most coveted girls of all of Paris," she had told us. I watched her with wide eyes as she floated around the room in the way only a classically trained ballerina can. She looked intimidating in her wealth, her crinoline rustling under her bustled skirt, yet her movements showed that she would always be a dancer. It was who she was at heart, and I wanted desperately to also develop into an elegant creature who commanded attention simply by walking. "Women want to be in your place and men become haunted by your beauty. You are the lucky ones. The chosen ones." She paused and opened her arms to all of us, eyes closed, smiling and nodding once before resuming her lecture. I remember how I beamed from within at having been one of the few who were chosen, no longer fading into the background. I realized I shared this sentiment with the other girls who were nodding with adoration in their eyes. She told us how dancing in the Paris Opera Ballet was the greatest experience of her life and she would forever be thankful that she had been chosen. "From a young age your parents saw something special in you; something that sets you apart from the rest of the girls. Many mothers *think* their daughters are special, but those girls are not really special, otherwise they would be here. Think about the girls you know at home, those who are not pretty or talented."

There were a few giggles from the audience. "You know what kind of girls I'm talking about," our instructor encouraged the laughter.

She circled around our class while we stared at her raptly, telling us things that no respectable young woman would utter. "You girls are in a unique position. You can have both wealth and love—something no other woman in the world can have. If you make it to the Opera you will perform for France's most elite. They will covet you and many will fall in love. They will look at you as they have never looked at another woman before." The room remained silent while we waited for her to continue, but she stared far away with a dreamy look on her face. "I had the opportunity to meet France's most influential men. I relished each performance as much for the thrill of dancing as for the possibilities of who I would be introduced to after the curtain closed. I met my monsieur when I was just sixteen and he remains my only love to this day. Here at the ballet the world is yours."

As the instructor went on to compare the Opera's ballerinas to a fine silk and those that didn't fit in as itchy wool, I saw my classmates' eyes glaze over. We all sat up taller, truly believing we were special as we looked forward to a life as coveted, loved women. I found the idea of dining out with educated, powerful men very enchanting. I imagined myself dressed in a lovely gown, talking about everything I had studied in my preparation for the ballet.

Now as I stumbled down the street, my mind was clouded with confusion. Were we being groomed not to be one man's *lorette* but to be available for every man who attended the ballet? Was it possible that my mother knew of this as well? I pondered the thought, recalling that when she had first broached the subject of the ballet she said that it would be easier for me to marry in Paris. Only when I was completely immersed in dance did I discover that most ballerinas become *lorettes*. Was this one more element that she failed to mention? Was she that desperate and selfish that she would push me into prostitution? I thought of myself at age twelve, dancing at the market, and of my mother, watching me, thinking that this would be the solution to her problem. I thought of her greedily waiting for an envelope to arrive from Paris, not caring where the money came from, as long as it ended up in her hands. I entered my room and urgently shook Noella awake.

"What do you think our culture classes are all about?" She looked at me in sleepy annoyance when I told her what I had learned. "Men don't want an old woman as a mistress. If we fail to become a *lorette* early on, then after our twenty-fifth birthday we have to carry on the tradition of post-performance. If every single dancer ended up in a grand apartment, the ballet would have no entertainers and there would be no reason to pay for expensive season tickets."

"If this is such a tradition, then why does no one speak of it? Why does everyone whisper around it?" I found my voice, angry that I had asked this same question about *lorettes* and knowing that I would not be able to simply decide for myself on this matter. What kind of world had I entered? Perhaps most people would believe that I was beneath the *abonnés* and would never be a suitable marriage prospect. But I was not so low that I would be their whore. Never.

"To acknowledge it among society is taboo. The *abonnés* have wives. Haven't you listened to anything? We offer these men an escape from their dreary life, and in return we get to live like fancy, rich women. We're their favorites who they spoil."

"And you're all right with this?" I demanded of her.

"There's quite a bit of flattery attached to it, wouldn't you say? We're the most talented dancers in the country. To men, we're goddesses who they can only dream of having," she said arrogantly.

I looked at her in astonishment. "How can you take this so lightly?"

She laughed while shaking her head as if I was a dim-witted child. "Don't be so innocent. Of course I want to be a *lorette* living an easy life within a year of my first performance, but I don't know if that'll happen. None of us do." She breathed in calmly, smoothed down her hair, and looked me directly in the eye.

"I won't do it." I steadied myself and met her stare. "It is one

thing to know that I will never be married. It's my choice to become a *lorette*. But prostitution is most definitely not how I want
to live my life."

Leaning in, challenging me with quivering lips, her words
turned to anger. "Then leave the *abonnés* to all of us whores-in-
training. If you come from such a great life, then why are you
here? I accept it because I have nowhere else to go." Her bitter-
ness toward me simmered as she explained. "My father hasn't
worked a day in his godforsaken life." I watched her absently
twist a strand of hair around her finger and roll her eyes as if she
didn't want to care. "My mother left home at sunrise every
morning to clean a wealthy family's house. She was having a relationship with the man of the house but she told me that he
wouldn't be attracted to her forever, so it would become my responsibility to support the family."

"She made you go to bed with him?" I blurted out, my eyes
wide in horror.

"No!" she cried. "Though we thought about it. My father's
drunkenness was notorious. None of the families wanted their
sons to marry me."

"No one would take me either," I sheepishly admitted to her,
realizing that whether it was Paris or Espelette, it was the children who were punished for their family's mistakes.

Noella gave me a small smile, and to my relief, asked for no
details. "I thought I would have to follow in my mother's footsteps until she told me that the man she worked for kept a young
woman in Paris who he had met at the Opera Ballet. I thought
that this woman had it so much better than my mother, who was
also involved with the same man, but had to return to her sad,
dank home each night. So my training for the ballet began and
my mother pushed me to be the best," she explained. "I went to

his mistress' apartment once. God, it was beautiful, with views far into the city, gowns and jewels in every color imaginable, and soft linens. She saw that I wanted to be a dancer more than anything, so she met with me and taught me how to dance and how to behave like a lady. I danced so one day I would no longer have to clean my father's vomit when he would fall asleep in his own piss."

I let her outburst go, looking at her with pity, thinking of her as a small, frail girl being burdened with the responsibility of cleaning up the mess her parents made of her life. For the first time, I saw myself in her.

"My mother tricked me into everything," I said, opening up to her. "She was so calculating about it all. After I had fallen in love with dancing, I found out that I would not marry and would need to become a mistress. This was years after I began my classes. And now that I'm living my dream of dancing in Paris, I have to find out on my own about these post-performances. She never said a word. She never even mentioned it, all she's ever mentioned is the money. And I know if I never talk to her again and never send her another franc, she will not realize what she did wrong. She'll say I'm a horrible, selfish girl who doesn't care about her family's well-being. When it's her that is so selfish and doesn't care about her children the way a mother should! I'm trapped. I can't go back to Espelette. And the ballet is not the kind of life I want to have, I know I won't be able to do it—how could you even think of it as an option?"

Noella looked at me thoughtfully. "Don't judge me for accepting the undesirable possibilities. I know what kind of life I'm striving for," she said philosophically.

Now it was my turn to shake my head. "If we have to face those possibilities I won't be able to stay here with you."

"Once you have tasted Paris, it is a hard lifestyle to leave," she warned. As she fell back asleep I lit the gas lamp next to my bed, careful that it remained dim so as not to wake her. Squinting to see in the faint light, I gripped my pen angrily and thought about what I would write in a letter to my "dearest maman."

But my conscience gave me pause. What if she really had not known the truth? I couldn't have my feelings about my mother written down as a permanent reminder of the thoughts I should censure. Instead, I wrote to the only person I knew to be familiar with the Paris Opera Ballet. Certainly these were not the sort of adventures she wished to hear of.

June 26, 1865

Dearest Alexandrie,

It seems as if it was only yesterday that you were in my studio, a fuzzy-haired girl with more determination than I have ever seen! I had no doubt you would be accepted into the Paris Opera Ballet. The concerns you wrote to me of remain just. First and foremost, you must know that your mother had no knowledge of this aspect of the ballet. She is as oblivious to it as you had been. She is so proud of you. She talks of her daughter dancing in Paris for the city's most prestigious all of the time. If you want to be angry at anyone, be angry at me, because I knew. But how can I tell a classroom of young girls about this? I prefer to teach my girls all of the tools they will need to make their own decisions once they leave my classroom.

I will advise you that you must remember to not follow in those post-performance dancers' footsteps and to always remain virtuous. Even when you have been accepted, you must not get caught up in what others are doing and lose your judgment. Many men will try to entice you into abandoning your morals and I have no doubt the authorities at the Opera will encourage such behavior. I tell you this in extreme urgency: Your virtue is the only card you hold in setting yourself up as a lorette. Understand that there are two types of men at the Opera. One will take a virgin away from the ballet's dwellings so she will be only his. The other goes to the ballet to be with a woman who has known many men, and he will only care to be with her for one night. You must understand this distinction.

While the ballet has offered you a world of opportunity, I beg you to not trust anyone in it. It is, underneath the costumes and lights, a business. The Ballet Master wants his dancers to give up their virtue because he knows once this is gone he runs no risk of losing them. He has no desire to see a dancer leave the ballet for a better life, as lorettes often do. He wants her to grow old at the Opera, entertaining the abonnés after every performance. The dancers that remain at the ballet provide him with a considerable source of income, more than the donation an abonné makes when he chooses a lorette, and this is the road he wants every ballerina to travel.

Do not fall into this trap. Your life is now just beginning and you must take every caution to maintain your standing as a young, untouched girl. It is the one thing you have in your favor and the only thing the ballet can take from you. If you do not follow my advice, you will be ruined.

I have revealed much of what the Opera does not want known, so I must request that you burn this letter promptly after reading it. I bid you farewell with much pride,

Madame Channing

Act II

No. 8 Scène:
The Unveiling

I did not come from a broken family. I attended church each week. I worked hard at my studies and training at the studio. So upon discovering the nocturnal activities of the ballerinas, a girl of my background surely should have packed up her belongings and hopped on the first carriage back to Espelette. What a wonderful tale it would make for generations to come! How my descendants would laugh with glee as they sat around the fire after a day in the fields, telling the story of how I went to Paris to become a star only to find out my fame would be as an infamous *courtesan*! They would speak of my strong values with pride as they described how I told the Ballet Master exactly what I thought of his production. A bit of excitement and a story to be passed down from my children to my grandchildren—this was more than any farm girl could ask for. I had experienced Paris and now I would return home, where people were grounded with morals. This was what any respectable girl from Espelette would do after all.

Instead I chose to stay. The truth was that it was hard to leave the promise of the Green Room for a cold room in my father's farmhouse. I could sip champagne with the *abonnés* as a true Parisian ballerina or I could laugh with pepper farmers about my brief life as a *petit rat*. It was true, I wished one aspect of the ballet didn't exist, but at the age of eighteen, I made the decision to emerge as a professional ballerina nonetheless. Now official members of the quadrille, Noella and I joined the Paris Opera's dancers, leaving our instructors behind and studying under the Ballet Master's critical eye. We moved from the students' building into the dancers', our days as roommates officially over. While I missed our late night talks, I loved having my own little space with its wood floors and wardrobe that I imagined would one day be filled with gowns of the most beautiful fabric with shoes and hats to match every one. I loved waking up to the large window overlooking the city. Having our own rooms was a privilege that came with becoming an Opera ballerina, but I thought the best part was that Noella was only a few doors down the hall from me.

As the year progressed, I quietly accepted how the ballet worked and heeded Madame Channing's warning as I watched the older dancers slip into costumes of vivid colors and fabric. While I still thought of my mother as too greedy for her own good, I guiltily sent money back to Espelette each time I received a stipend. She wrote to me frequently to tell me what was happening at home and I replied with details about practice and performances. I thought of my mother bragging about me, and while a part of me knew it was more to make herself look good, I mostly felt happy about it, knowing that I had not disappointed her. For as much resentment as I had toward her, I also wanted her approval.

Each time I performed, I thought of how proud she would be to see me waiting to go onstage as the orchestra's soft music began to fill the theater, letting everyone know it was time to move to their seats. I scratched at the back of my neck, the heat rising in anticipation. Unfortunately, as the newest members of the production we were cast in male roles, dressed in full tuxedos.

From backstage, I could glimpse the spectators in the balcony loges, the partially enclosed loge doors opening onto corridors where the notable patrons socialized, creating their own Green Room, eager to see who was with whom and what the women were wearing. "The Emperor is here," an excited dancer hissed and we simultaneously turned our heads to view an ostentatious military escort leading the Emperor and Empress to the three front stage boxes, which afforded the most privileged view. The Ballet Master scurried to the Emperor's side not one minute after he was seated and Cornelie chuckled at his display of obsequiousness. "The Emperor actually doesn't care about the Opera House but feels obliged to appear," she whispered into my ear. "The Ballet Master has much contempt for his lack of enthusiasm, but he makes quite a show so the government subsidies keep coming in."

"Even so, it's an honor to perform for such a powerful man." I was in awe to be only steps away from Napoleon III. "Does he join the *abonnés* in the Green Room so that we might speak to him?"

"No, he cannot move freely backstage; there are far too many political ramifications if he should. Instead he treats the imperial loge as a temporary throne where he can show off his power."

Cornelie's lips turned upward in a sly smile as she dropped her voice to a barely audible whisper. "However, he's not at all bashful about using his perch to scout out beautiful women. He'll stare at women through his opera glasses and he's so obvious about it that the Empress becomes embarrassed."

I thought that such actions confirmed his reputation as a womanizer, but my reaction was drowned out by the increased tempo of the orchestra, our cue to line up behind the curtain. My heart rate increased as the curtain slowly lifted, revealing satin dance slippers, bare legs, torsos, and finally the faces attached to the bodies. Much like at my audition, each time I performed I tried to block out the audience and automatically follow the routine we had practiced for so long. But I could not help but gaze out to the crowd, my eyes scanning each person's face in anticipation of a reaction to our dance. I felt as if I was miles away from the patrons as the principal dancers dominated the stage and I served as a prop to lift them into delicate poses and then became a launching pad for their exquisite jumps. As the final scene came to its end I stood motionless, waiting for the crowd's response, watching the main floor of spectators look toward the loges, and only when the notable patrons applauded did the rest of the hall fill with the sound of a performance well done.

"I cannot wait to get out of these dreadful pants! I feel like I'm wearing a suit of armor," I groaned to Noella in the dressing room. All the years I had been waiting to perform I had always pictured myself in tights, adorned with flowers in my hair, not dressed as a man.

"I completely disagree," she said with a trace of mischief in her eyes. "It sets us apart. We are the new, untouched ballerinas."

I cocked my head at her, a sly smile spreading across my face. "And what has you in such high spirits?"

"I am completely in love," she sighed dramatically while plopping down beside me. "It was so effortless. He has been watching me perform for weeks. Since our first performance, he has been in the crowd every time. We spoke very briefly at first, and now he is practically the only man I talk to in the Green Room. I'm surprised you haven't noticed. His name is Pierre; isn't that the most perfect name? He already inquired with the Ballet Master about making arrangements for me."

"Noella, don't take him back to your room!" I was stunned that she would even consider it. I was equally stunned that I had not seen this man monopolizing her attentions. The Green Room was so full of activity that it was easy to become overwhelmed. I found it hard to take in one aspect of it, and left each evening with only a little taste of everything.

She simply laughed off my warning while unpinning her hair. "I told him I was new to the ballet, completely new, and he was *so* thrilled and not offended in the least bit that I would not meet him after the show."

"How old is this man and what else do you know about him?" I asked as I gladly disrobed from the heavy wool of the tuxedo, a bit skeptical that this man had tried to book her for a postperformance.

"What else do I know about him? He's twenty and so handsome with shiny blond hair and hazel eyes," she continued, not noticing my skepticism. "He says he's married to a fat woman who is forever pregnant and he said he wishes he could be with someone as beautiful as me every night."

She sighed a second time, with even more of a theatrical flair, and leaned against the wall. "I must write my mother immediately; she will be so excited that it's happening so quickly. How sweet would it be if he was the only man I'm ever with and my future is secure within the year?"

"It would be everything you hoped for." I tried to sound supportive as I helped her button the back of her dress and we moved into the foyer of the Green Room. As much as I valued my friendship with Noella, she sounded like a stupid girl. In love with a man who tried to buy her for the night? I looked away so Noella wouldn't detect my disapproval and instead focused on the men in the Green Room.

Much like being onstage, I was not yet comfortable in the Green Room, although it was less intimidating than the first time. I had expected to enter as an observer, but after our first performance, the Ballet Master paraded his new girls around to the *abonnés*. Noella and I watched as finely dressed men entered the foyer, greeting one another and the dancers. "Girls, come along with me," the Ballet Master ordered, guiding the newcomers toward the center of the room. I followed him to a group of five gentlemen immersed in conversation. "*Bon soir!* Did you enjoy tonight's performance?" The Ballet Master beamed as the men murmured in the affirmative. I had never seen the Ballet Master so carefree, his face absent of the stern look he wore throughout our practices. "Have you met our newest ballerinas? Only months ago they were the ten most capable students, who now have proven themselves ready to join the production."

The men each introduced themselves, lightly kissing our hands and welcoming us to the ballet. They congratulated us on our first performance and teased us about being the young men of the ballet. "Aah, stop it now," the Ballet Master winked at them. "You shall scare them off! With a few more practices they will be the stars of the show."

Those who were currently the show's stars silently seethed behind their glasses of champagne. I wondered how many times they had watched new dancers enter the foyer, stealing attention from them. They did not have anything to be jealous of, for after the first night, we were too self-conscious to approach the men as the Ballet Master had, and we kept to ourselves while the lead ballerinas reclaimed the room.

Today, Noella is watching a man I guess to be Pierre in the midst of a serious discussion with another *abonné*. When he catches her eye, she gives him a huge grin, which he returns. I grow bored watching this game and turn my attention to Cornelie as she sashays up to a tall, distinguished-looking gentleman seated under an obnoxiously large military-style painting of a soldier on his horse. He's immersed in a card game with two other men and an older dancer but breaks out in an amused smile at her interruption. I immediately recognize his long nose and hair brushing just above his dark eyes. I watch him absently run his hand through his hair, brushing it away from his forehead and eyes. My pulse quickens and I can't help staring at the artist from the audience. I have seen him sketching in the loges and look for him after every performance. The older ballerinas have told me that he's an aspiring artist and usually leaves as soon as the curtain closes, after he has the images he needs to create a painting. I constantly think of the two types of men that Madame Channing wrote me of, and I scrutinize the *abonnés* to determine which type they are. But I sense that the artist in the loges is neither, that he is mesmerized by the beauty of the dance, not the girls. I smile as if I already know him, and I picture him turning the pages of his sketchbook, showing me all of the images he has created from the performance. I want to ask him if the colors dance in the light for him as well.

I move in closer to listen to the conversation. "You are quite famous with our production. Does it bother you that everyone finds you eerie?" Cornelie asks, and before I know it I can hear my own voice. "I don't find you eerie at all," I say as the group turns to look at me. "I always think dance is art, so what could be more fitting than to have an artist in the audience?"

Instead of inviting me to sit down to look at his sketches, he places his hand protectively on his book and looks at me oddly. "Of course," is all he says before turning away from me as if I am a child who broke into a conversation to show everyone a toy. Embarrassed, I take a few steps away from the group, who do not even notice, and am thankful to find Noella at my side wanting to talk about Pierre.

"I realize I must look like a madman sketching furiously throughout the performance," I hear him tell Cornelie arrogantly, and I decide that I do not like this man at all. "But I am trying to capture the movement before it disappears. The ballet is artistic gold. An artist has to have a high conception, not of what he is doing, but of what he may do one day. Without that, there's no point in working."

Cornelie looks at him as if he's an alien. "A yes or no would have done just fine."

"You should try to expand your horizons, my dear," he replies in a bored tone while studying the cards in his hand.

"Why don't you tell me what will be expanding tonight," Cornelie purrs, swishing her skirt seductively, and I cringe at how obvious and vulgar she sounds while nudging Noella to listen to this ridiculous conversation. We exchange a look and stave off hysterical laughter only out of curiosity to see how this haughty man will react. Before he can answer, the Ballet Master approaches and taps him on the shoulder. "Monsieur Degas, may I have a word?"

"Of course," he replies in a confused manner, setting his cards facedown on the table and rising to shake the Ballet Master's hand. I slowly sip a glass of champagne and try not to indulge in a tray of petits fours, intent on hearing their conversation.

"Fellow patrons have begun to complain about your presence," the Ballet Master tells him while guiding him away from the table. "Anyone seated by you is distracted from the performance."

"I will try to be mindful of my actions. I admit I do lose track of where I am while immersed in my work." He turns away from the Ballet Master as if the conversation is over but the Ballet Master steps forward, blocking his path. "We have to ask you to cease your work during our performances." He leans in close, dropping his voice, one hand on the artist's shoulder. "If complaints persist I will lose business. Surely you can understand my delicate position."

"Don't you realize that I am capturing the most thrilling aspect of our culture?" Monsieur Degas cries in outrage, looking at the Ballet Master in disbelief. "I have exhibits lined up with gallery owners expecting to see performance paintings!"

The Ballet Master studies him intently, eyes narrowed. "Exhibits? Of my ballet? Well, in that case . . ."

"So my work is merely free advertising to you?" Monsieur Degas sneers.

"And my ballet is only a place for you to find buyers for your art," the Ballet Master says unapologetically. He pauses for a moment, then adds, "What if you were allowed into our rehearsals instead?"

Monsieur Degas looks absently away, silent, seeming to mull this over. "I am not sure," he says, bringing his focus back to the Ballet Master as he motions for a hovering Cornelie to leave them be. "Could I also walk freely around the room if a certain angle isn't to my liking?"

My eavesdropping is cut short as Cornelie bumps me aside to help herself to the petits fours. "Excuse me," I say rudely. "Other people exist."

"Sorry," she says with her mouth full, barely looking at me. I still cannot help but feel like I'm witnessing a hurricane whenever I'm in the Green Room. I watch as the Ballet Master's conversation ends and Monsieur Degas rejoins the group of gentlemen playing cards. Cornelie has moved on to a surly-looking man with a round head and thick monocle. Noella quickly abandons me when Pierre motions for her to join him. It's as if I'm standing in the center of a storm while everything around me is being blown haphazardly. I want to step into the storm but am hesitant. Then I feel a hand on the back of my dress and I whip around, startled to face a man both older and slightly shorter than I. In my ballet shoes we would see eye to eye, but standing in my heeled boots I feel as if I tower over him.

"It was me," he says, taking my hand into his and kissing it lightly.

"Pardon me?"

"You could feel eyes on you during your performance. They were mine. My name is Julien." He says the last with a flourish and a bow. My immediate reaction is embarrassment and I want to pull him upright before the rest of the room sees him acting so dramatic. Instead I smile back at him, noticing that he has beautiful, piercing blue eyes framed with long dark lashes. Despite being prepared for this sort of encounter, I feel very young and vulnerable as he speaks closely to me in a low murmur, as if reciting lines from a play. I have to admit he's inarguably handsome, with thick dark hair that has yet to be overrun with gray, yet his aggressiveness makes me afraid of him.

"My name is Alexandrie, and I am overcome by your compliments." I collect myself and strive to imitate the dignified composure of the wealthy women I see throughout the city.

He leans on his cane to move even closer to me. "I watched the way the stage lights caught the golden highlights in your hair. It hypnotized me." He smiles knowingly and I blush in embarrassment. "So tell me how you became drawn to the Opera," I inquire of him in an effort to turn the conversation away from myself.

"Quite by default, really," he replies. "I'm a member of the Jockey Club and we have seven loges and share Monday, Wednesday, and Friday night seats in a regular cycle." I nod, knowing the Jockey Club is *the* social group to be aligned with if you are a man striving for power and status. "I joined because of my passion for horse racing and surrounding myself with fellow successful businessmen, but now it has offered me more opportunity than I had imagined. Would you do me the pleasure of joining me as I depart from the Opera House?"

Julien waits for my answer with a gleam in his eyes as if I'm a prized horse that he has to have. I must admit I'm flattered by his demeanor, but I also feel intimidated into accepting and agreeing to anything he says. "I am afraid I cannot. I am not one of the dancers who makes herself available for post-performances."

He laughs as if he is truly entertained by my statement. "I only meant that you join me for coffee. It's still early and I was planning on going to the café down the boulevard. The experience would be heightened if you accompanied me."

He notes my hesitation and puts his hand on my arm, and I reflexively tighten it. "I did not mean to be pushy," he smiles. "We can create our own café here."

I smile in relief. I do not know this man and, while he says he merely wants to go to a café, I cannot trust that he is sincere. The sun has set and if I leave the Opera with a strange man, I have no control over what may happen. I sit down on a tufted stool, sweeping my gown to the side, as he pours two cups of coffee from an elaborate porcelain coffee urn.

"The chill in the air is prophetic of a changing season." Julien sips his coffee, looking out to the party and back to me. "It is reminiscent of my favorite line, 'The most minute and trivial circumstance connected with those happy meetings, crowd upon our mind at each recurrence of the season...'"

"Yes, from *The Pickwick Papers*." I sip my coffee demurely, my lower back beginning to ache from sitting tall like a proper lady. Julien leans back in his chair and crosses his arms as if I have astounded him. "So you are familiar with Dickens? I'm quite impressed."

I smile to myself, knowing that all of the weeds I pulled in Monsieur Aston's garden were worth it for this one moment. I remember how sad his eyes were when he told me how he wished the world were different. As the steam from my coffee subsides, I glance up from my cup to meet Julien's eyes, knowing I am looking at the very thing that brought such worry to Monsieur Aston's face.

No. 9 Scène:
A Cruel and Subtle Analyst

A dark-haired man is furiously sorting through a stack of papers. I can't see his face but his brow is furrowed in concentration as a band plays loudly beside him. Dancers circle him, twirling ribbons around their bodies. They stop to watch a procession of carriages pull up, doors opening and richly dressed couples stepping out. The band gets louder, the dancers resume, and I move toward the man. "These are all of you," he says to me. I clutch a towel closely to my body, thinking that I should have dressed myself before entering such a party. He does not notice and pushes the papers to me. I cannot hold both them and the towel, so they scatter all over the ground, pictures of me, old and unhappy in tattered clothing, sitting in the center of a pepper field as chickens circle around me. "But I have no past," I tell him, trying to grab the papers. "But I know you," he replies and kisses me deeply on the mouth. I can't see his face, only the slight curve of his upper lip, as if he is sneering at me. The drumbeat gets louder and louder. I pull away from him and I can see his lips moving, but I can't hear him. "I can't hear you!" I scream, as the dancers flutter their ribbons over my face. I move my hands furiously, trying to get them to leave me alone, the drumbeat deafening my ears. "Stop it!"

"You are the hardest person to wake up." Disoriented, I open my eyes and see Noella's laughing face. "I've been banging on your bed, shaking your blankets—and nothing! Get out of bed or you're going to be late." She bounds out of the room, already dressed for practice.

I quickly scrub my face, slip into my drab tea-length practice skirt and tights, and run out the door. I smooth my hair back and pin it blindly as I arrive at the practice studio.

My frenzy comes to a halt and my body freezes when I see him front and center, sketching feverishly. Cornelie is posed in the middle of the room holding one of the multi-colored fans used in the performance, her feet planted in fourth position. The classical stance ends there with her shameless attempts to seduce the artist. She throws her head back and places a hand behind her neck with her elbow up, as if in the throes of passion. But her blatant attempts do not distract him. He looks at her the same way one would look at a tree or a sunset, studying and sketching, back and forth, his eyes squinting at her and down at his pencil.

Keeping a curious eye on him, I join the group of dancers and we practice our steps monotonously as Cornelie continues to bask in the glow of his attention. If he had been at our practice a week ago I would have been delighted and would have wasted no time in introducing myself and inquiring about his drawings. But after my attempt at conversation last night I don't want to go anywhere near the man. Soon the Ballet Master storms in, clapping his hands. The music starts, and we rehearse for hours until we achieve the right mix of energy and grace. As the music gets louder, I find myself concentrating on how the lines of my body look as I move through the routine. Launching into a *cabriole,* I imagine I'm an exotic bird, extending its legs and beating them in the air. When our routine begins to slow, I steal a look at him, wondering if he's too arrogant to notice that I'm creating perfect lines for him to draw.

We finally break and Noella and I collapse on a bench in exhaustion. As I begin to tell her about Julien, I notice Monsieur Degas is studying us and drawing rapidly. I stretch my legs as if I am warming up because I feel compelled to make him see me as a beautiful dancer and not a worn-out prostitute like Cornelie. Noella sits slouched down, glad to give her feet a rest and not caring to put on airs. "He is drawing us right now," I whisper to her. Her eyes roll over without moving her head and she gives him a skeptical look. "So what? That one is not right in the head. His fascination with the ballet is only a guise. He thinks he's better than everyone else who comes here because he pretends to be here for his art."

I know this isn't true based on the conversation I overheard with the Ballet Master. I glance up at him and his eyes hold mine for a moment, as if seeing me for the first time. My heartbeat accelerates but I don't break from his gaze until his eyes drop down and he begins to draw again.

"He most certainly is a disagreeable man, but I think he truly is here only for the inspiration," I say to Noella while at the same time peering out of the corner of my eye at him. His ability to look past Cornelie's overt gestures and focus completely on his drawing not only validates my suspicion that he is mesmerized by the act of dancing, but it also reminds me of Monsieur Aston's belief that what lies underneath one's physical appearance is far more valuable. Perhaps I had judged him too quickly.

Noella grins and dismisses my musings with a wave. "Perhaps, but don't ponder the thought for too long. Have you seen any of the work he has done?" I shake my head. "I suggest you familiarize yourself with his masterpieces before you get swept away with romantic inclinations of him."

"I don't have romantic inclinations!" I hiss, but Noella only gives me a doubtful look.

"He's just...different, that's all," I say, still watching him draw. Noella has become obsessed with men and romance ever since our first performance and it's really starting to annoy me. I love the idea of our performances being captured on Monsieur Degas' canvases for eternity—but inclinations, I do not have for him. I don't want to explain to her that you can be interested in someone without wanting to become involved with them. Before finding him in such bad humor, I simply wished to talk to him as two artists discussing their craft. This is something I cannot do with the investor, stockbroker, or diplomat in the Green Room.

I take a longer walk home after practice, wanting a few minutes to myself before returning to the dancers' building. I breathe in the fresh air and appreciate the quiet hum of the city around me. Passing a newsstand, I take a closer look at one of the newspapers and am surprised to see an article about our very own artist and his recently exhibited works dedicated to the Opera Ballet.

While there are no images of the paintings that the article refers to, there is a lengthy critique of his work titled *The Stage*

Does Not Hide Their Origins. My face reddens with embarrassment as I read:

> He shows all the real ugliness underlying the stage pageantry—the unhealthy precociousness of these little girls, their childish limbs topped by faces of little old women, too delicate, too bold, or too dreamy. Most of his dancers are minor supernumeraries who appear in the group scenes and the back row of the ballet, with their soiled feet and anemic pallor.... With an audacity that is both strong and attractive, he shows her emerging from a lower world, proud of appearing in the glow of the footlights, with a sly, common expression on her vulgar monkey-face.

A vulgar monkey-face with a common expression and soiled feet? Is this how he sees us? I read on, expecting the critic to savage his paintings for depicting us in such an offending way. Unfortunately we don't deserve the respect that a woman of a higher station would, as the critic continues to say,

> How true, how alive it is! The figures seem to exist in air. Light bathes the scene convincingly. The expressions on the faces, the boredom from their painfully mechanical work, the scrutinizing look of the mother whose hopes will harden when the body of her daughter wears away, and the indifference of their companions to the drudgery they know, these are emphasized and recorded with the pointedness of an analyst who is always both cruel and subtle.

The article reveals that Monsieur Degas declined to comment on the paintings, saying they "spoke for themselves and to explain them would only be insulting to their artistic representation." A fellow exhibiting artist, Paul Gauguin, explaining his interpretation, tells the critic how the series captures the true sense of the Opera Ballet and all that lies underneath the costumes and makeup. "Nothing is real but the effects they create, the skeleton, the human structure, the movement, *arabesques* of all sorts," he tells the critic. "What strength, suppleness, and grace! If you are aspiring to sleep with a dancer, do not permit yourself to hope, for a single moment, that she will swoon in your arms. That never happens; the dancer only swoons onstage."

Fuming, I purchase the paper and head back to our building, storming into Noella's room, thrusting it in front of her. "This is what you were referring to?"

I read the review to her and she looks at me like the insults are nothing more than a mere annoyance. "You're worked up about this? That's the artist's whole agenda. He gives us low foreheads and pig faces to show we are members of the criminal lower class. He thinks of ballerinas not only as sexual deviants but as threatening social deviants. He paints us as the lowly creatures that he views us as. I told you he's mad. Why do you care so much about what he thinks?"

"I don't care about what he thinks," I say evenly, trying to recover myself. "I care that now the entire city will see us as monkey-faced creatures!"

"Don't be ignorant," Noella scoffs. "Those are the paintings of a deranged lunatic. Don't let it upset you. Just accept the fact that your beloved artist is not here because he respects the ballet and idealizes us. He thinks you're a pathetic, lowly creature."

I shoot her a disgusted look and lock myself in my room. But I know it isn't her flippant comments that have me so upset. I don't want to believe that he is allowed to visit our rehearsals each day only to search for the ugliness in our lives. I feel degraded in the knowledge that he views us as animals performing for his own entertainment. We have to face degradation from men every time we perform, men trying to convince us to entertain them as if we are common whores. The one person who I thought looked at us as living works of art is only searching for our faults so that he can display them for the entire city to see.

No. 10 Scène:
A Model Dancer

When I notice him the following day at practice I look at him in disgust. Here I had thought there could possibly be something underneath his self-important attitude but now I understand that the only thing that lies there is malice. After years of being told that we are brighter and more beautiful than ordinary girls, that we have a certain something about us that makes us shine, we not only begin to believe it but we live by it. It is quite difficult to accept that someone sees me as a common, poor girl, and I'm filled with an irrational fear that soon the entire city will begin to think that way and I will become the ordinary, fuzzy-haired child from Espelette once again.

I refuse to acknowledge his presence as I practice my steps and run through the routine we are perfecting for the night's performance. When we are dismissed, I sit down to remove my slippers from my aching feet. Turning to leave, I nearly jump out of my skin as I find Monsieur Degas in front of me, blocking my path.

"You shouldn't sneak up on people," I say, trying to keep my voice level even though my heart speeds up so rapidly it is hard for me to catch my breath. He is the last person I want to speak to.

He gives me a sly smile. "You always pose throughout your rehearsal, yet you ignore me today. Have I done something to offend you?"

He is scrutinizing me with a teasing intimacy that makes my head buzz and leaves my hands cold and shaking. I can feel the color rising to my face and, as I mentally become aware of my blushing, it grows hotter, turning my face a deep crimson. He must notice this because his smile becomes broader and he looks at me with the air of a man who knows he has the upper hand. This infuriates me. Even though my physical appearance is that of a silly girl, I hate this man for thinking he is above me.

"I read the article from your recent exhibit," I say, my eyes challenging him to deny the ugly images that he had painted.

"Ah, yes, the writings of a neophyte journalist," he replies, his face unchanging. "This has made you upset with me?"

"I don't care for the entire city to view us as you do. We may be dancing monkeys in your eyes but there is beauty beyond our staged exterior."

His smile fades while his eyes narrow, and he takes on a thoughtful look as if turning my words over in his mind. Calmly, he smooths the tails of his jacket and looks back at me. "I see your point. Let me remedy the situation. You must come to my studio and pose for me and show me this hidden beauty you speak of."

"Monsieur, that is the last thing I wish to do," I say crisply and move to the side, but he steps with me, blocking my way again. I look at him with impatience. "Give it some thought. Talk to some of the other girls who have posed for me; you will find that I am the utmost professional and will not take liberties," he says while resuming the look of superior teasing that makes me feel like an awkward young girl. It further enrages me, as I had not been referring to liberties. How incredibly conceited of him to think that would be the only reason I declined. "I would formally introduce myself but I assume you already know my name," he says, his face remaining the same.

I will the color not to rise in my face at his self-assured intro-duction, not wanting to admit that I had been watching him for some time now. "Indeed, Monsieur Degas, I make it a point to learn the names of every patron," I reply smoothly.

"How very enterprising of you," he says, the corner of his mouth rising in a smile. "My name is Hilaire-Germain-Edgar Degas. But you may simply call me Edgar; there is no need to be so formal, Mademoiselle. Mademoiselle...what name should follow?"

"Alexandrie," I say, as he takes my hand in his outstretched fingers, covered with pencil lead, and kisses it lightly. Instead of defensively tightening up, my heartbeat immediately quickens at his warm touch. Trying not to look at his eyes, I concentrate on the side of his middle finger, which is indented from drawing. "I do hope to see you later," he says and gathers his pencils and sketch pads, preparing to depart for the day.

Highly unlikely, I think to myself as I watch him casually place his top hat upon his head and saunter out the door. That evening, I watch top hat after top hat being removed as I step into the storm of the Green Room. "I think they're sick of us al-ready," Noella says and I have to agree with her. The men are gathered around the lead dancers, praising them for their performance, as we huddle on the outskirts of the group. "How do you girls do it?" one gentleman refers to the rigorous production. "Pure stamina" is the reply, followed by dazzling smiles. "We practice every day," I hear myself saying. "It can be incredibly draining, and you need to be dedicated in order to wake up every morning to put your body through the workout. You have to love it. As Emily Dickinson said, 'My labor and my leisure too.'"

"Alexandrie is quite bookish," I heard a fellow dancer whisper to a thin gentleman, who chuckles in her ear. "No one wants to hear a dancer," he whispers to her. "They only want to look at a dancer."

Noella gives me an annoyed look as it's made clear we are now completely ostracized from the circle. "What are you doing?" she asks. "Why are you quoting people like an old man?"

"I was just making conversation," I reply, bewildered. "No one else was."

"Can't you see what is happening here? This entire thing"—she grasps for the right word while moving her hands in a circle to encompass the ballet and Green Room—"it's about being seen. Unless we're in the front of the production no one remembers us after the show. We need to be in front of the patrons' faces for them to show any interest in us."

I know she's right as I hear the loud laughter from the men gathered around the lead ballerinas, but only a twinkle of conversation from the few men who speak to the rest of us. It looks as if we are lined up, ready to dance at a formal ball. One side of the room is dominated by black tuxedos, while the other is filled with the bold colors of dresses. I know how I can be seen by the entire city, I think scornfully, taking a long sip of champagne.

I tell him I will model for him, but I first question many dancers to see if modeling for Edgar alone in his home will bring about an unwanted reputation for me. Walking across the street to the dancers' building, they all answer the same, with great laughs, telling me that he is so reluctant toward women that I am just as safe in his home as I would be if I spent the afternoon in church. Some girls only have complimentary things to say about him while others share my nascent opinion of him.

"During one session," a fellow dancer says, "I questioned him about why he hated women so much. He didn't even look at me when he replied, 'Women always think that men despise them. On the contrary, we're obsessed by them. They're our only danger, women. They have goodness when we are no longer worth anything.' "

I linger outside my room as Paulette, a twenty-year-old dancer, tells me he lives in a beautiful three-story home where he has made his living quarters on one floor, displays his impressive collection of art on another, and has converted the top floor into his studio, where he spends most of his time. She says the studio is cold and when she modeled, he became angry when she asked him for more coal to heat up the room.

"His studio is a disaster; I could barely find a place to put down my clothes. I cannot believe that such a fine home can have one room that looks like it hasn't been cleaned for decades," she tells me. "When I finished modeling, I had to change in a dark, dirty corner which that maniac called a dressing room."

She further tells me that he would sing while he painted but then became frustrated with her fidgeting and screamed, "You pose so badly that you will make me die of rage!"

She smiles away the criticism. "He's overly dramatic. In all honesty, he is not hard to get along with. Just hold your pose and do not offer up an opinion of his art, or else he will fly into a fury."

Paulette speaks of another dancer who had modeled for him and felt the need to criticize the final product. "She thought he would paint her as an idealized version of herself. She had a huge hook nose and he painted her exactly as she was. I suppose the ugliness in her is what drew him to paint her in the first place. He was so offended by her ignorant critique that he pushed her out of the room and threw her clothes out after her. She said she had to dress at the top of the stairs while his maid cleaned the railing."

After hearing Paulette's tales, I'm dreading the modeling session even more. Noella is right behind me as I enter my room. "I cannot believe you're going to his studio after the stories Paulette just told you," she says as I sit on my bed and unlace my boots. "She had nice things to say as well," I reply.

"We have one bad evening and you go running off to a lunatic," she says, looking at me with a raised eyebrow. "I don't want you to waste your time with this man. What about Julien? He seemed so taken with you!"

I remembered when Julien touched my arm and I felt nothing but hostility, but when Edgar touched my hand, I couldn't describe what I felt and I can't explain it to Noella either. "You're as protective as a mother," I laugh. "Don't you realize that if I am seen in paintings around the city it will increase my popularity at the ballet? Everyone will want to meet the girl in the painting."

"Conniving," she smiles wickedly.

That Sunday my legs are heavy as I walk past the Paris Opera House through the neighborhood's crowds. I feel self-conscious in the limp skirt that I practice in, falling just above my shins, but it's what he wanted me to wear. Hugging my long walking jacket to my waist, I take in everything around me. While I don't find Paris as intimidating as I did when I first arrived at its door in my tattered tutu, the massive building with its grand archways and sculptures of eight muses still seems to tower over the Rue le Peletier. I only know a few paths in the city, and recognizing the neighborhood's musical center, the Conservatoire de Musique, I make my way down the street. Turning toward a café, I see a tall woman walking out, exiting only after the door is held completely open for her. She gives the man a small smile and nod, and slowly passes, raising her head to the sky and flawlessly opening a parasol. It seems as if it is one long movement, and I stare at her confident, graceful stroll down the brick-covered street. I find myself making a mental note that a fine lady will move slowly, as if she has no place to be. Everyone in Espelette moved at a hurried pace to try to get each chore finished before the sun set. I admit that I run around near hysterical, trying to make it on time to practice and eat enough food during our lunch breaks, so that by the end of the day I am exhausted and have stomach cramps.

After the woman has disappeared from my view, I resume my walk, this time at a much slower pace. "*Bonjour,* Mademoiselle," several men smile slyly at me as I look away uncomfortably, realizing a slower pace gives adequate time for people to get a good look at me. I want to drop my head and pass by them quickly, but I force myself to lower my eyes and continue to glide past. When I raise my eyes again, I see that the street is so busy I cannot tell which way I am supposed to turn. I begin to feel panicked; I don't want Monsieur Degas to be angered by waiting for me. The streets seem to merge together and I can't tell which way is straight. I step up to a fruit stand and ask the man which way I should go to find the street I am looking for. He quickly waves me in a direction but it only confuses me more. "I'm sorry, sir," I say, my voice beginning to quaver. "I am unfamiliar with the city and am afraid of walking too far down the wrong street and not being able to find my way back."

"My lady, see the church on the corner?" I feel a hand on my shoulder and turn toward the voice. "That is the street you are looking for. It is odd to see such a young girl visiting Paris alone."

"I live here, although I am new to the neighborhood," I smile at him when I see that he is probably seventy years old.

"Then I welcome you. I myself am very old to the neighborhood," he chuckles in his slow, raspy voice. "It is easy to get lost here with so much commotion. Just remember that the church of Notre-Dame-de-Lorette is the landmark of the new Athens." I look at him questioningly. "Look around at all of the neo-Greek and neo-Roman architecture," he scoffs. "It is not exactly appealing. A tawdry re-creation of Greece."

"Is that the proper name of the church?" I ask, gazing over at it. While the building itself is not large, the front is dominated by huge vertical columns supporting a grand portico with relief sculptures of saints. I suppose this adds to the Roman aura of the neighborhood.

His laugh turns into a cough and I stand back and wait for him to clear his throat. He spits into a handkerchief and, noticing his teeth are rotted out, I am anxious to distance myself from him. "That's what we call it! These young men want it all today and hide away their mistresses all over this neighborhood. The mistresses always attend Sunday service at the Notre-Dame, probably out of guilt, and the locals referred to the church as Notre-Dame-de-Lorette so frequently that the name stuck."

"Thank you for pointing me in the right direction," I tell him and head toward the church, thinking this quarter is like a larger version of the dancers' building. I can picture life being exactly the same, only I would have to cross the street to visit Noella's apartment. It is a strangely comforting thought that we could all be neighbors and I could grow old surrounded by the girls who I currently live with. Now that I know which direction to go in, I decide that I love the energy of the new community establishing its own roots. I feel it's very emblematic of my own life in Paris. The church's nickname reflects the culture of Paris and my fellow dancers' role in preserving that culture. I now catch myself looking longingly at the three-story apartments housed above ground-level shops. I've heard rumors that the *lorettes* have their own servants and seamstresses who live on the attic floors of these apartments. Would the locals gossip about me if I lived here?

I try to maintain a slow stroll while holding the directions to Monsieur Degas' home in my hand. Each block seems to go on forever as I anticipate the next street I am to turn onto. My path ends in front of a large iron gate. I check the directions and peer inside the gate to see the road that I stand on continuing past the gate, turning into a secluded private lane separating rows of grand homes from the city street. Hesitantly, I push open the gate and enter this private community. Lush gardens and neatly kept houses sit side by side away from the noise of carriages and street vendors. I feel as if I have left Paris and have entered an entirely different world. My nervousness begins to escalate as I reach a large home whose numbers are identical to the numbers on my directions.

Taking a deep breath, I knock on the large wooden door. I wait on the front steps, concentrating on keeping my breathing even. An old woman answers, looks at me questioningly, and I tell her I am here to see Monsieur Degas. She studies my face and I wonder if perhaps I am at the wrong house, when she turns from me and screams, "Monsieur!" Startled, I take a step back, but she motions for me to enter the house. I hear footsteps and my attention turns to a spiral stairway whose elegance far surpasses even those at the Opera. I cannot take my eyes from it as I try to understand how it is functional. The underside seems to flip over, yet the stairs are large and solid. The staircase conflicts against itself, and for that reason I am mesmerized by it. Edgar appears, arriving at the bottom of the stairs, formally dressed in matching trousers and a long jacket, with a large smile on his face. "Mademoiselle Alexandrie, I see you are satisfied with my reputation," he says as he approaches me and I smile politely. "I also see you've met Zoe, the only woman I tolerate." He winks at Zoe and she shakes her head at him. "God bless you, Mademoiselle," she says to me as she walks slowly up the staircase.

"Is Zoe your mother?" I ask, a question which is answered with laughter. "My dear, Zoe is my maid," he replies. "What kind of thirty-one-year-old man lives with his mother?"

I blush. "I am not used to being in homes with maids," I reply quietly and his eyes soften as he watches me.

"Then today is your lucky day," he says, assuaging my embarrassment. "We must go up this Rococo absurdity of a staircase to reach my studio and I'll show you my home along the way."

I look to both sides of the foyer we are standing in. There is a door on either side of the wall with the staircase prominently displayed in the middle. "Those doors are always locked," he says, following my eyes, and I begin to tell him I did not mean to enter but he cuts me off. "My bedroom is behind that door and the other door holds the museum. Only favored visitors are allowed in. My art collection is very delicate and the temperature must be controlled so as not to ruin anything. Come along." He nods toward the staircase and I follow him up the winding steps until we reach the second story. I find myself further amazed at his bad humor—to have a museum inside his own home and to only share it with certain people whom he deems worthy!

"This is the public area," he grins as he sweeps his hand out and I take in a set of warm, wood-paneled rooms with deep windows. The rooms are decorated with expensive oriental rugs and gilt-framed paintings, leather-bound books, sculptures, and wall hangings. "It's so opulent," I say as my eyes land on a silk-covered chaise longue and marble fireplace.

"I would describe it as more of a cultured formality than opulence," he replies while guiding me back to the staircase. "The furniture was handed down to me from my family. I admit I am not much for decorations."

We climb to the top of the staircase and enter his studio. I am shocked by the disorder of it compared to the rooms below. "I don't allow Zoe to clean my studio," he shrugs, taking in my expression. "I'm afraid moving around dust will damage the canvases. Now, by the windows, we have work to do."

I cannot tell if he's teasing or annoyed with me. I don't want to be difficult, so I hurry toward the windows, which are spread over an entire wall and almost completely covered by a linen curtain. The sunlight seems to enter as if through a film, and dust specks flicker in its subdued beam. Edgar rummages through a deep cupboard as I survey the massive studio—easels jumbled together, sculpture stands, tables, armchairs and stools piled with screens, picture frames, rolls of canvas and paper. The click of my heels echoes on the wooden floors. I try to slow my breathing but feel as if my every movement reverberates off the high ceiling, and I am sure he can hear me swallow my nervousness. I don't see a place to sit down, so I change into my ballet slippers by leaning over on one foot. In the large studio, I feel very small, yet the center of all focus. He pulls out a large roll of paper and quickly sharpens a few pencils. I watch him as he moves the knife with strong, sure strokes, so unlike Monsieur Aston's slow and shaky sharpening technique. He moves to the only open space in front of windows and grabs a dust-covered chair and table, positioning himself quite close to me. I stand uncomfortably between him and the windows and nervously scratch my back.

"Hold that pose," he cries, and I freeze at his intensity. "You're a natural; I love awkward gestures like scratching your back."

Immediately my arm begins to cramp, but I ignore it and try to take my mind off it by observing the studio. Even though Paulette warned me, I am still amazed that it is so unkempt. The high walls are completely bare even though he must have so much artwork to hang. Wouldn't he want to be inspired by his accomplishments as he creates more? My eye is drawn to a small stove with its pipe running through the air into the wall. Amidst all of the clutter I had not noticed the most curious thing of all—giant steps leading toward nowhere. They look as if they belong in a fairy tale, waiting for a snooping child to climb to the top and discover a new world. Only when I see a canvas taller than the ceiling of my room do I understand that he must climb the staircase to paint something that size. Of course! I had always wondered how artists paint large canvases. Do they move around like a clock, painting all sides? How do they get to the middle? Do they sit on it? It turns out they have fairy-tale staircases. I unconsciously nod and Edgar looks up from his drawing.

"I'll be still," I whisper, and he resumes his drawing. As he lowers his head, I think I see the side of his mouth turn up as if suppressing laughter. I watch from the side of my eye as his pencil moves rapidly with one hand, the other alternating between holding the paper and erasing unwanted lines.

"You must be getting stiff. Let me just get one last detail and you will be free," he says as he holds his pencil still and moves his chair toward me. I keep my eyes fixed on the window while he studies my face intently. All I can hear is the scratching of his pencil. He is so close that if I lower my hand it will touch his shoulder. I catch my breath as he leans toward me and then feel a fool when I hear the screech of his chair on the wooden floor. I had thought he was going to kiss me. And what would I have done if he had? Before I can think rationally, my mind automatically answers, return the kiss.

No. 11 Scène:
The Green Room

A never did tell Noella about my romantic inclinations toward Edgar and instead maintained that I was conniving. It was easier that way, since I myself did not even understand how I could be attracted to such a disagreeable man. As Edgar worked on my painting, my mother wrote to me of her dire situation, describing how my family was only eating vegetables now and chastising me that the funds I sent back hardly made a dent in the debt. *Are you making any progress in securing a monsieur?*

After many evenings in the Green Room, I no longer find it intimidating and have begun to relax, enjoying watching to see who is spending repeated amounts of time with whom and observing familiar faces. Standing amidst a group of Julien's fellow Jockey Club members I realize that no one expects me to contribute anything to the conversation, simply to nod as points are made and laugh when a joke is said.

"There is quite a bit of purifying involved in the creation of a new city," one man says while looking at a crowd of men descending on a nearby dancer. "A newly constructed city comes at great costs, of which the least significant is the monetary one. Many tens of thousands of people were evicted from old buildings to make way for the new—nearly fourteen thousand from the Île de la Cité alone." He waves his hand back and forth as he lists the new improvements.

I try to hide my disgust at his nonchalant description of purification. The loss of land along railroad routes to Paris had devastated the people in small towns where I grew up. I remember my father describing how ferrymen, towpath workers, and owners of riverside inns and village stagecoach shops attacked the railroad bridges and stations outside of Paris when their livelihood was threatened by new rail routes serving others, not local people. Today's boom in commerce has shifted vast sums of money into the coffers of entrepreneurs like this man, who increasingly dominate society.

"You know my standing on the new Paris," Julien says, rolling his eyes.

The other man chuckles and slaps a friendly hand on Julien's shoulder. "We are not all as fortunate as you to have a thriving business waiting for us. The new city is coming, so I might as well profit from it."

Julien musters a small laugh for the group but I can tell he's offended. "Keeping my grandfather's legacy intact by not allowing the franchise jewelers to trample over my stores with their cheap knockoffs is hardly fortunate," he replies.

I try not to let my eyes grow wide as I imagine the extravagant jewels that he could shower upon me. "I did not know you are a jeweler," I say to him, and immediately am made to look stupid as a loud man in the group bellows, "Suddenly you are much more attractive to her; she's going to expect to be covered in jewels!" The group laughs at this joke and turns toward me for a reaction. The pit of my stomach is in flames as I think not only are they treating me like a greedy girl, but I'm acting like my mother. I deserve to be laughed at. I cannot think of a witty remark to correct my statement, so I say in a quiet voice that it is the creation of jewelry that intrigues me.

Julien's eyes light up and he runs his hand over my hair. "Such a curious girl." He studies my face. "All my life I have been surrounded by jewels and I am constantly searching for the perfect one," he says and I blush, ready for him to compare me to a jewel, but he does not. "It's amazing that the most dazzling objects are nothing more than chemicals. Take the lovely gem Topaz for example, deriving from silicate. It's a dense mineral, very hard and high in specific gravity. Topaz in its original state comes in many different colors. When they are put under intense heat to be made into gemstones, most become a yellowish brown. The Imperial Topaz contains an orange hue and is the most valuable form of the gem. Garnets are more than just a stunning red accessory; they're actually a silica mineral."

Now more than ever I wish I were the kind of girl who could pull a witty comment out of the air. I find it hard to pretend to be entranced with Julien as he drones on about the various elements that form a gemstone. I murmur a "very interesting" or "is that so" from time to time in an effort to stop my eyes from glazing over.

To my great relief Noella and Pierre join the group, giving a break to Julien's lecture. "Pierre wishes to be formally introduced to my very best friend," Noella says while gazing up at Pierre's face, even though she's speaking to me. Noella barely speaks to the other *abonnés* anymore and spends her time huddled away with Pierre. The two of them whispering closely to each other has become a permanent fixture in the foyer. She counts the days until our next performance, not because she cannot wait to go onstage, but because it is when she will see Pierre again.

"Two such beautiful girls! How does the Ballet Master get any work done when he is surrounded by such beauty?" I smile and offer my hand to Pierre, only because it is the polite thing to do. I cannot fathom how someone as street smart as Noella can be flattered by such obvious, even cliché, compliments. Their relationship consists of Pierre complimenting Noella's looks and her returning the compliment. I doubt either one knows anything more about the other.

"Pierre, is it?" Julien interjects. "What is it that you do?"

"I enjoy the ballet each Saturday! What more is there to life?" Pierre smiles easily and puts an arm around Noella. "Alexandrie, it was a pleasure to finally be introduced, but I must retire early this evening." Noella watches him depart with a sulky look on her face. "Odd gentleman," Julien says as his eyes also follow him. "He seems quite young to hold season tickets."

"He comes from a long line of aristocrats," Noella replies proudly.

"Is that so? And what is their name?" Julien looks at Noella with excitement, but she glances away in embarrassment. "I am not sure," she says quietly.

I am about to tell Julien that Noella isn't the kind of girl who pries into someone's life, which I hope will soothe her embarrassment, but I see Edgar enter the room and my words never surface. His dark hair is swept back from his forehead and he firmly shakes the hand of a fair-haired gentleman. As he turns away, smoothing his large necktie, his eyes catch mine and I give him a small smile of recognition. He nods to me and catches the gentleman before he leaves, and to my great surprise I see them approaching my group. I realize both Julien and Noella are staring at me. I do not have time to recover before Edgar maneuvers the gentleman in front of me.

"Here is my inspiration." His arms are stretched toward me as he grins at the gentleman.

"You have captured her likeness brilliantly," the gentleman says with a sharp accent that I cannot place.

"Forgive us for interrupting," Edgar says but does not give the group time to reply. "Alexandrie, this is Monsieur Taylor. How do you Americans say it? Meester Taylor."

Monsieur Taylor laughs good-naturedly at Edgar's imitation of his accent and gives me a slight bow. "Alexandrie, it is a pleasure," he smiles. "I have just arranged to purchase some pastels Monsieur Degas has created of you. They are exquisite. They'll be the envy of my collection."

"Yes, American art is so foul that this poor soul needs to travel to Europe to find real art." The two men laugh together and Julien attempts to enter the conversation. "Paintings of Alexandrie? I should like to see those." He moves closer to me and I wish he would go away.

"Pastels, not paintings," Edgar says rudely to him. "Alexandrie, since our Yankee friend here is so impressed with your features, I should like to draw more of you. Perhaps you could come by tomorrow morning."

"It would be my pleasure," I smile demurely at the pair.

"Wonderful! Bring along your costume from tonight's performance." He exchanges a look with Monsieur Taylor. "Since the sound of a pencil is so much louder than an entire orchestra."

"I would also be interested in seeing these portraits," Julien again says to Edgar. "Would it trouble you greatly if I stopped in to see the finished product?"

Edgar looks at Julien as if he just noticed he has been standing beside me. *"Beaucoup!"* He takes a sip of champagne and leaves. Monsieur Taylor gives the group an apologetic look and follows Edgar out of the room.

"It would trouble him greatly! What an arrogant man," Julien seethes as his friends nod in the affirmative. "To treat a potential buyer with such a lack of respect! Alexandrie, how can you stand to be in the same room with such a horrid man?"

"He's not that horrid." I reach into my small purse and apply powder to my face, smiling to myself. A buzz around my portraits has begun.

No. 12 Scène:

Science as Art

I awake early in the morning, full of excitement that my art has been purchased. The walk to Edgar's home seems quicker this time, since I know where I am going. He greets me at the door, still in the trousers he wore to practice, shirt tucked in, but his morning jacket is nowhere to be seen. Without his jacket on, I can see the broadness of his shoulders and I try not to stare at him as we move to his studio.

"I want to pay you for your time," he says while pulling an envelope from his pocket. "No, I couldn't accept that," I say, waving my hands for him to stop. "You deserve to benefit from the sale," he says, looking at me in confusion. "I did nothing but stand here," I reply. "I will not take your earnings, and that is final." The truth is that I'd already been paid—in exposure—and I knew I would feel guilty accepting money from him.

"I have to say that has never happened before. But, as you

wish. Let's get started. Today I want you to act as if you are getting ready for a performance," he says, beckoning me toward a
pile of canvases. He flips through them and pulls one out from
the middle. "I started this image years back but haven't gotten it
right." He points to a rendering of a young woman with long,
dark hair assessing herself in front of a mirror. "I need to capture the innocence of dressing."

"She appears to be scrutinizing herself, rather than dressing,"
I say, my eyes locked on the image. I don't recognize her from
our production and wonder if she had been part of the ballet before I entered.

"Exactly!" He places the canvas back in the pile and turns to
me with raised eyebrows. "If you wish, you can dress behind that
screen, or I can leave the room if you feel more comfortable."

"If you wouldn't mind," I say shyly. I suspect changing in the
same room as him would send me into a frenzy of nerves so severe that my hands would not be able to unbutton my dress and
he would wonder what is taking so long. After he has left the
room, I step behind the screen and change into my costume,
which is all white—a white bodice and layers of white tulle, with
the blue from the large sash at my waist as the only touch of
color. I had worn this costume for several weeks now in my role
as one of the wedding guests for our production of *La Sylphide*.
I tie the sash into a bow on my lower back and walk toward the
large window, feeling out of place. The only other time I ever
change into a costume is when I am about to walk onstage. I
suppose this is a bit like being onstage, I think to myself. Except
that I am the only performer and he is the only one in the audience. It's incredibly quiet and I notice he has given me a lot of
time to change.

When he enters the studio, he is all business and directs me into various poses. I think of the unfinished painting and try to emulate how I would prepare myself for a performance if no one was there to watch me. He becomes particularly interested in my pose as I move to bring the strap of my satin ballerina's bodice up to my shoulder. I repeat this action over and over at his request.

I strain to hold my pose quietly even though my limbs have been aching for what seems like hours. I focus my eyes on the floor, amusing myself by tallying up how many different colors of paint it is stained with. I count twenty-eight, if shades of the same color can be categorized as a new color. Since it's my own game, I decide they can be. My eyes wander over to him as he draws, adjusts his view and the window's light, all the while humming what I recognize to be Italian opera. I want to ask him if I am correct, but I bite my tongue, suppressing the urge to break his concentration.

As he rummages through his paints, he speaks to me about his friends and the new style of painting they are bringing to Paris. "We're going in a completely different direction than every artist before us," he says excitedly while mixing colors. He doesn't speak in the teasing tone I am used to; instead his words are rapid and almost agitated. "We're not painting rigid portraits or religious murals. Observing life is what we are striving to do."

"I do that too!" I cry out in excitement and words fly out of my mouth before I can stop them. "Even when I was little, I was always observing the people in town. I barely spoke to anyone at all because I was so busy watching them. And their faults," I add sheepishly.

He chuckles, while never taking his eyes away from his canvas.

"My dear, if I recall the first time I met you, you were quite angry about my paintings because they showed the faults of the dancers," he says, the familiar tone coming back. "Yet it turns out you do the exact same thing."

"I don't broadcast them! Seeing them and exploiting them are two entirely different things," I say defensively.

"If someone appears as one thing, but in reality they are something completely different, how is that exploitation? I think my work is a realistic representation of life," he argues. "I observe society through critical eyes, just as you do. This is how I paint, as a scientist of sorts, dissecting those around me to reach into what they actually are instead of what they appear to be. No one likes to see their true selves, even though it is much more appealing."

"And the ballet has not escaped your critical eyes?" I ask with much contempt, peering at him through the side of my vision. I know this man, I think to myself. Not from the ballet, but from somewhere else. Gypsies talk of everyone having had another life and that, contrary to what the Bible teaches, no one ever really dies. They are born over and over and over again so that sometimes you run into someone you knew in a past life. Could this be the case with him?

His eyes shift away from the canvas to focus on me and I stand still, waiting for him to scream at me to leave. Instead he looks as if he is suppressing a smile. "Now, now, you are much too sensitive. All dancers try to hold on to this image of otherworldliness, as if you are mythical beasts. Just think— one of the Opera's dancing wonders was once a small girl spying on her neighbors. This is far more interesting to me than a staged persona. The girls in the painting that you are so worked up over are terrible pigs who overindulge in men, money, and vanity."

The shock of these words pulls me out of my daydream and I want to protest, but then I think of Cornelie and I have to admit that she is a terrible pig. I watch his hands move quickly over the paper and a thought occurs to me that I have not seen how he draws me. True, the American collector was impressed by my pastels, but what did he mean when he said Edgar had captured my likeness? I have a terrifying thought of portraits of a piglike version of myself surfacing all over the country. I peer at him suspiciously, watching the curve of his upper lip and, all of a sudden, I know the gypsies were right, because I remember the dream I had of the dark-haired man who drew me in Espelette and then kissed me.

My heartbeat quickens at the memory, and even though I know it was a dream my face reddens and I forget the point I had wanted to make. "I have seen paintings of landscapes with many bright colors in the galleries by the Opera House," I say as if I am a stranger interviewing him. Yet I keep replaying how he pulled me to him in my dream, and how I thought he was going to kiss me at the end of our last modeling session. "They are different from other works of art," I continue awkwardly. "Is this the new style of painting you are referring to?"

"Yes, although I would never put my name on those particular paintings. I prefer to lean on the lessons of the great masters and not have colors throwing up all over the canvas." He chuckles to himself. "Many of my colleagues will spend an entire day ruining a landscape with too many colors running into one another until the entire picture becomes a complete blur."

I smile to hear his take on the work of his friends, yet I remain on edge. "It sounds like heaven to spend an entire day outside painting and absorbing all that nature offers," I say, pushing the dream out of my head and instead thinking about how incredible it is that all of these artists have found one another to share in their talents and criticize one another, much like the girls of the ballet.

"That sounds terrible to me!" he exclaims, and I stiffen, ready for him to lose his temper and paint me as a feeble-minded pauper. "I have no use for the outside. Give me a warm summer day and I feel like sleeping all day long with the shutters closed."

I peer at him inquisitively. Edgar's cantankerous comment doesn't fit the youthful glow that emanates from him as he paints. As he continues working, he breaks into a great smile and tells me he believes that true art is created only in an artist's studio. "If I were the government I would have a special brigade of gendarmes to keep an eye on artists who paint landscapes from nature," he says with a glint in his eye. "Just a little dose of birdshot now and then as a warning."

He tells me sometimes he paints landscapes, but he does not feel compelled to camp outside with bugs getting stuck in his paints and the sun beating down on his face in order to produce a proper rendering. "I get along very well without ever going out of my own house. With a bowl of soup and three old brushes, I can make the finest landscape ever painted. When I want a cloud, I take my handkerchief and crumple it up and turn it round till I get the right light, and there's my cloud!"

I laugh out loud, this time at the absurdity of re-creating something that is in its perfect form steps from his front door. "If that is how you would paint a cloud, then tell me how you would paint a beach?" I tease him, not entirely sure if he is serious.

"That's easy. I spread my flannel coat on the floor in my studio and make the model sit on it." He leaves his canvas and sprawls on the floor, imitating how the model on the beach might look. "You see, the air one breathes in a picture is different from that outside."

He stands up, winks at me, and returns to his drawing. He has such energy about him, I notice. It reminds me of how Monsieur Aston flipped through pages of books and raked through his windowsills to find the right lesson. Perhaps he was like Edgar when he was young, full of movement and passion for his trade. Yet I could never imagine Monsieur Aston being rude like Edgar.

"Tell me this," I say boldly. "How can someone who despises the outdoors be so knowledgeable about it to re-create it in his studio?"

"So the deep questions arise! Young Alexandrie, I am a well-traveled man," he says mockingly. "While I despise, as you say, painting on location, I do not despise the outdoors. Do you understand? I love to see new places and cultures; I just don't like to waste an entire day painting one particular spot. I don't want to limit myself to one place in the world—I want to see them all."

I find myself seduced by his words and wish I could travel all over the world. I marvel at how he has a way of making his own way of life seem less an eccentricity and more a model of how everyone should live. He speaks with such enthusiasm about his beliefs, I find it hard not to be swept away with his ideas and agree with him.

"I have never been out of the country, so I would love to hear about your travels," I say eagerly.

"Well, I just returned from America, where I visited family in

New Orleans," he replies, dipping his brush in the paints. "I spent two days in New York. What a degree of civilization! It's like England in her best mood."

He proceeds to tell me of his train ride from New York to New Orleans, which he says took four days, but seemed to go by in the blink of an eye. He explains how he rode in something called a sleeping car where travelers lie down in an actual bed at night, the carriage being magically transformed into a dormitory. My mouth drops open slightly, mesmerized at the thought of lying down to sleep in one city and waking up in entirely new surroundings. One day I will also travel to grand places, I think to myself.

"The train alone made the trip worthwhile, but once I arrived in New Orleans it was an entirely different world," he continues, enjoying the fact that he has impressed me. "The odd thing about discovering something new is that it initially captures your fancy but then bores you by turns. I was captivated by the Indian women behind their half-opened green shutters, and the old women with their big bandanna kerchiefs going to the market, and orange gardens and painted houses. I was excited to paint a bit of local color, but the light was so strong that I was unable to do anything on the river. Eventually I became bored with it."

"You mean the sun was in your eyes?" I ask.

"I mean my eyes are failing me," he says sharply, and I recognize the man I had decided I did not like. He jumps up to sharpen his pencils, moving the knife at a rapid pace, and continues. "Do you remember in the *Confessions*, Rousseau is at last free to dream in peace, beginning work that would take ten years to finish and abandoning it after ten minutes without regret?"

I search my brain to remember what the *Confessions* are, but it doesn't matter because he doesn't give me a chance to reply. His words are like a steam engine, rolling slowly at first and gaining more speed until they take off on their own, unable to stop for anyone. "That is exactly how I feel. I saw many things there, I admired them, and I shall leave it all without regret. Life is too short."

"I find it hard to believe that you left without one drawing," I comment dryly, now that he has finished his story.

"You have found me out," he says sheepishly and I'm somewhat surprised that he chooses not to argue with me. "I filled a notebook or two with drawings. The women there were almost all pretty. But I fear that their heads are as weak as mine." He gives me a quick smile and a shrug of the shoulders, then pauses, reflecting on this thought.

"Alas, I have just let out something that could earn me an atrocious reputation. On your honor never repeat that I told you the women of New Orleans were weak-minded," he says dramatically, teasing me.

I am actually glad to hear the insult, though I do not say this. Here he had been going on and on about how captivating these women were and I felt a stroke of jealousy toward an entire city of women who I would never meet. To hear that they are not intelligent sets my jealous thoughts at ease. "You have nothing to be worried about," I say calmly, realizing that if he should choose to paint me in an unflattering manner I will be quick to remind him of his opinions before my likeness is displayed for the entire city.

"Monsieur," his maid's voice yells up the stairs. "I told you never to bother me when I am at work!" he growls in reply.

"Monsieur Monet is here to see you," she says with annoyance. "He says it's important."

"Tell him to leave," Edgar says and returns to the easel. "Monsieur?" I hear a deep voice say and I turn to see a plump man with a dark beard that looks as if it has not been trimmed for some time. "Jesus Christ, Claude, you look like a pauper," Degas says in disgust as the man places several canvases against the wall and then shakes dirt off his cape. "You don't clean yourself up when you go to call on people?"

"It's a long walk," Monsieur Monet replies. "I brought some of my work in the hopes that you'll change your mind."

Edgar sighs and motions for him to approach. I peer over in curiosity and see canvases thick with greens and blues. "No," Edgar says and Monsieur Monet's face falls. "These are just decorations, they will not be suitable for an exhibit."

"The rest of the group disagrees with you," he glares at Edgar. "And only because you are organizing the exhibit I have to come here and beg for your acceptance. It is ridiculous."

"I think they're beautiful," I say, and Monsieur Monet beams at me. "You see there, Edgar, this girl knows art when she sees it," he says, obviously glad to have someone on his side.

"Exactly," Edgar replies. "A girl would decorate her walls with this type of thing. It is not art."

I want to hit him across the face. "Yet, it is the woman of the house who does the decorating," I reply. "And if a very wealthy woman was to attend an exhibit, I'm sure this would be exactly what she was looking for."

Monsieur Monet sends me a grateful smile as he stacks his canvases, preparing to leave. Edgar gives me a curious look, and I stare back at him with dead eyes. I know I need his paintings to gain exposure in my circle, but I do not have to play the part of the silly girl who knows nothing and pretends to be impressed or intimidated by him. "Hold on a second." Edgar puts his hand on Monsieur Monet's sleeve. "She may be right about that. Perhaps I was too quick to dismiss you."

"Then we shall exhibit together. I would thank you, but it wouldn't be sincere," Monsieur Monet says and, nodding his head to me, descends the stairs.

I turn toward the window, embarrassed at how Edgar spoke to this man, and I see that it is growing dark outside. "*Bon Dieu,* the sun has set already. I'll barely have time to make it back to the theater to change."

"I have kept you too long," he replies calmly, setting down his paintbrush. "Let me give you my carriage."

"That's very kind of you," I say in surprise. Then I remember I have a performance to get to and I hastily move toward the door but Edgar stops me. His hand on my arm, I remain still as if he has turned me into a statue with his touch. I pray that he cannot hear my heartbeat as I feel it growing louder and louder. "Do you want to see?" He motions toward his painting and I am astounded by how closely this moment resembles my dream. I hesitantly peer over his shoulder, half expecting to see myself surrounded by peppers, and am delighted to find that he has not painted a pig or a monkey, but rather an angelic figure whom I barely recognize as myself. My white skirt has pale yellows and blues swirled in, as if the colors are dancing in the tulle. "It's beautiful," I breathe in relief, and he looks at it with the scrutiny of a professional. He does not divert his gaze from the painting while he speaks to me, "Didn't I tell you? I dissect a subject to uncover what it really is."

That night I dance with a passion I have not had since becoming consumed by the Green Room.

I picture myself at gallery openings, being introduced to an entirely new crop of men beyond just the ballet. There I will meet men who appreciate art and don't look at ballerinas as objects to acquire. The *abonnés* are not the only option; there is an entire city outside these doors. With marriage on my mind, I wonder why a rich man of Edgar's standing is all alone. Probably because for every kind gesture he shows there are a dozen rude ones to follow.

But there's a certain victory to be had in breaking through a cantankerous man's shell. After seeing my painting, I know that he is the artist I first thought him to be, and he has inspired something in me. I am full of new thoughts and possibilities.

My daydreaming ends when the curtain falls and I return to the dressing room to change for the night. For a moment, I contemplate skipping the Green Room party and going to bed, as I am growing tired from the day's excitement. I'm glad I don't have to worry about entertaining Julien, since it is not his day to use the club's tickets.

I peer into the Green Room to make sure I will not be missing anything by departing early and am delighted to see Edgar's tall frame. All of a sudden, I am not too tired for the party. As I approach him, I can see he is drinking a glass of wine and speaking to several gentlemen. But each time I move toward him one of the Jockey Club members steps in to say hello. I smile and talk to them politely, but by my third attempt to break away I'm becoming very annoyed with them. Cornelie bumps into the arm of the current member who has stopped me in my path, causing him to spill champagne on his jacket. For once I'm happy for her interruption. "I'll get you a napkin,"

I tell him and scurry away. But I stop with my hand frozen on a stack of napkins as I watch Cornelie then take Edgar's arm and lead him out of the building. Their figures retreat, close together, arm in arm, and I feel as if I have been punched in the stomach.

No. 13 Scène:
The Guest of Honor

I stretch at the *barre,* dreading Edgar's appearance at practice today. As much as I try to think rationally about the situation, I can't help but be hurt. My eyes keep drifting over to Cornelie—the star of the show, I think bitterly, yet so unrefined. The *abonnés* think she's hysterical and brings so much personality to the ballet. But I see her leaving the Green Room with so many different men, without any shame. I look away from her, not wanting to remember that Edgar left with her last night. I want him to be the person I thought he was when I first laid eyes on him, someone who would not indulge in such vile things as Cornelie.

When he arrives, I expect him to move toward her, but instead his focus is turned entirely to me. "There's my star," he says softly as he approaches me. "I was looking for you after the performance, but you were nowhere to be found."

"I saw you. It didn't appear you tried very hard to find me," I reply coldly, looking levelly into his dark eyes.

"Such sad eyes," he cocks his head at me. "What has you so upset?"

"I'm not upset," I say, turning from him and resuming my stretch.

"I would wish for nothing less than to see to it you are always happy," I hear his voice behind me. "Your paintings are like nothing I've ever accomplished before. I wish to do an entire series of you, and you cannot fall into bad humor on me now. No one else will do."

He stresses the last point in such a way that I turn around, looking at his small, sharp eyes. "Is that so?" I ask, thinking of Cornelie. Is it she who will not do?

"I would never lie about such things," he answers and I conclude that last night was a terrible mistake on his part. One he wishes never to repeat again.

And over the next few months, he does not. When he attends practice, his eyes follow every movement I make. A year stretches on and I nearly forget about his indiscretion as our friendship grows deeper each time I arrive at his studio to model. My confidence rises every time I see him watching me, and I dance as if he's the only one in the room. But he's not the only person observing me and soon the Ballet Master announces that I have been promoted to a *coryphée*. I'm the only member of the quadrille to advance, moving ahead to perform in small ensembles while my old quadrille dances behind me as the *corps de ballet*. I feel as if I'm the center of the universe and there is no end to my good fortune.

I spend every Sunday in Edgar's studio and, much to Julien's dismay, he interrupts our conversations to describe how he cannot paint fast enough because galleries and collectors are so taken with my likeness. To my great relief not one of the paintings remotely resembles a pig. Instead they show me stretching or adjusting my slipper, things I do every day, but somehow Edgar is able to make the light hit me in a way that makes these everyday movements look beautiful. I receive so many compliments on the paintings, but each time it seems another man is about to extend an invitation to dinner, a Jockey Club member appears, making it impossible for me to go out with anyone but Julien. They're in the Green Room, the galleries, and even cafés. Soon other men stop approaching me and I reluctantly join Julien at cafés all around the city.

"A boulevard café is *the* appropriate rendezvous spot for illicit lovers," Noella wiggles her eyebrows with excitement, as if she is a woman of the world since she has been frequenting such places with Pierre.

She may be correct, but Julien is most definitely not my lover. While Noella is focused on one man, I'm trying to keep my options open, as difficult as that may be. I don't want to discard Julien, but I find it hard to spend less time with him. It's as if Julien has branded me and I wish I could announce to everyone that I am not his mistress. I want to find my own way, to meet many people, and decide for myself if becoming a *lorette* is what would make me happy.

It would most certainly make my mother happy. Every week like clockwork I receive a letter from her in the mail, reminding me of my family's debts and asking about the men I'm meeting, and why I am not a *lorette* yet. I made the mistake of telling her about Julien's attentions, and now he's all she asks about. She knows if I am taken care of by Julien, then my newfound status will trickle to her and there will always be francs and gifts in the mail. "If you send us one diamond earring that he gives you, it will feed us for a year!" she had written, and I could see her excitement leaping off the page. It wasn't enough that I was sending more money home each time I advanced to a higher level, and salary, in the ballet. She wanted more, and the jewels, money, and gowns that came with the life of a *lorette* made her salivate. It would be so much easier if I could cease all correspondence with them and never send another franc. But they are my family, and I feel it's my duty to take care of them. If I bought a new dress with what I earned, as I so wanted to every time I received my payment, I knew that each time I put it on, it would remind me of all that it could have brought to my family instead. The relief they would have felt in paying off a debt wouldn't be known because I would be wearing it. Besides, it would eventually go out of style, becoming worthless, and so I kept my wardrobe to a minimum, borrowing dresses from the other girls when it became necessary.

Just when I'm beginning to give up hope that I'll never be anywhere that is free of Jockey Club members, Edgar invites me to a dinner party at his home.

"It's the guest of honor," Zoe says to me as she opens the door. "All of the guests are upstairs."

"It smells delicious," I say as I remove my lace shawl and hold it over my arm. Zoe motions to take it from me and I smile sheepishly while handing it to her, still not used to homes with maids.

"Monsieur has a team of chefs in the kitchen for tonight's

dinner," she explains while moving me toward the stairs. "Go on, now, they're waiting for you."

I slowly ascend the stairs, smoothing my full white skirt and admiring how the red trim catches the light. It's one of my favorite outfits, with the matching long jacket's red band cinching my waist and sliding perfectly over the skirt, as if it was one gown. I wear it whenever I am not sure what I should be wearing, because it looks both formal and subdued at the same time. I'm glad I chose it when I arrive at the second floor to see everyone dressed formally, as if attending the ballet. I notice easels standing around the perimeter of the room and am delighted to see my own face displayed in heavy frames, ready for patrons, collectors, and exhibits. It's as if someone has been spying on me and has captured my every movement and framed it. I look at myself dancing, stretching, preparing to go onstage, and examining my costume as if no one else is around, as if I hadn't spent hours posing in Edgar's studio for each portrait.

The aroma from the kitchen is stronger and the room is full of conversation. "Edgar, I will never understand how you can live in two different worlds," one man says more to the crowd than to Edgar. "Your home is impeccable but your studio is in disarray."

"It suits me. I entertain in my home and lock myself away in the studio," Edgar replies matter-of-factly. I have never seen him look more handsome, dressed in a dark three-piece suit that accentuates his tall, slim build. His hair is brushed away from his face so that his eyes are clearly visible. His face is glowing; perhaps from attention or the glass of red wine he holds in his hand. But it's his contented smile that makes him look so handsome.

"Some would say it is reflective of your dueling personalities—isolated and mean versus the life of the party," a man with a large nose says while stroking his great beard. "How do those at the Opera House describe you? Ah, yes, 'circulating with deceptive smiles and sparkling asides.'"

"Perhaps I want people to believe me wicked." He raises his eyebrow to the group and turns to see me beside the staircase. "There she is! Alexandrie, come over here and save my reputation."

"The portraits come to life!" one woman exclaims. "She is stunning, Edgar. Wherever did you find her?"

"When I was circulating with a deceptive smile," he answers as I smile at the group. I feel less than stunning in comparison to this refined woman. Her dress is very simple, but I can tell the fabric is expensive and, while nervously pulling my jacket down, I glance at her shoes and notice the way they shine as if never worn before. She most likely throws out her shoes as soon as a scuff appears, I think, instead of polishing them over and over like I do. "Alexandrie does not share your sentiment," Edgar continues. "Why, I do believe she finds me delightful."

"I do not believe it! Alexandrie, tell us the truth," the man with the beard exclaims. "He is a bear of a man, is he not?"

"I have seen no such evidence," I lie, happy to be included in the conversation despite my obvious shortcomings. "Although I do know some models who would agree with you."

"You see," he cries, and the crowd erupts in laughter.

"Do not believe it for one minute," Edgar laughs. "The muses never talk among themselves; when they aren't working, they dance."

He introduces me to his art dealer, Paul Durand-Ruel, who has a small mustache and appears to be no older than Edgar. The man with the great beard is another painter, Camille Pissarro, and there are several collectors and society hostesses. I also recognize a few faces from the ballet, librettist Ludovic Halévy and bassoonist Desire Dihau. I greet them and to my great relief they don't act as if I'm out of place in Edgar's home. In fact, everyone at the party treats me as an equal and I'm thrilled that Edgar keeps me by his side. I feel completely at ease in his home without any of Julien's friends in sight. Even though the evening has just begun, I find myself wishing it will never end.

The party moves to a grand dining room with an enormous arrangement of flowers in the center of a freshly polished dark wood table. Edgar pulls a chair out for me and sits beside me as the chefs carve fresh roast beef onto each plate, topping it with a spicy sauce. I know Edgar doesn't eat all of his meals in such a fashion, but I can't help imagining that he does. The image of a grouchy man in pajamas being poured coffee and custom-cooked eggs makes me laugh to myself.

"Of all of your work, you have stayed away from self-portraits," Monsieur Durand-Ruel implores of Edgar. "I would love to see a grand oil of you at work in your studio. It is practically a prerequisite!"

"I refuse to play out the artist's role for the benefit of the public," Edgar replies nonchalantly.

"Please," the well-dressed woman, who I have learned is Berthe Morisot, rolls her eyes, "if you are too afraid to paint your own likeness, then have another artist do it. Ask any one of us! Édouard Manet painted a beautiful portrait of me."

"True, but you're practically family," Edgar replies while cutting his roast beef. "He's almost obligated to paint you."

"I've worked with Édouard far before I became involved with his brother." She looks put off, her large eyes focusing on her plate. I, personally, am happy to hear that she's not available. After having watched her closely, I found her delicate features quite pretty and her bourgeois background appealing. I had wondered if this was the type of woman that Edgar is drawn to.

"Yes, yes, I know that you come from an artistic family," Edgar says condescendingly. "The master of Rococo runs in your blood! But, honestly, Berthe, you do not need to prove yourself to me, I already think you're extremely talented. Even if you are inclined to self-portraits."

"All of the old masters have at least one studio portrait of themselves," Monsieur Pissarro steps in to her defense. "Surely you want to follow in their footsteps. I know I do."

Edgar grins at him. "How could you compare the two of us to the old masters? We paint like pigs. In fact, I will never touch a brush again and shall work exclusively in pastels."

The two men become involved in their debate as the rest of the table engages in their own conversations, so I take this opportunity to speak to Mademoiselle Morisot. Now that I know she has not been invited here as a love interest, I'm less intimidated and curious as to how she has inserted herself in this male-dominated profession. "It must be quite difficult being the only woman artist here," I say softly to her. "Indeed," she smiles kindly at me. Even though she is not much older than me, she has that air of a sophisticate that makes me seem like a child in comparison. "I've gotten used to working twice as hard just to make a name for myself. Often I feel as if people only humor me, yet I have just as many, if not more, gallery showings as they do."

"I think it's quite inspiring," I smile at her. "Even though I haven't seen your paintings, the fact that Monsieur Degas respects your talent speaks very highly of your abilities. I've found he can be pretty picky about the artists he surrounds himself with."

I think back to Monsieur Monet's visit as she chuckles. "Perhaps, but the truth of the matter is that he's lucky that *I* respect *him*," she says and now it's my turn to chuckle, happy to see that she's not intimidated by him. "I have far more contacts than he. I think, underneath his talk, he believes that the best place in art for a woman is as the model." She takes a small sip of wine, pats her lips with a napkin, and looks at me. "Not to slight you at all," she adds.

I'm not sure if she's insulting me or merely didn't think about how her words would be taken. "Of course," I reply smoothly but feeling a little defensive. "The ballet is, of course, my first priority. But I've found that modeling can offer me many opportunities beyond that." I want her to see that we're both women who strive for something more and that we could be friends. But her look of amusement makes me see she thinks otherwise. "I doubt you will find any opportunity from Monsieur Degas. But don't let it upset you. Believe me, you're not the first naive girl to think that."

My face reddens as she turns away from me, signaling that our conversation is over. I look down at the gleaming table and glimpse my own defeated face. I was nothing but nice to her, I think angrily, and she's implying that I only spend time with Edgar in the hope of becoming his mistress. I want to tell her sharply that I have refused payment from him for modeling, but instead I turn my attention back to Edgar, still arguing with Monsieur Pissarro, who is shaking his head. "Enough. I want to talk about these masterpieces you have created," he says, ending the debate.

All eyes turns toward me as the table eagerly waits for Edgar to explain his inspiration. He places his hand on top of mine and I feel chills run up my arm. "Seeing these young women onstage was so inspiring," he says, taking a moment to smile at me. "But Alexandrie has a special quality about her. You should see her practice! I have never seen such raw determination before. As soon as I saw her, I knew I had to paint her."

"So it's raw determination that you have, now?" Monsieur Pissarro grins at me.

"It's my strongest attribute," I smile easily back at him. "I see the stage as a blank canvas, and it is up to me to create a master-piece on it. I cannot tell you how incredible it is to see Monsieur Degas' work because it's exactly as I imagine the stage to appear while we're performing. Dancing has been my dream since I was a young girl, and I would like to tell you that I cannot believe I'm living my dream, but that would be a lie. The truth is that I work every single day to improve my form and become a better dancer. One day, I would like to be named the lead ballerina and have my name be synonymous with the Opera. I think it's time we had a strong, independent woman representing the ballet." I look Mademoiselle Morisot directly in the eye as I deliver the last sentence. She shifts uncomfortably in her seat and I sit taller, knowing she realizes she misjudged me.

"And you would fit the bill perfectly! You must be grateful for Alexandrie's influence, Edgar. These works are more alive than any of your previous paintings of dancers," says Monsieur Durand-Ruel. "I have to say I was not particularly moved by the earlier ones. While a clever and accurate satire of theatrical life, they didn't speak to me. But these paintings show more closely the being apart from the dancer. One can see the world through the gaze of this girl seated amongst us. Genius, once again."

"It seems as if Alexandrie has altered my relationship with the dance." While he is speaking to the table, his eyes remain on me and I meet them with a sly smile. "You no longer see the Opera dancers as monkey creatures?" My comment is met with laughter from the table as Edgar replies quietly, "No, I do not. I see the ballet through your eyes—as a work of art." For a moment, Edgar and I are the only two people in the room. The warmth in his eyes flickers for a moment before he turns away from me, speaking to the group in a businesslike manner. "These paintings have all been created from numerous sketches from our modeling sessions. Drawing is the foundation of my art," he says seriously, and I think that despite his intentions he is very much playing the role of artist for public satisfaction. "It's a transformation in which imagination collaborates with memory. There, your recollections and your fantasies are liberated from the tyranny that nature imposes. And that is why paintings made in this way by a man with a cultivated memory are almost always remarkable works."

Before I know it the food is cleared from the table and guest by guest begin to bid their farewells. I keep waiting for another moment between the two of us, but everyone wants to talk to me just as much as to Edgar. It's thrilling to be part of this world of artists, but when the last of the guests leave I'm afraid I've overstayed my welcome. Gathering my lace shawl, I look over at

Edgar in deep conversation with his art dealer. I move toward the stairs and am happy to hear him call out to me, "Don't leave just yet."

I walk over to the two men just as Monsieur Durand-Ruel bids us farewell. Edgar puts his arm around my waist, hugging me toward him, and my hand naturally rests on his chest. "Tonight has been quite a success," he gushes. "I cannot tell you what you have done for my career. All of these paintings now have homes. It seems I am not the only one who is inspired by you."

"I can't believe all of these people would want a picture of me," I respond shyly.

"Who wouldn't want to hang a portrait of the most beautiful dancer?" He lets go of me and looks directly into my eyes but I glance away. Even though I want him to look at me like this, I cannot help feeling embarrassed at being the center of attention. When I have the courage to look back at him, he's already moving toward the stairs, beckoning me to follow. "We'll need to get started on making more sketches immediately."

To my great delight, immediately means first thing in the morning and, when I awake early the next day, I can't think of a better way to spend my Sunday. I float all the way to his home, wanting to hold on to the feeling of belonging to this new circle of artists, as well as this new side of Edgar. I had thought that after he sold all of his paintings, he would be done with me, that he would think it had paid off and now he could move to another subject. I hope this means that perhaps I am not simply a subject to him. Making my way to the iron gate, I spot a thick girl pulling on it, her hair wild and crazy. She looks familiar but out of place. But when she slips through the opening in one swift movement, graceful despite her size, I realize it's Cornelie. What would she be doing here? I want to run up and ask her, but at the same time I don't want to talk to her, so I slow my pace and follow while she saunters down the street as if she lives here. She turns naturally to Edgar's home and knocks on the door. Not a gentle tap, but a series of loud knocks that ricochet throughout the street. My eyes narrow as she cocks her head to the side, twirls a thick strand of hair, and looks over her shoulder at me.

"It looks like you're not enough for him," she calls out, slowly twirling her hair around her finger, letting it go, and repeating. "Why are you here?" I spit back at her. "Every single painting of me has been sold. I doubt anyone wants to hang your face on their wall. I certainly wouldn't want to look at it by choice."

Her mouth curls up in an evil smile, which I know by now is preemptive of an especially cruel remark, but the door opens, evaporating her insult. We both turn at the same time, our faces changing to sweet smiles. Zoe looks at us and I think I see her roll her eyes before ushering us up to the studio. Edgar's greeting is far more welcoming as he excitedly moves around his studio, sharpening pencils. "This is going to be my best work yet," he says, not able to stop grinning. "It just came to me—how do you top a masterpiece? By adding to it! The two of you, dark and light, against each other, will come together beautifully."

I stand silently, holding my coat over my arm, unable to answer. Something that had seemed so good has now turned terribly wrong. Cornelie begins to take off her coat but her arm gets stuck in the sleeve. "I can't get my clothes off!" she giggles while pulling at her sleeve. I watch her with disgust while she grasps at her sleeve, laughing and probably thinking she's sending subliminal messages.

"Be careful, my dear, that comment can be taken the wrong

way," Edgar chuckles and helps her out of her coat. My insides stew to see him touch her, and she gives me a haughty look before turning back to him, stepping in closely to take her coat back. "I don't think there's a wrong way to take it," she whispers in his ear, just loud enough so she's sure I hear. At this point I can't even look at them, so I turn toward the window pretending there's something really interesting to look at. I hear Edgar laugh as their footsteps come closer to me. "If you two ladies will change into your costumes," he begins, and Cornelie immediately begins to unbutton her dress, which is met by loud laughter as Edgar protests. "Hold on there! Give me a moment to leave the room!" "You don't need to leave," she grins at him. "We're not all as frigid as Alexandrie here."

"Ah, but she is nearly half your age," he says pointedly, then smiles kindly at me and leaves the room. I step behind the dressing doors and change, happy that he defended me and insulted her increasing age. "You sound like an idiot," I say to her as I emerge in my costume. I look over at her in revulsion, bent over putting on her skirt, making her rolls of fat more pronounced. Yet this horse of a woman is the one that Edgar chose to leave the Green Room with. Would he paint her as a horse, as I see her, or would he glimpse angelic features underneath her rough appearance? The world makes no sense to me.

"Men only understand directness," she replies, standing up without any shame and adjusting her skirt. She moves past me, the rose tulle brushing against my blue. "Otherwise they'll never know what you want from them."

"And what is it you want from Monsieur Degas?" I retort. "I know you don't have any feelings for him. Why come on so strong if you don't care about him?"

"I never let another girl win." She flips her hair back and looks evenly at me, warm and cool colors facing each other. "This is not a competition," I say quietly.

She walks slowly toward the window, then turns to address me. "Everything is a competition."

No. 14 Scène:

The Intruder

As we travel down the street on our way to a show, Edgar holds my hand comfortably, as if we've been together our whole lives. He points to a row of pale yellow shuttered homes. "We should get one of those," he smiles at me and I squeeze his hand in response. I'm the happiest woman on the earth and I can barely believe that I have him, that we're together and making plans for the future. Inside the building, I move to where Edgar and I were sitting, ready for the show. Looking around, I notice the seats are not traditional theater seats but long rows of tufted cushions. It looks like a brothel in here, I think to myself. Where is he? Being left alone on this cushion when the show is about to start is making me anxious. I notice that everyone is facing the other direction, so I turn around as well. I had thought I had a front row seat, but now I'm in the very last row and can see everyone in the

audience. Music begins to play and I squint into the crowd, looking for Edgar. A wave of relief floods over me when I see him
seated with a group of people. Smiling, I get up and make my
way to him. He always knows someone wherever we go. But I
freeze in my tracks when I get closer and, standing above the
group, I see Cornelie seated on his lap. He looks directly at me,
then pushes her onto her back and lifts up her skirt.

My eyes flash open. My heart is racing while I look around my
room and then sink back into my pillows. You need to get ahold
of yourself, I think as I get up and cleanse my face. I let the cool
water wash away my night sweats, and I cannot help but wonder
what the dream means. Am I looking in a different direction
than everyone else?

I tell Noella about the dream, which is burned into my memory, as we walk to practice. "You're just being insecure," she tells
me. "That's all it is. He would probably love that dream, since he
enjoys pitting you against her to watch you get jealous."

"That's not true." I look down at my feet. "He's only being a
professional and has used her for so many paintings. I mean,
she's so blatant that if he had any feelings for her he would just
be with her already."

"All men love to have women fighting over them." Noella
trots ahead of me up the stairs, her way of saying she's bored
with the topic. I want to talk to her further and alleviate the
anger I'm carrying with me from the image of him lifting up her
skirt. Looking directly at me.

My anger worsens when I see Edgar leaning over Cornelie, in
deep conversation, as the pianist tunes the piano for practice.
"Move it," Noella hisses at me, giving me a push toward the
barre. "You look like an imbecile."

I move quickly and begin stretching, embarrassed to realize I had been glaring at them. I bend down to a *plié,* beginning to relax, and gradually lose myself in the moment. I practice bringing my chin up to extend my *relevé* but jump when I see Cornelie's horse face in front of me. *"Bon Dieu,"* I say in true shock. "Where did you come from?"

"You should be more aware of what's going on around you," she grins slyly at me and I have an urge like never before to reach out and hit her across the face. She's so close to me that I can almost hear the satisfying noise of my palm making contact with her cheek.

"Move over." She doesn't wait for me to answer, simply pushing me aside. I open my mouth to object but before I can get a word out she motions toward Edgar, moving in the direction of our corner, ready with his sketch pad. "You look flustered today, Alexandrie," he smiles flirtatiously at me, to the point that I wonder if he knows what I dreamt of. I scrutinize his dark eyes, crinkled at the edges, and then turn to Cornelie's smug face, and I have no words. I ignore both of them and stretch, with Cornelie invading my space and stretching alongside me so he can map out his next masterpiece.

I notice she keeps looking at me oddly and doesn't stop once we are fully immersed in rehearsing our performance. "What?" I hiss at her as we sashay past each other. "Just sizing up the competition," she whispers back as we simultaneously rise to our toes in a perfectly synchronized move. She leaves my ensemble, moving to the front for her solo. I keep in step with the *coryphées* and watch her leap into the air, whip around and pause a moment to glare at me. We all come to a halt and watch her descend, as if in slow motion, our faces scrunching up in pain, knowing what is about to happen. Our eyes are glued to her foot, hitting the floor at an awkward angle and collapsing underneath her.

Her cry of pain wakes us out of our trance and, for a moment when she's hunched over gripping her ankle, I think of her as a human being who can feel pain. "Don't just stand there gaping at me—get me a doctor now!" Her loud, demanding voice diminishes any sympathy I felt for her as one of the younger girls scurries out to find a doctor. Another runs from the kitchen, carrying a bag of ice and places it on her ankle. "You moron," she slaps it away, "that's going to make it worse. You would love it if I am injured, wouldn't you? All of you!" She looks like a complete lunatic, not making any sense, lashing out at the group. Tears begin to fall down her face while she sits shaking. "Where is the doctor?! Every second that goes by is crucial," she screams and spit falls from the side of her mouth. No one answers her and we all stand wide-eyed watching her outburst, not knowing whether to feel sorry for her or be afraid. "Calm down," the Ballet Master crouches next to her. "I am sure it's only a sprain and you'll be back on your feet in no time. What happened? You never miss a landing."

"You know why she is so upset, don't you?" Noella says to me at lunch. "Because it will disturb her post-performances?" I say cattily. Noella giggles at that. "Perhaps that's part of it," she grins. "But I think the real reason is that she knows she's not invincible and she's well aware of how much older than us she is. She gets to practice so early because she needs all of that time to stretch out. She's an old woman with stiff limbs. Her time as the star is over and she knows it."

My entire face brightens at this. "Of course! And she may never heal from an injury," I sit back, smug, while Noella nods excitedly. "While she's sitting out of practice, you had better stand out." She drops her voice so no one will overhear us, "I don't care about becoming the lead ballerina," she waves her hand away. "I just want to find my monsieur and be done with it. But you actually love dancing and are good enough to get to that level. And you would make a much better *étoile* than she ever did."

I become giddy with the thought. "The funny thing is that if she were not trying so hard to intimidate everyone she would never have put herself in this position," I whisper as we return to practice. "You see, she has no one but herself to blame," Noella says while raising her eyebrows to me and we line up to stretch our muscles, renewed with strength by the possibilities that lay ahead.

"We're going to need to reorder our production," the Ballet Master says, and I cannot help but glance over to Cornelie, seated with her crutches beside her, glaring at us. "I'll be healed in no time," she yells. "Yes, yes," the Ballet Master dismisses her, "but until then we have a performance to put together. For this weekend's show we'll have to work around the lead, cutting down the solo parts. There isn't time to get anyone trained in a matter of days, so for now, I need the ensemble to be ready. Alexandrie, move to the front. Practice in this role for me." I gladly step to the front of the group and assume a lead role. My heart is beating wildly and Noella grins excitedly at me. I take a deep breath and wait for the music to begin, glancing over at Edgar, who gives me a quick wink. I try to suppress a smile. At this moment it seems as if everything is coming together for me, and I can hardly contain my excitement.

"You did an adequate job," Cornelie says, hobbling over to me once we have finished. "But the crowd will be disappointed. I know I would be, if I was expecting to see the most famous ballerina in the country and instead had to settle for a drab replacement."

"Or perhaps they'll forget all about you," I shoot back. "How could they! My exposure goes further than just the Opera House," she says arrogantly. I raise my eyebrow to her, insinuating that she is certainly exposed during her post-performances. "I'm a guest at every prominent function there is," she says meanly to me. "In fact, tonight I'll be dining at the Emperor's home. I wonder who I shall ask to accompany me?" She feigns confusion, casting her eyes toward Edgar making the final touches on his last sketch. She looks back at me, grinning ear to ear. "You know, after Saturday's performance I had the opportunity to really get to know your little friend's companion. Pierre is his name?" My body goes cold as she looks at me with mock innocence in her eyes.

"Yes, it was Pierre," she nods her head. "Handsome young man. We got to know each other quite intimately." My hands are numb, knowing Noella will be heartbroken to hear of this. "You're more vindictive than I gave you credit for," I whisper to her. "If you hate me, then fine, but leave Noella out of it."

"Believe me, Noella wasn't mentioned at all," she laughs, and I wish she would lower her voice. "Excuse me, I think I'll invite our Monsieur Degas to the Emperor's for an intimate little dinner party."

"She did *what?*" I had expected to see tears, but instead Noella's face was bright red with anger. "I don't know if it's true," I say while motioning her to sit down. "But she certainly wants us to think it is."

"What is the point of that? So she can say, 'Take that—I slept with him, I'm better than you, I win'?" Noella had been pacing back and forth ranting on and on ever since we returned to our rooms and I told her what Cornelie had said. "She is the most insecure, callous woman I have ever met." I nod in agreement. "She's trying to do the same thing to Edgar tonight," I reply. "Just the thought of her trying to get to him makes me sick to my stomach."

"She's a horrible monster," Noella seethes. "You have to do well on Saturday. Maybe the Ballet Master will force her to leave and you can take over her role. Then we'll never have to be bothered with her again. We need to get her out of here."

"I wish it were as easy as stealing shoes," I say, which makes Noella laugh. "I'm serious! Remember when—" A knock on my door cuts me off and I rise to open it. "So sorry to bother you." Cornelie is on the opposite side, standing too close to Edgar, who looks uncomfortable. "We were just on our way to the Emperor's, but my stockings have a tear in them and I thought you might have a pair I could borrow."

"I doubt anything of mine would fit you," I reply evenly, keeping the door only slightly open to show her she's not invited in. I can't even look at Edgar; the sight of them together makes my skin crawl. "Noella, perhaps you can help me out?" She feigns sweetness while looking over my shoulder at Noella, still red-faced with anger. "You've always been generous in letting me borrow your things."

At this comment, Noella jumps to her feet, and I quickly move to shut the door before she attacks Cornelie like a caged animal, although I would enjoy watching that. But Edgar's hands move quicker than mine, steering Cornelie in one direction while stopping the door simultaneously. "There's no reason to make a commotion," he says sternly. "Cornelie, go to the carriage and I'll meet you there in a minute." She scowls but hobbles slowly down the hall, probably knowing she'll look like an idiot climbing into his carriage unaccompanied. As if he's ashamed of her, I think spitefully.

"I apologize," Edgar whispers to me while Noella moves toward the window to glare at Cornelie making her way into the carriage. "It looks as if the three of you have a personal war going on, one that I do not wish to be a part of, and it seems I have been purposely put in the middle of it."

"It certainly appears that way, doesn't it?" I say with narrow eyes. "She's vindictive; you have no idea how much so. How can you stand to even be in her presence?"

"She amuses me, so I enjoy her company," he says matter-of-factly. "She's overconfident but I like to be entertained." I look at him with disgust. "Quite honestly, it makes me think less of you," I say, somewhat surprised at myself for letting my thoughts surface so easily. "It makes me question your character."

"You're being oversensitive," he replies shortly. "I just want to let you know that I'm sorry for disrupting your evening, and had I known this was a ploy of hers, I wouldn't have let her knock on your door."

"Open your eyes. The entire night is a ploy," I say meanly and shut the door, not caring if I offend him.

No. 15 Scène:
Privileged Company

The invitation arrives in the mail—Cornelie and I standing with our backs to each other and far-away looks in our eyes. Printed over our bodies is a formal invitation to Edgar's home to view his latest works.

"It appears he's not holding a grudge against you," Noella says while looking closely at the invitation and nodding her approval. "This is really good."

"It did turn out well," I admit, peering over her shoulder. "I don't know if I even want to go after that whole scene."

Noella cringes in agreement. "But you're somewhat obligated to go," she tells me. "And you know that Cornelie will go, and if you're not there then everyone will ask where the other model is. Do you really want her to speak on your behalf?"

"I hadn't even thought of that," I groan, running my hand through my hair while contemplating the situation. "I don't know how their night ended, but just the fact that he voluntarily spends time with her makes me want to not be around him."

"You know I think that's a smart decision," Noella replies. "If he had wanted to pursue you, then he had the perfect opportunity to spend time alone with you, but instead he invites Cornelie along. He's a waste of your time, and I'm glad you see that."

"I know," I admit. "It's going to be hard to see him, though."

"Just go to his home and be perfectly polite, and then your obligation to him will be fulfilled and you can distance yourself from him," she says. "Then this will all be over with and you won't have to worry about him anymore."

Over the next several days, I avoid Cornelie as much as I can. Thankfully, our modeling sessions together have ceased, another benefit of her injury. With his party approaching, Edgar is in painting mode and, to my great relief, is not present at our practices. Some of the older dancers told me that Cornelie arrived home quite early, and by herself, the night she left with Edgar. Like me, she has not seen him since. "I don't know all of the details," Paulette tells me while stealing glances at Cornelie. "All I can say is that he looked very annoyed when he dropped her off and didn't even walk her to the door. I would be shocked if anything happened."

I relish watching Cornelie fall out of favor, both with Edgar and the ballet. I can see her face grow dark when the Ballet Master praises how quickly I've caught on to my new lead role. I smile demurely, not telling him that I've stayed up until after midnight every night going over the routine, tiptoeing into the Opera House, repeating each step in the mirrors. Although she's not in the production, Cornelie shows up to practice every day, stretching at the *barre* while we perform. It's awkward to see her leaning on a crutch while steadying herself, but I have to give her credit that she has the determination to not let her limbs go weak. Even though she favors her injured leg, her presence remains a constant reminder that she is not out of the picture yet. *Yet* being the operative word. Noella and I hold on to the hope that my first lead performance will be superb and the Ballet Master will dismiss Cornelie altogether.

"Are you ready?" Noella asks me eagerly while we fasten flowers to our tightly pulled-back chignons. I look at her in the mirror, pausing at my reflection in the fuller skirt, more decorated than the other girls, and nod calmly even though my insides are shaking with fear. The lights seem brighter in the front and my heart definitely beats louder. As the show goes on, without solos, I keep up with the girls in the front row and soon I feel as if dancing in the front is exactly the same as in the back. Only the recognition is greater.

Roses are waiting for me on my dressing table, so many that I can barely see the mirror. I grin at the other lead dancers, who are also admiring their arrangements. "How will you ever get them all back to your room?" Noella leans in to smell the flowers. "I think I'll leave most of them here. As a reminder that I've come this far," I reply. "As a reminder to Cornelie," Noella raises an eyebrow wickedly. "Exactly," I laugh.

"You have done a marvelous job," the Ballet Master approaches and Noella quickly leaves for the Green Room. "It has been many, many years since I've seen someone with your potential." I smile widely at the compliment. "Thank you, Monsieur. This may be the proudest day of my life," I answer sincerely.

"And I have no doubt you will surpass this day. Keep practicing hard and behaving as you are by avoiding skirmishes between other girls and remaining professional. We at the ballet view you as a true professional handling adversity with grace." I lower my eyes and smile, proud of myself for portraying such an image to the ballet's most influential men. His words remind me of when Madame Channing told me to ignore the other girls and remain focused. It had worked then, and I pray that it works now. "I see you achieving great things here," he continues. "Your time will come to be the star and I would be nothing but pleased to have you represent the Opera."

As if the evening couldn't get any better, with a successful performance and praise from the very critical Ballet Master, the Green Room soon becomes my own as every *abonné* congratulates me on my performance. It takes me some time to make my way through the doors, but once inside, Julien finds me and tries to take me to a quiet corner. "She's a natural. This girl is going to be known throughout all of Paris one day," a Jockey Club member says, stepping in front of our path, and I see Julien force a smile.

"Are you not happy for me?" I ask him when we have a moment alone. "Happiness can rarely be found in the public eye," he replies coldly. "This is my greatest achievement," I reply, bewildered. "And you're the only person who has not congratulated me. Forgive me, but I find that quite odd."

"Apparently you measure success by how well known you are," he says while his eyes roam throughout the crowd. "First you whore yourself out to that artist. God knows how many people have paintings of you in their homes, and who knows how many more have seen them. And as if that's not bad enough, now you're center stage for the entire audience to see." I blink hard and turn from him, unable to believe the words coming out of his mouth. "I think I've heard enough," I say evenly and move away from him, but I feel his hand on my arm. "Please wait," he says quietly. "Forgive me, I spoke too hastily." I turn back around, waiting to hear what his explanation is. "You need to understand my position as a married man. I thought you were happy dancing in the middle of the group. Why try to push through to the front? Anonymity has its benefits too, if you'll let me show you them." I know that he is referring to being the anonymous mistress. It's the first time he's spoken about arrangements out loud. "I'm sure the benefits are more than I could hope for," I say hesitatingly. "However, this is very important to me. I have worked toward this my entire life, and I see that I can go far with it. I understand your situation; however, you must also understand mine."

My hands are shaking when I walk away from him. I decide to end the night as the star, instead of chancing a spat in the Green Room. If Julien cannot support my goals at the ballet, then I won't entertain the idea of becoming his *lorette*. It's better to end it now, I think as I leave the foyer. I walk back to my room, weary with the thought that another relationship will be ending this time tomorrow.

I'm astounded at the number of people at Edgar's. I was expecting a small party like before, but I can't even find him in the crowd. But of course I can find Cornelie, or rather she finds me, barreling over with a slight limp but no crutches in sight. "Not exactly on time, are you?" she says rudely to me and I ignore her. "You should have been here early to greet all of the guests. As the model in these paintings, that was your duty. You should know these things. If I were you I would apologize profusely to every single guest."

"The invitation says to arrive anytime after seven," I reply with annoyance. "You would love it if I went up to all of these people and made a fool of myself, saying how sorry I am that I'm late when half of them have never even met me before. I would never take advice from you on how to behave." I walk briskly away from her. A waiter passes me a glass of champagne, which I gladly take.

"Here she is." I feel Edgar lightly touch my forearm and guide me into a circle. I nod uncomfortably at him. "Alexandrie has been kind enough to model for me for quite some time now," he tells the group. "Yes, I remember you from Edgar's last gathering," Monsieur Pissarro says to me. "It's wonderful to see you again, Monsieur," I reply sweetly, trying to remain dignified even though I am having a hard time standing next to Edgar. It would help if I didn't find him so attractive. Suddenly I'm desperate to find out how his night with Cornelie ended. "Forgive my manners, you have the unfortunate luck of being stuck with a group of artists," Edgar smiles easily at me and I wonder how he can talk to me as if there's no hostility between us. "This is Alfred Sisley, the only landscapist I've met that I like! And here is Paul Cézanne, an artist of my own mind who fled the banking world." I smile at both men. Monsieur Sisley, a chubby man with a boyish face and dark, slender eyes, takes my hand and returns the smile, but Monsieur Cézanne diverts his eyes from me. I study the strange, scowling man, so dark that he must be foreign, and wonder why he's so rude. "I'm trying desperately to convince them that we should join forces and have a grand exhibit together. Look at the crowd I brought to my home. This has to prove that I can get five times this many into a gallery."

They all laugh except Monsieur Cézanne, who looks at Edgar as if he's about to hit him in the face. "We never doubted you could pull off an exhibit," Monsieur Sisley chuckles. "You only invited us here to show off your success."

"It's not mine alone! Alexandrie is the one who made all of this happen. Without her I would have nothing." Edgar beams proudly at me and I return the smile, somewhat confused. I think about responding with something about how I'm not always the perfect model so that I can see if he picks up on my reference to his night out with Cornelie, but as I try to find the right way to word it, a thick accent blocks my way. "Don't let her take all of the credit," Cornelie's voice interjects and the group turns toward her. She's trying her best to look demure, but instead I think she looks like a painted clown. "Right," Edgar replies shortly, looking at her briefly. "You all know Cornelie," he says flatly to the group.

"Ah, yes, the ballet's *étoile*! It is an honor, Mademoiselle," they murmur and each man nearly knocks the other over for a chance to kiss her hand. Edgar makes no motion to greet her properly. "You like my paintings?" she asks them, looking up through lashes as they nod enthusiastically. "I thought it would be a good idea to have both girls model, but I feel these are lacking in an emotional quality," Edgar says, now being blatantly mean to Cornelie. I try really hard not to smile, knowing Paulette's gossip was true. Cornelie falters for a moment, then regains her attitude. "Such a temperamental artist," she says to the crowd, who laugh along with her, all eyes on her as if she is a magnificent creature. "I'm so glad all of the paintings are done so I don't have to spend another minute alone with him!" She looks directly at me when she says the word *alone* and I look back at her evenly. I maintain my composure, seeing us as if from above the room.

Me, standing quietly with a glass of champagne, my dress perfectly pressed and covering my body. Cornelie, already tipsy, sloshing a glass of vodka back and forth as she dominates the conversation, moving too close to the men, shoulders forward, her dress slipping away from her shoulders. Their eyes follow her movements, waiting for the strap to completely dislodge and for her to fall out of her dress.

Without addressing anyone further, Edgar steers me away from the group. "You were right about her," he whispers in my ear and I breathe a silent sigh of relief. "The night was a ploy and I wasn't even able to make the contacts I had hoped to with her around. Her behavior proved to be quite embarrassing and, believe me, I find her less humorous and more annoying because of it." I nod my head, taking a moment to form the proper answer. I want to jump up and down and yell, "Of course I was right—why did it take this long for you to see it? Anyone who spends one minute with her can tell she's nothing but a brash whore." But, knowing that I'm now in favor, I hold my tongue and remain composed, the opposite of Cornelie. "It's a shame that she's the one who represents the ballet," I reply. "She is indeed an embarrassment."

"That's an understatement!" Edgar guffaws. "When I made it painfully clear that my accompanying her was a business dinner and nothing more, she proceeded to take one of the guests into the bathroom and, let's just say, he returned to the table with a smile on his face."

"You cannot be serious," I gasp. "Did everyone there know what happened?"

"She made sure of it. It seems she wanted to show me what I was missing, so she made quite a production of flirting with him during dinner, and as soon as he excused himself to use the bathroom, she was practically running after him." Edgar shakes his head, frowning at the memory. "She hardly bothered to fix herself before returning."

"That's appalling," I say, absolutely disgusted yet elated to hear that her behavior was even worse than I could have imagined. "That was the general opinion," Edgar replies, guiding me through the room. "Monsieur, there's a matter of a sale," Monsieur Durand-Ruel interrupts us. "Pardon me for a moment," Edgar says, kissing me lightly on the cheek and moving to a corner of the room where they speak in hushed tones. It was such a natural move, I think to myself. It seems as if everything is working out for me. First the ballet performance and then, mere hours after I leave Julien behind, Edgar finally comes to his senses. I take a sip of champagne, look around the room, and think that it's going to be a wonderful night after all.

"Everyone thinks these paintings are overpriced," Cornelie's slur snaps me out of my daydream. "Probably because you're in them and everyone knows you're cheap," I mutter under my breath but just loud enough so she hears me. She looks at me, glassy-eyed, and then takes a gulp of champagne. If it were Noella or another girl I would gently take the glass away from her, but I'm rather enjoying watching Cornelie make a fool of herself. "Where did Edgar go?" she asks sloppily, squinting around the room. "I would stay away from him if I were you," I say wisely, a small smile creeping up. "Why is that?" she questions me with lazy eyes.

"I think you made quite an impression on him at the Emperor's dinner," I reply. "So much so that he doesn't want anything to do with you."

"Doesn't matter," she says loudly, like a child. "He's just embarrassed because he wasn't able to perform. And, believe me, he wanted to. But I can't waste my time on a project like that when every man in the city wants to be with me." I roll my eyes at her. "Sure, Cornelie, sure. You know as well as I do that's a lie." I move away from her, wanting to distance myself as much as possible. "Where are you going? We're supposed to be here together to show off these paintings," she says angrily. "I don't want to be seen with you," I hiss at her. "The last thing I want is everyone thinking I'm like you. Just to be associated with you is a guaranteed way to ruin a reputation." I quickly walk away, not giving her a moment to retort.

A waiter passes and offers me an hors d'oeuvre, which I reluctantly decline. After reading "cocktail reception" on the invitation, I had eaten an extra helping at dinner so I wouldn't get hungry. I hadn't expected there to be any food here tonight and now I feel stupid for not knowing what a cocktail reception was. "Our business matter has been settled," Edgar says, rejoining me with a tired smile. "Are the paintings selling as well as last time?" I ask him. "Not quite as well," he admits. "Although there are a lot more to choose from. It seems I overestimated my abilities."

"It sounds like someone is trying to swindle a compliment from a lovely young lady," a blond man laughs and slaps Edgar on the shoulder. "You're one of the problems," Edgar banters back. "You haven't purchased a single thing!"

"You're mistaken! I've just acquired that small portrait over there." He points across the room at a still of me stretching at the *barre* with Cornelie posed in the background. "Wonderful choice," Edgar beams. "It's a shame you weren't in town to see my last show. Alexandrie, you remember Monsieur Taylor?" I smile at the American I met in the Green Room and he leans past Edgar to reach for my hand, only he's too far away and bends toward me while Edgar watches him, amused. I feel embarrassed for him, so I move a few steps in and he quickly kisses my hand and then takes a step back, quite flustered. Edgar immediately engages him in conversation by trying to persuade him to buy another painting. I glance around the room, noticing Cornelie sitting on the lap of a man with scars all over his face from a skin condition. Amazing, I think to myself, it doesn't matter what a man looks like; as long as he's fawning over her, she'll encourage him. They look completely out of place, his hand holding a drink and steadying her at the same time as she rocks back and forth in drunken laughter, while the rest of the party assesses the paintings as if visitors in a museum.

As much as I love being on Edgar's arm, I don't want to seem presumptuous and I can see it's growing late. "I'm afraid I'm going to have to be on my way," I say politely. "I was just about to leave myself," Monsieur Taylor says. "I'll be happy to give you a ride home."

"That's very nice of you, thank you," I reply. "Actually, I need to show Alexandrie some sketches I've been working on of her," Edgar interjects. "I'll make sure she gets home safely." He smiles down at me, then turns toward Monsieur Taylor. "Shall I have Zoe bring your coat?" Monsieur Taylor hesitates a moment, then smiles easily. "I had no idea you consult your models about your work," he says.

"You see the finished product," Edgar replies shortly. "The process, my friend, is none of your concern." I begin to feel uncomfortable as the two men eye each other. "Very well, then," Monsieur Taylor backs away. "Thank you for such a wonderful party; I enjoyed myself as usual. Alexandrie, it was a pleasure to see you again." He gives me a slight nod of the head, but I notice he doesn't try to take my hand this time.

When the last of the guests trickle out, I smile expectantly at Edgar. "I'm very curious to see these sketches," I say, and he smiles coyly at me while reaching to a high shelf. I expect to see a roll of paper, but instead he produces a key. "This would make you favored company." He waves the key and takes my hand as we descend the stairs. My head is spinning in circles as he unlocks the door on the first floor. I feel as if I've been chosen for an honor far higher than entering an enclosed room in a man's home. I no longer think he's arrogant to shut off this part of himself and I realize that, to him, admittance into the museum is an honor, and I'm thrilled that he's allowing me into his personal life.

I slowly inhale and step into the vast space, the click of my heels the only sound in the still room. He leads me through by the light of a large lantern. The windows have dark, heavy curtains over them so that no light can enter. The room is as dark as a cave, but as a new treasure is illuminated with every turn of his hand, I decide I wouldn't want it any other way. I walk through a forest of easels, holding every size painting imaginable, from landscapes as tiny as a book to life-size portraits. He tells me which artist has created each work as we pass it. "This is my favorite Ingres, and beside it is a Corot that I'm quite taken with," he speaks very softly and closely to my ear while looking stoically at each piece. I can see how proud he is of his collection.

The museum follows an L shape, ending at a large door. He opens this door and I can see it's his bedroom. Suddenly I'm not sure if coming into the museum was a good idea. I begin to panic, thinking this is a man who was alone with Cornelie, for God's sake, what if he expects the same of me?

He looks at me and smiles gently. "It's fine to come in, the museum extends into my room."

I feel a great wave of relief sweep over me, oddly mixed with a little disappointment. I step through the door while he explains that this is where his most personal and sentimental work hangs. He shows me a pastel portrait of himself as a child and one of his father seated next to a guitarist. I look at the portrait of his father, hands clasped while solemnly listening. His eyes have the same vacancy as Edgar's do when he's not working.

"Did you paint these?" I ask, and he nods. "It's the only room where I hang my own work, because no one can judge it," he admits.

"Are you not afraid that I will judge it?" I tease him. He takes my hand and smiles at me. "You are too kind to judge harshly," he says softly. Chills run up my arm again and I can't control my movement as I lean toward him. I close my eyes and feel his lips brush against mine, only for a second, before he pulls away. Standing up, my hand still in his, he smiles shyly at me. "I don't want to get you into trouble for keeping you late," he says and opens a door on the opposite wall and before I know it we're standing next to the staircase as if we never entered the museum at all.

"I want to thank you for inviting me tonight," I say, feeling a little awkward after having kissed him. "It was a wonderful night; I enjoyed myself so much."

"Of course, I was so thrilled that you came tonight," he replies, and I see that the color is rising in his face. Seeing that he also doesn't know how to act after our kiss gives me confidence and I tell him I hope we'll see each other soon.

"As do I." He moves toward the front door, then abruptly turns back to me, practically bumbling. "Actually, I'm going to be attending the Salon tomorrow. It is a horrid art exhibit, but a popular event nonetheless. Perhaps you would like to go with me?"

No. 16 Scène:
The Annual Salon

Edgar had downplayed the Salon so much I'm astounded to see it's the social event of the year. Posters advertising the exhibit are plastered on all buildings leading to the show, creating a medley of colors. I feel so lucky to be accompanying Edgar as we enter the building and begin to walk, arm in arm, through eight miles of paintings. It's impossible to move with crowds blocking the hall, but I wouldn't trade the slow pace with its starts and stops for anything. It gives me more time to be beside Edgar, gently bumping into him when the crowd comes to a halt. Still under the spell from the evening at his home, I had broken down at practice this morning and told Noella that my interest in him has extended beyond friendship. She clapped her hands in delight to hear that he has finally opened his eyes, but warned me to tread carefully. Being close to him today, I don't heed her advice as I imagine the two of us like this for the rest of our lives, inseparable, a fixture at every prominent exhibit in Paris.

"I had no idea this would be so grand," I say to him, as I rest my closed parasol on my shoulder.

"Don't be so excited," he laughs. "The Salon is known for insignificant paintings, but artists obsess about being accepted into it."

"So it's not an honor to have your work exhibited here?" I ask.

"Hardly!" he laughs. "It does give artists some recognition. But the real dream is the Louvre. Any artist who tells you he has not spent endless afternoons studying the paintings at the Louvre is a liar. That, my dear, is the ultimate recognition."

I look at him in confusion. "If the Salon has such a bad reputation, then why do more people not exhibit in smaller circles as you do?"

"Not everyone has the advantages that I do," he explains. "Most artists are not able to bring collectors to their homes and studios. The studios in Montmartre, for example, are unfit for any human. I can't imagine bringing a collector there!"

Once I'd become especially brave when exploring the city and crossed over to Montmartre, mesmerized by the windmills I saw in the distance. After climbing a hill so steep stairs had to be built into it, I saw a whole street lined with dilapidated little shacks held up by leaning pieces of wood. Beggars dotted the street and chickens ran wild in the yards, reminding me of Luce's childhood home, only worse.

"Each time I visit those studios I'm afraid that the walls will collapse," Edgar says. "Inside is even worse. The kitchen and bedroom sit right in the studio. There is something reassuring about them, though. It shows the artists' priorities—art at the center, sleep and meals shoved to the corners as man's basic necessity."

We continue along the slow path and it proves hard to see most of the paintings. Edgar explains to me why the placement of pictures is so important at the Salon. "See over there," he points upward. "That one is so high in the corner we can't even see it. No doubt whoever made that painting thought this would be the proudest day of his life, yet no one can even see his work."

"Why did you want to attend if you're so against the Salon?" I murmur to him while squinting at the small painting so high above us.

"I'm trying to find one or two artists who stand out amongst all of this." He waves his hand toward the wall covered with paintings. "Camille and I have plans to open a group exhibit of artists who are disenchanted with organized exhibitions and conforming to the rules of an outdated standard of what art should be. Keep a sharp eye out, there has to be a realist in here somewhere." He nudges me playfully and we peer at the various pictures.

He studies each painting we pass with a critical, professional eye, taking in the technical brushstrokes. I listen carefully to his assessments and try to determine what it is about each painting that has set it apart from the rest to earn such coveted wall space.

"Exhibitions can make or break you," he mumbles, more to himself than to me. "They can ruin a career or make you a fortune. There's quite a lot of risk involved."

"I can see this would not be the type of show for such an isolated man as yourself," I tease him.

"You must understand that my life has not always been so

isolated," he says, unsurprised at my comment. "My father expected me to treat my career as an artist in the same manner as I would if I had become a businessman like him. I saw this as too structured a way to create art. I visualized my life as relaxed and free and wanted to travel and wait to be inspired. I would come home late from nights out with friends. We gathered at house parties and cafés, drinking and talking of our big dreams, although none of us had any idea of how to go about achieving them."

I watch him closely as his eyes remain fixed ahead, glancing down at me occasionally, while we slowly move with the crowd. I find it hard to believe this focused man I know had been viewed as a free spirit by his friends.

"My father would berate me the next day for sleeping well into the afternoon. But I disregarded his criticism. I needed to work the way I wanted to, as it came to me and when I felt like it. There were some nights when I would stay up until dawn working on a painting. Then I would leave it for months and find that I was not as interested in the subject as I had been when I first began it, so my studio in my father's home was full of half-finished works."

I can't help but think of his current studio, the vast open space with palettes of dried paint strewn about, crumpled pieces of sketching paper, canvases leaning against the wall with cloth draped over every one. I wonder if the canvases underneath are only half finished.

"My father would argue that if I never finished a painting I would never start a career. He told me if I remained stagnant by the end of the year, then he would no longer support me in my career choice. Instead, I would attend school and make a career

for myself in banking, as a businessman. I was enraged by the ul-
timatum."

Edgar continues, his eyes focused on his hands, nervously
wrapping around each other as we walk, and tells me that he
wanted to get far away from his father's judging eyes, so he made
arrangements to stay with his uncle and aunt in Naples for the
summer. "I told my father that I was going to get away from the
Paris scene and submerge myself in my art away from the pull of
my friends and the distractions of the city."

"So you lied to him and took a vacation instead?" I ask, my
eyes narrowing.

"The atmosphere was so different from the pressures of Paris
that I relaxed, observed, and drew whatever it was that intrigued
me. But by the middle of the summer, my family began to see
where my father's concern lay. While I had so many ideas, I never
saw any of them through. I continued to start a painting, only to
leave it when something else caught my eye.

"One day, searching for stamps to mail a letter back home, I
saw a letter my uncle had begun writing to my father. Among the
updates of life in Naples, one passage caught my eye and to this
day I remember it word for word:

" 'Edgar is still working enormously hard, though he does not
appear to be. What is fermenting in that head is frightening; I
myself think—I am even convinced—that he has not only talent, but genius. But will he express what he feels? That is the
question.' "

Edgar pauses for a moment, obviously transported back to
that day. "I reread the sentences and quietly put the letter back in
the drawer. I had planned to venture out in Naples for the afternoon, but instead changed into my painting clothes and went to

my room, pulling the half-finished canvases out of the dust. I got to work and soon found myself back in the streets of Naples, feeling the same excitement I had on the day I tried to capture the inspiration in my sketchbook. I was transported and lost track of all time and by the end of the day I completed the painting."

I look at him curiously. "What made you change?"

"Something got through that day, and while my father had hounded me day after day, something about my uncle's words affected me. I never thought my family saw talent in me to the point that they would call it genius. I knew that if I could break through to a group of middle-aged bankers, I could break into the art world, and it was time for me to go after my dream with full force, to make this my life, and to let nothing stand in my way. So, I returned to Paris armed with dozens of completed canvases and never returned to late nights with my school buddies. I had changed that summer." He smiles with pride.

"I think at some point in everyone's life, they begin to believe in themselves when others do not and that is the moment their lives begin," I say to him. "You speak from experience?" he smiles at me. "I do," I return the smile. "I would not be here today if I had not believed in my own abilities. My mother thought that I would take to dance immediately and was disappointed when I wasn't a virtuoso after only a few lessons. I knew I could master it, but I had to work at my own pace." I told him how I cleaned the studio because I knew that, with time, I could succeed.

"I think you have it wrong," he replies after listening intently. "True, everyone hits that point in their lives where they need to begin to believe in themselves and venture out on their own. But very few do. You would have been the only girl in that class if everyone had to clean the studio to pay for classes. That is what separates people like you and me from the rest of the world, and that is why we both wake up every morning and think 'There is nothing else I would rather be doing with my life.' "

He shifts his focus to a man peering closely at the paintings while writing thoughtfully in a small notebook. The man looks up and sees Edgar, and immediately begins to fight through the crowd toward us. "Wonderful, here comes an art critic. Simply smile and say you are delighted with the Salon," he whispers to me. "If he asks you any questions, try to keep it to a simple yes or no. Art critics are the worst."

"Monsieur Degas, it's wonderful to see you today," the critic shakes Edgar's hand. "You're in such lovely company," he briefly turns his attention to me but it's apparent he doesn't wish to speak to me further. "And are any of your works on display today, Monsieur?" he asks, pencil poised over his paper.

"I try to avoid showing at the Salon and instead exhibit independently through dealers," Edgar replies. "I would like to organize a group exhibition, if only I can find the right group of artists."

Edgar tries to guide me away from the critic, but the crowd is too thick and we make no progress.

"Now, it's well known that you are somewhat of a difficult exhibitor," the critic says with a sly smile. I peer up at Edgar and can tell he's getting annoyed, but he gives the critic a calm smile. "And what would give you this impression?" he asks genuinely.

"Gallery owners talk, Monsieur. You have a reputation for being pedantic over the details of your exhibits." The critic seems to enjoy telling Edgar what was most likely never meant to be made public. "Surely this is why you have so few public exhibits."

"Your assumptions have no basis. I prefer alternative approaches to the market. I would never hang an article in the brothels that picture shows are, exposing my work to the incomprehension of the crowd. I see no need to lose consciousness in front of a lake," he gestures to a group cooing in front of a landscape painting. I can see that now he's boiling mad and I wonder if I should steer him away from the critic. "I don't give a damn about the public," he continues. "All people talk about now is popular art. What criminal folly it is."

Edgar finds a break in the crowd and we escape. I expect him to be in a foul mood, but instead he's in high spirits. "Tomorrow it will be in all of the papers that I abhor public parades like this and everyone will wonder what kind of group exhibit I'm planning," he grins.

"And just what is it that you are planning?" I tease him with a sly smile. He gives me a wary look and imitates my tone. "Exactly what you know I paint?"

"Of course," I stammer. We walk through the rest of the exhibit in silence and I wonder where the man I was with yesterday has gone to. Back outside, we reach his carriage and he asks if I would like him to drive me back to my building, but he says it in such a way that it sounds as if it's an obligation he would rather not have, so I tell him I enjoy walking. "As you wish." He turns toward the carriage and I wish he would offer again.

"Will you be at tomorrow evening's ballet?" I inquire. "I'm afraid I won't have time tomorrow," he says while climbing into his carriage.

"Then I'll plan to see you at practice," I smile sweetly at him. He picks up the reins and sighs. "I'm conflicted in continuing our sessions," he says while squinting at me in the dusk of the setting sun. "Your image will eventually become a threat to my originality, but my good business sense tells me to continue on with what the public embraces."

"You don't mean that," I blurt out, surprised at his words.

"Ah, but I do." He gives me a wide smile and flicks the reins. "I suppose time will tell."

I watch his carriage pull away through the busy street and stand with my mouth open. What had I done to make him become distant?

No. 17 Scène:

A Matter of Convenience

I still don't understand," I complain to Noella while walking to practice the following week. Her face takes on a weary expression because I haven't stopped speculating about Edgar's behavior for days. "I'll stop," I grin at her and she throws her hands up in the air. "Thank God!" she says dramatically, making us both laugh.

"Just promise me that you won't tell anyone," I whisper. "You're the only person I speak to here," she snickers. "Who am I going to tell?"

As soon as we enter the practice studio, Edgar approaches me and I exchange a quick look with Noella before she departs to the *barre*. I greet him and hear my voice coming out a bit too loud and overly cheery. He doesn't seem to notice and asks in a great hurry if I'll model for him after practice.

"I thought you were conflicted," I cannot help but say with a hint of animosity.

"It would appear I'm more of a businessman than you would think." He gives me his small smile that makes me think he's suppressing laughter, which always causes me to smile back, then he resumes his rushed tone. "I can't stay for the entire afternoon. I'm meeting a friend for lunch. Can you meet me at my studio once practice has ended?"

I consent, and while I join the group at the *barre* I can't stop watching him. His hands alone astound me; they're always stained with paint or lead, with a fresh indentation from the pressure of his tools. Yet as he works, they float gracefully across the paper with such care. I watch as his face appears to be that of two different men, his brow furrowed as he analyzes his subject but his mouth remaining completely relaxed, the curve of his lips opening slightly when he takes a moment to look at his art, then gently closing as he continues to work.

Noella and I sit at our regular table during the lunch break, biting into the mushroom and goat cheese sauté provided for us. I hate mushrooms, but as the summer ends they appear everywhere, and I expect that dinner will be a stew overrun with mushrooms. Taking a sip of water, I watch Cornelie waltz up to Edgar on his way out the door, lean into his ear and throw back her head in laughter, her big teeth overtaking her face, her hand on his shoulder. As much as I hate her, a part of me envies her because I wish I could be as sure of myself as she is, to be able to easily walk up to him and make a joke. To my great disappointment I can see he's amused by her and I wish it was me who is making him laugh.

I quickly look away from them as Cornelie saunters over to our table and plops herself down, talking about the dance we've just practiced and her opinions of what would make it better. Underneath her brash exterior she truly cares about the dance and is always looking for ways to improve. She is undoubtedly the favorite of the Ballet Master for her dedication, but he also loathes her opinions on choreography. She has been in the ballet for over a decade and feels that she is as knowledgeable, if not more so, than the Ballet Master, and often butts in with her suggestions. He constantly chastises her publicly for disrespecting his expertise, but he can never stay mad at her because he respects her drive and recognizes how she benefits him.

"So, Alexandrie," Cornelie turns to me, talking through a mouth full of sauté, while preparing to shove crackers in as well. I divert my eyes so I don't have to look directly into her mouth. "What's this I hear about you being the last guest to leave Monsieur Degas' home? This is a bold move for such a chaste young woman. Are you exploring different avenues?"

I shoot Noella a quick look and she immediately shakes her head to tell me she did not give Cornelie this information. "It was completely respectable," I reply shortly, letting her know I don't want to engage in conversation. Every time she opens her fat mouth I wonder what it is that Edgar had seen in her. Part of me wants to tell her I was there so late because he showed me his museum. It would definitely make her jealous, but she thinks everything is a competition, and who knows what she would do to try to get back at me.

"He seems to be perplexed by why you would take such a social risk," she laughs, raising an eyebrow at me. I stare back at her, wondering if Edgar had just now told her I had been at his party or if, perhaps, Cornelie had been with him this weekend. "He thinks the other men may get ideas about you. He remarked that perhaps this is what you want."

My mouth drops open. "He said that?"

She erupts with laughter. "I told him perhaps you have your eye on a *specific* man who has not noticed yet."

I try to hide my anger but am unable to. "Why would you say that?" I snap.

"Settle down. He's too preoccupied with his work to even contemplate a little lovesick girl," she grins viciously.

Noella shoots me a matter-of-fact look that I know too well. "You're just jealous that you weren't asked to stay," I snap at Cornelie, immediately regretting that I let her get to me.

She laughs so loudly that the other girls look over at us and I wish I could shut her up. "I feel sorry for you, not jealous. To me, you'll always be nothing more than a *petit rat,*" she gloats at me.

I decide it's safer to not reply, and I study the melting cheese as if it's the most interesting thing I've ever seen. Having won the argument, she gets up to leave, but not before leaning over my shoulder. "The funny thing about artists, Alexandrie, is that the thing they find inspiration in one day, they come to despise the next." I can smell cheese on her breath and I turn away from her as she laughs and finally leaves me be. I don't want to admit that there may be some truth to what she said. But what gives her the right to gloat over me? She made a fool of herself at the party and could possibly lose her position in the ballet.

I throw myself into the last half of practice. I concentrate on each step, thinking of nothing but the strength of my body. I soon become lost in how each step tells the tale, a slow extension of the leg translating into longing, a series of *ballons* to and from the air describing frenzy. How one fluid movement leads to another until the entire story is told. But it's not enough to still my mind. Even though I'm not entirely convinced that Edgar finds

Cornelie in bad taste, I cannot let go of the notion that he and I are drawn to each other on a deeper level and he can't go very long without spending time with me. It was only a matter of time before he asked me to model for him again.

When practice concludes, I can hardly wait to spend the afternoon with Edgar. I brush my hair until it shines, then pin it up and apply color to my lips and cheeks. I study myself in the mirror, thinking I looked quite pretty and surely he'll think the same. I gather my things and set out to his studio, passing a fruit stand on my way. The bright glow of oranges catches my eye, which reminds me of his story of New Orleans. I impulsively purchase a bag to take to him, stiffening at the high price, but thinking it will be worth it to watch how happy he'll be to see the fruit from his travels.

When I'm let into his home, I stand nervously in the foyer holding the oranges awkwardly while he walks slowly down the stairs with a confused look on his face.

"Oh, Alexandrie, I completely forgot," he says hurriedly. I try to hide my disappointment as he speaks even more rapidly. "My brother has just arrived for an unexpected visit to sort out a mess he made of his latest business venture. He's upstairs unpacking his bags. I must cancel our session, I do hope you understand. He mentioned wanting to see a play this evening, as if this is a social visit for him. But perhaps I could call on you then for a rescheduled session? We could work in the practice room from around six to eight this evening, that wouldn't keep you too late, would it?"

My nervous energy deflates and I cannot help but feel hurt that he seems to be sneaking around to see me when he should be inviting me to the play.

"Of course, don't let me stand in your way," I try to smile through my disappointment.

"I greatly appreciate your kindness. So, if I am freed of my brother's presence I'll see you tonight at six o'clock in the practice room, and if he decides to stay in, then we shall make other arrangements." He smiles, then looks at the oranges as I try to hide them behind my back, feeling stupid for buying them. "What are those for?"

"Oh, I saw them at a fruit stand on my walk here," I stammer, my face and ears growing hot. Why does my face always betray me? "They reminded me of New Orleans. When you told me about the oranges there. On your vacation." *Bon Dieu,* I have to stop talking, he's just standing there staring at me while I ramble about oranges in New Orleans and he looks as if he's never heard this story before. "It just sounded so beautiful when you told me of your travels that I felt compelled to buy these." I remain still for a moment, then hand him the oranges and turn to leave.

"That's very sweet, *merci,*" he says, a bit bewildered. "You're welcome!" I say, again much too cheery and loud, while walking through the door. I march hastily down the street, catching my breath. I know I looked like a bumbling idiot and I'm completely embarrassed at having listened so intently to a story that I don't think he even remembers telling me.

My face is still burning with shame when I see Noella bidding farewell to Pierre outside the entrance to our building. Her face glows as well, but with happiness, and I feel even more foolish when I fill her in on the recent events.

"Obviously he thinks of you as a model and nothing else," she says simply.

"I know," I admit quietly.

"Everything with him is for his own convenience," Noella nods with conviction.

"He expects me to stay in waiting for him, just in case he grows bored and decides to visit me." I am outraged as I replay the uncomfortable encounter over in my mind. "I should decline any invitation to model for him. This isn't going anywhere."

"You've said this before, but this time you really must decline," Noella stresses. "A man like that has no regard for anyone but himself. You'll end up in this exact place again. If you allow him to drag you along, your bruises will just grow deeper and deeper each time he drops you."

No. 18 Scène:
A Salon of Realists

I sit in the middle of the hard floor of the practice room that evening, my eyes returning to the clock. Six o'clock, it says, then six-fifteen, then six-thirty. He never arrives.

As weeks pass by with no sign of him, I wonder if, perhaps, he went to the play with his brother and an elegant woman in the audience caught his eye and he now has no use for me. It's a thought that disturbs me and I know I need to let it go. I know I have no hold on him. I feel foolish for hoping that he thought I was special. I cringe at how I tried harder than usual during practice, dancing for him, feeling loved when his eyes rested on me. My thoughts had moved to the possibility that, because he is not married, perhaps he would marry me. I would become the new *étoile* and he would become a famous artist, and we would come home to each other every day. Tears flow from my eyes as I think about how stupid I've been to entertain such an idea when I obviously haven't entered into his thoughts at all. I hate that he frequents my mind and has hurt my heart, and to make matters worse Cornelie has fully healed and resumed her spot in the ballet. It's painful to watch the lead dancers as a *coryphée* after having been up front with them. I feel as if I've been betrayed, both by the Ballet Master and Edgar, for having dangled something I want so badly in front of me, only to yank it away. So I'm very much relieved by the distraction when I receive a huge bouquet of flowers from Julien, along with a letter apologizing for his outburst and hoping I will forgive him and accompany him on a Sunday stroll. He writes that he has accepted the fact that I want to become a lead dancer and he has missed me greatly and knows I'm worth making a compromise for. I smile at the words, thinking that at least one person sees that I'm worth something. Perhaps, as in my dream, I had been looking in the wrong direction.

When Sunday arrives, I force myself to think of Julien in the same way I do of Edgar. Rain is knocking against the glass and part of me hopes it will be a reason to cancel today's outing. I want to be excited to see Julien, but I consider my wardrobe halfheartedly. Only when I pretend Edgar has requested my company do I begin to have fun picking out what to wear. I stand in front of the mirror, pinning up layers of hair until it all rests on the crown of my head and the lace of my high neckline is exposed. I move to my glass double doors and open them to see the rain has stopped. I sigh and touch the railing separating my room from the city. From my room, I can see into the Opera House's windows. I will a smile to appear as I see Julien seated on the Opera House stairs, but instead I want to cry. This is the wrong man waiting for you, I think, but soon I join him and we venture out arm in arm.

"When the rain chases people off the streets, there's a calm about the city that seems almost unreal," Julien comments. The still air gives an animated look to the trees and flowers, making me feel like I have walked into a vibrantly colored painting.

"We're the lucky ones. We've braved the wet sidewalks," I reply, giving him a bright smile. "And our reward is this glorious day. Perhaps on a sunny day the sky takes up so much color that when it pales it lets the rest of the world shine."

"You do amuse me," he chuckles as he takes my hand. We make our way through Luxembourg Gardens, leisurely moving by tree-shaded arbors where people gather, gossiping with one another. I feel so much better, and decide that fresh air was the best thing for me. Everything is renewed from the rain, and I hope it will have the same effect on me so I can leave the last weeks behind me and start anew. I smile as I look around the huge garden within the city, with white sculptures standing in flower beds and long avenues of chestnut trees. We walk adjacent to the Seine, making our way past the enormous steel and glass pavilion of Les Halles market to my favorite café, the one with the striped awning. "A spectacle like that can ruin the most charming outing," Julien says with disgust as we walk past a woman wearing an outfit so showy that it's almost comical, prancing back and forth in front of the customers seated by the windows of the café. "It's so blatant that I wonder if she's an actress hired to play a courtesan," I giggle, quite amused, but Julien doesn't laugh. "Public women run rampant no matter the time of day," he says, shaking his head. "It's no wonder the city is contaminated by plague."

"Sidewalk cafés certainly provide a front seat to the theater of the streets," I say in agreement, while thinking that the older girls of the ballet are not so different from this street woman.

"And now they're even soliciting *inside* cafés. Unbelievable," Julien whispers to me as we sit down. I glance in the direction he's glaring and see a woman seated by herself, drinking hard liquor. This is all it takes for people to assume she lives a fast life. In Espelette, no one would dare utter the word *prostitute,* much less become obsessed with spotting one.

"Why is everyone so preoccupied with spotting a public woman?" I ask in annoyance, mainly because I feel like a fraud criticizing them only to turn a blind eye to what's happening a few doors away from my room. "People can't get enough of it. They suspect everyone and look for small indications to validate their suspicions. It seems you cannot have a conversation without being interrupted by someone pointing out a possibly deviant woman, explaining why she's deviant, and watching her for further evidence. What does it matter?"

Julien keeps his eyes on her for a moment, while she sits with her thumb resting on her mouth, scanning the crowd, looking almost bored. "She's the effect of the new Paris," Julien turns back to me, spitting out the word *new* as if it's a rancid piece of meat. "Nearly everything has a fresh tint of paint and the stonework has been renewed, virtually erasing the past of each structure. Soon whole quarters will be demolished to make space and substitute modern elegance for history." Julien becomes angrier with every word. The opposition to the industrialization of Paris is a conversation I have had too many times in the Green Room. While I had first been opposed to the improvements as well, believing they were leaving poor families on the street, I now see that they are moving us toward the future and will open up many more opportunities. Julien fears change because, after all, he has become successful in the old Paris and he can't help but be apprehensive that new ways of life will leave his enterprises obsolete.

"There is also much good," I say, trying to open his mind to new possibilities. His unwillingness to see beyond his own life annoys me.

"Don't be stupid. Paris' rampant prosperity and public show is just a disguise for the destruction of the old Paris. All of the sites will be torn down and the pieces sold off as souvenirs. If that is your idea of a business opportunity, then you embarrass yourself, Alexandrie."

"I see your point," I reply to end his tirade and judging. I pretend to look at the menu, but instead peer at Julien. I love that he wants to be with me and is straightforward with his intentions. However, the thought of spending the rest of my life with a closed-minded man who's unwilling to listen to my opinions disgusts me. I don't think I sound stupid; in fact, I think I'm making a valid point. One of the things I love about Paris is that it's such a modern city. The longer I live here, I realize that the old Paris offered nothing to me but a secure life of squalor; the modernism of the city will bring more jobs to people of my class. I know Julien doesn't care to hear this and I really don't wish to reveal my lowly roots, so instead I focus on the café's menu and let the subject drop. When I look up, I'm startled to see Edgar seated nearby with a group of men, most of whom I recognize from his parties, so I assume this must be his exhibit group that he was so excited about.

My heartbeat increases and I immediately divert my eyes. Only a few weeks ago I would have greeted the group with confidence. But now I have no idea what my standing is with him. Perhaps I'm being overly concerned and he's simply been busy.

Then again, Julien has a wife, children, runs a company, and still finds time for me. Because he wants to find time, I think, remembering how Edgar pulled away from me at the Salon and then completely forgot that he asked me to model. I'm glad our table is hidden from his view so I don't have to make the decision to politely say hello or act like I didn't see them. Plus it offers me the opportunity to eavesdrop shamelessly without it being obvious to Julien. I pretend to read the menu while listening to them talking about bringing their new movement in art to the critics and collectors.

"We'll show life for what it is," Edgar says excitedly. I smile at Julien and when his eyes drop to the menu, I focus back on Edgar's table. Leaning slightly to hear better, I see that Edgar seems to be the leader of this table. "We admire your talent for portraying new subjects, but we cannot deal with your high criticism and unrealistic perfectionism," a man with a full head of thick, wavy hair says to Edgar.

"You have such relaxed attitudes toward painting. Simply sitting around, daintily painting landscapes whenever the mood strikes is not going to get you to the level you need for the exhibit," Edgar replies. "You need to put less emphasis on color and turn your attentions to studio work. Especially you, Claude."

"We respect how you can become completely absorbed in your work, but the way you close yourself off is unnatural," replies the man Edgar criticized, his beard wild and unkempt. I recognize Monsieur Monet and I think to myself how Edgar can be welcoming to some, yet seem to take pleasure in ostracizing those he doesn't like. Yet it would seem that everyone, including myself, wants to be favored by him. "I'm more of the mind that in order to paint one's surrounding one needs to insert oneself into it," he continues. "We'll have plenty of works completed for our opening. I won't change my way of working."

"Good for you, defending your little decorations," Edgar says haughtily. "Most people think if they defend their practices I will argue with them until, out of sheer exhaustion, they'll defer. Most learn it is easiest to just appease me and silently go on with their own plans."

I realize that I'm not paying attention to Julien and look over at him in time to see him spill a drop of coffee onto his hand and immediately take a kerchief from his pocket to wipe away the liquid. He motions for the waitress to clean the tiny pool of coffee that has landed on the table. Julien could never be an artist, for he would spend so much time cleaning the paint from his hands that he would never complete a picture. Edgar always has traces of color on his hands and arms, yet it never seems to bother him. I prefer that abandon to the rigid stiffness of keeping everything perfectly clean and pressed. I would let Edgar smear paint all over my body and roll around the floor with him until my room became a painting of unrestrained desire. I feel a warm blush moving its way up my face at the thought, so I quickly push it out of my head and smile at Julien, who looks back at me as if the blush was meant for him.

"I have very exciting news," Julien leans in toward me. "My wife will be visiting relatives in Milan next month and, for an entire week, I'll be free to see you anytime my heart desires. I was thinking we could go away together. Have you ever visited Spain? Its beaches are the best in Europe."

"That's so generous of you." I take a sip of coffee because I can't think of anything else to say.

"I thought you would be more excited." Julien leans back in

his chair and crosses his arms. "We've been spending so much time together for several years now. I enjoy our outings and our evenings in the Green Room, but I want to move our courtship further along."

I slowly place the small cup on its saucer, my hands shaking slightly. I knew eventually Julien would become bored with our chaste routine and would move forward with the arrangements for me to become his mistress. If I leave with him for a week, no doubt that fate will be sealed. While it would offer me some relief from worrying about how I will be taken care of, my heart is not in it.

"I am beyond excited," I say to him, my hand flying to my chest. He sits taller, his eyes lighting up. "But it's impossible for me to leave the ballet for an entire week. Sunday is the only day I have a moment to myself."

"I could speak to the Ballet Master." Julien leans toward me, placing his hand on mine. It feels like a weight holding my hand to the table. "Surely he could get by without you for one week."

"We're in the midst of quite a project. The Ballet Master is working to adapt the Russian production of *Le Corsaire* and every dancer is needed for it to be a success," I say seriously.

"I cannot wait much longer," Julien says angrily to me, as if I am making excuses, which I must admit I am. Before I can answer him, we're interrupted by raised voices.

"Enough nitpicking," Monsieur Cézanne yells and now the conversation is so loud that everyone in the café turns toward the table of artists. "Edgar, you were supposed to find a dealer to exhibit our work, but it's only been met with resistance. You take each refusal personally and, in your arrogance, are alienating many of the dealers in town. We're becoming doubtful about securing a venue. Instead of making progress, you're making enemies along the way."

Edgar waves the insult away, "Paul, a painting is a thing that requires as much knavery, as much malice, as much vice as the perpetration of a crime."

Monsieur Monet and another man, dressed in a paint-covered shirt, leave the table in a noisy fit. "He sees himself above us because he has money," I hear one of them mutter as they pass behind me.

I'm embarrassed to have witnessed such a public outburst, but it doesn't seem to bother Edgar. "Do you invite those people to your house?" he asks the rest of the group, as if the two artists are gypsy trash.

The group begins to protest and Monsieur Pissarro jumps in to defend Edgar. "He's a terrible man to say such things, but need I remind you he has always been frank, upright, and loyal."

"Thank you, dear friend," Edgar smiles smugly. "If I weren't rude I'd never have any time to work."

He sits in silence, seeming to enjoy watching the group grow hostile and frustrated. Just as they appear ready to disband, he announces that he's found a gallery and they're booked to hold their first exhibit in Nadar's photographic studio on the Boulevard des Capucines. Their spirits restored, the group quickly forgets how only minutes ago they were about to abandon Edgar and go their separate ways. They now praise his efforts and make plans for which paintings they'll exhibit, how they'll be framed and hung and how they'll spread the word about the grand exhibit. "The realist movement no longer needs to fight," Edgar says. "It already *is*, it exists, it must show itself as *something distinct*, there must be a *salon of realists*."

"To the salon of realists!" they cry out, raising their glasses to a newfound opportunity. Their boisterous cries draw looks from the entire café, and Julien glares at the group as if they're being inappropriate. I shrug my shoulders as if to say, "What can we do?"

"He's a horrible, self-righteous man," Julien says, looking at Edgar in disgust. "Are you still modeling for him?"

"Not as much anymore," I say, casting a glance toward his table.

"Smart girl," Julien replies with a smirk. "Even someone as kind as you cannot tolerate his vile disposition for too long."

I nod, thinking to myself that it wasn't my choice and it is Edgar who has not wished to see me lately. "Today has been quite enchanting," he turns his attention away from the artists and cocks his head at me. "I rarely have time for such idleness. It's truly refreshing."

"That's a shame," I say, glad that he hasn't revisited the topic of vacationing in Spain. "I've made it my religion to leave everything behind each Sunday and venture outdoors. I find it clears the mind."

"Perhaps you can clear your mind of its simple thoughts in just a day, but for me I need much more time." It takes all of my abilities to remain composed and I smile back at him like a statue. "Yes, you have far more responsibilities than I do," I reply. It's excruciating to play the submissive role and I muster up all of the advice and training I've accumulated to appear a subdued lady enchanted by a powerful man.

"What little sun we have today is beginning to fade, and I'm afraid that my wife will begin to wonder where I am," Julien sighs, but I silently thank his wife for ending our afternoon. "Forgive me for not being able to walk you back. I do hope you understand."

"You don't need to explain yourself to me." I smile at him, grateful that I can walk home in silence.

"Think about what we spoke of," he says as he pays for our lunch and rises to his feet. "I *cannot* continue to wait."

I nod as he kisses me farewell on the cheek. His lips are wet and cold, and as soon as I see his figure disappear from the café I instinctively wipe my hand over my face. I lean back in my chair for a moment and then feel self-conscious sitting alone, so I grab my gloves and go outside. The sun has broken through the clouds and I open my parasol to shield my face.

"Lovely day, Mademoiselle," I hear a voice say to me. I'm startled at the interruption and even more shocked to see Edgar's beaming face. Cornelie's words replay in my head and I hope he hasn't assumed that I followed him to the café like an unstable young woman. I decide I'll look even more unbalanced if I try to explain this is not the case, so I don't even bring the topic up. "Indeed, what a surprise," I say nonchalantly, resting my opened parasol on my shoulder. "I was afraid your brother has been holding you hostage."

He looks at me in bewilderment, then appears to connect that the last time I saw him he cast me aside for family arrangements. "I've been doing the same thing I do every day," he replies defensively. "It is well known that I lunch at the café de la Rochefoucauld nearly every day. I was just there telling my friends that we have been booked for a group exhibit next month. If you were truly concerned as to my whereabouts, you could easily have found me there if you inquired with that beast of a concierge; it is understood I am there between twelve-thirty and one o'clock."

I'm relieved that he had not seen me inside the café, so I smile up at him in feigned kindness despite his rude manner and he matches his step with mine. "I didn't ask for your daily schedule," I say sarcastically.

"Oh, it was implied." He gives me a familiar smile, yet his eyes do not warm. "You've become quite presumptuous about what I do with my time. Now you'll always know where I am, since you have such a good memory for details."

I know he's referring to my visit with the oranges. I grit my teeth in embarrassment. "I was really more teasing you than anything else," I say evenly while keeping my gaze straight ahead. "Congratulations on the group exhibit. You must be so pleased." Out of the corner of my eye I see him smile at me and we continue along the street together.

"And now the weather is magnificent, but I have no real confidence it's to continue," he changes the conversation to less personal topics. "One should believe in nothing but rain, in France."

"You speak like a man three times your age," I muse. "How can you be surrounded by the excitement of Paris and only see the negatives? I live for the days when I can be outside all day long, taking it all in, and your words personally offend me."

He laughs loudly at my rebuttal and places his arm around me briefly. "I didn't mean to cause you offense. I sympathize deeply with your Parisian prison. Let us talk of something else."

I give him a genuine smile. "You are forgiven. So, are your paintings ready for the exhibit?"

He gazes straight ahead with a worried, faraway look on his

face. "Not at the moment. I'm trying a little to work. I find that I need to devote more time to taking care of myself. I thought I was far too young to worry about health, but my doctor has convinced me that I need to get out of my studio more often and get a little exercise."

"Is it your eyes?" I ask sympathetically. "It would seem so," he replies, still staring straight ahead. We walk a few steps in silence.

"Is it something that can be corrected?" I ask. "Will getting outside or wearing spectacles help them to heal?"

"It will prolong the inevitable. You see, I'm going blind," he says quietly and I look at him with pity, shocked at his words. "But you're an artist, if you can't see, then you can't..." I don't want to finish the sentence and he nods solemnly. "Then I can't paint," he sums up. "I'm so sorry. It is good that you're following your doctor's advice," I say, trying to be positive.

"It's not an accomplishment," he says curtly. "I shut myself up too much in my studio. I don't see the people I love often enough and I shall end up by suffering for it."

I start to ask about his brother, and whether his visit is making Edgar wish he saw his family more, but he quickly changes the subject. "You are quite right. What lovely country," he comments.

I choose not to comment on this because I'm crushed at the thought of him not being able to paint anymore. I can't imagine how he would spend his time, what he would talk about, where his passion would lie. Perhaps in a dark world all he would see is what lies beneath the surface of things, and he'll begin to dissect a subject until all he can see is the pain and despair of life. Beauty, to him, is only a veneer.

"Edgar! Perfectly timed," a boisterous voice booms. "I really need to be going," Edgar says to me hastily but he doesn't move fast enough and the man who bounds up looks so similar to him that I know this has to be his brother. I smile, expecting an introduction, and his brother looks at me expecting the same thing, but Edgar begins to walk away, beckoning his brother to come with him. His brother follows in confusion, and I stand watching their backs in complete humiliation.

January 14, 1869

Dearest Maman,

I have enclosed half of my earnings from this month. I know it is meager, but I hope that it helps some. Forgive me for not sending more, but the Ballet Master pulled me aside after a performance earlier this month to tell me he is tired of seeing me in the same dresses each evening. It seems my image was not meeting the ballet's standards. He told me that the abonnés *will assume he is not paying us properly and it will hurt his standing amongst them. I have purchased new gowns and am again in his good graces and I have happy news to report. I have been promoted to a* sujet, *a soloist, Maman! This will bring me a little more pay, and a lot more recognition within the production. I am so happy at my accomplishment, and I hope you share in my joy.*

I know you will not be able to fully share in my joy until you see that I am settled, but please know that I am moving toward that. It is not as simple as I had thought when I arrived here. The last few years have flown by and I see now why I was at such a disadvantage to start my training later in life. If I had arrived here at the age of fourteen like so many others, I feel I would have so much more time to get this right.

With love,
Alexandrie

No. 19 Scène:
The Highest Honor

"Y ou ran out of rehearsal so quickly this afternoon. First I see you at the café yesterday in the company of another man and then today you don't even acknowledge my presence. It's as if I've ceased to exist." I look curiously at Edgar as he approaches me in the Green Room after the performance, his tone lacking the haughty tease that I'm used to, especially since he had known I was in the café the entire time. I would expect him to have a bit of fun with that.

"I do apologize; I have many obligations and thoughts to consider," I say vaguely. Part of me wants to tell him how rude it was to leave me standing in the street as if he was ashamed of being seen with me. But the truth is that I'm so exhausted by putting on airs for Julien, obsessing about Edgar's behavior, and keeping my mother apprised of my progress that my energy is utterly drained. I don't want to bother with him.

"Life wouldn't be interesting if there were no obstructions," he replies, looking around as if he's bored. "Shall we go to your room; I'm eager to get started."

I'm taken aback at his bluntness but regain my pride. "We most certainly shall not," I hiss, hoping no one overheard him. "You have apparently gotten the wrong idea about me. I'm not someone who you can hide away and then call on when it suits you. I am unlike your friend Cornelie in *every way*." I emphasize the last part with such force that he takes a step backwards.

"My dear, relax," he says. "There is an incredibly high demand for your portraits. I came to draw what you did not let me this afternoon. If you had not been so hasty to disregard me, I wouldn't need to be here right now. But the complete exhaustion you wore on your face captured my attention. I won't be able to rest until I get it on paper."

I should be relieved that he's only referring to a modeling session, but the prospect of having him observe my own private space makes me feel very self-conscious. The recognition from his portraits has helped me to become known, and some patrons have even told the Ballet Master that they attended the show after seeing Edgar's paintings. I know I must continue to model, but a familiar fear creeps back that perhaps a painting of myself in an exhausted state would only produce a less than desirable picture. "We couldn't have a session at your studio after tomorrow's practice?" A glimpse of his grand home enters my mind and I wince at the thought of him entering my own small room with just enough space for a table, wardrobe, and bed.

"My brother is still at my house. Besides, tomorrow you'll be refreshed after a night's sleep," he says, his voice growing steelier with each word. "I ask for only a brief moment of your time before I lose the urgency that has haunted me all day."

"Fine," I say sharply, his mention of his brother reminding me that he does not wish for me to be a part of his life. As we leave the Green Room I can't help but see eyes following our departure. I imagine how it looks, and immediately rethink my actions. The painting will be evidence that I haven't lost my virtue, but I wouldn't put it past a jealous dancer to lie about an indiscretion on my part. Does he know I am putting myself at risk by doing this? Stop, I tell myself, you're overreacting. Pierre visits Noella in her room all of the time, and all she has to do is leave her door wide open so everyone can see the two of them seated at her table playing a game of piquet.

Once inside my room he either chooses to not comment on my minimal living conditions or fails to notice how small it is as he unloads his pencils onto my table. I glance toward the open door and see a figure pass by with a glance inside my room. Now I know any possible lies will be unjust, since others have seen with their own eyes that I'm only having a respectable modeling session.

"If I were not here, how would you spend a night to yourself?" he asks.

"Quite honestly, I would just wash all of the makeup off of my face and go to sleep," I reply.

"Then do that, I want to draw you as you would be in real life."

"If that is what you want." As I splash cold water onto my face I begin to question his professional manner and wonder if he had, indeed, been haunted by me. I lie down on my bed and wonder if perhaps Edgar had been haunted not by me but by the idea of a grand painting.

"You sleep fully clothed?" he scoffs at me.

"No, but don't you wish to draw a dancer?" I say, confused.

"Don't assume you know what I do or do not wish," he snaps. "I said I want to draw you in real life, to capture your complete exhaustion. Actually, if you are as exhausted as you say, you would not have energy to change."

"Now who is assuming?" I say in what I mean to be teasing, but once my words hit the surface my annoyance is hard to mask.

"Don't be difficult. While this is not your normal post-performance booking, you do not have the night off," he replies in a small voice, through tight lips.

I feel like a child being chastised for not washing her hands before dinner. "I don't engage in post-performances," I say coldly. He nods, looking chagrined as if he regrets that remark, but quickly resumes a mask of impatience as I make no move to undress. "For heaven's sake, Alexandrie, I'll only be painting you lying on the bed. There will be no other details," he says as if reading my mind. I've learned a lot about art since moving to Paris and I'm fully aware that a nude is the most celebrated subject to paint and the most respected by critics. While I confess to not understanding how a completely naked body can be called classical and a fully clothed woman can be labeled deviant, I know that it is the details that matter in nude paintings. Depicting the form by itself is a work of art, and an honor to model for. However, if there are minutiae present in the painting that suggest deviant behavior, the model is labeled a public woman. Gallery owners have been known to study the clothing that has been cast aside in a painting for signs of deviance. If there's any hint that these clothes have been removed hastily in a moment of lust, they'll ban the piece from being shown. To know that Edgar is planning on a classical nude is quite enticing to me for two reasons—he has bestowed quite an honor upon me and it will no doubt be accepted into an exhibit where viewers will learn I am the model, increasing my fame exponentially. It will put me in the right position to become the *étoile* one day.

I rise from the bed, glancing at the hallway again, and open the door of my wardrobe so that I can step behind it as I would a screen. I disrobe and my excitement turns to embarrassment to be alone with Edgar in my room, utterly naked. I automatically move my arms up to cover myself and self-consciously resume my position on the bed, but he looks at me as if I'm fully clothed. His demeanor remains the same as if he were painting our dance class, brow furrowed and only focused on his art as he arranges the blankets around my body. I hold my breath until my head becomes dizzy while his hand brushes against my skin. Even the movement of the blanket causes my skin to tingle. He takes no notice and retreats to sit down in my chair, beginning to draw.

"So what turn of events brought you to the café de la Rochefoucauld?" he asks absently.

"Just an invitation from a friend," I reply vaguely.

"A friend, you say? Is he a patron of the ballet?" he continues to question me with a slight smile, as if he is enjoying the interrogation.

"Yes," I say, not offering any more information. Wouldn't he have recognized Julien? I think. Why is he being so coy? "And I trust you and your brother found your way home safely? You know, it was very rude of you to not introduce me. I was standing right there, and he was obviously waiting for an introduction. You ran away like you were embarrassed to be seen with me. It was humiliating."

He looks at me with sympathetic eyes. "Please don't think I'm embarrassed by you," he says. "That is not the case at all, quite the opposite in fact. You don't know my brother. He's not a gentleman, and let's just leave it at that. Trust me, you should be thanking me for not introducing you."

"I doubt anything scandalous would have happened from shaking his hand," I reply sarcastically.

"Then we have a difference of opinion," he says, concentrating on his sketching. "Luckily he will be leaving in a few days and I won't have to deal with him anymore. Let's please talk of something else. Tell me about your friend from the ballet. Will you soon be unavailable to model after your performances? Or perhaps in a few more years you will become extremely available."

I sit up in anger at these words. "I take great offense to your insinuation, Monsieur; I will never entertain a man as part of the ballet," I say defensively, refusing to even look at him.

"Is that a fact?" He cocks his head to the side and he studies me intently. "I thought all of you girls strive to become *lorette*s only to turn to prostitution."

"Not all of us," I manage to say clearly, as a lump builds in my throat. I realize that he sees me as no different from the rest of the girls. He doesn't say any more, and I rest my head, bothered by his words and opinion of me. I close my eyes to calm my wounded pride, but he insists I keep them open because my tired eyes lend themselves to the overall theme. He tells me if I close them, he will simply be drawing a sleeping girl, and he needs me to be an exhausted girl. So the session continues on with my position changing every now and again, and with him drawing and humming as if he has done nothing to offend me.

"So tell me why you don't aspire to remain in the ballet," he brings the topic up again.

"I very much want to remain in the ballet. I want to be the lead ballerina one day. It is the post-performances that I don't want because I don't want my life to move away from dancing to revolving around ... making a man happy," I tell him.

"Such an independent young mind, yet you contradict yourself since you're obviously comfortable in becoming a *lorette*." He never takes his eyes away from his drawing but I see the sides of his mouth turn up as if suppressing laughter, a tic that used to delight me but now enrages me.

"It's easy for you to speak in such a demeaning fashion because you have no idea what it's like to be a girl born into a poor family." My eyes remain fixed on the ceiling, not giving him the satisfaction of analyzing my face as my anger grows.

My mind wanders back to Espelette when our next-door neighbor was suddenly seen about town in brand-new clothes buying bag after bag of food at the market. I stood with my mother watching our neighbor buying fish and steak as we counted out our francs and tried to talk the merchants down so we would have enough bread and beans for the week. "I know their farm is not doing better than ours," I heard my father say to my mother that night after she described how the woman was weighted down with so many bags she could barely carry them all home. "I suspect the added income is from other activities," my mother replied cattily. "When I woke up the other morning to make breakfast, I saw her slipping into her back door. The sun hadn't risen yet and she was completely disheveled. Hair all matted up in the back and clothes wrinkled. Others have seen her leaving her job as a maid for the big house at the edge of town at unusual times of the night. Apparently she's working additional hours."

"Perhaps we should get you a maid's job," my father chuckled.

"Oh, please, then who will run the house?" my mother teased him.

At the time I didn't understand what working additional hours meant, but from the tone of my parents' voices it sounded like something dishonest and shameful. After hearing that conversation I always stared at our neighbor and tried to figure out what it was she was doing at her job.

My eyes leave the ceiling and I turn my head self-importantly toward Edgar. "By contrast, the ballet offers a way for women to meet these men without having to hide their activities and endure the stigma of being a cheating wife or the pity of having a husband who will put you up to such things to lessen his workload. Every girl who has been accepted into the Opera Ballet has a bit of independence about her, and a love for dancing. We all share the drive to move to a higher station than our parents are in. We work just as hard as any businessman does yet we will never attain the riches to support ourselves in the manner of those we associate with. If we want to continue performing and enjoy everything Paris has to offer without worrying about finances, there is no other choice but to become a *lorette*. It's nothing more than securing our lifestyle."

"I do express sympathy to your plight." Edgar rests his pencil on the table and wipes his brow, leaving a streak of ebony across his forehead, and looks at me calmly. "But I don't think you realize that the only difference between *lorettes* and *courtesans* is the master they report to. I suspect you will be happier finding a nice young man to run off with. Money and status are fleeting."

"I grew up in a house where my mother literally served my father day and night. He never once considered how much work she did in making sure his meals were always on the table waiting for him and his clothes were always washed and pressed. Never once did I hear him say thank you. He just expected it. I don't want to end up like that for any man."

I have never opened up to a man before about why I came to Paris. Conversation with the patrons of the ballet was always limited to politics, dance, and their careers—all safe topics so my imperfections would not be discovered. I had never defended my practices because I was so afraid that one wrong word would ruin my chances of becoming a *lorette,* and I always ended up agreeing with men so I would not run the risk of seeming stupid. Furthermore, no man had shown interest in where I came from, he was only interested in the girl onstage and would like to believe that I materialized in the Opera House solely for his eyes. I had always preferred this arrangement, but as I talk of Espelette and the mundane family structure that I am responsible for supporting, I realize how refreshing it is to open up to someone. I notice that Edgar seems to be listening with interest. The pressure I carry with me is slowly released as each word escapes my mouth.

"I suppose the role of the patriarch is similar in all walks of life," he says while sharpening a pencil, its peelings falling on the table. He sweeps them up with one hand and shakes them into his pencil box. "I spent my childhood watching my father dedicate his time to the bank he owned. If someone couldn't benefit the bank, then they were of no benefit to my father."

"Did you grow up in Paris?" I ask.

"Yes," he shifts his head to the side, analyzing his drawing. "I enjoyed the days when my mother would work in the garden and I could spend the day outside with her, drawing the different flowers that she was planting. I remember her soft humming. Those are some of my best memories."

"You make the garden sound so lovely," I say, fully aware of the different classes we come from. Our garden was a source of food, filled with vegetable plants. Edgar's mother was free to plant flowers in any color because she didn't have to worry about how she would feed her family. "My time in the garden was spent working. My memories are of my mother ordering me around while I was covered in dirt."

He chuckles at this. "I'm very lucky to have had that time. My mother was a Creole southern belle to the core. She never pinned her hair up or fastened hats over it. She swept it above her head and would pluck flowers from the garden to put in her hair for that extra touch. Her friends called her Spanish-style."

I understand now why he had become so distraught when he spoke unkindly of the Creole women. I thought his concern was overly paranoid and a bit dramatic, but knowing his mother is of that descent, it now makes perfect sense. I wonder how a man can show such respect for his mother yet retreat to the room of a disrespectful woman like Cornelie. I look at Edgar's dark hair falling into his eyes and think that he must resemble his mother, giving him a look of a distinguished Parisian with an exotic touch. I completely relax on my bed; it is wonderful to hear him tell me about how he grew up. Most men only mention their family if they're hinting at the wealth they come from. I know they don't want to reveal too many details because, as a dancer, I will never be involved in that side of their lives. Listening to Edgar speak of the day-to-day nuances of his childhood makes me wonder if perhaps I was too hasty and he was actually being protective of me by not introducing his brother to me. Maybe I shouldn't discard the notion that he would have me as part of his life. I no longer think of how the completed nude will enhance my career and only wish to hear more of his upbringing. I listen attentively to learn that his mother had two sons after Edgar, but neither survived and when Edgar was four, his brother, Achille, was born. But she again lost another baby after Achille.

"The loss hit her hard and she left abruptly one morning to stay with my uncle, my father's brother, also Achille. There must be a curse on that name," Edgar sniffs ironically while pressing the pencil more firmly across his sketch pad. "My father was enraged. He told her that her enchantment with his brother was a disgrace to him."

"Did he leave her?" I ask in shock, thinking that my father became enraged if his soup became cold and such a great infidelity would be met with a wrath that would have surely left my mother stoned to death.

"No. My father was a quiet man and my mother was this beautiful woman that people were drawn to. On some level he always felt that he was not good enough for her, so in his attempt to not lose her he turned a blind eye to her," he smiles sadly at the memory. "One night I awoke to shouting and crying. My mother was on the floor with blood-soaked towels around her, crying in pain while my father crouched by her. 'It's died inside me,' she wailed. All he said to her was 'It's what you deserve.'"

Edgar stops drawing for a moment only to resume with heavier strokes, and I'm sure the pencil will rip right through the entire sketch pad. "Edgar," I say softly, thinking only of his well-being and wanting to console him. I wonder if his parents' marriage is the reason he hasn't married. I want to ask him this but bite my tongue because I don't think he'll appreciate such a bold assumption based on one story.

Instead of wrapping himself in my arms, he snorts at me. "My pain is nothing compared to the guilt my father carries with him. She died when I was thirteen."

"Edgar, I'm so sorry," I sit up slightly, clutching the blanket to me, but he gestures his hand down and I return to my pose.

"My father knew no other way of life than the bank," he

explains as if his childhood memories are insignificant. "I hated to see the guests filing in, remembering how my mother would select which piece of jewelry to wear and how she would spray herself with perfume before going downstairs to greet each guest at the door. I missed hearing her laugh over the dinner conversation. I would retreat to my room and copy the old masters' works while I tried to block out the laughter and clinking glasses of dinner conversation in the background. I soon came to see my world as empty, with the parties and dinners only masking the sad life we lived."

"If we felt no pain we would have no motive to better our lives," I say to let him know I understand. He looks at me with a bit of surprise. "That's a very accurate statement." He reaches into his breast pocket and glances at his watch. "The evening is growing late and I know you're tired. Thank you for your time; now I do hope you get some rest."

I sit up, holding the blanket to me, and watch him collect his supplies in one great swoop and rush out the door. Why did he depart so suddenly? What is it that I keep doing wrong? I ponder this question as I quietly close the door. Moving toward my French doors, I can see him climbing into his carriage and I wonder if his behavior has less to do with me and more to do with the burdens he carries with him.

Intermission

Wartime Correspondence

August 1, 1870

My dearest Alexandrie,

   I write to you under extreme conditions as I have left the
comforts of home and have joined my family in Milan. The
declaration of war could not have come at a worse time, as I
had hoped to speak to the Ballet Master regarding our long
postponed trip to Spain. I respect that you have been cautious
and do not want to disappoint me, yet I know such a lovely
young woman as yourself could never be a disappointment.

   It pains me that I was not able to say good-bye to you, but
you can understand my delicate position. I want you to know
that as soon as it is safe for me to return to France, I will waste
no time in resuming our plans as if I had never left at all. I am
so incredibly happy that you have finally made the right decision and accepted my offer. When this war is over, I'll have you

living in opulence, and you won't have to wait for me to attend the ballet to see me. I know you will be well worth all of my waiting. Now it is your turn to have patience.

Do not be afraid, for I shall return to you,

Julien

August 5, 1870

Dear Monsieur Aston,

I wanted to write to make sure that my letter finds you well in this difficult time as the conflict between our country and Prussia grows. My mother keeps me updated on everyone in Espelette, but she did not know if you are being taken care of. I hope that your vegetable garden is thriving, even without my exceptional gardening skills (I'm teasing of course), and that you will not go hungry.

So often I think of your story of the ballerina you once loved and remind myself that I will not turn out that way. But I must admit that it is hard. I have met an aspiring artist named Edgar, who I have modeled for and imagine myself marrying. But it seems he does not share my feelings, and as much as I hate to admit it, I may have no other alternative than to become a lorette. There is a gentleman named Julien, older and powerful much like your love's monsieur, who is pressuring me to become his mistress. I have used every excuse I can think of to hold him off. I feigned a headache in the Green Room so we would not be able to have the conversation regarding arrangements. I explained how I had so many more responsibilities in my new soloist position at the ballet. When I ran out of excuses, I finally relented. I know this is not what you want to hear, nor is it how I want to live, but I hold the hope that Julien will be respectful and I can lead a happy life. I do not know of any other way to continue to perform at the ballet and not have to worry about supporting myself when I can no longer dance.

While I have found some success in dancing, I struggle with love. As I tried to avoid Julien, Edgar did the same to me, becoming more melancholy and distancing himself from the ballet. Time is what I wish for over and over again and sometimes I cannot help but think that I have single-handedly brought on this war. The Emperor sometimes attended the ballet and I had felt so honored to dance for him. I realize that I have been truly blessed to have had that opportunity. Now Napoleon III is rumored to be greatly ill and cannot defend his soldiers. Both he and his soldiers have become prisoners of war, news that hit the city with great force. Panic has ensued since word reached the streets that the Germans are nearing Paris and there are barely enough French soldiers left to stop them.

Everyone in Paris is stocking up on food and firewood as if they will be shut in their homes for years. It looks as if a great storm is heading our way and everyone is preparing for the worst. I read the papers and know that the German Army is three times bigger than ours and our soldiers are cornered near Sedan. I had assumed that Paris was untouchable. Rationing food and firewood seems a bit hysterical to me. The Opera has always been unaffected by everyday concerns. We continue to receive donations while ordinary families struggle to feed themselves. To imagine that I would wake one morning and not have an abundance of food waiting for me is absurd. The Opera is untouchable.

But as the days go on, I can see that the Opera is becoming more vulnerable. All of the men have left and even Edgar is based in one of the battalions. He never even told me he was leaving and as hurt as I am by that, I fear that he will be injured. I try to hide this from the other girls, keeping up my ruse that I am only interested in him for the fame his paintings can bring me. I cannot admit to the other ballerinas that I love him, because I don't trust them. My only friend at the ballet taunted me with this, saying, "Did you expect him to come running over here in a grand show of love and sweep you off of your feet asking you to wait for his return? Then you'll run off together and have lots and lots of babies?"

This is the very thing I wish for. But instead of admitting that, I insulted her in return, saying that I didn't see Pierre, the man she loves, running to her room, because he was spending his last night with his family, not his whore. She reacted more fiercely than I had expected and she came after me physically—right in the dance studio! I tried to defend myself, while the other girls pulled us apart. My lip was bleeding and my head rang loudly as I looked at her in disbelief, even though I knew I deserved it. She didn't apologize and only glared back at me. Tensions are high across the city and we're no exception. Our world revolves around dancing and wealthy men and suddenly we have no one to dance for. Last night we performed to a near-empty theater since almost everyone has left to fight and other less courageous men, like Julien, have simply fled to safer areas.

I'm relieved to have a break from Julien and his demands, but not at this cost. I wish I could leave all of this to sit at your table with tea and biscuits and hear you tell me that everything will be all right. I'm having such a hard time navigating my life and those words would mean the world to me right now.

All my love,
Alexandrie

P.S. I have just returned from practice, where the Ballet Master announced that the Opera House will be closing briefly due to the war and, while we will still hold practices so as not to lose our abilities, we will not be performing. For the first time since hearing of the war, I have become afraid that perhaps we are not as untouchable as I had thought.

October 5, 1870

Dearest Maman,

Forgive me for not writing sooner, but I must ration the last sheets of paper that I have. I do hope this letter finds you safe and well. I am not able to enclose payment due to the wartime conditions. I still cannot believe the Second Empire has been overthrown and the Third Republic is now in power. Even more so, I don't understand why, instead of negotiating a lenient peace settlement, the republic mobilized the people to continue the war. Those of us who remain in Paris have seen a tide of change. The Opera House is still closed and, in a patriotic gesture, the general public has been allowed to use the grand building for political lectures. Many days when I leave practice, I can hear crowds inside our theater singing *republican hymns and reciting Hugo's poetry. I cannot tell you how upsetting this is to me. The nights of grand performances are over and now common people dirty the seats that were once reserved only for notable patrons.*

I admit that at first I enjoyed a break from performing. Every afternoon became a free day where I could read and wander. The other girls are also frustrated and lie on their beds staring at the ceiling waiting for the ballet to reopen. The fire has gone out and our practices are lackluster, which really doesn't make a difference because we don't have a specific performance to practice for. The entire practice is merely an attempt at keeping up our routine.

Paris is beginning to resemble the farmland where you read this letter and each afternoon the changes become more and more pronounced. Food shortages are at the forefront of everyone's minds. The authorities have built pavilions in the marketplaces and filled them with wheat and flour. Would you even believe that livestock have been brought here! Sheep and cows roam through the public parks, munching on grass and leaves. I am no longer able to sit in the parks because sheep amble over to me and try to eat my clothes and books. At first I was able to shoo a few animals away, but before I knew it the parks were overrun. The sheep have eaten all of the grass and pedestrians yield to oxen that walk the city, confused and out of place.

We are just waiting for everything to return to normal.

Much love,
Alexandrie

October 12, 1870

Dear Madame Channing,

My mother has told me that your classes continue and I am glad to hear that you are well. I am sure you have heard that the ballet has shut down temporarily, but it has oddly brought all of the ballerinas closer. I suppose as the lack of heat and nutrition weakened our bodies, the closing of the Opera House has weakened the cunning of our minds. Without anything to compete for, we have become a family looking out for one another, as I had envisioned so long ago. Each day we take notice of who failed to show up for meals and we run to their rooms to see if they have become sick. Many times the missing girl has been so tired of potatoes that she chose not to eat, or she has taken her own savings and purchased rat meat.

I have had an ongoing rivalry with one girl in particular, the etoilé, Cornelie. She has been a very vindictive, self-involved person who is threatened by the younger ballerinas and has made no secret of her dislike for me and her desire to see me fail. But now she has assumed the role of mother hen and, as the first to arrive to practice each morning, she fixes her eyes to the door and tallies each girl as we filter through.

The other day she noticed that one of the members of the corps, Ginette, didn't show up to class, so the Ballet Master told us to go check to see if she was in her room. We hurried back to our building and knocked on Ginette's door. We heard nothing and, exchanging glances, knocked again. This time we heard a low moan and, recognizing the sound of someone gravely ill, Cornelie threw open the door and rushed in. Ginette lay on her bed, her face flushed into a blotchy mess that shined so brightly with sweat it matched her deep red curls, which hung limply around her face. I watched Cornelie cover Ginette with blankets, her gold bracelet sliding up and down her forearm, an odd sight, as I'm used to seeing it pushing into her flesh. But Ginette protested weakly, saying she was burning up, while looking at us through bloodshot eyes. I put the back of my hand to her forehead and felt her skin on fire. When she told us that she had felt like this for days, Cornelie told me that we needed to get her to the doctor immediately, so I ran to tell the Ballet Master that her fever was so high even her eyes had turned red.

"Take me to her," he replied in a businesslike manner and followed me back to her room. I watched as Cornelie wrapped her in blankets before the Ballet Master picked her up and carried her away. In his suit and top hat, he seemed out of place in her room. I could have mistaken his actions as fatherly concern if I had not seen the rigid way he lifted her out of bed and his stiff manner as he walked down the hall with her. It reminded me of the way my father acted when he brought a sick animal to the veterinarian—a man protecting his assets.

As the weeks stretch on, each time girls fail to show up at practice we know something is wrong and we inevitably find them sweating in their cold rooms, overrun by fever, alternating between shaking with cold and kicking blankets off their bodies because they're overheating. Girl after girl has been transported to the doctor and in our desperate state of mind many of us think that becoming ill would be a blessing because the fever will warm us. Even so, we're better off than most that don't even have the option of a doctor and simply die in their cold homes.

I wanted to share this story with you so you can tell your students that friendships can be forged despite competition. It is a shame that it has taken such a dramatic situation for this to happen, but I would like to think that there is a lesson in this and perhaps the next generation of ballerinas will be more kind to one another and will not single a girl out because she has to clean the studio (a small attempt at humor on my part).

All my best wishes,
Alexandrie

October 28, 1870

Dear Alexandrie,

It is hard for me to sympathize with your hard times in Paris. I think that here you are complaining, yet you're provided with living quarters and three meals each day. No one is buying peppers because of the war and our garden has been wiped out by an early frost. Luce and I have a supply of canned vegetables, but that is it. We are practically starving and I check for a letter from you every day, hoping for some relief. Imagine my happiness when I see that you had written, yet nothing is enclosed because of "wartime conditions." We have children in our home, your nieces and nephews, who are hungry. Are you saving your francs for more dresses? Think of your family, and all that we have done for you. How could you be so thoughtless?

Maman

November 21, 1870

Dear Maman,

This is not the response I had expected from you, to say the least. I should send your letter back so you can read it and hear how cruel you sound! We are all looking out for one another here and making sure everyone is safe and healthy and you accuse me of being thoughtless for not sending any money along with my letter? How about writing "I'm so glad to hear you're safe" or "I can't believe the Opera House has closed"—anything but what you wrote to me. Let me tell you what I thought when I saw your letter—"I'm so happy this letter arrived because now I know my family is safe."

By now you've seen that this letter also does not contain any money, so I am going to remind you again that I cannot send you anything because I do not have anything to send. When the Opera closed, they ceased payment to everyone, including myself.

Alexandrie

December 15, 1870

Dear Alexandrie,

Of course I am glad to hear that you are safe. Things were hard before, as you know, and the war has made a bad situation so much worse. I suppose hunger and a cold house are all I can think about.

Denis has joined the service and I worry about him every day. Luce worries about him constantly, so I need to put up a strong face and pretend that he is perfectly safe. My nerves are frazzled from it all and I didn't mean to take it out on you. I suppose I assume your life is easy compared to ours.

So, on to better topics. Espelette is quieter than usual since almost all of the boys have left for the service. Has Julien left to join the service also? You should use what paper you have to write to him so he won't forget about you and will make you his *lorette* when he returns. Everyone here has also banded together, much like you and the ballerinas, and we share news that we hear about the war and letters from our sons. I'm the only one who can share a letter from my daughter, so please do keep me apprised of conditions in Paris. Everyone loves to hear of what is happening in the city.

I need to boil potatoes for lunch, so I must end this letter. Continue to be safe.

Love,
Maman

January 10, 1871

Dear Maman,

It pains me to hear that life is so hard. I pray for Denis each day so that he will return home safely. Julien is not in the service, but he left the country to get away from the war. I keep *waiting for the war to come to an end so that we can all return to our normal lives.*

What I found at first to be a historical experience, and at times even comical, has turned scary since winter arrived. I am quite frightened of what will become of us, Maman. The city entered a severe coal shortage and we are freezing in our rooms. Each night I bundle up in five blankets and try to fall asleep while I shiver. I fantasize about bathing in hot water, staying in the tub all day, about sweating in the sun, running my hand over the hot flame of a candle, anything but this. My body is too cold to move, and I've lost so much weight that I'm incredibly weak, and sleep won't come because of the discomfort. I wake in the night to rhythmic thumps; look out my window to see residents chopping down trees from the public parks, which are now nothing more than fields of dirt after the livestock ate all of the flowers, grass, and leaves. Now they're bare, with frozen snow-covered stumps. The few remaining trees hold no branches except for the tops that were too tall to reach. Soon these too will be gone when desperate mothers and fathers cut down the trunk to warm their freezing children. Fences have disappeared from homes and shops to be used for firewood. Anything that could be burned has been stolen.

The flour and wheat supplies have dwindled and the roaming livestock have long been slaughtered. Without heat and food, the winter seems to never end. I agree with you that a food shortage would have been much more convenient if it had been in the warm days of summer when families could get by with what they grew in their gardens. Overtaken with hunger, people have become desperate and have slaughtered their own horses, giving their families enough meat to eke out the long days of winter. When reports came of zoo animals gone missing and butchers selling elephant steaks and tiger cutlets for insanely high prices, I felt as if we would surely die. The rich will take whatever meat is for sale, or travel away to warm locations, but girls like me will either starve or freeze to death. I took for granted the ballet's kitchen that supplied us with breakfast, lunch, and dinner. Now the kitchen serves us nothing but potatoes. Without butter, oil, or spices we force down dry, flavorless baked potatoes morning, noon, and night. The potatoes have become a metaphor for our lives. I'm even envious of the girls who purchase rat meat at the market. Without any income coming in, dining on a dirty rodent is a luxury. This experience has made me realize that I am too dependent on the ballet. Without it, I have nothing, and cannot take care of myself. If it never reopens I'm going to be in a horrible situation. I feel like a fraud, acting as if I'm on the same level as the patrons, when in actuality I'm not even fit to clean their homes.

I wish I had glamorous things to write to you of, and lots of francs to send, but it would seem that during this time our lives are not terribly different from each other's.

I do hope this time shall pass soon,
Alexandrie

Reopening the Doors

Christmas passes without a gift to be received and the New Year arrives without a celebration to speak of. Still there has been no news of Edgar, but I can't stop my mind from thinking of him or my heart from hoping he has made it through the war safely and that I will see him again. We sit on the floor before practice, not bothering to stretch. I look around at my fellow dancers and notice how unkempt and thin we have become. There's no reason to spend time pinning our hair back, so we wear it long. Some girls have not bothered to bathe and their hair is matted with knots. Would the world look so ugly if there was no one around to impress?

"Do you realize if the ballet remains closed for another year we'll be twenty-five when it reopens?" Noella whispers to me.

"You don't think that will happen, do you?" I ask, turning my attention to her.

"Jeanine didn't think it would happen, but she turned twenty-five last week," Noella says quietly, looking over at a dark-haired dancer. "Her monsieur is stationed at one of the battalions and was supposed to make arrangements for her before her birthday. Now she doesn't know when, or if, he's coming back."

I think to myself that this sounds like an appropriate punishment for being so relieved that Julien has fled the country. Just as my anxiety level is rising at the thought, the Ballet Master walks in with a determined look in his eye and a confident stride. "Ladies," he says, clapping his hands for our attention. Normally, we would have left our positions at the *barre* and lined up in front of him. But today we barely move, some girls lie on their stomachs and only prop their heads up with an elbow to listen to him.

"I have wonderful news," he says, his eyes moving back and forth through the group. "The French provisional government has given up and entered into peace negotiations with the Germans. It has just been confirmed that the troops are dispersing and returning home. Firewood is being delivered to your rooms as we speak, the kitchen will resume, and most importantly, the ballet will reopen in exactly one month!"

We all sit up straighter and exchange looks of relief, glad to have a purpose again. "We will shoo the common people out of our theater and reopen with a grand performance," he explains to us. "We'll welcome back our patrons with a grand post-war debut. It will be called the Second Coming and will be the most important performance of your lives." He walks back and forth, ramrod straight, swinging his cane as he lectures us. "I must be firm in ordering you all to avoid going outside while the German troops are still visible throughout Paris. The peace negotiations did not go smoothly when the Second Empire surrendered, and if things should turn violent, I cannot risk any of you getting caught in the cross fire. We need everyone to be healthy, ready for the Second Coming."

Noella and I quickly exchange looks and stifle laughter. "God forbid he be concerned with our personal safety," she says later as we walk back to our rooms. "Dreadful man," I agree.

"I would never admit it to him, but I'm more than happy to oblige and stay inside, warm in our newly heated rooms," Noella giggles as she enters her room.

I couldn't agree more, I think, sitting in front of the fire, basking in its warmth. When my feet begin to get too hot, I walk across my room and crack open the French doors. A cold wind bursts through, my curtains flailing in all directions, and I quickly close the door. Looking through the panes, I see that the shop owners have closed their doors, refusing to offer their services to the Germans. With all shops shut down posting signs of "Closed for National Mourning" and black flags raised, Paris looks like a truly deserted city. I sink down to a seated position and gaze out at the quiet streets.

The Second Coming

The following morning the city remains still. I splash cold water on my face in an attempt to wake myself up and then walk across the deserted street in silence. The Ballet Master has become obsessed with the reopening, his "Second Coming," and has required us to arrive at the Paris Opera House at five o'clock in the morning, fully dressed in costume, to rehearse. Pamphlets filled with illustrations of battles and maps showing the areas of Alsace-Lorraine that have now been claimed by Prussia remain scattered underneath the seats, but aside from that small reminder of the hard times, the theater is just as I remember it. I yawn and silently curse the Ballet Master's demanding ways but perk up when I see he has provided a large pot of coffee and pastries for a burst of energy on this early morning. I have an overwhelming urge to steal the entire tray and run with it back to my room in case we encounter another food shortage. "That's a tricky one," Cornelie says as she drains her cup. "He knows we can't think badly of him if he shows us a nice gesture."

After practicing lazily for almost an entire year, our rehearsal is less than perfect. Our timing is off and we can't hold poses or leap very high. We have lost our strength from a diet of potatoes, and it shows. Our minds have also been elsewhere, searching for something to keep us company during the cold nights.

"How could you sluggish girls let this happen? How you perform is a reflection on the audience," the Ballet Master chastises us, forgetting that he led the lethargic practices. "If you go onstage with as weak an attempt as you have shown today, the audience will take this to mean that you have no respect for them. We will meet here each morning and work twice as long!"

I'm more exhausted than I ever have been before when I leave the theater, my muscles aching from suddenly being paid attention to again. I see Cornelie coming toward me, and I quickly turn the other way, separating myself from the other girls and walking toward our practice studio. I can't handle a conversation with her about how we need to strengthen ourselves and improve. Passing by the studio doors, I notice a tall figure in a suit standing inside the studio and my rapid heartbeat tells me it's Edgar. I'm so happy to see he's safe and I hope he has come to tell me how he has missed me this past year and how he's dreamt of me each night as he sleeps. I run toward him, ready to embrace him, but my steps slow as he makes no move toward me.

"Good afternoon," he says, looking at me in confusion. "Are you not practicing today?"

"We started earlier today and have just finished," I explain, tugging nervously at my tutu while my spirits deflate at learning his only reason for coming to the studio is to return to his normal routine. "We rehearsed in the theater instead."

"Ah, so I'm too late," he deduces. I attempt to make small talk as I walk toward him, planted in the middle of the room, his re-flection multiplied by the studio's large framed mirrors so it ap-pears as if he's everywhere. "Was your grand exhibit successful?" I ask, my voice echoing in the empty room.

"It was canceled," he replies. "So we must start the gallery search again."

"I'm sorry, I know it meant a great deal to you," I reply.

"Yes, well, with everything that has happened since, I would be a horrible person for wallowing in the misery of one canceled exhibit," he snips and I blush in embarrassment that I should have brought up his exhibit as the first topic and not something more pressing and important. "Very true," I say in an attempt to recover myself. "It has been a terrible time. Did you serve in the war?" I hide the fact that I know he had been based in one of the battalions, where he never once wrote to me.

"As a republican willing to die for my country, I joined the National Guard," he states arrogantly. "Are you familiar with it?"

"I am." I try to hide my contempt for his assumption that I know nothing of the history of France. I search my brain for all that I have learned about the National Guard, thinking I will make him look the fool for assuming I'm just a silly girl without any knowledge. "It has never been fully supported by our coun-try's leaders, from Bonaparte not trusting the untrained soldiers, to Charles X completely banishing it, to Louis-Philippe reestab-lishing it. Napoleon III had tried to limit its influence by allow-ing no more than sixty battalions in the city, with only the best of those receiving arms. But this year, with France under siege, the city took advantage of the National Guard and the battalions grew to two hundred and fifty with almost two hundred thou-sand men."

"Thank you for the history lesson," he says sarcastically, raising an eyebrow at me. I suppress a giggle because I suspect I sounded a bit like Julien droning on about the new Paris. "Thankfully, as soon as France knew surrender was imminent I was released, so from the comfort of my own home I read the news that they have officially surrendered. Unfortunately, the inexperienced soldiers have spun out of control and the Guard that remains has become a revolutionary army. Right now France is trying to hold on by its fingernails with a new government that's not even legal and the National Guard is running rampant." He sighs and looks at me. "And you? How have you fared?"

I tell him how the Opera House closed and that there are still pamphlets strewn about the theater as evidence. "It was quite a lonely time," I say, looking up at him. "Do you not agree that wartime puts everything in perspective? It makes you reconsider how you live your life. Yearn for those you love?" I am dropping hints so loudly I feel as if I'm throwing them onto the floor, but he only chortles.

"Please! This war has not put anyone into grave danger," he laughs. "I was assigned to Bastion One and we found ourselves in more of a camping situation than a war. I ended up drawing during the days to get away from some of the other men, who I found to be extremely pampered individuals. They whined about not having a hot meal from a restaurant or clean, pressed clothes ready each morning." He makes a disgusted face as he remembers.

"So you're stronger than most men and able to cope," I reply, treating him as I would Julien, fully aware of the flattery I'm giving. "But I find it hard to believe that your mind never wandered home, for those you left?"

"Alexandrie, if you're searching for a compliment you mustn't be so obvious," he teases me roughly, and heat rises to my face. "Now, there's no need to get upset," he says in a softer tone, taking my hand and making an overexaggerated display of bowing and kissing it, and I am now positive he's making fun of me. "I'm thrilled to once again be in your presence." He winks at me, then walks out the door without another word.

I wait in the studio, my face burning, until I feel he has distanced himself enough and only then do I begin to walk back to my room. I had been waiting for the moment when I would see him again. After an entire year, it is not so much to ask that he be overcome to see me. I have thought of his well-being every single day—three hundred and sixty-five days of wasted thoughts. The funny thing about separation is that you only remember the good in people. As the war raged on, I was filled with images of Edgar's concentrated look when he drew, how his lips brushed mine, how he gently arranged the blanket over my body. Pictures of him leaving the Green Room with Cornelie or the mortification I felt when I stood in his foyer holding the bag of oranges never surfaced until now. These images come rushing back and I tell myself that our meeting today is proof that I must not focus my efforts on Edgar. I mull this over bitterly until a hand grabs my arm and I'm shaken out of my inner rant.

"I should murder you," Noella cries, popping out of nowhere and pulling me into her room. "I had to listen to Cornelie go on and on about where the flaws lie in our performance and what we need to do to correct them. You must promise to never leave me alone with her again!"

"I'm sorry! You're just not quick enough!" I laugh, choosing not to tell Noella that I have just spoken to Edgar. I'm too humiliated at his lack of excitement in seeing me to rehash the entire conversation. Luckily Noella's mind is on other things, as she holds up an invitation. "We've all been invited," she says with excitement in her eyes. I look at the invitation, dark with grays and thick black words that read:

"Gray, cold, starving... Victor Hugo describes us best as *Les Misérables*. But history will not repeat itself! We hereby require your wretched, miserable presence at the *Conservatoire de Musique* to celebrate the end of the war and the beginning of a prosperous new time."

"It should be fun," Noella gushes. "What better way to welcome everyone back to Paris? I love it!"

"But what is it, exactly? I mean, it doesn't say anything about dinner or entertainment," I flip the invitation over to see if there's any more information. "It doesn't even say what to wear. Is it a costume ball or just people gathering together to talk?"

"I think it's just a large gathering," Noella replies. "It's being hosted by the owner of Au Lapin Agile, so it should be quite fun!"

"His cabaret can be a little raunchy," I look at her with apprehension. "I'm not sure we'll fit in there."

"That's exactly why we should go," she stands up, exasperated. "Don't you ever get tired of being so sheltered here? All we do is practice, perform, and then repeat. I don't think I've spoken to a single person who isn't tied to the ballet in some way for years! Sure, it could turn out to be horrible, but we were personally invited! I've never been personally invited anywhere."

"I don't know, my guess is that they think it's an easy way to pack women into the theater so the men will arrive," I say, nervous to leave the protection of the ballet. "It's going to be a lot different from the parties at the Opera House."

"Think of it as a day off! We don't have to impress anyone or watch what we say," she says. "We can just show up as guests—not hostesses. It will be so refreshing."

On the night of the party I'm still nervous but try to hide it from Noella while we peer out my window, watching crowds of people on their way to the Conservatoire. The thought of arriving to a party with just Noella, and no one to even meet there, makes my stomach knot. "Everyone is dressed so casually," she says. "It looks like they're going to the market! We should definitely change."

"I'm so glad we can see the party from here!" I exclaim, pulling a walking dress out of my wardrobe. "Could you imagine how snotty we would look if we arrived in full ball gowns?"

"We'd be laughingstocks! I can't believe I spent all of this time on my hair and now I'm going to have to let it down," she scowls while pulling at pins. I bite my tongue from telling her that this is more evidence that we don't belong at this party. In fact, when we finally arrive, I see we're two of the few ballerinas who have accepted. I spot some of the younger girls standing in groups together, looking uncomfortable and out of place. I want to join them, but Noella pressures me to walk around so we can see all of the guests. "We're not ballerinas tonight," she says firmly. "We can be anyone."

"Ironic that the whole reason we're in the ballet is so we can be something we're not," I whisper to her. "And here you want to be just a common resident."

"I *am* just a common resident." She grabs my arm tightly and pushes into the crowd. "And so are you."

Even without music to fill the building, the noise level is deafening. Everyone is talking about the war, and the hard times they've endured, their voices getting louder and louder with each drink. Noella nudges me. "Isn't that your artist?" I nod, looking at Edgar laughing with a few bearded men, and Monsieur Cézanne standing rigidly next to him. "Let's go say hello," Noella starts to move toward him before I can stop her. The last thing I want is to interrupt him after he embarrassed me so much in the studio. "See, we're not so out of place here. You had nothing to worry about." She forges ahead unaware of my last encounter, and I reluctantly follow a few steps behind her.

"I had no idea you frequented such places, Monsieur," Noella grins at Edgar and I'm amazed at her confidence. "I could say the same for the two of you!" He moves to the side to allow us space to join the conversation. "Alexandrie, two days in a row of unexpected meetings, I daresay I'll begin to think you're follow-ing me." His eyes narrow flirtatiously and I see Noella look curi-ously at me. But she doesn't have the chance to tease me because Monsieur Cézanne steps in close to her, taking her hand. "I don't believe we've met," he says, staring at her intensely. I exchange a quick, shocked look with Edgar and we stifle laughs while Noella introduces herself. "You should be extremely flattered," Edgar nudges Noella. "Paul isn't a man known to strike up a conversa-tion." The other men laugh, and I feel sorry for him to be teased in front of everyone, especially Noella. But he gives a little smile and ignores them, his eyes locked on Noella. "I've never seen anyone as light as you before," he says and I can see she's grow-ing uncomfortable. Her eyes dart to the side as if looking for an escape route. "I would love to paint you on a canvas washed en-tirely of black. Your white hair would leap off the painting and your eyes would look like the sky. It would be extremely power-ful."

"Oh," Noella says, somewhat shocked. "Well, that does sound interesting. But I really have no time to model."

"What were you gentlemen talking about before we interrupted you?" I interject loudly enough for Monsieur Cézanne to look at me in annoyance, giving Noella the chance to step to the side and escape his severe eyes.

"What else but the war?" Monsieur Cézanne addresses me as if I'm an idiot, but I merely smile at him. "Yes, I was telling them about how the 'harsh' conditions have been so greatly exaggerated. In fact, my time at the Lycée was much worse than at the Guard," Edgar laughs. "My father told me how it was the most prestigious school in the country. Only when I entered the school, I began to have second thoughts and wondered if my father had simply been trying to get rid of me."

An image flashes into my mind of the green dress slipping from my hands when I first discovered the secret of the ballet. For the first time I'm able to see the parallels in our lives. How is it that two people who have grown up in such different backgrounds can have such similar experiences?

"I had imagined grand buildings full of learning and encouragement, great minds at work," he sweeps his hand through the air to convey the magnificence he believed he would find. "So when I sat drawing the surroundings of the fort, I remembered back to those days and how the students were only allowed to bathe every three months, how the rebellious ones would be beaten in front of the class, and if they did not subside they were thrown into solitary confinement. I saw the boys returning to class after a stretch in the Lycée prison, mute, with dark circles under their eyes. None of the guardsmen at the battalion had such pallor, so I never joined in the reminiscing of pampered city life."

"You never tried to leave?" I ask, seeing myself years ago writing to Madame Channing with a shaky hand.

"I never considered leaving," he replies.

Even though he had not picked up on my hints, I'm glad to be welcomed into his group and see that he's safely back in Paris. Listening to him now, I wonder how the Lycée and the ballet, both prestigious Parisian traditions, can also hold such horrid secrets. He now dismisses the bad side of the school as if it was nothing more than an inconvenience. My greatest fear is how I will be able to remain at the ballet past my twenty-fifth birthday without relying on post-performances for long-term support. I know I will not be able to wave away the downside as simply the way it is. It seems no matter what kind of conditions Edgar is put into, he can easily retreat into himself and tune out the rest of the world.

I'm eager to hear more, but the clinking of glasses gets louder and louder, making it hard to hear the conversation. "Attention! I have a few words to say!" We look toward the stage to see the party's host. Noella takes this opportunity to distance the two of us from Edgar and his friends. "That was the creepiest man I have ever met," she whispers to me as we slip away into the crowd. "He's very weird," I whisper back, then begin to laugh. "He seems to have taken quite a liking to you, though." She rolls her eyes and we peer up at the stage to hear the Au Lapin Agile owner's speech. He clears his throat and I recognize the words from a book I had read while huddled under blankets with nothing else to do.

"So long as there shall exist, by reason of law and custom, a social condemnation which, in the face of civilization, artificially creates hell on earth, and complicates a destiny that is divine, with human fatality; so long as degradation of man by poverty, the ruin of woman by starvation, and the dwarfing of childhood by physical and spiritual night are not solved; so long as, in certain regions, social asphyxia shall be possible; in other words, and from a yet more extended point of view, so long as ignorance and misery remain on earth," he pauses and smiles widely at the crowd. "And might I add, as long as Prussia muscles its way into our country," he drops his head and laughs as the crowd cheers noisily, then brings his hands up and speaks in a softer, matter-of-fact tone, "then parties like this cannot be useless."

The curtain opens and I watch a peasant being released from prison. He hobbles away, carrying a yellow card to show he's a convict. The crime? Chopping down houses for firewood. The audience roars. "It nearly had gotten that bad," several people murmur, thoroughly amused. "What is this?" Noella whispers to me. "It's a farce on the book, *Les Misérables,*" I whisper to her. The convict continues his walk, meeting a dying woman who explains she has a child and has turned to prostitution. I go cold when she stands up and takes off her robe to reveal a shabby reproduction of our ballerina costumes. As she prances onstage, the crowd laughs but Noella and I look at each other with frightened eyes. "He specifically invited us here," she whispers. "He can't possibly think we would find this amusing."

"I told you this is a different kind of theater than the Opera," I whisper back. "He thinks he's being smart and satirical. But it's only hurtful." We watch as the prisoner vows to take care of her and she slaps him at the shabby quarters he invites her into. "This isn't the Notre Dame de Lorette!" she squeals and stomps offstage while the audience roars. "Let's get out of here," Noella hisses. "I can't stand here and watch this." I nod and we slip out the back as the prisoner just shrugs at the prostitute and arranges to take her daughter, who is being held by a rich hotelier.

A Civil Affair

Attending that party turned out to be the best thing for Noella and me. In our minds, it made us fully aware that we are of a different ilk just as we had been taught to believe so long ago. We hadn't known how envious everyone was of us, and how they could hurt us out of jealousy. It reaffirmed for us that we are best kept behind the walls of the Opera House, and it made us more than eager to work on the dress rehearsals for the Second Coming. As the weeks pass, our coal supply remains intact, our meals offer more variety, and we begin to resemble the graceful dancers we once were. We smile proudly at one another, excited to get back to our lives as coveted ballerinas. In our satin tops and with flowers pinned throughout our hair, we would never have recognized one another as the starving girls shivering under cold blankets.

Each morning, we gather in the Opera House before the sun rises, our legs aching but getting stronger by the day. Each day word comes that another *abonné* has returned to Paris. Jeanine's monsieur came back for her and she cannot stop crying in her relief. Edgar attends many practices, quietly sketching, but leaves before it's over, so I never have a chance to speak to him. His presence rattles me less now. I suppose the closing of the Opera House has given me a new perspective, and I now yearn for something stable. The only thing I can depend on from Edgar is that he'll shower me with attention and then promptly leave me. Before the war I had reluctantly given in to Julien's demands. Now I see that I will be wise to choose that path.

March arrives and I awake on the morning of the Second Coming full of excitement. The day cannot pass fast enough while Noella and I spend the morning speculating on the success of the reopening and choosing which gowns to wear after the performance.

"There are posters all over the city announcing the reopening," I say with excitement as I hold a pair of pumps up to a gown. Noella shakes her head, "No, those don't match," she says. "Everyone is calling it the grand performance that will reestablish Parisian theater!"

I sort through numerous pairs of shoes and hear Noella moving toward the French doors. "Alexandrie, look," she says seriously.

"Traitors!" I hear a muffled tone through the windowpane, and quickly open its doors to hear more clearly. "Everyone who loses a battle to the Germans is a traitor! We will reclaim our city!"

An astounding number of poorly dressed men have gathered in the street and speak to the growing crowd as if they are onstage. The cheers grow louder and soon we're joined by our entire hall as we cluster around the doors.

"We revolt against your government for peace! The government and National Assembly have stabbed the nation in the back by surrendering! They have removed the cannons from Montmartre—cannons paid for by private citizens, aimed at the German besiegers' victory parade into Paris. Traitors! We have held our own elections! We are the Commune of Paris! Behold the Parisfication of the whole of France!"

We watch the demonstration in confused awe. "Are they trying to continue the war?" Noella whispers. "I don't know," I say, peering over several dancers' heads to watch the crowd on the street grow larger. "They're speaking of the French government. It doesn't make sense."

"They're revolting against their own," Cornelie observes. The sound of hooves clicking on the street becomes louder and the well-dressed officers of the National Assembly move in on the crowd. The demonstration soon appears to be a battle between social classes, the working-class Commune trading insults with the bourgeoisie military.

"The Commune of Paris is nothing but the tyranny of the scum of the earth using brute force, no negotiations or compromises!" a member of the Assembly yells to the crowd. "To revel while the nation is lying defeated is treasonous!"

"I warn you—do not come closer!" The Communard speaker motions toward a group of men who step forward to make themselves visible. I gasp to see them holding several monks, bound and tied.

"Treasonous, out-of-control revolutionaries!" the Guardsmen yell.

I watch the speaker calmly look at the approaching Guardsmen, and it seems as if all movements are slowed. When the speaker turns toward a monk, placing a long rifle to his forehead, I am not sure if I'm seeing correctly, but then everything speeds up as the monk falls to the ground.

We scream and shut the doors, running into the hallway as the Communards and Guardsmen shoot at one another, not even caring that the crowd is witnessing the entire thing. We stand against the walls, shaking with fear. I have never seen anyone die before and I can't control the sobs that overtake my body. My mind can't get rid of the image of the man, seeming so far away from the monk, breaking the distance with the ominous long nose of his weapon. Many of the other girls have the same reaction, while others stand dumbfounded, unbelieving of what they have just witnessed.

"I thought this was over," Noella moans. "I know," I say, looking at her worried face. Shots continue to ring out, followed by screams and wails. We remain frozen in the hallway. Eventually they become more muted and we assume the battle has left our street. When the noise finally stops, we cautiously move back to my room and peer out the window. We're met with the most gruesome sight of all—bodies lying bloodied in the street and the faraway horizon of the city engulfed in flames. We all stare in disbelief, no one uttering a word.

"It's eight o'clock," Cornelie whispers and we look at her in silence. The curtain should be rising as we assemble into our opening poses, ready to greet the audience once again. Our heads should be held high as we wait in anticipation, the music of the orchestra filling our ears, the curtain ascending past our heads. But the Opera House is filled with nothing but empty seats. For all of the Ballet Master's planning and grandiose ideas, the "Second Coming" never materialized.

Spring never reached Paris. When the flames died out and the city was left in a blanket of smoke, the Communards had burned the Palais des Tuileries, Hôtel de Ville, the Conseil d'Etat, the Palais de la Légion d'Honneur, the Cours de Comptes, and a section of the Ministère des Finances in the Rue de Rivoli. When the fighting came to an end in May, thirty thousand men perished in the Commune. Roughly one out of thirty Parisians was killed in the course of the uprising and its suppression.

The culmination of the war has left everyone exhausted and on edge. As life slowly returns to normal, fears subsiding, sun shining, food growing, we resume our routines. As I awake each morning for practice and prepare for the night's ballet, it almost seems as if the last year has been a horrid dream. But I fear the events will have a lasting effect, leaving the population in a rage of paranoia that is quickly bubbling to the surface.

Act III

No. 20 Scène:

Even Dreams Become Burdens

A cautiously approach the dancers murmuring in hushed tones, their eyes darting toward the door while some wipe tears away. I move closer to the huddled group, my eyes intently searching their faces. I've seen far too many tearful exchanges of information about backstabbing. We constantly look over our shoulders because girls will rob one another whenever the chance arises. One day we'll reach out to one another, sharing our deepest feelings, only to wake up the next morning to betrayal. I had witnessed one dancer, Marielle, pack her belongings in anticipation of leaving the ballet after securing a rich landowner. Marielle had a reputation nearly as scandalous as Cornelie's and she made the mistake of confiding to Cornelie that the reason he was going to take her as a *lorette* was because she had told him that she was so in love with him she'd refused any other man. Cornelie promptly seduced the man the following night and conveniently lost her key, so she and the man went to Marielle's room, where Cornelie told him she had left it, and found Marielle in flagrante delicto with two men. The landowner cursed her for the whore she was and never returned. I assume a similar situation has been brought to the attention of the group today.

"Alexandrie, something terrible happened last night," whispers Ginette, fully recovered from pneumonia and full of freckles. "You know the thin, pale man with the round head and monocle?"

I nod. We all know him, and despise him for berating us, calling us cheap, stupid women. I had listened in horror as the older girls told stories of nights with him that were full of tension for fear of saying or doing the wrong thing. When something wasn't to his liking, he would slap their faces, beat them, and while pinning them down, he finished hurriedly and proceeded to throw them onto the floor. Many nights I awoke in a sweat as his face loomed down on me in a dream and I recalled a particular story Paulette told me about when he threw her onto the floor and spit on her.

She spoke of the pure hatred in his eyes and the story has haunted me ever since. The evenings when I saw his huge, round head silhouetted in the audience with his monocle gleaming I prayed that he would not approach me.

"He went to Cornelie's room last night after the ballet," Ginette continues, pausing for dramatic effect, obviously enjoying delivering this piece of news.

I look at her impatiently. This is not out of the ordinary. Cornelie scoffs at our fear, calling us oversensitive princesses. "Do something to anger him and he'll finish up instantly," she had laughed. "Just prepare to be thrown to the ground afterward. Who cares? It's over and done with and you can get a full night's sleep. I'll take a quick beating over turning tricks all night any-time!"

I look around and realize that Cornelie isn't at rehearsal. Ginette draws a deep breath and squeaks, "She was found stran-gled to death this morning."

I look at her unbelievingly as the rest of the girls nod that this is the truth. I can't get air into my lungs and I feel as if I'm breathing in tiny little gasps, but nothing is reaching me. As much as I hated Cornelie, I had always thought her to be invin-cible. Her life never got to her. In fact, she had embraced it.

"She must have taken it too far," Noella whispers to me. "Made him so angry he strangled her."

I become numb; it doesn't seem real. I expect to see Cornelie plow through the door, her voice preceding her. My trance is broken by the rapid claps of the Ballet Master's hands. We auto-matically line up to perform. "Be seated," he says. Bewildered, we sink to the ground. "I'm sure you have heard of the unfortu-nate happenings of today. We will be canceling practice so you can all grasp the gravity of the situation."

We relax into the ground, thankful that he's empathetic to our loss. "As you can well imagine, this situation will not portray the Opera favorably. Cornelie had quite an adoring crowd and her absence will not go unnoticed. It's unfortunate that a crazed fan somehow managed to enter her room. For that is what hap-pened last night and anything else is a lie. Anyone who's caught telling lies will be removed from the ballet without any questions asked. Do I make myself understood?" he asks us slowly and clearly, his eyes resting on each dancer as we become rigid and nod.

"Let this be a lesson to you all that you must always do what-ever it takes to please the patron. For he is why we dance," he con-tinues. "You each understood this when you entered. Cornelie has paid for her complete disregard of all that the ballet was built upon. Remember her whenever any of you get the notion in your head that you can make your own rules. There are no short-cuts."

He pauses and breathes heavily, his chest moving up and down, then turns sharply on his heel and exits. We remain seated, absorbing that the Ballet Master believes Cornelie deserved to be strangled to death and the round-faced man with the mono-cle had every right to do it. But none of us dare say it aloud. A clear line has been drawn. We are replaceable. We cannot begin to comprehend what had happened that night in Cornelie's room, but we all understand that it is to be covered up to protect the ballet's image, and any one of us can be tossed aside at any given moment without a further thought.

We file out of the room and, in my daze, I run directly into Edgar. He steadies me and meets my eyes as he says gently, "The Ballet Master told me why there is no practice today." All I can do is nod. He stares intently at my face. "There is great sorrow in your eyes."

I gaze up at him. It's the first time his eyes are still and not feverishly moving to take in every detail of his surroundings. They're such a deep, dark shade that I can't tell their exact color and are fringed with eyelashes so heavy that I feel I would have to move them like a curtain to see into his eyes.

"I'm very sorry," he says. "Would you like to get away to take your mind off things?"

I blink away tears and follow him outside, not caring that I'm in my plain practice skirt amongst the elegant women of the city. He guides me to a café with his hand on the small of my back in almost a protective way. The gesture makes me feel like we're a familiar couple on an ordinary day stopping for a cup of coffee.

As we sit down, I'm so drained that I can't even register how excited I would have been an hour ago if I knew we would be seated at a café in public together, conversing in plain view of the entire city.

"Are you all right?" he asks, looking at me with an almost fatherly concern.

"I just can't believe it," I reply. "I've never been friends with her, or even wanted to be. I've wanted her out of the ballet for so long, but not like this. I feel so guilty now. This may sound absurd to you, but during the war she was like a mother to us. And now she's gone and we're supposed to go on as if she never existed."

I feel defeated and make no attempt to sit properly or portray myself as a perfect lady. I'm too shattered from this morning's events and it no longer seems that important to me.

"It's not absurd." He is still for a moment, his eyes looking into the distance, reviewing my words in his head. "Sad, but not absurd," he continues upon reflection. "You shouldn't feel guilty either; this was not your doing. I know she made things quite difficult for you. The way she lived, and the risks she took, was an invitation for something bad to happen. I don't mean to speak ill of her, she was a friend of mine. Believe me, I tried to tell her to be more careful, but she treated it like a joke. I wish she would have listened so we wouldn't be having this conversation. The thing about powerful men is they think they're entitled to anything they want and don't have to deal with any repercussions. I don't want to see you get yourself into a situation where you can be harmed. Don't talk so much to these men. Don't give them anything to use against you."

"Yet I'm sitting here talking to an *abonné,*" I say with a small smile.

He smiles an easy smile that completely changes his features, breaking the concentrated look he wears and shedding years from his face. "True, I suppose you'll have to trust that I'm not a crazed lunatic."

"Sometimes it's hard to trust anyone," I reply, breaking the brief moment of lightness and dropping my eyes down while tracing my finger over the rim of the coffee cup. I breathe a deep sigh and look at him quizzically. "You do know what happened to her?" I ask and he nods sadly. "I believe we both know the Ballet Master's version is not entirely accurate," he says. "Normally I wouldn't care to keep such a secret, but I don't want to see girls like you being pushed to the street or worse. I need to know that you'll be safe."

"I don't want my life to end up like hers," I confess. "It would be nice to think that I could rise above it and do anything my heart desired, but I have lost so much time, I fear I won't be taken as a *lorette* at all. Without that, I don't know how safe I'll be on my own."

I sigh and think that, for all of the pressure he put on me, Julien has yet to return to the ballet. I had taken my relationship with him for granted and assumed I could turn to it as the last option when time ran out. I never thought I would look for Julien at each night's performance, but now my eyes search the loges and when he is not to be found, I become more convinced that he has made Milan his new home.

The way Edgar looks at me with a cross between pity and concern affects me and I'm afraid I have said too much. "I apologize for being so long-winded," I quickly add, pulling myself together. "I suppose I feel comfortable talking to you."

He gives me a small, sad smile and places his hand over mine.

"Anytime you need someone to talk to. You do realize how important you are to me, don't you?"

"I don't," I say, looking curiously at him. While I want to reach out to him, a part of me holds back. Why is he being so kind to me now? Is he the type of man who needs to save people? Is he drawn to women in distress? Does he need to be the powerful man protecting a helpless woman from danger? I suppose all men need to feel important, yet the fact that he has never reached out to me until now, when I am in my most vulnerable state, makes me wonder if he preys on the weak. And when I have moved past my pain, will he move toward another distressed girl?

"Never doubt that I care for you," he says softly, holding my hand in both of his. "You know I'll always be here to help you if you should ever need it. After a night's rest you'll feel better. We all wish we could escape from our lives at some point."

"You have everything that I strive for," I say, amazed. "You're able to follow your dream. Your whole life is dedicated to what you love. What would you want to escape from?"

"Even dreams become burdens. I want to escape from myself. Each day the urge to create a better work of art burns through me until my fingers are full of lightning. If I could escape my own mind, then I could rest. Even as I sleep, I dream of colors and wake anxious to re-create them before the memory fades."

"Perhaps your restless mind is your best asset," I comment, glad the focus has turned away from me. "If you were able to escape from it, then you would be one of many whose art is only still landscapes and posed portraits. What you have is a gift."

"You understand how my mind works, and that's a frightening thought," he laughs.

"Edgar, may I ask you a personal question?" I say, looking over the table at him. "I'll tell you anything you want to know," he replies, opening his hands to illustrate that his life is an open book.

I take a quick breath, slightly afraid of being so direct, but I need to know. "Why is it that you are not married and live alone in such a large home?" Once the words are out I feel relieved. This is the question I have wanted to ask him from the first day we met. "You've found your drive and have left your careless ways behind," I say to him. "Wouldn't marriage be the next step for a responsible man?"

He smiles sheepishly at me. "The truth of the matter is, there's no time for marriage. Perhaps you'll say this is selfish, but I don't desire it. My future lies in my art, and I'm not compelled to put that aside for marriage and raising a family. An artist's income is notoriously sporadic, and my greatest fear is giving up my dream to support a family by taking on stable work. I would be miserable, and that would make me a terrible husband.

"Now I would like to know what it is about the ballet that you're so drawn to," he changes the subject and turns his attention fully to me. "I look at you and think that you don't belong in that world. That you would make a nice, honest man happy. I know you have to support your family, but why through the ballet? What is it that you're striving for?"

I hesitate for a moment, wanting to argue that if he thinks so highly of me, why hasn't he pursued me at all? Why doesn't he understand that I wouldn't make him stop his art? But I decide that a confrontational argument is not the way to reach him. "It's the dance that I love," I reply instead. "I, like you, want to create something beautiful. I understand completely why you wouldn't want to be in a marriage that would hinder your dreams. Dreams are the most precious thing we have, and having the chance to achieve those dreams is unlike anything I could ever have imagined." I watch Edgar's eyes light up and I smile to think that it has taken years to get through to him; he's seeing me as an artist, as different from other women. "If you had seen where I grew up, and the few luxuries my family had, you would never believe that I would be sitting at a fine café in Paris today. I focused all of my energy on becoming a dancer in the Opera Ballet."

He listens intently as I tell him everything—about Denis and Luce, Madame Channing, my mother's greed, and Sunday afternoon studies with Monsieur Aston. In the bright light of the café, I become more exposed than when he drew me on my bed. We remain fixed to our seats, exploring the inner workings of our minds, the thoughts that run rampant through them, and the fears that we could never share with anyone. I see that through both our dreams and our loneliness we have much in common; my life is becoming increasingly more isolated, not knowing who to trust, and he has sought out his own world of isolation, trusting only in his art. It is at this moment that I realize I don't feel curiosity or awe for him. I feel love. I smile at him and he winks at me while drinking his tea, and I think that perhaps he has fallen in love with me too.

No. 21 Scène:
A Secure Future

*H*ow I have longed for this moment!" Julien embraces me, sweeping me off the floor and turning around as I giggle with embarrassment at the looks we're receiving from everyone in the Green Room. "I cannot tell you how ecstatic I am to be back in the city for an evening at the ballet! Oh, how you appreciate all of the richness in life after being away."

"Life in Milan didn't suit you?" I ask through tight lips, resenting him for running away when things became tough, only to return from essentially a holiday and act as though he had been in the deep trenches of war. After Edgar's return, I heard news that Denis was back in Espelette, and each day we saw more and more of the men we knew arrive safely back in Paris. Each arrival was cause for a celebration, but not Julien's.

"It has qualities, but it's nothing compared to Paris," he

replies without noticing my resentment. "Italian life is so relaxed I found myself growing bored."

"You didn't see Paris at her worst," I say bitterly, knowing I should be demure but letting my offense overtake my ladylike demeanor. He gently takes my hand and his eyes narrow, giving me a silent warning to cease. "It does sound as if you endured trying times," he tells me evenly. "I presume those times are behind you now."

I gather myself and smooth my hand over my hair, becoming the picture of grace. "Yes, I don't believe our family here at the ballet can see much worse." He looks at me with annoyance and thrusts his shoulders at me as if to ask why I would make such a negative statement. I explain to him that just when everything appeared to have returned to normal, we were struck with news of Cornelie's death. I expect him to embrace me and console me for the loss but he only smirks and turns his head away. "I'm surprised that it hasn't happened sooner. A woman who acts like refuse will be treated as such. It's hardly anything to mourn."

The hatefulness of his words hits me hard, and I want to scream at him and tell him how kind she was when so many of the girls fell ill while he was gallivanting in Milan. I want to tell him that she is better than him because she treated these girls as human beings while he only treats us like figurines that he can own. But I remain silent as I hear firsthand what the patrons truly think of the older girls. As much as I want to defend Cornelie's memory, I don't want to become her.

"Yes, it's a sad existence," I agree meekly. Pursing my lips together, I watch the patrons courting dancers and hear the hum of low conversation that is now synonymous with the closing of the curtain. I entertain the thought of telling him I have found another, but what would I say? There's a chance I can win the heart of the man I truly want to be with? I have not forgotten that the war has shown me that I desperately need stability. In a perfect world, I could have stability and happiness, but nothing is secure with Edgar and I cannot do away with Julien just yet. I smile broadly at him and think that if I do end up with him, I'll be safe from freezing rooms and meals of potatoes. I hold my head up high and swallow any lingering doubts as I tighten my grip on the strangulation that sent Cornelie to her grave. "You're exceptionally distinguished to see her as what she is," I say and his eyes brighten at my sly words. "Someone like her is so very beneath you. You, my dear, have impeccable taste and shall be rewarded with only the purest, most adoring of women."

"This pure adoration that you speak of," he glides toward me until his face is so close to mine I can feel his breath on my lips. "Is this something that you hold for me?"

"It is," I whisper, my eyes remaining steady but my stomach tightening.

"Then let's waste no time with our arrangements," he whispers, making a firm statement rather than an inquiry, as if he's testing me to see if I'm speaking from the heart. I falter for a moment, not expecting that my praise would have been construed as an invitation, although this is *the* invitation I need. Noella is dying for an invitation from Pierre. The tales have been passed on from dancer to dancer. As she readies herself for a romantic excursion, he visits the Ballet Master, offering a sizable donation to the ballet in exchange for exclusivity with his chosen dancer.

"Are you able to leave for Spain as we had planned, since you have only just now returned?" I ask cautiously.

"No, I am not," he answers. "We will go to Spain another time. Accompany me to dinner instead. I can have all of the arrangements taken care of in two weeks."

"I was so looking forward to Spain," I lower my eyes, but immediately jerk my head up when Julien grabs me forcefully by the arm. "Do not play games with me," he whispers harshly into my ear. "I have waited years for you and you will be joining me two weeks from tomorrow."

Julien looks at me with such intensity, daring me to deny him. I agree, more out of fear of what he will do or what will become of me if I do not comply than out of excitement to join him. My mind immediately begins to spin. I cannot wait for Edgar to come to me as I had done before. Thankfully, we've arranged for several modeling sessions this week. I have only two weeks to turn Edgar to my favor.

Julien kisses my cheek and departs from the Green Room and I hurry over to Noella, who immediately becomes enraged with me. "Any other dancer would have been his mistress years ago. He's handsome and a *jeweler,* for pity's sake."

"A forty-five-year-old egocentric man with a wife and two children," I remind her and she shrugs as if this is a non-issue.

"He's a man to whom people never say no," Noella points out. "He saw what he wanted and he went after it."

"And I'm most grateful he chose me," I assure her. "But I could do better."

"You can't possibly be considering casting Julien aside because of Edgar?" Noella looks at me as if I am crazy. "I know you're drawn to him, although I have no idea why, but you cannot seriously consider him."

I'm about to tell Noella that I believe he sees me differently now, when we hear the clink of silver against champagne flutes, calling attention to the center of the room, where the Ballet Master stands.

"I hope everyone is enjoying the evening," he booms, turning throughout the room to address everyone. "I have an exciting announcement to make."

The room becomes quiet as everyone focuses on the Ballet Master, resting on his cane, his small eyes barely visible as his wrinkled skin swells up from champagne. "The Board Members and I will begin the search for the prestigious position of the Paris Opera Ballet's new *étoile*. All *sujets* will be considered for this position."

I gasp to myself and hold Noella's hand. I finally have a chance to become the star of the ballet, the most talented and well-known dancer, guaranteed a lead in every production. My ultimate dream is right in front of me, and I immediately want to tell Edgar. A lifelong arrangement between the rising artist and newly anointed *étoile* seems so right.

"We will be judging every performance for the next month, looking for grace, beauty, and talent," the Ballet Master continues. "The *étoile*'s responsibilities will extend beyond the stage, as she will represent the ballet throughout the entire city. It will be demanding both physically and socially, with mandatory attendance at the most prominent events in Paris. Every *étoile* is unique. In the past, we have looked to dancers with large personalities. But times have changed. Paris has changed. We want an *étoile* with dignity and culture to become the new image of the ballet."

"It's as if he is speaking of me," I bubble over to Noella once the speech is finished. Noella looks at me in surprise. "Hopefully they're not looking for modesty as well," she says and I blush. "That sounded horribly conceited; I'm just so excited," I reply.

"Of course," she smiles at me. "And I think they'd be crazy not to pick you. But the selection is a month away, and you have more pressing matters to deal with before that. As I was saying before, Edgar is a silly flirtation, not an option. Julien is far wealthier than Edgar, who is living off of an inheritance. His paintings could not possibly be worth half of what the items in Julien's stores are worth."

"I'm talking about something much more, something that no other dancer has ever achieved," I say excitedly with a glint in my eye. "Edgar does not want the hassle of a traditional wife and I do not want to behave as one." I smile to myself, thinking that I will be a famous ballerina with paintings of myself in galleries throughout the city. I'll be the only dancer who is living exclusively with an *abonné,* not as the other woman. The thought of being with Edgar every day and reaching my dream without having to deal with wifely duties makes my spine tingle.

"That is the most ridiculous thing I have ever heard of," she replies, not sharing my enthusiasm. "Go to dinner with Julien and be done with it."

"But I love him," I say to her seriously.

"Need I remind you that time is not on your side?" Noella stresses. "Perhaps you could convince Edgar to be with you. And there is a good chance you will become the new *étoile.* But if that doesn't happen, and the year ends, you know where you'll be standing, or rather lying."

My confidence is muted with the thought of bringing man after man back to my room. "We're making a better life not only for ourselves but for many more generations to come," she speaks to me gently. "The anxiety you feel is simply the weight of this responsibility. You are about to capture a man who is well established and wants to take care of you. You should finally be able to breathe. You have accomplished what you set out to do."

I nod and try to think rationally about my dueling futures, one risky and one being handed to me. While I'm only twenty-four, I can see the toll the ballet is taking on me. I'm visibly aging, my face becoming more angular, and my body is not as strong as it once had been. The ballet's atmosphere has caused me to become obsessed with my looks. I scrutinize every inch of my skin, analyzing dark circles under my eyes, spreading thick cream on my feet every night to counteract the blisters and cracks I'm prone to from dancing every day. Is this the only opportunity I have to become a *lorette*? If I follow my instinct to turn my back on Julien and seek a greater alliance with Edgar, will I find that it's unreachable and I've passed up my only opportunity for a better life? While my future motivates me every day, it also scares me terribly. I can only see a few days ahead in time, anything beyond that is an indistinguishable blur. I have no idea what lies in that hazy atmosphere, but I do know that it frightens me beyond anything I have ever known.

⁓

August 20, 1871

Dearest Maman,

First I want to tell you the good news. I'm being considered as the new étoile! *I am so excited and am working twice as hard as usual. The selection will be one month from now, and I hope I will make you proud. These past years have been the wonderful opportunity you wished for me, but there have been* many things I have learned about the ballet since my arrival that I never told you of. I wanted to find my own way, and I think I have done a good job of it.

I know you are eager to see me settled as a lorette and sending more money to support you, but it seems that both of us have been misinformed about many things. I have learned that it is not up to me to choose a monsieur. The abonnés have all of the power, and they choose which girl they fancy and all other men stay far away. It isn't like you think it is, or what I had been led to believe it would be. I don't have dozens of men asking for my hand and I'm not dining with a different gentleman each day. Julien laid claim to me long ago and if I am to become a lorette, I have no other choice than him.

The next thing that I am going to tell you is the most difficult for me, but you must know. The only way a dancer is permitted to remain at the ballet after the age of twenty-five is if she becomes a courtesan, allowing the Ballet Master to hire out her services to any patron of the ballet who wants her. Madame Channing can verify this if you do not believe me. Please, please do not tell anyone else about this. It's kept quiet at the ballet and I am ashamed to have you know this.

I have found a way around both dilemmas, and that is to not become a lorette at all, but instead to be happy. I have found myself falling in love with the artist I told you about. I want nothing more than to live with him forever, as a lead ballerina and the model for his art. He both intrigues and inspires me and the more I get to know him, the deeper I fall in love with him. I think he feels the same way about me. The extra money that I have been sending home is thanks to him. He took it upon himself to have his influential friend Ludovic Halévy plead with the ballet for a raise for me. Surely, this is cause for *you to see that he cares deeply for my well-being. He's supportive of my work and truly respects me as a dancer. With him, I can continue to devote myself to becoming the lead ballerina and he can become a world-famous painter. Neither of us will have to compromise.*

I know this letter has brought some shocks, but it feels good to be so honest with you and I hope you will want the same thing for me that you wanted for yourself at my age—for me to be true to myself and follow my own path.

Much love,
Alexandrie

Alexandrie,

Your letter has me in a state of perpetual panic. What are you doing in Paris and with whom are you surrounding yourself? How can you be so influenced by girls who are selling themselves to make more money? I am mortified that things like that are going on, and I highly doubt the Paris Opera Ballet condones them. I know I've pushed you to send money back here, but not in that way! Becoming a lorette *is as much for your security as it is for ours. Is this artist you are so in love with pushing you to give yourself to him? I am certainly not happy that you're "following your own path." If anything, I can see that you need my help more than ever.*

You are nothing but a dreamer. Might I remind you that you are not a young girl anymore! When I was your age I already had a family to take care of and could not be concerned with such idle thoughts. This artist that you speak so highly of is doing nothing but using you. He's getting all of the rewards and you are getting nothing. Yet you continue to traipse to his studio to model. Julien has been begging for your hand for so long now and I cannot believe you would even question such an opportunity. And now you write to me of your doubts, and nonsense about wanting a chance at happiness and love? If you cannot do this for yourself, then think of us. What good is a grand painting of you going to do for your family? Are we going to hang it in our home that we are forced to abandon when we cannot pay to maintain our fields?

You seem to have become violently stricken with modernism. Your dreams of becoming the new étoile *are admirable but not realistic. What happens if you land wrong during a performance and break your leg? You will never be able to dance again and that is why it is so important that you have Julien to turn to. This is your only option. So you do not like one aspect of being a* lorette—*grow up and make a sacrifice. I have been sacrificing for you your entire life. Do you think I enjoyed taking you back and forth to practice every day and then returning on the weekends to clean the studio in order to pay for your classes? I have bent over backwards to give you a better life and I am tired. I am so tired, Alexandrie.*

You will go to dinner with Julien and you will throw yourself at his mercy and accept all of his terms. You need to live your own life, yes—the life I sacrificed for. You owe me this. I have worked too hard for you to throw this away on a whim. I cannot do any more for you. I have molded you for this occasion and I am exhausted.

You have your fancy existence in Paris now and if you

choose to turn your back on opportunity in order to chase a silly notion, then understand that you are not to ever contact me again.

Maman

The rustling of paper fills the silence of the night as I sit on my bed, my hands shaking as I grip my mother's letter. Why had I thought I could write to her as an adult and she would treat me as if we were on the same level? Shame surfaces through me as I reread the letter. She hadn't even believed me about the post-performances, and the fact that her opinion of me is of a flighty girl who is going to get sucked into any kind of deviant lifestyle and be persuaded to become a prostitute is truly crushing.

She's a closed-minded old woman from a small town, I think to myself. She has no pull on me anymore; her grip is gone. She isn't able to steer me toward Julien, she has no idea the world I live in and is clinging to her own stereotypes—the jeweler as the responsible man I should be with, the artist as the crazy bohemian, the Paris Opera Ballet as the prestigious production, the bad ballerinas influencing me, and me—the girl who cannot make a decision for herself and would be lost if it wasn't for her mother to guide her. Had she forgotten that it was me who cleaned the studio, who thought to model for Edgar in order to be seen when the rest of the young ballerinas blended into the background, who moved her way toward the front of the stage? I've been making my own decisions for some time now, and I don't have to answer to her anymore, I think. She wants me to do the easiest thing, become Julien's mistress, so she can benefit without waiting for me to figure out my life. She doesn't care if I'm happy or not.

I tear the paper up, thinking that I will follow one of her orders. I won't contact her again. I'll live my life for myself, not her, and I'll make my own choices without thinking about how it affects her.

No. 22 Scène:
A Work of Art

"**W**ould you accompany me to the Bal Mabille?" Edgar sets his pencils down and rubs his eyes tiredly. "I've been shut up inside and would like nothing more than a lively outdoors dance."

I remove myself from the *barre,* trying to control my delight. I have modeled for Edgar every day since Julien's offer. With only one week left before I'm due to meet him, I feel that I have become closer to Edgar, sharing with him my hopes for becoming the next *étoile* and encouraging his new ideas for painting. The only thing I can't share with him are my feelings. So many times I've wanted to say something, but I become so nervous that he won't feel the same way that I end up saying nothing. But an invitation to a ball gives me renewed confidence—it's the perfect night to tell him of my feelings for him.

"Do I have time to find a costume to wear?" I've seen the

wealthy couples promenade at the stroke of midnight each Saturday for the Opera's most prestigious ball. The tickets are beyond my means; therefore, I'm left with the crowds in the street to watch in awe as the costumed attendees arrogantly ascend the stairs.

"You're thinking of the pompous balls. You don't need a costume to enter the Bal Mabille." He grins happily and hurries me out the door. "Come along, you must change out of your practice clothes."

I emerge in a tasteful beige swept-back skirt topped by a jacket and he looks at me skeptically. "Need I remind you we are attending a ball, not a lecture. Perhaps you can borrow a flashier gown from the other girls."

"I would never be seen in a revealing gown! People would surely think you had bought me for the night."

He laughs at my protest. "You do not behave as a public woman, *une grue,* correct?"

"I most certainly do not!" I blush at his blunt words. "However, appearing in a flashy dress is an invitation to be judged vulgarly. It's practically deadly in polite society."

"What you choose to clothe yourself in doesn't define who you are. You're going to need to remember that when you become the new *étoile* and everyone will want to wear what you have on. Take me, for instance. I dress the same as the Jockey Club members, but I'm most certainly not a pretentious follower who needs to surround himself with other pretentious followers to feel important. I also don't dress as a bohemian so people will think I'm an artist. When they see my paintings they will know that I am an artist. Appearances are only that, what you *appear* to be."

I smile at his slight of Julien's friends, picking up on the jealous undertones. More evidence that he shares my feelings, I tell myself, and then quickly return my focus to my dress. I have to admit to myself that he makes a valid argument about the ways of society, but I can't bring myself to go against the moral labeling that I am surrounded with. "I'll add a few accessories, but that's it." I compromise and choose an elaborate, wide hat and shiny, royal blue gloves to match the feathers in it. I unlace my dark boots and slip into blue satin pumps with a bow and look at him matter-of-factly.

"You're strong-willed, but for all the wrong reasons," he chuckles at me and offers me his arm to depart to the ball.

It's a perfect summer night and I can hear music long before we approach the Bal Mabille. "This is what the best dance in Paris looks like. Forget about your preoccupation with society's rules and Jockey Club members and just have fun." Edgar waves his hand in front of him to reveal the ball in full swing and, as if on cue, fireworks burst from the sky and I jump at their thunderous proximity. The couples stop dancing to look up to the sky, whistling and applauding. When the fireworks dim, an orchestra seated under a mock Chinese pavilion begins to play and the dance resumes in the form of a four-person cancan, which I observe curiously to see that it's quite similar to a balletic *pas de quatre*. "This is truly amazing," I say to Edgar of the enclosure marked by trees and baskets of flowers, illuminated by the glow of gas lamps hanging from imitation palm trees. "What did I tell you?" he yells over the music and clapping. "It is the best Paris has to offer!"

Edgar must know everyone in the city; I stand by while he stops to chat and pay his respects. As we move through the crowd I wonder how I could have assumed so long ago that he was a loner. If I had not known him, I would mistake him for a charismatic official. It's not until late in the night that he finally pulls me onto the dance floor. Once we find an empty spot to place ourselves, the orchestra changes its selection to a slow, classical song. With one hand on Edgar's shoulder, I feel as if someone is squeezing my lungs when his hand rests lightly on my lower back and I close my fingers around his other hand. We move gracefully to the music and I identify this moment as the one I would choose if I had to stop time and remain in one element for the rest of my days. I'm dancing much too close to him, but I cannot bring myself to pull away.

"I want to show you something I completed last night," Edgar says into my ear, and I can't stop the huge smile from spreading across my face.

"Come with me," he says excitedly, leaving the ball and leading me to a nearby gallery. It hasn't opened yet but a few of its staff are inside, and they welcome Edgar's early-morning appearance. "Monsieur Degas, to what do we owe this unexpected pleasure?"

"I don't want to disturb your work," Edgar politely shakes the gallery owner's hand. "Would you permit me just a minute to show my model her painting?"

"Of course, take as much time as you need."

I nod demurely and follow Edgar through the gallery. The clicks of our footsteps ring throughout the empty corridor, the pounding of nails in the wall the only obstruction to their easy patter. As I walk behind Edgar, I imagine that he's bringing his beloved into the gallery to show me his work before it's made public. I see this visit as an intimate gesture on his part, opening up a secret part of his life to share with the only person who understands him.

"I brought this over today," he says, pointing to an enormous canvas leaning against the wall, waiting to be hung. "I call it *Four Dancers.*"

My vision is flooded with four nearly life-size images of myself bringing the strap of my costume to my shoulder. My mind wanders back to our early session and how he made me repeat this movement over and over. I had been so nervous not to say anything to set him off, as Paulette had warned. As I look at the finished product I think that he has indeed captured a fleeting moment, and I'm amazed at his acute perception. The image of me in the back of the painting shows my face reaching up in a look of utter happiness. The entire painting speaks of a grace and peace that I rarely feel I have.

"The right side of this painting is a landscape," I notice, my voice ringing loudly through the empty gallery. "Are you contrasting what the other artists of your group are painting with what you choose to depict?"

"That is an interesting take on it," he studies the painting thoughtfully. "But no. I have captured the love that you cannot hide in your face when I am with you and the complete happiness you have during our time together. I know it's fleeting because I'll leave you. For a moment you are as serene as the meadow in the painting, but it is only an illusion."

He looks back at me matter-of-factly as if we are debating a piece of art that neither of us has any emotional regard for. My eyes widen and I stand staring at him, completely speechless. I cannot believe these words have come out of his mouth. Slowly, my eyes narrow and I find my voice. "Why would you bring me here to show me this? Are you trying to humiliate me?"

"Calm down," he looks at me as if I'm overreacting. "You have a face that doesn't hide emotions and that's why I enjoy using you as a model for my work. I thought you would enjoy seeing it brought to life, but apparently I've offended you in some way."

"No offense taken," I say coldly, fuming that he's using my emotions as a tool to further his career. Was my mother correct? I am so angry that he should be so cruel. To be fully aware of the love I have for him and to want to crush it only because he feels he has that power over me. I turn away but I can feel his eyes boring into me.

"Now, Alexandrie," he says gently. "Don't be upset with me. This face haunts me throughout the night. You, such a free-thinking young woman, trapped in a costumed brothel. Me, the isolated artist, pretending I'm not lonely when the sun sets each night. You and I can join together and become fueled by our strong wills. We'll establish a fitting union—a marriage of a true bohemian with a mild touch of the bourgeois. We can leave everything at a moment's notice and become consumed with the adventures to be had in the world. It is a lovely little dream, is it not?"

"How are you so certain it can only be a dream?" My voice comes out small and choked. These are the words I have been waiting to hear from him. It's as if he has read my mind, only he has delivered my thoughts as if they are the greatest impossibility.

"You know I can't escape from myself," he shrugs his shoulders sheepishly. "And you would be a very wicked girl if you were to consider a distressed artist while being seen in the frequent company of a certain jeweler. I would give anything to be in his place, yet I cannot give anything, it is simply not in me."

So he is cognizant of Julien's intentions and his constant references to the Jockey Club were only to show me this. "You know it's not him I want to be with." I lower my eyes, aware that at the end of this week I will be joining Julien for dinner, securing my future. I wonder if Julien is arranging his donation with the Ballet Master at this very moment while I am here at the gallery. A wave of guilt flutters through me and Edgar guides my face toward his with the tips of his fingers and looks me directly in the eyes, speaking seriously, "That which draws us to each other cannot be sustained. It will drive us apart."

No. 23 Scène:

The Bather

It has barely been a month since Cornelie's death and rehearsals have resumed the same as any other day except for the strained atmosphere. We perform with a stillness and discipline that has not been present since first entering the ballet as scared young girls. We are no longer innocent, but our fear has resurfaced, reconnecting us with our youth and insecurities.

Throughout our obedient preparation, Edgar sits in the corner, an observer to our performance. I wish I didn't have to see him after our conversation at the gallery. He had refused me. But I had already committed to model for a series of paintings he had been using Cornelie for. He told me she had been eager to be the subject of his idea for various paintings of a woman bather. I had not known, but many nights while I seethed with jealousy, thinking she was entertaining him, she was posing while he sketched furiously. She didn't have to worry about her reputation, so the door to her apartment remained closed, leaving me to think the two of them were in her bedroom. But she was only modeling in her private bath.

"That was absolutely perfect," the Ballet Master tells us. "Good work, Mademoiselles, you are free to go." I take my time, conversing with the other girls, stalling out of nervousness at spending time with Edgar. He has revealed a side that I did not know existed, a side that desires me as much as I desire him. I take a deep breath, reminding myself that he will not give himself over to his desire, and I have no hope of being with him. "It is a nice little dream, is it not?" I smile sadly as his words replay in my head. Yes, that is all it is: a hugely unattainable dream that poses such a high risk for my future that I cannot consider continuing with it. Julien is my reality and I must remember to not lose my judgment.

As I finally round the corner to meet Edgar, I come to a halt when I hear the Ballet Master speaking to him. He tells Edgar that he had seen me leaving for the ball with him and is prying for details of his intentions. I am appalled that the Ballet Master is attempting to glean information to determine whether I will become Edgar's mistress. I can picture his brain working overtime, thinking of how he might raise the donation by pitting two men against each other as if I am cattle at an auction. Although I'm aghast to hear this interrogation, I listen eagerly for Edgar's response, hoping there's a chance that he wishes to remove me from my tiny room.

But Edgar only waves away the Ballet Master's concerns. "The dancer is for me only an excuse to draw." To hear him not even use my name, as if I am interchangeable with the other dancers, cuts into me deeply as I'm bombarded with images of the two of us—our flirtation with the idea of a life together, my hopes that he'll love me, the way my heart rate increases in his presence. But his words reassure the Ballet Master, who leaves the conversation and, approaching me, corners me. "Careful not to waste your time on that one," he hisses. "A certain patron has spoken to me of making a large donation to the ballet in return for your exclusive affections. I would hate to see you send such an important man mixed messages. This is a dangerous game you are playing."

I nod in understanding and walk away shaking from the confrontation. I now know that Julien has wasted no time in speaking to the Ballet Master and negotiating a suitable price to make me his own. Between Edgar's statement and the Ballet Master's urgent warning I feel tears of defeat brimming in my eyes. I hold them back and gather my strength, catching up to Edgar. "Shall we go to your building?" he asks. "I don't have a private bath, so I assumed we'd go to your home," I reply.

"Can we just work in the public bath," he says wearily to me and I make a face that it's less than desirable. "Please don't be difficult. I've already had more hassles this morning than I would care to have in an entire year."

"Is everything all right?" I ask and he nods. "Yes, yes, it's fine," he waves away my concern. "I just spent the morning negotiating a sale to a customer I despise, that's all."

"Well, hopefully you got a good price for it," I joke as we enter the public bath. "The highest price," he mumbles and scrutinizes the scene for his drawing. "Perhaps the calm atmosphere of the bath will let you escape from your mind," I smile at him, beginning a familiar conversation to put my defeated thoughts at ease and cheer him up at the same time.

"That would be counterproductive," he says absently, as he adjusts the shades for proper lighting.

"Oh, I just . . . because you had talked about escaping when we were at the café," I stammer.

"I want nothing but my own little corner of the world, and I shall devote myself to it," he replies, looking at me through narrow eyes. "The artist must remain thus all his life, arms extended, mouth open, assimilating everything that passes by and living by everything that surrounds him."

I stare, unblinking, at him. I feel as if I have been slapped in the face. It's as if he's warning me that our interaction is purely professional and our exchange at the café and gallery were nothing more than the ramblings of a lonely person. The last glimmer of my dream of a life with him slips away, like finely ground powder falling through my fingers.

He nods toward the bath, ready to draw. "Bathe as you would normally. Pretend I'm not here."

I comply; my cheeks flush with embarrassment as I remove my robe and lower myself into the tub. As I wash myself slowly, I hide my head from him so he will not see the tears that are fighting to escape from my eyes. I hold on to the side of the tub, head turned away, and pray that this will be over soon. I feel so exposed and can feel his eyes scrutinizing me while I hear the scratching of his pencils. My arm begins to quiver from maintaining the pose and I squat down into the tub, steadying myself with my left hand as I hold my hair up with my right. I concentrate on my feet as I hide myself from the malice that is emanating from him. When I had pictured the bathing series, I envisioned romantic paintings of myself classically posed. But Edgar's vision is intrusive and raw. Girls flow through our public bathroom and I am ashamed that they hear him talking to me so terribly.

My emotional discomfort becomes physical with my legs

cramping and I stand, leaning on the edge of the tub with one hand, the other behind my neck, turning my head away from him. I cannot do this, I think to myself as I bite my lip to keep tears from falling. The silent session seems to go on forever. When my body is shaking from the tears as much as from the cold water, he tells me to remove myself and pick up the towel. I dry myself off, still keeping my back turned toward him. I cannot bring myself to look at him.

"Very good," he says after completing his sketches of me drying myself with the towel. "I like that you turned away from me. It enhances the feeling of observation that I'm trying to capture."

He tells me he wants to return the following day to make more sketches. "I don't know," I hesitate. The last thing I want is to spend another day in the bath, clothed in humiliation as the water grows colder with each stroke of his pencil. "You have so many sketches from today."

"It is essential to do the same subject again and again, ten times, a hundred times," he says aggressively. "Nothing in art must seem to be chance—not even movement."

"How can you just assume that I will have no problem being around you after what you said to me in the gallery? Perhaps you can shut people out of your life without a second thought, but I cannot. It hurts to be around you," I find my voice growing louder and angrier with every word.

"I thought we explained ourselves and got everything out in the open," he retorts. "You should be more mindful of keeping your promises."

"What is that supposed to mean?" I glare at him, surprised.

"It means that you have promised me that you would do this series. And you have been promised to Julien," he seethes. "You can't be flighty and change your mind each day about what it is you want. I'm sorry that you're hurting, but you need to realize that you've brought it on yourself." He storms out the door and I remain fixed to the floor in shock. I begin to see that he's spent his entire life pushing people away and today he has fallen back into that pattern with me. He had been empathetic to my sadness over Cornelie and maybe in his surprise to discover someone who understood him, instinctually opened up, glad to be able to get his frustrations off his chest. But that moment was fleeting.

No. 24 Scène:

A Parisian Lorette

I refuse to continue modeling for the bathing series. Edgar's artistic belief that nothing must be left to chance has become my own as I prepare for my night with Julien. Visibly jealous, but not able to ostracize me because they yearn to learn how I have ensnared this man, the younger dancers will not leave me alone, pressing for every last detail of our courtship. I hear a sharp knock on my door and open it to see a perfectly pressed man in uniform surrounded by curious dancers.

"Mademoiselle Alexandrie?" he asks. I nod, not knowing what is happening.

"Monsieur wishes you to have this," the man says clearly, without emotion. "He is very much looking forward to tonight." I take the large, exquisitely decorated box out of his hands. He gives me a slight bow and retreats down the hall, his step quickening as he gets closer to the exit.

"*Bon Dieu,* he's bought you a dress, open it! Open it! I have heard of men doing this," Noella is bursting at the seams. "You can't mess this up! He's completely in love with you!"

I carefully open the box, which is more beautiful than anything I own, to reveal a rose-colored dress designed by the prestigious Charles Frederick Worth. I remove it from the elaborate box and its weight surprises me. It is very heavy, heavier than the ugly gown I wore to the first ballet, and has a neckline trimmed with flowered mauve fabric and lace, creating a necklace on the dress. The skirt bustles delicately in the back, which produces a draping effect in the front, revealing layer upon layer of ruffles in contrasting light pink with a long train of mauve flowing from the back bustle.

"Alexandrie," Noella whispers, gently touching the gown, and I shoo the rest of the girls out of my room for fear they'll also touch the fabric. But her eyes do not rest on the gown and I follow their direction to the bottom of the box, where a smaller container lies. Cautiously I lift the box and open it, gasping with surprise and delight to see the sparkling brilliance of a diamond necklace and bracelets. Finally, I think, the hours of listening to Julien's droning on have paid off. I cannot wait to wear them but Noella tells me they are the final step in preparing myself, that I must wait until I am dressed and worthy of adorning myself with such jewels. I have never had even a kerchief of this caliber and I tell myself this is the life I am intended to live. Noella helps me maneuver into the corset, pulling tightly, my waist cinching in painfully with each tug so my hips become more pronounced. After excruciatingly reconstructing the shape of my body, the dress molds to me like wet fabric, gathering effortlessly at my waist by a form-fitted bodice extending all the way over my hip to contour my newly corset-fitted body, which pushes my breasts so far up that I look quite well endowed.

Seduced by the dress and my curiosity to see what an expensive night in the city is like, I spend extra time piling my hair up on top of my head and applying color to my lips and eyes so I look just as lovely as the dress. Noella helps me clasp on the diamonds and I gaze at myself unbelievingly in the mirror, at the jewels dripping from my neckline and forearms. I have never looked more elegant. I could easily enter the Notre Dame and blend in with the rest of the *lorettes* in their finery. I cannot help but think that mine is only a costume; underneath it all I'm still the girl grinding peppers into a powder.

My thoughts are interrupted by a quiet knock on my door. It is time. I take a deep breath and gingerly open it. "I knew you would look *magnifique* in that dress," Julien says, gazing at me with a wonder in his eyes that makes me uncomfortable to meet them. "The colors of the fabric bring out the intensity of your eyes."

"Thank you," I force a smile. The compliment catches me off guard because it's delivered so insincerely, as if he has rehearsed saying it no matter who opens the door. He offers me his arm, I oblige, and we walk slowly through the hall past piercing eyes of jealousy into the evening air. He leads me to a grand carriage parked outside, his driver in a top hat and tails. A brilliant pair of dark brown horses whinny and kick up their hooves lightly as if they cannot wait to depart.

"Good evening, Mademoiselle," the driver addresses me as he opens the carriage door. I step into the carriage as Julien guides me up with one hand in mine and the other on my lower back. I try to relax inside as I hear Julien's footsteps walking around the back, to the other side, and the door opening. He sits very close to me with his arm around my shoulders and his other hand resting on my leg, forcing me closer to his body. "I am so undeserving of your generous gifts," I lie to him. "I cannot think that I could possibly provide you with anything as lovely as that which you have given to me."

"My dear, simply being in your presence is the greatest gift you can give me," Julien says, smiling at me as if I owe him the world. I look out of the carriage window and see the Grand Hotel on the Boulevard des Capucines. It occupies the entire triangular plot between the Boulevard des Capucines, the Rue Scribe, and the new Place de l'Opera, which will be the site of the new Opera many, many years from now. I turn to him in confusion. "You had specifically said that you desired to take me out for dinner. Why are we at a hotel?"

"Your naïveté is so sweet," he gushes. I feel embarrassed; of course the finer hotels have restaurants as well as rooms. I suspect I have given him more ammunition to view me as much beneath him by exposing the fact that I have never frequented such well-to-do places. I walk with him, arm in arm, toward the hotel entrance. Two doormen open the ornate double doors for us and I hold back a gasp at the elaborate foyer I stand in. The ceilings are even higher than the Opera House's; they must be six stories tall. The floors are sparkling marble with staircases grandly swerving in all directions. Chandeliers drip from the ceiling, throwing beams of light throughout the room. The hotel workers move quietly throughout the building, tending to guests and speaking in hushed tones.

I look longingly into the restaurant, where I can see decadent couples being served by waiters in white gloves and full tuxedos. The maître d' guides us past all of these tables into a separate room where there's one grand table with a chandelier hanging over it. He pulls my chair out and I sit down delicately, my dress flowing around the sides of the chair, as Julien takes my hand from across the table. He smiles slowly while watching my face.

"I didn't want to share you with the rest of the restaurant," he says softly. "This is beyond any of my expectations," I reply honestly, overwhelmed by it all. The waiter approaches to show Julien a bottle of wine, which he inspects, then takes a sip from the proffered glass and spits it out. I'm taken aback. How rude to spit out an expensive glass of wine! "It is good, but I am looking for a tad bit more flavor in my wine," he tells the waiter. "Of course, Monsieur, I believe I have an exceptional Bordeaux in the back. One moment, please."

The exceptional Bordeaux proves to be up to Julien's standards and we toast to new beginnings. My face is beaming, but inside I want to burst into tears. I see Edgar's face when I told him this was my last modeling session. He became apologetic, almost manic. "Alexandrie, please forgive me," he pleaded in a frenzy as I stood defensively in the studio. "I have just undergone an interrogation by the Ballet Master and I promised my dealer I would have this series completed by the month's end. I am under an extreme amount of stress. I didn't mean to take it out on you." He moved closer to me, flashing me a charming smile. "Surely you can forgive my actions?"

Normally I would have. But, like my mother, I am tired. "I cannot give you any more," I told him solemnly and walked across the street to my room, leaving Edgar with a bewildered look on his face.

"Come see the view," Julien says and I follow him to the circular floor-to-ceiling windows and peer down at the city as if I'm the most important woman in all of Paris and am looking down on the city that I own. The bridge that I cross so often over the

Seine River appears astonishingly short and small. I can see couples dining in the amber glow of night at the outdoor cafés, which seem quaint and simple in comparison to my dinner plans. I could have gazed at the city all night. It's a magical experience seeing the streets that I explore each Sunday from an aerial view. I'm almost upset when the waiters interrupt by bringing out trays of food.

Seated again, I look down at my plate with apprehension. The steak tartare that Julien requested doesn't look like it has been cooked at all and I wonder if he's trying to kill me. He remains still, fork poised above his plate, waiting for me to take a bite. I delicately taste the cold steak and find it to be like no other meat I have ever had. It nearly melts in my mouth and has so many flavors that I'm tempted to eat the entire platter. I sip my wine as the waiter presents the entrée, coq au vin, and I'm amazed to find that poultry does not have to be bland as I taste the delicate meat flavored with Burgundy wine, garlic, and thyme. I spread olive butter on the bread and meet Julien's eyes.

"You have made me a very happy man," he says, not breaking eye contact. "When I saw you onstage I could not take my eyes from you. You stood out among all of the other dancers. You move with a grace and concentration as if you know something that everyone else is oblivious to. I began to hear murmurings of an exquisite nude painting of you that has become quite famous in my circles. I fought for months with that terrible artist to get him to sell it to me, until he finally relented. I often look at it and think that soon I will have the real girl."

Why would Edgar sell him this painting? He loathes Julien. Furthermore, when did Julien purchase it? I think back to Edgar telling me he negotiated a sale with a man he despises, and then he told me I should keep my promises. Did Julien visit Edgar to warn him that I am now spoken for and he's entitled to own the painting of me? The thought sends chills up my spine.

"This is how I see you in my life," Julien continues with authority. "I still want you to dance so that I can point you out and boast to my fellow club members that you are mine. However, I cannot permit you to reach *étoile* status."

My mind, which had been trying to unravel how Julien acquired Edgar's painting, becomes frantic at the thought of not being considered as the new *étoile*. I open my mouth to object, but he does not give me the opportunity.

"If you are in the public eye I run the risk of being recognized in your company," he explains. "I've told you this before and have compromised with your recent promotion. But I cannot have the *étoile* as my mistress; it is out of the question. I own an apartment around the corner from the Opera House that I have been told is quite elegant and that is where you shall call home. As you prove yourself worthy to me your living arrangements will improve. You will acquire clothing and jewels and nights out at fine restaurants. You will not speak to other men; conversations in the Green Room will no longer be allowed. Your modeling will also come to an end."

He pauses to smile at me. "I know you are grateful, but let me finish. I'll have a key to your apartment and will come and go as I please. You will not interfere with my family or my life. I will not tolerate any whining that you feel neglected. I'll provide you with a wardrobe and you will wear what I deem appropriate for specific occasions. You represent me now and I do not want you looking like a common street person when you're shopping or getting a cup of coffee. I will outline what you are to wear for each task of your day. I need you to be freshly bathed, shaved, and perfumed before you go to bed each night. I may stop in for a brief rendezvous if I feel the urge, so I need you to be ready and waiting for me. I will provide you with lingerie that appeals to me and you are to wear these to bed each night in anticipation that I may visit you. I like my women to be very put together, and you will be no exception."

He clears his throat and looks down at his hands nervously, like a child admitting to misbehavior. "I am partial to certain practices in the bedroom, so you will find an abundance of silk scarves in the apartment for, ah, these purposes."

"You wish me to wear a scarf to bed?" I ask, thinking that it is odd, but not so much to cause such nervousness in his request. The side of his mouth turns up, "Again, I like your naïveté. The scarves are not for fashion."

It takes all of my strength to keep my gasp silent while Julien speaks with a faraway look in his eyes, lost in his own fantasy. "I often gaze at that painting of you, imagining you are tied to that bed, waiting for me. I see how you bend when performing."

"You wish for me to be tied to a bed for an indefinite amount of time?" I whisper, horrified at the picture he has painted.

"It only adds to my excitement," he says, his eyebrow raised at me. I cannot reply and only stare across the table at him, no emotion whatsoever on my face. This is not how I pictured the glamorous, adored life I have worked so hard to obtain. A life as Julien's *lorette* will go far beyond ownership and into a world where I star as the object of his sick sexual fantasies. What if he were to be interrupted on his way to the apartment? Perhaps a family emergency would divert his plans to visit me and I would be left tied to the bed. I could starve to death and no one would ever find me! *Bon Dieu,* I cannot spend the rest of my life literally bound to his whims.

"I also do not wish to produce any children with you. The

ramifications of this would prove to be very uncomfortable; it would take much explaining if our children were to approach my own children at some point. My heirs will take over the jewelry empire as I did with my father, and I will not reciprocate this tradition with bastards, tarnishing my family's good name. To ensure this does not happen, I have made an appointment with a doctor who is a trusted friend of mine to perform a simple procedure that will render you unable to reproduce. It is nothing to be frightened of; he will effortlessly remove an organ or two and both of our minds will be set at ease."

Chills take over my entire body and I place my hands in my lap so Julien will not see how they shake with fear. My mother had told me that we all must make sacrifices, but I am faced with sacrificing not only my independence but my dreams and even my body. "Surely we do not need to go to such extremes," I say softly.

"This is not negotiable." Julien moves from his chair, leaning over the table, gently touching my hand. "These are my terms that you will live by."

I nod my head obediently. As if the bedroom arrangement was not bad enough, I will no longer be able to work toward becoming an *étoile* and will never be able to bear children. The only way out will be if he deems me unworthy, and now I know I must make that happen.

"I have booked a room for us tonight," he says calmly. "I have also made arrangements with the Opera for you to move your things to your new home."

Stalling for time, I take a long drink of wine. Suddenly I do not have nearly as much at stake, as the image of myself strapped to a bed waiting for Julien is in great contrast with one of accompanying Edgar on holidays and gallery openings. Although Edgar is not an option, becoming an *étoile* is. I think of Cornelie's space at the end of the hallway, which resembles more of an apartment with living quarters, a separate bedroom, and even a small kitchen. Most coveted is the large balcony with its bistro table and chairs, where I would sip afternoon tea every single day. I wouldn't need Julien because I could live happily there and dance without the fear of leaving with an *abonné* when the curtain closes. An *étoile*'s earnings would never make me wealthy, but I could live a modest life.

"Take it easy," he barks, "there's nothing more disgusting than a woman stumbling around drunk."

I smile at him, but more to myself, as he excuses himself to go to the bathroom and I gulp down another glass of wine and tuck the remaining steak tartare in the palm of my hand. Unsure whether I am at the stage of "nothing more disgusting," I pour another glass, immediately followed by a third, and I am wiping the corners of my mouth when he returns. As I close my fingers around the steak, I can feel my eyes becoming heavy and my speech slurring. He's ready to go back to our room, but I tell him I need a moment to freshen up. I stumble into the powder room, hastily break the steak into three pieces, and place the meat under my armpits and in my undergarments. The steak is extremely cold as I exit and make a quick turn down the hall, pleased to see it is long and empty. I run back and forth through the hallway, breaking a sweat quickly in my heavy gown, losing track of how many laps I have made, and finally return to the powder room. I look blurrily at myself in the mirror, my face flushed and my lips and teeth stained with red wine. Well done, I have fallen quickly from the poised woman who arrived in his carriage. I remove the now warm tartare pieces and bend my head toward the front of my dress to smell my armpits, then I jerk up quickly. The combination of sweaty meat and body odor has mixed with my perfume, creating the scent of an extremely dirty woman who has tried to cover it up with perfume. I hope this will be enough to make him rethink taking me as his mistress.

As we walk toward our room, I can see his eyes watching me swerve from side to side. I have never been so drunk before and part of me wonders if I have overdone it. Surely he will see through my attempt and know that I have done this on purpose because no one would become this intoxicated at dinner. Through blurry eyes, I see the room is just as gorgeous as the rest of the hotel. The bed is huge and I just want to lie across it by myself and sleep in the softness of feathers and mountains of pillows. The view of the city stretches into our room and I take it in, but immediately have to turn away because it is making me dizzy. I spin right into Julien, who kisses me on the mouth, long and hard, and I take in deep breaths when he breaks away. "I take your breath away, do I?" he whispers.

"No, you caught me off guard." He glares at me. "It is the wine talking. Take off that lovely dress and say no more."

I do as he says, trying not to laugh as I see the sleeves of the dress are a deeper shade than the rest of the fabric. His face takes a sharp hit as the smell of my impromptu run reaches him. He moves a step back and looks me up and down. "You have much to learn about hygiene. Do you not understand how important tonight is?"

He is taking my lack of grooming as a personal insult. I think to myself that things are going well. I do not answer him and only shrug.

"You must understand that the rules we went over at dinner are the rules that you must live by. I picked up a perfectly coiffed and perfumed woman. Where did she go? Now I am here with a sweaty pig."

"She only lasts for a few hours," I slur, plopping myself on the bed and lying down. My head is spinning and my ears are buzzing. He is lecturing me on how I must change myself for him, to not let him regret his decision to keep me, and that he is not obligated to follow through. His words jumble together in my head and I am not listening to him anymore. I lie on my back, the hard busk of my corset constricting me, my hands firmly pressed to my forehead, trying to make the room stop spinning while keeping an ear out to see if he's telling me he has changed his mind and I am free to go or if he is actually going to follow through with this. He begins to pull me up, talking about some nonsense of me getting into the bath. *Bon Dieu,* he's persistent, I think. He is literally going to drag me into his world. I want to tell him that I know how to take a bath, this is not news to me, but I choose not to because I don't want him pawing all over me and giving me rules to live by. I sit up and open my mouth, prepared to yell these insults at him because, after glasses and glasses of wine, this sounds like an excellent plan. But instead of insults, vomit pours out of my mouth, onto his arms and hands, which are pulling mine up.

"I've had it! You disgust me!" Julien pushes me away from him as if I'm a rodent full of disease. "Get out! You have just thrown up the most expensive meal you will ever eat! You are a common, stupid girl to not know what opportunity lies in front of you! Your looks may be deceiving but I will not be swindled by you."

He is shaking with anger as he reclaims the jewels he gave me and throws a bathrobe at me. I put it on and wander out to the hallway, wiping my hands on the robe. I dab my mouth with the sleeve and hiccup, satisfied that I have successfully driven him away.

I decide the night air is good for my spinning head and I meander through the elegant Paris quarter where people stare, horrified, as I clutch the vomit-crusted bathrobe to my body, swaying in my high heels. I draw fewer looks as I return to my less elegant neighborhood, where I belong for the time being. Loosely dressed waitresses stick their heads out of the partially opened doors of the opaque-windowed brasseries, revealing the sound of loud, boisterous customers inside. Had I not been so drunk I would have been scared to pass through the Boulevard Montmartre at this hour. "You forgot your clothes, darling!" "No need to be so blatant—everyone knows what you're selling!" Hoards of the boulevard's street prostitutes heckle me and laugh as I quickly walk past them. I've never been so happy to return to the dancers' building, with paint peeling in the hallways illuminated by the eerie glow of cheap gas lamps. I pass a light-haired man with his head down, walking quickly down the hall, and just as I recognize him as Pierre, I see Noella's door swinging shut. I glimpse her fingers catch the door before it closes all the way and she pushes it open and pulls me in, slamming it shut behind her.

"What are you doing here?" she exclaims.

"You would make a great captor; I barely blinked before I was accosted by you," I giggle. I suppose I am still drunk. "Was that Pierre? And why are you dressed as a *courtesan*?"

"Yes," she replies impatiently. "He took me to a masked ball, and I am not dressed as a *courtesan*. This was not one of your paltry courtyard dances that you attended with your artist."

My eyes find a sparkling feathered mask thrown haphazardly onto her table and I nod. "You would not believe how the Opera

House was transformed tonight. I felt like a queen. Pierre is so close to making arrangements for me, I can feel it." Her eyes glisten with excitement at the memory of it, then turn to focus on me. "But never mind that. Again, what are you doing here? What happened to you? You look a nightmare and you smell worse. Are you drunk? Did he beat you?"

"The short version of it is that I got sick." I hold up my arm to show the robe as evidence. "And he was disgusted, so he no longer wants me as a mistress. You know, too high standards."

She looks at me disbelieving. "Alexandrie. What did you do? You were in perfect health when you left. Was he that terrible?"

I stumble to Noella's French doors, leaning against their frame. Her room is identical to mine, only as I gaze out the window I don't see the Opera House, but white cafés and rows of pale yellow houses, spreading out smaller and smaller. The roadways cross in all directions and the dark silhouettes of pedestrians scatter across the ground.

"He was exactly as any of us would have expected." I move away from the doors and lie down on her bed, cradling my throbbing head. "He took me to the most beautiful hotel and I had food and wine that rivaled the feast my eyes took in. He told me the rules of how my life would be, which included dismembering my insides so that I will never bear his children. And he expected me to become his mistress that day and move into his paid-for prison tomorrow. I know so many of the girls here would give up both motherhood and independence for that life, but I can't. Please don't make me justify this decision by telling you the details of what Julien wanted. Just understand that it was horrid enough for me to throw it all away."

She exhales and nods in understanding. "Tell me you did not leave the dress there."

I laugh hysterically, partly because it strikes me as funny and partly out of relief that she comprehends my actions. "And he took the jewels. But I have this robe, which is just as elegant as the dress! Everyone in Paris was looking at me with envy."

She stands up and yawns. "I'm exhausted and you sincerely stink. Go to the bath. Try not to choke on your own vomit. Well, it seems you've gotten rid of most of it on your robe, so you should be fine."

"I am truly lucky to have such a caring friend as you," I grin and sway down the hall to my own room, eager to put the night behind me.

No. 25 Scène:
Shaky Ground

Aclosed my eyes with dreams of becoming the star of the ballet running through my head, but when I open them I can barely lift my head from the pillow as I lie in clammy sweat, my head throbbing and my throat raw. I want to stay in bed and sleep all day but we're not allowed to miss practice unless we have written notice from a doctor. I do not even consider going to the trouble to request a house call. I doubt I will qualify as greatly ill, but rather be chastised for receiving an excessive alcohol consumption diagnosis.

I peel myself out of my blankets and go to wash up. I feel like a filthy animal as I wash dried vomit out of my hair. I had sweated so much during the night that I smell on top of the intentional stench I worked up in the hotel. As I dry off, I run the night's events through my head. It's almost hard to believe it all happened. I hope Julien is still thoroughly disgusted with me and a night's rest doesn't make him think a second chance is an option. As much as I can remember from the blurry bedroom encounter, he was raging mad and completely revolted by me.

I quickly guzzle three glasses of water. But it does nothing to alleviate my scratchy throat and I leave to attend practice, hoping I can make it through. I find the outdoor air refreshing and I feel like a dog who sticks its head upward to catch the breeze as I make my way to the studio. I'm one of the last girls to arrive and I immediately take my place at the *barre* to stretch. The Ballet Master likes to see all of his dancers warming up so that we are ready to begin as soon as he stomps his cane to the ground. With one leg stretched out on the *barre* I lean backward, my head dizzy and throbbing. "How are you holding up this morning?" Noella whispers behind me as she *pliés* forward to graze her ankle. "I feel terrible, but I'm glad to have emerged unscathed," I whisper back. "I only hope it's completely over."

"Oh, I imagine it is," she chuckles. "I don't know many men who would give you a second chance after the antics you pulled. Ginette saw you return last night and assumed dinner went badly, and she's already making plans to insert herself into Julien's life. You have nothing to worry about. When one dancer falls there are a dozen more ready to take her spot."

"Vultures," I laugh quietly.

I had been caught up in my fear that I had not heard the last of Julien, but once the cane hits the floor twice and we line up to perform, I do not have room in my head to ponder the thought anymore. It takes all of my concentration to keep up with the routine and not fall out of step. Even though I accomplish this, I do it mechanically, and the Ballet Master chastises me in front of everyone for lacking passion and grace. I think I can just nod, apologize, and it will be over, but he snaps his fingers and points in front of him.

"To the center, please. I will not accept your halfhearted attempt. You are a disgrace to the ballet. You disrespect me with your pitiful performance. Do you think you can go onstage like that?" He imitates my rigid movements and lackluster face. My cheeks burn red as the whole group is silent, waiting for my response. As I contemplate if I should respond or if it was a rhetorical question, an alarming thought enters my head that the Ballet Master must know of the events last night. This will not raise me in his esteem, and I need that today more than anything as I prepare to replace Cornelie.

"No, I do not, and I apologize," I answer, more to stop the thoughts running through my mind than anything else.

"Then show me how you *will* perform," he says sternly. I walk with my head held high, cheeks burning, to the lineup with the girls and he cries out, "Not with the dancers. Show me *solo*."

I breathe in deeply, a mix of anger and embarrassment, pivot, and walk back to the center of the room. I take my stance, one leg bent; one pointed to the side, arm over my head, the other falling to my ankle, and look to the Ballet Master, waiting. It's as if I'm trying out all over again. I'm well aware that to be called to the front of the group is a severe warning that a dancer is in grave danger of losing her spot.

He nods to me and I begin to dance without the aid of music. I imagine an orchestra playing the notes of my feelings, the desperation and hope that clash against each other. I swoop down, letting my shortcomings take over me and leap into the air to show that I will not be held down, that I can rise above this obstacle and reach toward greater things. It takes every ounce of strength that I have to deliver what the Ballet Master wants to see. Everyone is silent and the sound of my feet on the hardwood floor echoes throughout the room. I finish, trying to hide my shakiness, partly from last night and partly from my fear. If I do not meet his approval, I'll be yanked from the night's show and out of the running for the new *étoile*. I could even be thrown to the back of the production, only one step ahead of a *petit rat* and will need to work twice as hard to advance to a *coryphée* position. The Ballet Master waves his hand for me to rejoin the group and I breathe a sigh of relief.

We have five hours before the night's performance and I rush out of practice to sleep, but the Ballet Master's voice stops me. "Mademoiselle Alexandrie," he bellows, and the rest of the girls whisper amongst themselves. "A moment, please."

I hesitantly walk toward him. "Leave us be!" he yells at the dancers who are meandering by the door, waiting to overhear the conversation, and they scurry away like mice. "Monsieur," I say to him.

"Early this morning, quite a large donation was removed from the ballet." He looks at me knowingly. "I am appalled at the behavior that caused such an abrupt change in the disposition of one of our most respected *abonnés*. Behavior that is neither refined nor cultured. Behavior that is unfitting to represent the Opera Ballet."

I bite my lip and try to keep my head raised. "Monsieur, please understand that I have never acted in such a way, and I never will again," I plead. "The ballet is my life, and dance is the only thing I love. Part of this *abonné*'s terms were that I could never rise to *étoile* status. If I had known that before, I would never have encouraged him, and you would not have lost your donation. I know I didn't go about things appropriately last night, and you have every reason to be embarrassed by my actions, but please don't take me out of the running. Becoming the new *étoile* means everything to me."

He sighs while running a hand through his thick white hair. "You have put me in a terrible position," he looks at me intently. "There are still many performances to be judged before the ceremony. I suggest you do not make any more mistakes."

"Thank you, sir, you have no idea how grateful I am," I blubber, overcome with gratitude. The Ballet Master waves his hand toward the door. "Don't thank me, just leave and be prepared for tonight's performance."

I hurry back to my room, knowing I will need to regain my strength. I lie down in my blankets and close my burning eyes, thinking of how I slowly stepped closer toward the audience throughout the years and how in one day I was almost pushed to the back. I want to ask the other girls if they have any medicine that will ease my symptoms, but I know they will never share anything to help me perform better. If I have a bad day and am thrown out of the ballet, it will only benefit the others by moving them into a more visible role in the performance and with the patrons. The background dancers will jump at the chance to move closer to the audience, just as I had.

I awake hours later feeling much better. My headache has subsided and I'm not as dehydrated as before. I take extra time preparing for the performance, pulling my hair tightly back and making sure it's securely fastened with hairpins and flowers matching the light blue of tonight's tutu, giving off a look of both elegance and innocence to show the Ballet Master that I take my station seriously. When he walks backstage he takes notice of my clean, fresh look and I can see approval in his eyes. The performance goes flawlessly and for the second time in the last forty-eight hours I thank God that I have emerged unscathed.

As I check my reflection in the mirror of our dressing room,

I see Julien huddled over a very young dancer, whispering in her ear. My heart beats rapidly with fear and I try to move out of the dressing room quickly, even though I know he has been in attendance for the entire performance and has seen me dance, so he obviously knows I'm here tonight.

He must have felt my gaze on him because he looks away from the young dancer and fixes his eyes on me, giving me a dirty look as if I'm a disgusting rat. The young ballerina also looks my way and smirks at me. I drop my head and exit. I'm content knowing the truth and leading the other dancers to believe that Julien has such high standards that I cannot meet them. The young dancer undoubtedly views herself above the rest of us to have entranced such a finicky man. I have no desire to defend myself, I'm only thankful to be rid of him, I tell myself as I enter the Green Room.

I circle around, paying my respects to each group, trying to portray a refined lead ballerina. Relieved when I have greeted each person, I prepare to retire to my room. Walking toward the exit, I see Ludovic Halévy, who tells me my performance tonight was outstanding.

"Thank you, Monsieur," I beam at him. "I never was able to thank you for speaking to the Ballet Master about my raise. Thank you so much, that was extremely kind of you and I appreciate it so much."

"It was all Edgar's doing. It is quite important to him that both you and your family are taken care of. You have grown up quite a bit from the shy girl I saw enter Monsieur Degas' party," he smiles back at me. The smell of wine on his breath makes me feel nauseous, and I notice he's very drunk.

"Yes, that was some time ago," I reply. "Are you a collector of art?"

"No, Edgar and I have known each other since we were children," he slurs. "He's one of my oldest friends. He's a wonderful man, wouldn't you say?"

"I am not entirely sure what to think of him. Sometimes he looks at me in such a way and opens up completely, but just as suddenly he closes himself off from me," I reply without thinking, then regret it. I cannot speak to this man as if I'm speculating with Noella. "Forgive me. I should not have said that, I suppose I only want to understand why he does this to me."

"Don't feel that you have to censure yourself," he says kindly as he puts his hand on my shoulder. "There are many reasons, I am sure. He told me that he had an unwelcome visitor to his home who threatened him to stop spending so much time with you, as you were no longer able to choose who you kept in your company. Even before this, once talk of arrangements being made for you surfaced, Edgar began to feel pressure from the Jockey Club to not meddle in the affairs of its members. Julien knew Edgar was the reason you were stalling and he wanted to put an end to your time with him."

My face burns with anger. My suspicions were correct, but I had no idea they ran deeper than the one-time visit to purchase my painting. "Forgive my bluntness," I say quietly to him. "But if Julien had not interfered, would I be with Edgar today?"

Monsieur Halévy looks at me with concern and takes a deep breath. "I'm afraid not. I have asked him that same question. He went into a long explanation, saying that he saw something in your eyes, that look of adoration, and it made him afraid. He likes your outlook on the world and would want nothing more than to talk to you all night, every night. But he said he fears that falling into that pattern would lead to pressure from you for a stable life, which he is loath to provide. He doesn't blame you; he blames the atmosphere of the ballet. He said it's ironic that the same ambience that drew him into the world of theater has ruined the one person he believes he could spend his life with."

"But he said I am the one person he can envision spending his life with," I say, a hopeful smile rising on my face. "I must go speak to him."

"Alexandrie, no," he says softly, as if talking to a child. "You have to understand that he won't. You can't change his mind."

I nod to him, but cannot forget his words. My heart races as I think of just how I can convey this message to convince Edgar that a life together is not just a little dream.

No. 26 Scène:
Nothing Must Be Left to Chance

I tell Noella about the conversation I had with Monsieur Halévy. "I do think that you both would be happy together, but I still believe the chances of him changing are minuscule," she says doubtfully. "You've been through so much this week; it would be wise for you to take a day or two and think clearly about this."

I take her advice, but when Sunday arrives, I still disagree with her. I find myself walking quickly down the street, my heart beating rapidly in anticipation. If he rejects me I know I'll be distraught, but I need him to tell me in no uncertain terms. I need to confront him.

I don't want to wonder anymore if this is the day that he has become bored with me and realizes I offer nothing for him. I don't want to spend nights thinking of him and how he's so different than other men with their superficial talk. Each night I hold on to the thought that he is feeling the same way, seeing me as the inspiration for his art, needing me to be with him, knowing no other woman can ever make him as contented as I can, only for him to close himself off completely from me. But I ignore these underlying thoughts and believe that my instincts have to be right and we are to be together.

When I arrive at his house, his maid leads me to his studio, where I see him poring over the bathing sketches. "I was just looking at you," he says while shuffling the drawings away, as if he's not at all surprised to see me here. "The sketches are exactly what I wanted. Cornelie's sketches were good, but her outlandish personality had gotten in the way. She tried too hard to pose with her leg propped on the rim of the tub or her back arched as she dried her hair. Yours are more realistic, the way a woman would look if she thought no one was there watching her."

"I need to speak to you about something other than the drawings," I bravely delve into the reason I have paid him a visit, my hands shaking and voice quavering. I try to be poised, but I am so nervous my ears ring.

He looks at me standing rigidly in his studio. "I saw your shoulders shudder and I suspect that it was less from the cold water and more from my cold manner," he refers to the bathing pictures in almost a tender way. "I had not wanted to, but I felt compelled to, and the sketches are proof that this attitude produces the best art."

"This is actually what I'm here to speak to you about," I interrupt before he can say more. "I come to you today free of any entanglements with Jockey Club members. I wish to only follow my heart and live a life of happiness. You don't need to isolate yourself from me."

"But I do," he says sternly. "Sometimes I think, could I find a good little woman, simple, calm, who understands my whims, and with whom I could spend a modest life of work? I always respond, 'Isn't this a nice dream?' "

"It does not need to be a dream," I stress again, moving closer to him. "I understand you. I wouldn't hold you back. And you would not control my life. Can you not see that it would work? Remember you spoke of us joining together when we were at the gallery. I know you think of it, I know it's what you want; why can you not give yourself to it, to me?"

He sits down and shakes his head, running both hands through his hair in a frustrated manner. His fingers are covered in paint and I half expect to see blues and greens streaked through his hair when he raises his head back up at me.

"Alexandrie, of course I think of you and entertain the idea of you and me together. What man would not? I would be lying if I said I wasn't drawn to you, but that isn't enough to spend a lifetime with someone. You have a determination that I envy, you have pushed through obstacles to get yourself to the position that you are at now. The truth of the matter is that I am not good with relationships. I'm not that man, for you or for anyone. I don't want to be that man."

I begin to fight off tears. "I love you, completely, with everything I have. You have been at the forefront of my mind since the first time I saw you, before I even knew who you were. And don't you see that I'm not like those girls? I would never hold you back; you and I can exist together," I plead in an attempt to change his mind, my frustration growing. Why could he not see things my way? Why can I not turn his mind to my position? If only I could crawl into his head and make him see things as I do.

"I cannot exist with anyone, it is not in me," he replies coldly, looking at me through narrowed eyes. "You are a dreamer who tries to be strong and independent, but I see that while you're determined, you are also weak and too controlled by your emotions to be involved with either the ballet or my way of life."

"You can be very cruel," I say, meeting his gaze and challenging him, my voice rising. He's infuriating me so much that I want to hurt him, to belittle him, to show him he is not extraordinary, that he is an idiot for not wanting me. "I see your way of life as a myth—this lifestyle of solitude toward the practice of art has come into existence only when writers began to describe it and painters to depict it and you are using it to hide. I think you care deeply for me but are afraid to tell me. I'm afraid that time will pass without anything being said and I will move completely past you and these feelings. I will be completely gone when you finally come to me with the nerve to bare your soul. I haven't forgotten how we danced together, the conversations we have had as if we are close friends, these moments of tenderness that only last a brief instant before you become afraid that you have been too kind to me. I know that is not who you are, I can see below your surface, just as you can see below mine. I fear that you are the one I am supposed to be with and that I was cast in this role in the ballet for the sole purpose for our paths to cross."

I take a deep breath and do not break my eyes from his. I am at once both afraid that I have gone too far and proud that I have stood up to him. He looks at me with startled eyes and immediately rises from his chair and walks toward the window, gazing outside at the dimming light. "I have decided to not see you again for both my own good and yours," he speaks without turning away from the window. "I have filled a book of sketches and will have plenty of material to complete the dance series. Professionally, there is no reason for me to return to the ballet."

"Why does it have to be either one or the other with you?" I rise and storm over to him, not willing to let this go, believing I can still convince him. I want to crack through his exterior, and the fact that he has withdrawn from the conversation sends me into a rage. "You are making a huge mistake, one that you will no doubt regret. You will be left alone, in this studio, thinking of this day and what would have happened if you had not behaved in such a stubborn way. You'll look around at your work and think to yourself, 'This is what I refused her for?' Yet I am offering you a chance to do both. What if there is a chance that you could be happy with me and continue to live the life you do now?"

He turns from the window and looks at me with such anger that I take a step back. "Do you think I've never been in this situation before?" he screams at me, and I cannot answer. He storms to the other side of the studio and throws open a door. His breathing is heavy as he lights a lantern and moves inside a closet. "Come here," he says, his voice more even.

Hesitantly, I move toward him. My eyes follow his arm, to the lantern, and gasp in horror at what it illuminates. I look at his face, then back into the closet. "What is this?" I whisper, my eyes locking on stacks of canvases with the central female figure washed out of the picture. I want to slam the door closed again, to lock this vault of dusty paintings with the ghostlike woman staring back at me.

"She was once everything to me," he says while gently closing the door. "Until she ran away with my brother. Why do you think I didn't want you to meet him?" He leans forward and blows out the flame in the lantern. My tears return as I realize Julien was not the one who hurt my chances with Edgar. They were ruined far before I even arrived in Paris.

"Love has ruined those paintings, and they are worthless now.

I have erased her from my life. Quite literally," he attempts a small joke, but it is only met with my tears.

"But I'm not her" is all I am able to squeak out, looking at him through blurry eyes. "And you will not become her," he says sternly as he moves toward the window again.

"I would never leave you," I sob, quite pitiably, but I don't care. He turns away from the window and looks at me with sad eyes. He smooths my hair back and gives me a wistful smile. "As I told you before, nothing can be left to chance. Not even you."

Act IV

No. 27 Scène:
Clarity in Absence

I wipe my eyes and try to remain calm as I leave his home. There's a lump in my throat, growing and growing. I try to hold it in as I walk down the street. Just wait until you get back to your room, I tell myself, then you can cry as much as you want. A part of me suspected things would turn out this way. I wish they hadn't, and even though I anticipated it, it doesn't make it hurt less. The tears well up in my eyes and I try to distract myself. Make it home, I think, only a few more minutes. If I run into someone from the ballet, they'll wonder why I'm crying, and I don't want to tell them. And I can't think of any reason that would be acceptable. I can't cry. I distract myself by trying to become entranced with a fruit stand. "Why such a sad face?" the vendor says to me and I force a smile. "I know you! You are going to be the *étoile*. You are so beautiful, you have a wonderful life, everything is ahead of you. You should be smiling from ear to ear, not filled with sadness." He's so right, I think while bringing my hand to my lips, the tears that I've been holding back pouring out like a river gone mad. I have everything to hope for, all of my dreams are within my reach, I shouldn't be crying right now, yet I can't control it. "It can't be tears from a man," he says, which only makes me cry harder. "Surely no one would ever cause such a pretty girl this much pain." I move quickly away from the vendor without answering him, my vision blurred. By letting one tear escape, they turn into sobs where I have to catch my breath, my nose running, and I pray I don't cross paths with anyone I know. Get home and go to sleep, I tell myself. Get it all out now and tomorrow is going to be a much better day. It has to be because I don't think it can get worse than right now. I try to think rationally, telling myself I know that this is for the best, that I needed it to be final, that years from now I'll look back on this and be glad that he told me what he did so I can move on with my life. Despite all of this, it doesn't make it any easier. My chest seizes while I sob and now I know where the term *heartache* comes from.

As each day goes by, Edgar remains true to his word and to my great disappointment he does not come to the Opera House. I have never been so direct and aggressive to a man before and I wonder how it is that he has not chased after me, and even more so, how he's able to cease all contact.

As the weeks continue on, any last fear of Julien completely subsides. He pursues the young ballerina vehemently and soon she's removed from the dancers' building and we only see her during rehearsals and performances. The rumor is that she plays by every single one of his rules, devoting herself to his every wish, and that he sees her as a young, impressionable woman who will not betray his idea of a dutiful mistress. She shows off the jewels and clothes that he buys for her and arrives to practices wearing ostentatious earrings. Her diamonds sparkle so brightly that the Ballet Master has made her remove them because they reflect light and distract from the dance. She smiles smugly at the rest of us, takes them off, and makes a big show of finding a place in her shirt to hide them, because "They are so dear, so expensive, that I dare not leave them out in the open. One of you jealous girls will steal them." I expect the Ballet Master to yell at her, but he's tied to Julien by this donation and is unwilling to upset his mistress. Now she has power over not just us but the Ballet Master as well.

While I don't envy her position, I am jealous of her accommodations, which she describes as having floor-to-ceiling windows, with a balcony overlooking the city. I can imagine myself seated on that balcony with a cup of tea, relaxing in the afternoon sun. But I know the serene moment will be interrupted by Julien entering at any moment with his key.

Any chance she gets she describes to the girls how Julien tells her that her skin is so soft and that she smells like roses. "Unlike other girls he has met who were so foul he nearly became sick," she giggles, looking directly at me. I never defend myself to these claims. I figure if I make it known that I had intentionally made myself foul, the other girls will think I'm lying and trying to make excuses for the fact that I was rejected and should have been the one in the lavish apartment wearing brilliant jewels. Eventually the fascination with her newfound life will wear off and everyone will stop asking her questions. I decide it's better to remain quiet and wait for it to pass.

Instead I listen eagerly as the Ballet Master announces the

roles for Saturday's performance. My stomach is in knots as I wait to hear if I have attained a lead role. Saturday will be the last performance before the decision for the new *étoile* will be made. The papers are full of speculation and Paulette, Jeanine, and I shriek with delight when we read our names in print as the most likely contenders. The ceremony will be held this Sunday, and the papers describe it as an exclusive event, with only Paris' most prestigious receiving an invitation.

The Ballet Master is naming the solo acts and I lean forward in anticipation, thrilled that my name has not been called yet. "And finally," he says with a sly smile, "if you have been paying attention to the names I have called, it will come as no surprise that Paulette will be dancing a lead role as Coppélia and Alexandrie will join her as Swanilda."

Paulette and I cannot contain our excitement, and jump up and down hugging each other. "Ladies," the Ballet Master chuckles. "Please control yourselves, you are rivals after all."

We let go of each other, still laughing, and I run over to Noella. "Isn't it wonderful?" I exclaim.

"So now it's fine for you to talk to me," she scowls at me. "Why have you been avoiding me? You've closed yourself off in your room and will barely look at anyone. You went to him, didn't you?"

I reluctantly nod. "You were right, he doesn't want me."

"I'm so sorry. I shouldn't have said anything." She moves me toward a quiet corner and sinks to the floor. "Men bring nothing but heartache," she sighs. "I've been doing everything in my power to seduce Pierre and do you know what I just found out? He hasn't a penny to his name. His season tickets were given to him as a gift. He's an imposter and has wasted years of my life."

"Noella! I'm so sorry. Why would he do that to you? You've been up-front about your intentions from the beginning," I cry out in shock.

"I know," she seethes bitterly. "He blubbered like a pathetic child when I found out. He said he was enjoying posing as a rich gentleman and having a beautiful young girl respect him and want to be kept by him. He was so charming that no one suspected him. The Ballet Master is furious that he allowed such a man into the Green Room. God, my mother is going to kill me. She's so anxious that I have not become a mistress yet."

"Why can't they be honest and up-front?" I muse, realizing how much I miss our talks.

"Edgar was! If he told you that he does not want to be with you, then you know your answer," Noella says angrily to me. "He's a coldhearted man. And now you know."

I look down at my hands and think that my girlish notions of a happy life with Edgar are only that of a young dreamer. I know now that it's impossible to bend someone to your will. He had correctly pegged me. "You seem to be coping well," Noella studies my face.

I give her a small smile. "Years of no encouragement eventually lead to giving up on the situation."

She twirls a strand of pale hair around her finger. "I suppose that's true, although I only have a sense of what love might be," she admits and I nod in agreement and think that I'm ready to stop looking for Edgar and wondering about how he's leading his life, what he's working on, where he's traveling to, and who he's spending his time with. How had I let him engulf my entire being? "My mind will be glad to be free of the pull of Edgar Degas," I say confidently.

"Soon your mind will be consumed with much more important matters," Noella looks at me gravely. "We will both be turning twenty-five soon."

"Your birthday is months away from mine; there's still a chance that you'll leave," I remind her.

"Alexandrie, I gave myself *completely* to Pierre. I'm tainted and have given up my chances." I exhale deeply, realizing why she is so bitter toward Pierre. "I was so stupid. When he went off with Cornelie, I thought I wouldn't be able to hold his interest if I didn't. He has taken much more than years from me," she says. "I'll be speaking to the Ballet Master shortly to let him know that I am now available to the *abonnés*."

I look toward the ceiling, wondering how the two of us have gotten to this place. I think of the day I first met Noella, how intimidated I was by her beauty and self-assuredness, and how we have stuck together throughout our time here. We had always been so sure of our abilities, so sure that we would never have this conversation. "It's deviant and everything that we did not want to be," I remind her.

"We started out disadvantaged and we continue to be at a disadvantage," Noella says. "Remaining at the ballet is clearly the best option."

As Noella leaves to speak to the Ballet Master, I return to my room. I stand against the door, scanning my belongings and taking in all that my life has been since arriving in Paris. The room strikes me as that of a vain person, with perfume and cosmetics cluttering a small mirrored stand, and hats and dresses bursting from the wardrobe, which is filled so full its doors will not close. My eyes wander to the table and focus on a book used to raise bottles of fragrance above hairbrushes and eye color. I remove the bottles and open up the book that Monsieur Aston had given to me so long ago. I had not thought of academics since I arrived at the ballet, and I realize how much I miss it. Making myself comfortable in my small bed, reading the tattered pages under the glow of my small bedside gas lamp, my mind wanders back to what Monsieur Aston said to me about not losing sight of who I am and always remaining true to myself. Always wise, he knew what my fate held, as I recall his sad eyes telling me he wished the world was different. He would be greatly let down to see where I am today, what kind of a person I have turned out to be. My throat tightens as I realize I *had* stayed true to myself. I wish that I could have been the person he saw me as, but I chose to stay in the ballet, and his teachings were only one more element of my training. I grew up to be like my mother.

My thoughts are interrupted by a knock on the door and I find Noella on the other side looking weary. "It's official," she says as she sits down at my table, crossing her legs and leaning her head down. "After the next performance, I will be a *courtesan*. My innocence is now a thing of the past."

"I'm not sure what to say. I suppose congratulations are not in order?"

She smiles at my dry comment. "It's not so bad. There is a certain mystique that comes with being a veteran dancer." She raises her head and curiously takes in the book lying open on my bed. "And what is it that occupies your time tonight?"

"A former teacher of mine gave me this book when I was only a child." I drop my eyes, remembering his kind smile and encouraging words as he shakily sipped his tea. "Everyone else always focused on what I looked like and how I presented myself. That's what I've always been focused on. But he didn't care about things like that. He taught me how powerful an educated mind is and that I can use my thoughts and ideas to create something beautiful. I used to become so inspired that I would return to my home and write poetry for hours."

I close the book and sigh. "I've lost myself along the way. My mother wrote to me ages ago that Monsieur Aston, my teacher, passed away. I was only upset for a brief moment and then turned my attention back to my tryst with Julien and the possibilities of Edgar."

"Don't be too hard on yourself," she says sympathetically. "It's our way of life."

No. 28 Scène:
In the Public Eye

"It seems the public has a low opinion of the Opera these days. They think we are above them and full of ourselves," the Ballet Master tells us.

"I thought we wanted people to think we are above them," Paulette questions him.

"We want them to envy us, to want to be like us," the Ballet Master explains. "We don't want them to hate us. There's a difference and, with the publicity from the competition, we can correct this. I've issued statements to the press that we have narrowed the *étoile* competition to three finalists. Congratulations, ladies, one of you will be the star of the show."

I cannot help but clasp my hands together and smile from ear to ear, and I see that Paulette and Jeanine both have the same reaction. When the Ballet Master asked to speak to us alone, I had automatically assumed I was in trouble again.

"You are all going to be very much in the public eye, and their opinion of you will factor in as much as the ballet's. I've invited the most prominent reporters to be introduced to you three at the Opera, and then you will need to conduct further interviews as requested before our performance. This is a bit out of the ordinary for both you and the ballet, but I've told you before how this is a different time, and we must take the proper measures to remain in the city's fair graces. I have also arranged for the three of you to perform in a cabaret number at the Au Lapin Agile."

"Oooh! A cabaret! How exciting," Jeanine giggles, and I look at her with disgust. She sounds so stupid, and she wasn't there to see the Au Lapin Agile's little production where they made fun of us.

"We'll show the city that we are a part of them and in turn promote our *étoile* finalists. It is really quite genius," he says more to himself than to us, proud of his idea.

"Monsieur," I ask carefully. "Have you given any thought to our safety?"

"Of course," he answers. "You will not be left alone at the Au Lapin. You'll be taken there by carriage, which will wait for you right outside the building. Here's the most important part to remember: You will go onstage, performing one cabaret number, you will smile and laugh and act like it is great fun. But then you will immediately depart to the carriage. Do not stay afterward and drink with the patrons. There is a fine line between respecting the public and becoming one of them. The press will be there and they would much rather write about how the three of you made lewd asses of yourselves after the performance than about the actual performance. We want the press to say what an honor it was to have you there, how much fun you had, and how talented you think the cabaret dancers are, and the audience will say how they loved watching you onstage. That will be what is published and if I read anything other than that, then my decision regarding which one of you will be made the *étoile* will be much easier."

Thoroughly frightened to say the wrong thing, we meet with a coach to prepare us for interviews with the press. "Everything must have a positive viewpoint," he tells us. "The image we want you to portray is one of confidence and gratitude. Remember those two words in every answer you give. The tricky part is to do this and also let your personality come forth. Let's practice. Tell us why you think you should become the new lead ballerina."

"Dancing is my first love," I answer. "From the time I was a young girl, I dreamt of being onstage in Paris. My determination and hard work have brought me this far, and every time I perform I can hardly believe that I'm lucky enough to be dancing with the Opera Ballet. The ballet is my entire being, and I will put every ounce of myself into leading the performances and representing the Opera."

This question is the first to be asked while we sit nervously at our press conference. "I am so happy to be part of ballet," Jeanine gushes through her thick accent. "They give me a place to live and many opportunity I would not have in Russia." Her eyes begin to water and I want so badly to roll my eyes, but I have to remain composed, so I look at Jeanine with a smile on my face as if she is speaking profoundly. "The girls are like sisters to me and the ballet is like family. To be *étoile* would mean I will never have to leave my family. I want to make my family proud, in Russia and in ballet."

To my great dismay, the crowd is eating it up, looking at her as if they all want to give her a hug and take her home to their families. Paulette gives a confident smile and smooths her hair back, looking slyly out to the audience. "I deserve the best of everything," she says arrogantly. "And if I am going to be a ballerina, then I will be the best. Nothing else will do." She smiles and raises an eyebrow, which is met with laughter by the audience.

And so we are branded—Jeanine as the simple, sweet girl from Russia who only wants a family to call her own, Paulette as the glamorous woman with expensive tastes, and me as the overly ambitious dancer.

"You're being overshadowed," Noella tells me. "Everyone I have spoken to either favors Jeanine because she's like a little lost orphan, or they like the idea of a fashionable *étoile* like Paulette so they can see what she's going to wear to each outing. You're hardly mentioned. And when I mention you they say, 'Oh, the other one.' They can't even remember your name."

"I know, I completely messed this up," I moan. "But I don't want to come off as arrogant like Paulette and I would rather pull out my own teeth than blubber on like an imbecile about being poor like Jeanine."

"You have to give them something," Noella says. "They don't know anything about you."

"I don't want anyone to know about my background," I reply, thinking of the stares I endured when Luce was with child. "I don't want anyone to look down on me."

"You can't be in the public eye without them knowing anything about you," she puts her hand on my arm and looks at me with sympathy. "I know it's scary, but you weren't born at the ballet. They need to know who you are, and it will be better if you are the one to tell them. If you become the *étoile,* which you will not if you don't offer more in your interviews, then they will find out for themselves. They'll dig into your past and print it. Why not be the one to say it? My past is worse than yours. You really have nothing to be ashamed of."

I nod, knowing she's right. My stomach is in knots when we leave for the night's performance because I know the press will be there to judge the abilities of the finalists for themselves. The Ballet Master has granted them time to speak to each of us before the show, in a balcony loge so the *abonnés* are not seen in the dressing room and the mysterious Green Room is not found out.

"Lovely to meet you, Alessandria," the reporter says. "It's Alexandrie," I correct him. Noella was not exaggerating and I know I have to face my worst fear. "If you had not become a ballerina, what do you think you would be doing with your life?"

I swallow and lay my palms flat on my knees so the reporter doesn't see how I'm shaking. "I probably would be illiterate, working on my father's pepper farm, without any prospects," I reply, straining to not sound embarrassed or nervous. I see his eyes respond and he suddenly becomes interested in my story. I describe Espelette, making it sound a bit more magical than it really is, and then I tell him about my training in the small studio, my education with Monsieur Aston, and how my family's survival depends solely on me. "You see, I studied every possible angle so that I would one day be able to be a model ballerina. This preparation has put me in the position to become the *étoile.*"

Dance and academics have been her childhood, and since arriving in Paris she has been immersed in the culture— all combining together to create a lead ballerina. She is someone who can physically carry the performance, is learned and knowledgeable to attend the grandest events in Paris, and one who respects the city's culture. Alexandrie has created her own academie, *and were she to receive a certificate, it would surely read* étoile. *As the sole means of support for her family, her determination has never been about herself. Watching her dance, one can see that this is the only moment she has to be completely selfish, to love what she is doing, and have her burdens lifted away. Alexandrie, no longer the third finalist, is an inspiration to all young girls who cannot see beyond the farmland of their backyards.*

"Bravo," Noella says after I read her the review. The tide has shifted and my candor now makes Paulette look spoiled and Jeanine stupid. The entire city is rooting for me and I am more than glad to step to the front. Unfortunately, first I must step out as a cabaret dancer.

"Now, I know the rumors about you girls are false," one of the cabaret dancers had laughed good-naturedly. "You have zero seduction in your dance! You're so technical, if this is going to work you all need to loosen up a little and have fun."

We had all laughed bashfully. Despite my reservations, I actually liked these girls. They were easygoing and weren't threatened by us. I stood with Paulette and Jeanine, watching them show us the steps we were to do. They were not as talented as we were, but what they lacked in ability they made up for with attitude. I studied how they engaged the audience with each move and then I practiced it over and over in my room, all so I can have a stellar review written.

"All we have to do is show up," Paulette says as we ride in the carriage to the Au Lapin Agile. "It doesn't even matter if we know the steps or not."

"It will be funny to wear the skimpy costume," Jeanine grins at us. "Why would that be funny?" Paulette spits at her and rolls her eyes at me. "Because they're so much louder than ours," I smile kindly at Jeanine, and give Paulette a look that says, "Humor the child." Jeanine annoys me, but I know she means no harm. Plus, she has a way of making her face completely fall when someone is short with her, and that automatically makes me feel guilty for getting impatient with her.

The night is hot and we all depart from the carriage, fanning ourselves. Backstage at Au Lapin Agile is like a colorful dream of the Opera House gone awry. We enter the dressing room where the girls are changing and Paulette looks around in disgust. "This looks like a good time," she declares sarcastically. "Just imagine, if we missed one step in our auditions this could have been our lives." I can't help but shudder at the thought.

"We've got a full house! Are you ready for your first cabaret?" The lead dancer grins excitedly at us while handing us our costumes. We smile back and take the clothes, corsets made from a scratchy synthetic material. With only red tights covering our legs and heels too high to serve any practical purpose, we walk toward the curtain, ready to go on. Instead of one large production, the audience enjoys many small ones, and we watch each group go on, being met with cheers and whistles. "I can't believe we have to do this," Paulette whispers in my ear. "It's so demeaning. Look at these people, not being able to control themselves. All these girls have to do is thrust a hip out and they go wild; yet the girls can barely even dance."

"They'll just make us look better in front of the press," I say motioning toward a large group circulating amongst the patrons. "That's the only reason we're here."

"Tell that to Jeanine," Paulette giggles and we look over at her dancing in place, thoroughly enjoying the performance. "I'd love to switch brains with her for just one day so I can know what it's like to be so simpleminded." Even though it's rude, I can't help but laugh.

"We're on," the lead dancer motions to us before she walks on the stage. "And now for our grand finale, please welcome our special guest stars from the Paris Opera Ballet," she says to the audience, who react with a mix of cheers and boos. I immediately become nervous at the negative sounds, and I imagine glasses and bottles being thrown at us. The bawdy music starts and our group goes into the beginning of the number. I wait for the cue, and then the three of us walk out, feigning extreme confidence while I watch the crowd's reaction. We push through the other girls and dip down, our bottoms guiding us back up, and apparently this is all we need to do to win over the crowd. The screams and applause get so loud that I can't even hear the music and I find myself laughing despite the ridiculousness of this performance.

"Anytime you want to leave the ballet and dance with us," the cabaret girls say, hugging us, and the press takes note. Glad to be out of the cabaret costumes, we talk briefly to the reporters before jumping back into the carriage, everything perfectly orchestrated by the Ballet Master.

I suspect he was pleased to read the rave review the following morning peppered with quotes from his three finalists playing into our fully cultivated images. "I love the costumes; they're so bright and fun," Paulette was quoted as saying. "All the cabaret girls are so nice," Jeanine piped in. "The whole atmosphere was playful and I'm so excited to have been a part of it," I said, showing both confidence and gratitude.

No. 29 Scène:
Presenting the New Étoile

The sun has barely risen as I stand in front of my French doors, nervous excitement running through my veins. Only days away from my twenty-fifth birthday, today could be the end of my time as a respectable woman. Or it could be the day I am named the new *étoile*. Either way, I cannot spend the entire day pacing back and forth in my room, waiting for the ceremony to begin. I had delivered my best performance at last night's ballet. I thought Paulette took the role as Coppélia, the doll, too literally and ended up looking stiff. Jeanine didn't even have a lead role, so that has to put me in the position to win.

Giddy with this thought, I decide to enjoy the day completely, without any more thoughts about the ceremony tonight. I feel the air is already warm and move to my wardrobe, selecting a short-sleeve dress in a rich shade of dark yellow, and a lace shawl to cover my arms. I put on a hat with yellow ribbons to shield my eyes from the soon-to-rise sun and venture out into the early-morning air.

"*Bonjour,* Mademoiselle," a café owner says to me as he opens its glass doors. "*Bonjour,*" I reply happily. "Are you open?"

"For such beauty, I will open early," he beckons me in. I giggle and enjoy being the first customer as I sip a cup of dark coffee and treat myself to a pastry. Any extra pounds it will bring on will not show themselves as quickly as tonight. I sigh to myself and wonder why I have not done this before. The streets are quiet, with only low rumblings of a few early-morning carriages. I watch as wagons of wares are set up along the streets, and I think that life outside of the Opera House is quite lovely.

When the noise from the carriages overtakes the morning birds and the people on the street multiply so that they lose all individuality, I take leave of the café, but am not ready to return to my room just yet. I tell myself there is one more extravagance that I deserve.

The door makes a clinking sound when I open it and I see there is a bell fixed to its frame to alert the shop owners that a customer has arrived. "*Bonjour,*" a woman who looks to be my mother's age when I last saw her appears. "What can I help you find today?"

"I am looking for a gown," I say excitedly to her. "But not just any gown, one fit for an *étoile.*"

"*Bon Dieu!* Will you be attending the ceremony tonight?" she asks eagerly. "I am a finalist for the position," I say, a little embarrassed to appear to be bragging but proud of myself at the same time.

"Then you will need a magnificent gown!" She claps her

hands together and begins to study my face closely. "I think green will look exquisite with your eyes," she says. I smile back at her and nod. It's fitting that I made my debut into the ballet in a green dress and now I will become its star in the same color. Only this time it will be the envy of the crowd, not an eyesore. Yes, green will be perfect.

As the daylight begins to fade, I give myself a final glance in the mirror, turning to see the entire dress. The dark green lace over the white fabric creates a lighter color. "For the summer season," the shop owner had said.

"You look beautiful," Noella says, seated at my table with her chin cupped in her hands. "When you return here tonight you will be a star."

"Thank you so much," I begin to tear up, which causes her to burst out laughing. "Stop that now! You have a big night ahead of you; now go, you can't be late to your own party."

I dab my eyes and give her a hug. I make my way down the hall and pause for a moment in front of the double doors leading to the *étoile*'s apartment. Wistfully, I drag my fingertips across the door. "Please God, let me live behind this door," I say to myself.

The Opera House is filled with music when I enter and I ascend its grand staircase and arrive at the ballroom. In all of my years at the ballet, I have never been to a party in the ballroom. The ceremony begins with a seated dinner, and I look at the rows and rows of round tables with long white tablecloths set up with beautiful candelabra centerpieces. The room glows in the soft light and I look around to see which of Paris' most prestigious have been invited. The Opera's Board Members are seated together at a table and I notice Edgar's art dealer in attendance. To my great surprise, I do not see anyone from the Green Room.

"Let's all sit together." Paulette and Jeanine are at my side and I smile at them in relief. "I was just thinking I don't know a soul in this room," I whisper to them. As we search for our table, every guest in attendance greets us. They ask us politely about our lives as dancers, and we answer each inquiry over and over. We tell them how we practice each day and how we could not be happier to be finalists for the lead ballerina. We find our table and while the guests dine on oysters, consumed with conversation of their own, I become incredibly impatient for dinner to end.

Once the chocolate soufflés are finished, the Ballet Master moves to the front of the room, clinking his glass for the crowd's attention. "Now it is time for the announcement that we have been awaiting." I sit higher in my chair and the gentlemen at the table wink at us as I reach to either side of me and hold Paulette's and Jeanine's hands. My heart is beating rapidly and I can feel the pulses of my fellow finalists racing. "This has been an extremely difficult decision," the Ballet Master says. "The Opera has so many talented young women that it is a shame they could not all be *étoiles*. But the Board and I have watched our talented soloists and have narrowed it down to the three most gifted. These three young women seated here have shown grace, beauty, and ability," he motions his hand toward my table and the entire room turns to look at us. My face reddens slightly, yet I enjoy the attention.

"But we can only have one lead ballerina," he smiles at us. "The young woman whom we have chosen dazzled the audience last night with her performance as one of the leads." I feel Jeanine sink down in her chair, and I bite my lip as I prepare to hear my name. "She captured the movement and the character of her role so fully that I felt she had become Coppélia."

My eyes widen in shock and Paulette brings her hands to her mouth in glee as the Ballet Master says, "May I present Paulette, the new *étoile* of the Paris Opera Ballet!"

Everyone rises to their feet and claps wildly as Paulette walks over to the Ballet Master and hugs him. Jeanine and I stand, numbly clapping as we watch the crowd descend around Paulette. I smooth my green dress and instinctively swallow back tears, but none are left.

I push open the heavy doors and move down the stairs of the Opera House, the summer night's air turning cool. "Mademoiselle Alexandrie," a man's voice calls to me and I turn to see Monsieur Durand-Ruel trotting down the steps. "I was sorry not to see you win," he says sincerely to me.

"Thank you, but Paulette is a wonderful dancer," I reply modestly. He smiles kindly and hands me a thick envelope. "Monsieur Degas wishes you to have this," he says. Curious, I peer inside and see stacks of francs. "It is his earnings from the sale of your nude portrait," he explains.

I shake my head, the memories of my heartache from Edgar and my experience with Julien resurfacing. "I can't take this," I tell him, handing it to him. He takes a step back with both palms in the air. "I cannot take it either," he says. "As his dealer, it's my job to see that the artist is paid for each sale. He told me to see that you receive this, for it is the least he can do." Monsieur Durand-Ruel quickly moves down the stairs and climbs into a carriage while I stand dumbfounded in front of the Opera House.

I return to my room, not as a star, and sit in my lovely green dress staring at the francs. There is enough here for me to live on for a year, maybe two if I'm careful. But then what? I will be in the exact same situation as I am today. Peeling my eyes away from the envelope, I think to myself that I have closed so many chapters in my life, with Julien, Edgar, and now the ballet. But there is one more chapter that I must close.

Dipping the tip of a pen into ink, I write *Forgive me for the choices I have made.*

When the ink dries, I fold the message and slip it in with the francs. I reseal the envelope and address it, writing the word *Espelette* for the last time in my life.

No. 30 Scène:

Joyeux Anniversaire

The following Saturday, I sit rigidly at my table hearing footsteps approaching closer and closer to my door. I am as attentive as a bloodhound waiting to take off when the hunt begins. Even though I'm expecting it, the knock on my door is so loud that I startle before standing, smoothing down my skirt and answering.

"Happy birthday to you," the Ballet Master barely looks at me as he brushes past me and stands in the middle of my room.

"Thank you, Monsieur," I reply and stand awkwardly in front of the door. He motions for me to close it, takes a seat at my table, and speaks in a hushed tone. "You have quite a decision on your hands today. As a dancer of twenty-five years, if you stay with us you must enter into the practice of post-performances. It is not something we speak of, but I suspect you are familiar with the tradition?"

"Yes, Monsieur, and I am ready to enter into the ritual. I haven't spoken of it to anyone outside these walls," I reply.

"I should hope not. The Opera Ballet has a reputation of being the utmost in class and sophistication. We don't need to be associated with the municipal system's *réglementation* of public women."

"I see the gravity of following the rules of the ballet has never been more important as the second stage of the life of an Opera ballerina," I say as if reading from a manual, my heartbeat increasing with each word. "I am putting my trust in your experience, and you, in turn, can trust in my good judgment."

"I am delighted to hear this and that you have chosen to stay with us," he beams at me. "You will find it a profitable way to make a living. You are now one of the most desirable women in the country. Ordinary men can only dream of being with a dancer." I smile at him even though I cannot hide the sadness in my face.

That evening when I arrive backstage I'm filled with nerves. As intermission comes to a close and the orchestra alerts the patrons to return to their seats, I reluctantly go back onstage, looking out into the audience, wondering which man, if any, has booked me tonight. I do not want the show to end. I know I'll need to go through with the post-performance eventually, but I don't want it to be tonight. While I move gracefully through the second half of the performance I cannot hear the orchestra, only the Ballet Master's words: "At tonight's performance, the *abonnés* will approach me at intermission to schedule time with the dancer of their choice. You are not to interfere or speak to me at all. When the curtain closes, you will see an envelope on your dressing table. It will contain your payment and the initials of the gentleman whom you are to entertain that night. He will make himself known and you will take him to your room. The francs must never be seen changing hands and you must never speak to me of payment. There is to be no trace of the transaction."

As the curtain closes, I take a deep breath and tell myself to just get it over with, that I have to do this or I will be thrown out of the ballet into a world of no options. Either I entertain a rich patron or I live on the streets. Those are the only choices I am left with.

I approach my dressing table with apprehension and observe Julien's mistress as she changes into an evening gown rich with lace. As she steps into it, her face takes on a look of pain and she drops the dress and carefully lifts the bottom of her corset up, pressing lightly on her lower abdomen. My hand flies up to my mouth and my body grows cold as I see an ugly gash as the source of her pain. She sees me watching her and quickly steps into her dress, glaring at me. I immediately turn away, shaken with the image of the wound that I came so close to wearing.

I turn my attention to my dressing table. The white envelope seems to take up the entire area. I peer inside and see a stack of francs and a card with the initials *CT*. "Mademoiselle?" I hear a tentative voice behind me and hastily tuck the envelope into my small purse and turn.

"We've met before," I say, studying the man in front of me. He looks to be only a few years my senior and his full head of curly light brown hair looks so familiar to me, but I cannot place him.

"That we have," he answers and his sharp accent flashes me back to a laughing Edgar saying, "How do you Americans say it? Meester Taylor."

"Monsieur Taylor," I recall. "It's good to see you again."

"You remember," he smiles happily at me. "I do," I reply. "You were the first person to purchase the paintings I modeled for."

"Pastels, not paintings," Monsieur Taylor teases and I manage a small smile. "I'm afraid I am the cause for your frequent modeling sessions. I've created quite a demand for your portraits over the years."

I look at him curiously and become paranoid. He cannot know what became of my modeling sessions, can he? Is he trying to take the blame for the heartache it caused me? I look at his eyes, shining with what I can only call innocence, and I feel he cannot possibly know.

"I'm so proud of my collection," he continues. "Monsieur Degas is very talented, but I feel that it is you who brings those portraits to life. The same exact picture could be made using another girl, but it would never be a masterpiece. Your intelligence, kindness, and your elegance cannot be reproduced."

I smile sadly at him, realizing he is very naive. Those are the very traits I had wanted Edgar to see in me when he painted those portraits. Now I see it did not matter how he saw me, for it was only at Monsieur Taylor's request that he continued to return. "I am none of those things, Monsieur Taylor," I say as I move toward the Green Room.

"But you are, and so much more," he follows behind me. "Your lack of pride is what makes you so beautiful. And please, call me Charles."

I stop in my tracks and find the card in my purse, looking down at the initials, *CT*. "Charles Taylor, you have purchased my paintings for your collection, and now you wish to sleep with me?" I ask quietly.

He looks at me with a shy smile. "No, I wish to marry you."

No. 31 Scène: Searching Blindly

I never knew if Edgar returned to the ballet. My life's path took an abrupt turn that night and I welcomed the move to America. My whole life I had been concerned about being in favor, with my mother, Edgar, the Ballet Master, and the entire city. I wanted to leave and start over. Yet each time I visit Paris, I cannot help but look inside the gallery windows to see if the familiar strokes of vivid colors shaded with gray that he dreams of are present. As I read the paper over a cup of coffee one morning, my attention is held by the headline "Louvre to Acquire Degas Collection." I know I cannot stay away.

As soon as I enter the Louvre, I see him and my insides immediately tighten at the familiarity. He's surrounded by a group, talking animatedly as they listen to his every word. I see that he has aged considerably and, with a full white beard and a receding hairline, he looks very much the old man he now is. But he still has the vacant aloofness that had intrigued me the first time I laid eyes on him sketching furiously in the audience so many decades ago.

"He has since gone blind," I overhear someone say. "He spends his time walking alone through the streets of Paris."

This information causes me to freeze in my path. It had finally happened and my heart goes out to him. For someone who spent his life capturing the unseen emotion in the world, losing his eyesight is the worst betrayal of all. I linger, trying not to be obvious as I eavesdrop. The crowd's gossip moves on to say that he has turned to sculpture because he can still feel form even though he cannot see it. One man describes how he will feel the model's body and then mimic it in clay. "Even though he was seated very close to the model, he can only dimly distinguish her shape, and has to get up at every instant to feel with his hand the curve of the hip or the position of a muscle that his thumb will model in clay," he explains, as if Edgar is an atypical creature rather than a man.

"I paid him a visit one day and was shocked to see him dressed like a tramp, grown so thin, another man entirely," another pipes in. "He was a dirty, disheveled, sordid Prospero in his studio filled with bizarre sculpture, shriveled wax figures crumbling into dust, and unfinished, unwrapped canvases leaning against the wall in sad disorder."

"True, he doesn't go out. He dreams, he eats, he sleeps." I peer closer and recognize the man as Camille from Edgar's group so long ago, now known throughout the world as the Impressionists. "I visited him as well and found him seated in an armchair, draped in a generous bathrobe, with that air of the dreamer we have always known. His hair and a great beard, both of a pure white, give him great presence."

The familiar tug of anger resurfaces as I think it is fitting for him to go blind since he could never open his eyes to me. If he had looked, just once, deep into me he would no doubt have seen the love I had for him and that I would not do him injustice. He has chosen to grow old alone, walking blindly through the city instead of having had a life with me. Feeling hostility toward this decision of his, I approach him and congratulate him on his success through gritted teeth.

"Alexandrie? Is that you?" He reaches his hand toward me, finding my hand, while I reply that it is. "I recognize your voice," he smiles, looking at me through failed eyes, remaining still and focused with no trace of the rapid movement I had grown accustomed to seeing in him. "I am delighted you came today. Your kindness touches my soul deeply."

I blush at the unguarded compliment and suddenly feel like a young girl again. I'm glad that he cannot see how the decades have aged me, erasing any distinguishable feature I once had. "Thank you," I say shyly. "That means the world to me."

"I would love to have dinner with you after my show and hear about your journey," he says. "I will share with you all that I am capable of. I'm ashamed to admit that I am not very talented with words. Ideas I have, but words fail me. I have only memories these days to occupy my thoughts. You do not realize how terrible it is to be alone as you grow old. There is nothing to think of but death."

"We're all growing old with you," I say with amusement, thinking of how it has taken him an entire lifetime to openly admit to his shortcomings. I no longer feel the need to reassure him that he is talented far beyond any other man and I study him quietly as I wait for him to continue.

"Very true, but I've really made a mess of my life on this

earth," he looks down as a sadness washes over his face. "I ask your pardon sincerely if, beneath the pretext of this damned art, I have wounded your very intelligent and fine mind, perhaps even your heart."

"Now, now, stop with the self-pity. Wounds are meant to heal. It's funny, when I was a young ballerina those words would have brought me much joy. But today they seem quite empty to me. Monsieur, it would appear you have no effect on me." My voice is teasing and light, yet my eyes are narrow. He chuckles, not being able to see the truth of my words. I want to grab him by the collar and shake him, yelling at him that it was because of him it took me years before I could trust my husband. Each time he was quiet or late getting home, I automatically assumed he had grown tired of me and I began to mentally prepare myself to be alone, when in fact he had only gotten held up at work or was tired. I wanted to shake out all the years I wasted feeling this way. It was only when I knew what it was like for someone to love me, when I knew that I deserved to be loved and that the only thing he wanted was to simply be with me, only then did I want to live every minute of every day and stop hiding from everything by devising backup plans in case things didn't work out.

I agree to meet him after the exhibit, as two old friends catching up. I'll tell him every last detail about my life in America, and talk about how odd it is that the Eiffel Tower is now the symbol of Paris. I'll listen to how he has spent his years and the struggle of losing his sight. As I begin to look forward to being reunited with him, I take in the exhibit of what he has dedicated his life to.

As I walk through the exhibit I am swallowed by Edgar's perception of the world. I feel a wave of nostalgia as I see myself and the rest of the dancers in motion, moving to the orchestra. I realize how young and insecure I was as I scrutinize myself in the bathing series. I had felt old beyond my years, but the paintings show that I was just a girl, afraid to make the wrong move for fear of disappointing him.

My smile quickly fades as I arrive face-to-face with everything I do not want to be reminded of, everything I thought I had moved past. I hadn't posed for this picture. I stare with wide eyes at my room in the dancers' building and I feel as if I am back in that very room struggling every day to get out. Against the wall is my small bed, and in the middle is the table that I would spend hours writing letters at. Only I am not writing in this painting. I see myself, fully dressed, thrown over in despair, crying as if my heart has been ripped out and I can never find my way back to it. It is such a helpless image of the emotions that I had tried to hide from the world. I realize that Edgar had studied me beyond my form and motion. He has painted himself blocking the door, looking at me with those unfeeling eyes as if he does not know what to do with the pain I carry with me. He had known that he was the cause of my despair and as long as he was present I could never escape from it.

I am fixed to the ground, unable to move, transported back to the endless days of waiting for him, the elation of seeing him, the frustration of not being able to reach him, and the desperate feeling that I had to hold on to each minute with him because it might be the last time I was with him. My eyes burn from tears falling down my cheeks and I wipe the tears away, pushing through the crowd gathered in groups sipping wine and pointing at paintings, and I exit the Louvre. I walk briskly away from the museum, slowing down only when I sense I have enough distance from the building. I breathe in the city air and let it all out in a deep exhale. My nose is running and I wipe it with my sleeve. I have long stopped caring if I appear refined, and I blink back more tears.

I have learned that those things I refused to see shaped my life as much as what was clearly laid out in front of me. Looking back, I always wonder if perhaps I could have accepted a quiet existence amongst the pepper fields and how my life would have turned out if I had. I would visit Paris in awe, with eyes obscured by fuzzy hair. I would look at the buildings for their architectural decoration instead of seeing men slip out, hoping to go undetected. I would see the Opera Ballet dancers for their grace and beauty and not the scars that lie underneath their costumes.

As the exhibit closes and he is left waiting for me, I am boarding a boat, on my way home to the family I have raised far away from the underbelly of Paris. I think of the lush garden of flowers in my yard and my children and my grandchildren, all oblivious to my previous life. I feel a calm wash over me that only the closure of completing a life's journey can bring. I will never be able to explain to him why I needed to leave, that he had taken so much out of me that I cannot return to the girl in the painting, wondering if today will be the day he will leave me.

Sources

The following sources were invaluable to me in researching Degas and the Paris Opera Ballet and encouraging my imagination to take flight from there. *Degas Letters* was especially helpful in conjuring up Degas' character and allowing me to infuse the narrative with some of Degas' own words. I would particularly recommend *Impressionist Quartet* to anyone interested in learning more about the birth of Impressionism.

Adams, Laurie Schneider. *A History of Western Art*. New York: McGraw-Hill, 2006.

Clayson, Hollis. *Painted Love: Prostitution in French Art of the Impressionist Era*. New Haven: Yale University Press, 1991.

Gluck, Mary. *Popular Bohemia: Modernism and Urban Culture in Nineteenth-Century Paris*. Cambridge: Harvard University Press, 2005.

Guerin, Marcel, ed., Marguerite Kay Hilaire, trans. *Degas Letters*. Oxford: Bruno Cassirer, 1947.

Herbert, Robert L. *Impressionism: Art, Leisure and Parisian Society*. New Haven: Yale University Press, 1988.

Huddleston, Sisley. *Paris Salons, Cafés, Studios.* Philadelphia: J. B. Lippincott, 1928.

Huttinger, Edward. *Degas.* New York: Crown, 1977.

Kendall, Richard. *Degas Beyond Impressionism.* New Haven: Yale University Press, in association with the National Gallery (U.K.) and The Art Institute of Chicago, 1996.

McMullen, Roy. *Degas: His Life, Times, and Work.* Boston: Houghton Mifflin, 1984.

Meyers, Jeffrey. *Impressionist Quartet: The Intimate Genius of Manet and Morisot, Degas and Cassatt.* New York: Harcourt, 2005.

Miller, John. *The Studios of Paris: The Capital of Art in the Late Nineteenth Century.* New Haven: Yale University Press, 1988.

Schivelbusch, Wolfgang, Jefferson Chase, trans. *The Culture of Defeat: On National Trauma, Mourning, and Recovery.* New York: Metropolitan Books, 2001.

Shackelford, George T. M. *Degas: The Dancers.* Washington, D.C.: National Gallery of Art, 1984.

Acknowledgments

I'd like to thank my extremely supportive friends and family who encouraged me to pursue my first novel, especially my sister, Anne, who is always unconditionally loyal. Special thanks to my agent, Kirsten Manges, who saw the potential of this story and worked tirelessly with me to develop it. I'm also grateful to my editor, Caitlin Alexander, for effortlessly pulling the story together with her insight and knowledge. Thanks also to Emily Powell and Ali Bothwell Mancini for their developmental editing in the early stages, and to Leslie Taber, Katie Klumpp, Gina Kacamburas, and Anne Shaver for their feedback on the raw manuscript. I'm truly lucky to have such a wonderful group of people in my life.

Dancing for Degas

Kathryn Wagner

A READER'S GUIDE

A CONVERSATION WITH KATHRYN WAGNER

Kathryn Wagner sat down with Random House Reader's Circle at a café in Washington, D.C.'s Dupont Circle. No removing of gloves was involved, but they did attempt to sip their coffee with Parisian elegance as they spoke about inspiration, obsession, dance, and geographical contentment.

Random House Reader's Circle: *What inspired you to write a novel about Edgar Degas? Was Degas your initial focus, or did Alexandrie come to you first?*

Kathryn Wagner: I've always loved Degas' ballerina paintings, and in an art history class in college my professor pointed out that the man behind the curtain in "The Star" *(L'étoile [La danseuse sur la scène])* was a "john." I've always thought of the ballet as very sophisticated, so I never would have guessed that—not that long ago—some ballerinas had an ulterior motive for dancing. It had always been a goal of mine to write a book, and at the time I started to seriously consider doing it, I was reading a lot of historical fiction. I was drawn to the idea of filling in the gaps and speculating about what might have happened to great historical figures. I've always loved art history and I look at paintings less for the technical brushstrokes and more for the story of what inspired the artist. I wonder about the artist's relationship with a model or how he or she spent time in the landscapes that he or she chose to paint. When I was figuring out what subject to tackle, Degas' ballerinas immediately popped into my head. I thought the lives of the dancers would be the most interesting, so it was Alexandrie's story that actually came to me first. I really knew very little about Degas as a person. When I researched his life and found that he had shunned all relationships for his art, I knew that the story had to be about unrequited love. I wanted Alexandrie to be strong and to want something more for herself than meeting a john behind the curtain. When I began the story I was about to turn thirty and was starting to seriously think about the future, so it was easy for me to relate to Alexandrie's struggle to choose the right path—minus her *lorette* vs. *courtisane* predicament, of course.

RHRC: Do you think there's a connection between Degas' love life (or lack thereof) and the way he portrays men in his paintings?

Kathryn: That is a great theory. I think the way he portrays all his subjects, men and women, shows a connection, because Degas completely removed himself emotionally from his paintings—and the final product is one by an observer. The relationships he portrays, such as in *Absinthe,* are not romantic

or idealized; *Absinthe* is just two people sitting together looking kind of bored. I think it would be safe to assume that
Degas removed himself emotionally from the world in order
to paint as a realist.

RHRC: *What was the most surprising fact you learned
about Degas while researching his life? Was there anything
particularly juicy that you just couldn't find a way to incorporate into the story?*

Kathryn: I was surprised to find out that he struggled with
his sight and went blind late in life. It really struck a chord
with me, because he lived for his art to such an extreme and at
the end of his life he couldn't even see all that he had accomplished.

I actually didn't find anything juicy or scandalous. I think
Degas would be happy with what is written of his life, because it's all about his career and there is virtually nothing
about his personal life. There were a couple of themes that I
would have liked to explore, but that just didn't work with the
story. For example, he spent a lot of time painting racehorses,
because he liked capturing their movement. I think it would
have been really interesting to learn more about that experience in his life and tackle some of the characters at the racetrack and explore the lifestyle of going to the races. But I
needed this to be Alexandrie's story, and incorporating Degas'
time at the racetrack would have taken the story away from
her.

RHRC: *Speaking of those details, what did you find to be
the most challenging aspect of Degas' life to fictionalize?*

Kathryn: I found it hard to fictionalize his relationship with Alexandrie and still be true to his life as it was recorded by history. Some readers might want a grand, sweeping love affair, but it would have been just really inaccurate to write that. I had to do a lot of revising to make sure that Alexandrie's character didn't come off as pitiable in her unrequited love, and also that Degas didn't come off as too harsh. There were a few areas that I took liberties with, using the research I did and making imaginative assumptions to aid the story. For example, it is not recorded that Degas' mother had an affair with her brother-in-law, Achille. I invented that to create a little more depth behind why the character of Degas in this book would shun relationships. Also, Degas did not have a heartbreaking relationship with a former model who ran off with his brother. I added that to the story because he had a habit of washing out figures from previous paintings and painting over them. I always imagined that it looked like he was trying to erase a lost love.

RHRC: It must be an exceptionally difficult choice to make when history doesn't quite give you the leeway you need in creating a story—rein in the drama or change history to suit your plot. How do you choose?

Kathryn: I think one of the joys of reading—and writing— historical fiction is that it *is* fiction. While it draws from real events, it also has the advantage of being free to invent new outcomes and interpretations. Two instances come to mind where I chose to incorporate important historical events but slightly altered the dates or circumstances to fit the story— they were small changes, but they were essential to the novel.

The first is that the final phase of the Franco-Prussian War, known as the French Civil War, which lasted from March through May 1871, did not actually begin in front of the Paris Opera House as an antiwar protest. But the war was an undeniably crucial event for my characters and for Paris itself, and this change really brought its impact closer to home.

The second is that the first Impressionist Exhibit was held in Nadar's photographic studio in 1874. Although not well received, it was not canceled because of the war. However, Alexandrie's story follows Degas from 1865 through 1872. The fact that Degas poured so much energy into arranging this exhibit that was ultimately a failure seemed important to the development of his character and his art, so I took the essence of that event and fit it to the scope of the story.

RHRC: *Did you watch a lot of ballet as a young girl? Or have you attended the ballet frequently as an adult? I'm curious as to what kind of research you did in order to describe the steps and movements of the ballet: Alexandrie's descriptions while she's dancing are very specific and energetic, which seems especially impressive given that you're not a dancer yourself.*

Kathryn: Like a lot of little girls, I took ballet classes, so I was able to draw from my experience when Alexandrie was at Madame Channing's Studio. I wouldn't say I frequent the ballet, but I love going when I get the chance. Each time it is such a beautiful experience, so as I was writing those scenes I tried to imagine what it would be like to see them from a different perspective (onstage rather than in the audience). I read a lot about the various ballets that were being performed at the time in order to capture the energy needed to tell each ballet's story. For the more specific descriptions of steps, I went online. It doesn't sound very romantic, but there were videos of different moves that I studied in order to try to put their spirit into words as Alexandrie performed them.

RHRC: You mentioned earlier that you've always thought of the ballet as sophisticated. Do you think readers will come away from your novel thinking about ballet in a different light? Were there any historical aspects that didn't fit with Alexandrie's story that you chose to fictionalize?

Kathryn: I think readers will see that the ballet has its own history and has changed just as the role of women has changed over time. When I think of major changes throughout history I think of medicine, government, women's rights; but for some reason I think of the opera, theater, and ballet as always staying the same. I wanted readers to realize that just because a girl was a ballerina in the late 1800s didn't mean that she had any more rights than girls who were living at home with their families. In creating Alexandrie's story I did fictionalize her life at the Paris Opera Ballet somewhat for the sake of drama. Through my research, I learned that the mistress aspect of the ballet was indeed quite prominent during Degas' time—usually arranged by the young girls' mothers, in fact. And many of Degas' paintings depict the relationship between *abonnés* and ballerinas, including *L'étoile*. But the ballet never functioned as an actual underground prostitution ring. Young ballerinas were closely monitored by their mothers to ensure they stayed intact and, to my knowledge, were not living in dormitory-style housing, as is depicted in the novel. It was also not an absolute requirement for ballerinas to become mistresses. The Paris Opera Ballet was, and still is, one of the most prestigious institutions in France, and history has shown that there are many famous ballerinas who were dedicated only to dance. I also chose to bring the Au Lapin Agile into the story in a fictional way to show the contrast of the dancers as viewed by the public, and to further illustrate how isolated the ballerinas in my story were.

RHRC: *The issue of women's rights at the time being similar in the country and in the city is an intriguing one. Yet when Alexandrie is transplanted from her small farming village to the big city of Paris, she thrives despite the challenges. Your family moved around a bit when you were young—did you have that same experience of hitting one particular place that was the perfect fit for you?*

Kathryn: My family moved when I was fifteen, so I was able to relate to Alexandrie's mixed emotions of fear, excitement, and intimidation at a vulnerable age. But an experience like that also gives you the reassurance that you can move to a place where you don't know anyone and make a new life, which is what made Paris so enticing for Alexandrie. After college, I moved to Massachusetts for about five years and made a lot of great friends, loved Boston, hated the winter; but for some reason I just always knew that it was a temporary place for me. I'm living in Washington, D.C., now, and I feel completely settled here and don't have the desire to move anywhere else. I'm definitely an East Coast girl, and I think the combination of a smaller city and the fact that hardly anyone is born and raised in D.C. is what makes it work for me. It's an interesting question, because I'm not sure if it's hitting a certain place geographically, or if it's growing up and hitting a certain place where you're happy with yourself and where your life is. Most likely, it's a mix of both and I think if given the chance, everyone should try to live in a few different places to find out what kind of environment they thrive in.

RHRC: *Among other things, D.C., of course, has a lot of great museums. Do you have a favorite? What's your favorite Degas painting and why?*

Kathryn: D.C. is a great museum city—and most are free, which is amazing. My favorite museum is the National Gallery of Art, and I also love the Corcoran Gallery of Art and the Phillips Collection. I would have to say that my favorite Degas is *L'étoile* because besides being a beautiful painting, it got my imagination going and gave me the inspiration to write *Dancing for Degas*.

RHRC: *You mentioned that aside from writing historical fiction, you're also a fan—who or what are your favorite authors or books?*

Kathryn: I love Philippa Gregory's books, especially *The Other Boleyn Girl* and *The Boleyn Inheritance*. The Tudors are fascinating and I'm semi-obsessed with the six wives of Henry VIII and all the drama that surrounded them.

RHRC: *Can you tell us a little about what else you're obsessed with? Perhaps what you're working on next?*

Kathryn: I'm working on another historical novel that focuses on the Postimpressionist artist Pierre Bonnard and the love triangle between Bonnard, his wife, Marthe, and his mistress, Renée Monchaty. It's set in 1920s France, which is such an energetic time, and the setting goes beyond Paris into Provence and the Riviera. This book is a lot of fun to write because each woman brings out a different side of Bonnard's personality—Marthe plays to the responsible husband who is content living outside the city, taking walks, and painting landscapes, while Renée plays to the restlessness that made him travel from place to place in search of something new and exciting. The tone of the book differs from *Dancing for Degas* in that it is much more gossipy and lighter, but at the same time, Marthe has some big secrets that she kept hidden from Bonnard, and his affair with Renée ends in a shocking way. I have a lot more research and writing to do, but it's really coming together nicely.

TOPICS AND
QUESTIONS FOR DISCUSSION

1. From Jane Austen's England to Alexandrie's France and all over the world, children were historically responsible for securing the futures of their families. Is that still the case? Why or why not?

2. Could you cultivate an ambition like Alexandrie's? Under what circumstances?

3. Alexandrie's larger-than-life mother pushes her to be the financial savior of her family. Why does her father play so conspicuously small a role in this narrative?

4. Alexandrie's mother was hopeful that her daughter would be chosen as a *lorette,* but horrified by the idea of post-performances. To what degree do these roles differ? Is the morality in this book clear-cut or more complicated? How do the consciences of the various characters—Alexandrie, Noella, Cornelie, Julien's mistress—differ, and why?

5. Did the structure of the novel—with its performance elements of acts, scenes, and intermissions—affect your reading experience? How so?

6. As a child at the market, Alexandrie dreamt of being a woman like Monsieur Belmont's wife. Did she succeed?

7. In the end, has Alexandrie found true love or simply the best possible choice? In her (dance) shoes, what would you have done? Would you have become Julien's *lorette*? Pursued Edgar? Married Mr. Taylor?

8. Why did Alexandrie flee the Louvre, and Edgar, at the end of the novel? Do you think Edgar would have recognized and understood her reasons?

9. In the introduction, *Coppélia* shows the audience that a woman with faults is better than a flawless doll. Which of the female characters in this novel fall into these categories? Which are successful in their chosen roles?

10. Having read *Dancing for Degas,* do you understand Degas' paintings on another level? How so?

Kathryn Wagner is a senior fund-raiser for a child advocacy nonprofit in Washington, D.C. She holds a B.A. in journalism with a minor in art and has worked as a staff writer and columnist for newspapers in North Carolina, Massachusetts, and Virginia. Imagining what has inspired great artists has been a longtime passion of hers. She is currently at work on her next novel.

www.kathrynwagnerbooks.com

ABOUT THE TYPE

This book was set in Garamond, a typeface designed by the French printer Jean Jannon. It is styled after Garamond's original models. The face is dignified and is light but without fragile lines. The italic is modeled after a font of Granjon, which was probably cut in the middle of the sixteenth century.

ML

3/10